life
ruins

Danuta Kot grew up with stories. Her Irish mother and her Polish father kept their own cultures alive with traditional tales they shared with their children. For many years, she worked with young people in Yorkshire who were growing up in the aftermath of sudden industrial decline. She uses this background in her books to explore some of the issues that confront modern, urban society: poverty, alienation and social breakdown, using the contexts of the modern crime novel. She now works as a senior education consultant, work that involves travel to establish education and training in other parts of the world. She is a regular academic speaker at conferences and literary festivals, and has appeared on radio and television.

DANUTA KOT

life
ruins

**SIMON &
SCHUSTER**

London · New York · Sydney · Toronto · New Delhi

A CBS COMPANY

First published in Great Britain by Simon & Schuster UK Ltd, 2019
A CBS COMPANY

Copyright © Danuta Kot 2019

The right of Danuta Kot to be identified as author
of this work has been asserted in accordance with the
Copyright, Designs and Patents Act, 1988.

1 3 5 7 9 10 8 6 4 2

Simon & Schuster UK Ltd
1st Floor
222 Gray's Inn Road
London WC1X 8HB

Simon & Schuster Australia, Sydney
Simon & Schuster India, New Delhi

www.simonandschuster.co.uk
www.simonandschuster.com.au
www.simonandschuster.co.in

A CIP catalogue record for this book
is available from the British Library

Hardback ISBN: 978 1 4711 7590 9
Trade Paperback ISBN: 978 1 4711 7591 6
eBook ISBN: 978 1 4711 7592 3

Typeset in Sabon by M Rules
Printed and bound by CPI Group (UK) Ltd, Croydon, CR0 4YY

MIX
Paper from
responsible sources
FSC® C020471

Simon & Schuster UK Ltd are committed to sourcing paper
that is made from wood grown in sustainable forests and support the Forest
Stewardship Council, the leading international forest certification organisation.
Our books displaying the FSC logo are printed on FSC certified paper.

For Martha, Eleanor, Bethany
and Samantha

life
ruins

Chapter 1

Ravenscar, December 2015

The setting moon hung low in the sky, turning the rocks at the water's edge a ghostly grey.

It was almost high tide. The sea flowed over the beach and lapped at the bottom of the rough path that formed a scramble to the clifftop. The waves washed in, then drew away, rattling the shingle in the winter silence.

People rarely came here. It was a place where wading birds turned pebbles over in the water, and grey seals basked on the rocks, undisturbed by walkers on the path above.

As the moon waned, the silhouette of Raven Hall high above merged with the darkness of the pre-dawn hour. The foreshore lay in deep blackness as the sea washed up its secrets: some rope, a baulk of timber long seasoned by the saltwater, a piece of fabric, torn beyond recognition by its time in the water.

1

And there was something else, something that was carried onto the shore as the tide came in, lifted onto the rocks and stranded there as the sea retreated leaving its bounty for the birds and the beachcombers.

The woman lay supine on the rocks, her hair fanned out in the cold morning air so the breeze lifted it gently, tousling it. The sea had not been kind to her. Her face was gone and the empty sockets of her eyes stared up at the sky.

It was midday before a walker scrambled down the path to explore the beach. Later, as the tide was turning and the light was starting to fade, a coastguard boat out on patrol saw yellow and black tape flapping in the breeze and people moving in the growing shadows on the foreshore. The next day, they read about the body of the young girl taken off that foreshore, battered by the sea and nameless.

A week later, all that was left was ragged sections of tape, and after that, nothing.

Chapter 2

Kettleness, January

Something was coming. Something dark was carried on the wind.

Kay McKinnon stopped on the headland of the Ness and looked out across the North Sea, grey and turbulent in the winter chill. *A sea that is stranger than death* ... She could remember Matt standing there proclaiming Swinburne into the storm winds of autumn, facing the sea as defiantly as the cliffs themselves.

But in the face of the sea, even the cliffs give way.

She was well wrapped up in boots, waterproofs, scarf, hat and gloves, but the cold stung her face and crept into every gap in her defences. As she stood there, she sensed that same, elusive feeling again.

Something was coming.

Kay had no time for fey portents. 'If you feel something's wrong, it's because you know something's wrong,' was how she countered the nervy premonitions

3

of teenage girls in her care. 'Even if you don't know you know it.'

So where was this feeling coming from? It wasn't surprising really. Matt had died a year ago today, and here she was, doing some kind of morbid pilgrimage he would have laughed at if he'd known.

'Well, you're not here to stop me, are you?' She said it out loud, as she said a lot of things to Matt. She still wasn't reconciled to his death and saw no reason why she should be.

Milo, Matt's white Staffie cross, tugged impatiently at his lead. Like his late master, he had no time for contemplative gazing from headlands, not when there might be rabbits to chase.

Turning south, Kay trudged along the path of the Cleveland Way that followed the cliff edge. In the distance, under the louring clouds, she could see the second headland. Beyond that was Sandsend. It was too far to walk before darkness fell. Only an idiot would get caught on these unstable cliffs at night.

She left the official footpath and let Milo off his lead. He trotted ahead of her as she crossed a field to the track bed of the old railway. She whistled Milo to heel when she reached this path, hesitating as she tried to decide which way to go. They'd walked almost eight miles, and these days, a few days after her sixty-eighth birthday, they both felt it. If she turned towards the coast, it was only a matter of fifteen minutes' brisk walking to take her back to her car on the headland and home for a much-needed cup of tea.

Kay didn't believe in mourning – when bad things happened, you got past it by ... well, by getting past it. You worked, you went on with what you were doing, you got on with life, that's what you did.

But you didn't forget. Today she was remembering Matt by retracing the first walk they had ever done together in a lifetime of walking. And here she was thinking about cutting the walk short. 'I'm getting old, Milo,' she said. He panted up into her face, grinning. *Old age is not for wimps*, Matt used to say, and he was right. The trouble was, neither was the only obvious way of avoiding it.

She wasn't seventy. She had a few good years in her yet.

A gull swooped down and curved away on outspread wings, crying as it headed out to sea. Kay watched it go, then, making a sudden decision, turned inland onto the old railway track they'd followed all those years ago. Bother being tired. She was going to look at the tunnel. Matt had shown it to her as they were coming to the end of that first walk. *Want to see something?*

In the heady awareness that something special was happening, she'd nodded her agreement, and they'd shared a conspiratorial grin. They'd walked down this track and there it was – the entrance to the tunnel, bricked up and abandoned years ago. They'd promised themselves they would come back but in over forty years of marriage – forty-three to be exact – they never had, so today, just a year after his death – here she was.

Calling Milo, she picked her way across the rough

grass and followed the track into the cutting. Stunted trees grew above her as the ground began to drop away. The path felt boggy under her feet. Despite the poor conditions, at least one other person had come this way recently. She could see the remains of their passage through the undergrowth.

And then the tunnel was ahead of her, a deeper darkness in the shadows. Dead vines trailed across the entrance, and grasses brushed against her legs, soaking her boots and trousers.

The entrance itself was partly sealed by a brick wall, but there was a gap at the top. It had been easy enough for her younger self to climb over. The wall was no more than a warning really, a reminder that old, unmaintained tunnels were dangerous.

Someone had helpfully stacked a couple of rocks up against it to make access over the top easier. 'You *are* joking,' she said to the absent stacker and, just a bit, to herself. She could hear that voice at the back of her mind urging her on. *You can do it! Go on! You aren't too old!* She pictured herself getting stretchered out by a group of husky young cave rescuers and decided she'd better not take the risk.

On the old bricks, a graffiti artist had painted an image of a young woman against a background of flowers. In keeping with current tastes for the macabre, the face was a grinning death's head. The image was in greyscale, blending in with the sepia notes of the winter scene – a beautiful but transient work of art that was already disappearing. A more recent – and less talented – tagger had spray painted a heart and the words 'Bobby + Lisa'.

Kids.

The tunnels must act like a magnet for them – forbidden, so instantly attractive and, for the more desperate – and Kay had worked with the most desperate and knew what pressures drove them on – maybe they provided some kind of shelter.

No. Not even those kids could look at that dark mouth and see shelter.

Whatever might have happened forty years ago, she and Matt had taken their happy memories away with them. They weren't waiting for her here.

Milo had been standing still, watching the tunnel mouth, but then he pressed himself against her legs, whining quietly, deep in his throat. 'It's OK, boy,' she said, clipping him back onto his lead. 'I don't like it here either.'

The light was fading. She had to use her torch to guide her return along the uneven path. Milo moved reluctantly, dragging against her arm, then he started barking, his hackles up. She looked back and saw a light bobbing in the shadows a way behind her – another walker. The path led up to the tunnel and nowhere else, so whoever it was must have come from there. She was half tempted to wait and ask about the conditions beyond the portal, but there was something about the darkening landscape ... and Milo was still barking. He could be tricky with strangers.

She pulled him smartly to heel. After a moment of

resistance he came, and they continued on their way, moving briskly. Just before she emerged from the cutting, she heard the walker behind her whistling. It was something Matt used to do, whistle absent-mindedly as they walked together – something he always denied.

She recognised the tune at once. It was an old Celtic melody about the transient nature of love. As the whistling faded behind her, the words ran through her head: *And what can't be cured love must be endured love, but my own true love I will ne'er more behold ...*

OK, now she was really wallowing in it. She blinked her eyes to clear them – daft old biddy – and followed Milo's urging as he pulled hard on his lead. She looked back and saw the figure emerge on the path behind her, just a silhouette in the dusk. She raised her hand in acknowledgement, and saw whoever it was do the same. Milo barked, and she turned back to the path.

Time to go home.

When she got to the car, she felt dissatisfied. Her walk hadn't really been in memory of Matt. There had been too many changes and too many recent events intruded. She couldn't shake the sense of foreboding. If anything, it was stronger now.

It wasn't that something was coming.

Something was here.

Chapter 3

In the darkness, the cliff edge was barely perceptible. Jared Godwin shone his torch onto the broken shale ahead. There were roped paths down to the foreshore, and an undulating, dead landscape that spoke of old mine workings and tunnels.

He'd spent the afternoon exploring the cliffs and the shore. It had been a long drive up from Bridlington but it looked as though it was going to be worth it. This coast had a history that suggested it would be ripe for exploration – old mines, old tunnels, military posts sealed off and abandoned. There would be an opening in the cliff somewhere, he was certain. He just had to be patient. He'd find it.

He always did.

Jared was an addict. Not for him the illegal street deals, the petty crime, the inevitable decay and death. His high came from danger and from fear, from the adrenaline surge of insane risk balanced against skill, experience and sheer dumb luck. Oh, his habit would kill him one day, he knew that, but until it did, it was the only thing that made life worth living.

People said it was like a rat inside you, clawing your guts, demanding to be fed. Jared had been feeding the rat since he was twenty but it couldn't be satisfied. Now it gnawed in his brain. Now it drove him on.

His moments on the edge – moving across a rock face with nothing but a thousand metres of air beneath him, climbing along ledges a hundred metres off the ground, buildings where the stone was crumbling away, places not meant for human presence, high above cities in those gaps in the world that the maps ignored, these moments were the ones when he truly felt alive.

Until the day he fell.

They were in the old steel works. They'd come in down the rails, climbed along the abandoned conveyors to the blast furnace. They'd had to climb to reach the ladder, and the ladder was rusting away.

He could still feel the rung snapping in his hand, the safety rail breaking as he swung back against it. Sixty metres below him, the rusting hulks waited. He had hung on, his other hand welded to the rung above, his feet scrabbling for purchase on a ladder that crumbled at each touch. Skua edged back – 'Hang on mate! Keep hold!' – but Skua couldn't reach him and could do nothing but watch as the last rung broke.

And then there was the drop.

He had fallen almost fifty fucking metres. He should have been killed. Instead, his attempts to break his fall, grabbing at the ladder as it snapped again and again, slithering down the metal, snatching at any hold he could, had turned a plummet into a series of shorter falls. He broke both his legs, his shoulder, his pelvis, smashed his ribs, cracked a couple of vertebrae and twisted his back.

Now, over a year later, he was walking again, walking on legs that were feeble compared with their previous strength, a body that had lost its suppleness and power, a body that doctors had told him, in no uncertain terms, would not survive the stresses of living the way he had. On the forums, they were calling him Phoenix, but he'd made his decision in that moment when he realised he had lost. If I survive this – never again.

Never again.

But the rat came back. The rat was hungry.

Two weeks ago, Jared had made his way to the east coast and ended up in Flamborough, just outside the small seaside town of Bridlington, where he found accommodation in a run-down caravan park that was more or less deserted in the winter months. But not that deserted, as it turned out. Night after night he was woken by the sounds of people partying on the far side of the site – loud music, shouting, screaming. The noise sometimes went on until three, four in the morning.

The guy who rented the van to him had just glared at Jared when he'd mentioned it. He was a big, slabby man with a massive beer-belly whose fat didn't conceal the hefty muscles underlying it. Jared had taken one look and dubbed him Greaseball Harry – GBH for short. GBH seemed to resent Jared's presence at the site altogether, but not enough to make him leave. Money was money, Jared guessed. And the van, run down and dilapidated, was cheap enough. But some nights he lay there unable to sleep, listening to the music, wondering who the partygoers were, what they were doing.

Today, he had come north to recce the old mines dug into the Kettleness cliffs, and the abandoned railway tunnels cut through the crumbling coastline from Sandsend to Runswick Bay. It was better up here than further south around Bridlington. Tomorrow, he'd leave the caravan site – it was so cheap at this time of year he could forget about the money lost. He'd find an accommodating farmer who'd let him camp in one of these fields. He'd get a better night's sleep in a tent on the ground than in that shithole of a caravan park.

It was getting late – it was already dark and he should really head back, but he wanted to take a look at the entrance to the Kettleness tunnel before he left. He checked his map. He was on the south side of Lucky Dog Point. He turned off the footpath and headed across the fields, his torch making a wavering beam on the ground.

He felt the air chill as he descended into the cutting. The portal was ahead of him now, a dark gap with wings of stone. As the light from his torch played across the wall, the figure of a woman jumped out at him, making his heart jolt with shock until he realised it was a painting, a piece of graffiti art, the kind of thing some urban explorers left to mark their passage. He'd check it out later.

At the foot of the wall, someone had left a handy

stack of rocks to make access easier. It would be simple enough to climb. He'd come back tomorrow, and . . .

In fact . . .

He glanced at his watch. It was after six. The idea that was creeping into his head was crazy. He wasn't here to explore; he was here to check out some sites. He was tired, his back was starting to hurt, he didn't have his equipment, he just had . . .

It's only a railway tunnel, for fuck's sake. It didn't matter that it was dark – it would be dark in there if he went in at high noon. He was wearing decent boots, he had a torch and a lighter. He was wearing his water-proofs. What more did he want?

The rat stirred, and he knew what he was going to do.

Carpe diem. It may never come again. He remembered the feel of the rung, solid under his foot one moment, gone the next. A prickle of tension touched his neck, apprehension clutched his stomach. He grinned.

He was going in.

He checked the batteries of his torch and made sure his camera was zipped securely in his pocket. Before his accident, a quick push of the arms would have seen him over the wall, but now it was a struggle to reach the top.

Once he was astride the wall, he had to stop to catch his breath.

A couple of months ago, he couldn't walk without a stick. It was getting better and it would go on getting better.

He dropped down into the tunnel.

Chapter 4

Kay lived in a small cottage near Lythe, north of Whitby. She and Matt had bought it two years ago, just after Matt's last big project had ended, and just before his illness made itself known. It had been advertised as having 'period charm', which meant, as far as Kay could see, no mod cons and doors and windows that didn't fit. But Matt had loved it and talked her into it as a project for their long-delayed retirement.

The cottage was cold as she let herself in. She took off her waterproof but left on her big jumper and changed her boots for warm slippers. Milo shook himself dry and hopped up onto the armchair, curling up small, his eyes watching her from under his tail. Matt had always been indulgent with Milo – Matt who could lecture for hours on the necessity of training and obedience as Milo sneaked biscuits off plates and curled up to sleep in forbidden places – and Kay hadn't the heart to change things now.

She checked the phone for messages. There were just two. The first one was from Becca, one of her long-term foster-children who had just started a new job: *Where are you? You aren't answering your phone.* Kay grimaced. Becca had called while Kay was out walking, and she had had ignored it. The other message was unexpected.

'Er ... Hello. Is this the right number for Kay McKinnon? Sorry to call out of the blue like this. It's Shaun Turner. You probably don't remember me. I used to work with Matt – with your husband – and I only just heard ... Look, I'm messing this up. I hate these machines. I'll call later.'

Kay sat there looking at the phone. Matt had worked with a lot of people over the years and even now, even a year later, she got calls from people who remembered him.

The name didn't mean anything to her. This Shaun Turner would either call back or he wouldn't. She didn't need to do anything.

She went through to the kitchen and made a cup of tea, taking it with her to the front room. She piled more wood in the stove and opened the damper until the fire was blazing, then began sorting through Matt's CDs, still stored in the bottom of the bookshelves. Milo groaned happily as warmth began to spread through the room.

Remembering the whistled tune she'd heard earlier, Kay selected a Dubliners album and slipped it into the player.

She evicted Milo and sat in the big armchair herself. Carefully avoiding her gaze, Milo climbed laboriously onto her lap and curled up, shuffling to get himself comfortable as music filled the room. Ignoring the dog, Kay tried to concentrate.

But again, Matt eluded her. She'd hoped the music would bring back other memories, but all she could hear was the edginess beneath the jaunty tunes, the scraping fiddle and the harsh voices. When the disc reached the song she'd heard earlier, she couldn't bear it anymore.

> *'For love and porter makes a young man older,*
> *And love and whiskey makes him*
> *old and grey,*
> *And what can't be cured, love, has to be*
> *endured, love . . .'*

She stood up and turned the player off. What can't be cured can bloody well be changed. You couldn't recreate the past, and you shouldn't try.

It was almost a relief when the phone rang. Caller ID told her it was Becca. After the message, Kay had been expecting – but not looking forward to – this call. She braced herself. 'Becca, love. How are you? Are you settling in?'

'No. I'm lousy. I'm not staying here. I'm leaving.' Kay sighed and let Becca run on until she wound down with a final, 'It's a dump.'

'What did you expect from a seaside town in winter? Yes, Bridlington's a dump in January. Everywhere's a dump in January. What you mean is, it isn't Leeds so you're not going to like it even if they serve it up with dancing boys and fairy lights.'

Kay waited for the angry explosion from the other end of the phone. It was Becca's way to let off steam before she calmed down. When Becca responded with a sullen, 'Suppose', Kay felt a niggle of worry.

'It's a big change. It's not what you planned … No, I'm not getting at you, I'm just saying – it's *not* what you planned. Is it?' Kay waited as Becca's voice chattered angrily at the other end of the line. 'It's what … What? You're … Don't be daft.' She took a mouthful of tea, but it was tepid. She made a face, partly over the spoilt tea and partly over the way the conversation with Becca was going. Matt had always been much better at calming Becca down. The trouble with Kay was she had a big mouth and didn't know when to keep it shut.

She'd known Becca for eight years, from the day she'd arrived at their house, a thirteen-year-old bundle of anger and aggression. She'd run away from home on her twelfth birthday after being accused of setting a fire at the house where she lived with her mother and stepfather, spent a few weeks on the streets, several months in a secure unit and had a string of broken fosterings behind her. Her first action on coming to Kay and Matt's had been to wreck her room with a thoroughness that had managed to impress them, veterans though they were of angry teenage room-wreckings.

Kay had left Matt to deal with it – he was better at the quiet reason that could calm kids who were wound up beyond anything they could bear.

Later, when a blank-faced, red-eyed Becca came down, hiding her distress behind the mask so many of them wore, all Kay had said was, 'I hope you like pizza.'

Becca's gaze checked her over. 'Has it got them olive things on it?'

'No,' Kay reassured her.

'They taste like shit,' was all Becca said. But she ate her tea quietly, with just the occasional hitch in her breath to show how distressed she had been.

But in the end, Becca had been one of their success stories, settling down at school, passing her exams, starting a college course, and then ...

In the past few weeks, something had gone wrong. Kay didn't know what had happened, but Becca had suddenly announced she was leaving college and had no interest in further training.

Now she was in Bridlington working in a café at a drop-in centre for homeless kids, a job Kay had found for her by dint of calling in some favours. Kay still had contacts in all the youth groups and charities up and down the east coast, which came in handy at times like this. 'So what's the job like?'

'It's a café. What do you think it's like?'

'Like most jobs, I expect. Good bits and boring bits. Better than being a filing clerk.' Did they even have filing clerks these days?

'What?'

'Nothing. Never mind. It's what you chose, Becca. It's not a bad job. You need to work. And it's not just any café, is it? Think about it. You know all about this, right? Imagine it when you were sleeping rough – you come through the door of this drop-in place and what do you see?'

'Me, looking like a loser in an overall.'

'Don't put yourself down Becca. Even if you do look like a "loser" – which you aren't, by the way – you can talk to a loser in an overall, can't you? She isn't the police, she isn't a social worker, she's just . . .'

There was silence at the other end of the phone as Becca absorbed this. 'Yeah, OK . . . but they keep talking to me like I'm stupid, you know? Like I don't know anything. I know more than they do. They've never been on the streets. They've never—'

'As far as you know.' Kay cut in before Becca could really get started. 'And they don't know you yet. Give them a chance. They're just trying to take care of the kids, trying to make sure you don't get it wrong.'

'They keep telling me, do this, do that, they don't give me a chance like I'm some kind of—'

Kay intervened before the metaphor arrived. Becca's metaphors tended to be more than colourful. 'What worked for you?'

Becca's teenage years had been marked by a recklessness that Kay had become familiar with over her years of working with damaged children. It spoke of, if not a desire to die, a lack of interest in staying alive. She could hear the shadow of it in Becca's voice even now.

Down the line, Becca was mulling this over. 'Knowing someone was bothered,' she said after a long pause. The anger had gone out of her voice and she was thinking again.

Becca had always had a problem with impulse control. Even at twenty, she was prone to quick, destructive acts when she was angry, like her sudden decision to leave her college course. She would throw biting insults at people who hadn't even realised they'd upset her, or, as now, threaten to walk out of a job that could get her back on track. At one stage, a psychiatrist had suggested she was bipolar, but Kay thought this was a load of rubbish and an excuse to quieten down a difficult kid by pushing drugs down her throat. Psychiatrists were one step up the evolutionary ladder from cockroaches, as far as Kay was concerned.

'So you can be someone who's bothered, right?'

'Suppose.' Becca's voice was grudging, but she was calmer. 'They don't go on like that at Alek.'

'Alek?' Kay knew most of the staff at the centre, but she wasn't aware of an Alek.

'The caretaker sort of guy. Alek.'

'He probably doesn't work with the kids.'

'Yes, he does. He's got this like workshop with all old engines and stuff that the kids work on. If they want to.'

'OK. And you get on with him?'

'Yeah. He doesn't say much. He's foreign. But he's OK.'

A bit of an outsider – that would appeal to Becca. Becca disliked and mistrusted anyone with authority over her, starting with her police officer stepfather and expanding outwards with almost no limit.

'And the users?'

'Mostly they don't talk to me. Much. There's one or two . . . like there's this kid, Paige, comes in sometimes. I don't get her, but she likes to talk. She thinks I'm cool because I come from Leeds.'

'You see?' Being cool carried a lot of currency. 'What don't you get about her?'

'I dunno. She seems together, and then she doesn't seem together, know what I mean? She used to come in with another girl, but now it's just Paige on her own.'

'What happened to the other girl?'

'Dunno. She was there when I started but she hasn't been around for a bit. It's not like school or something. You don't have to go.'

Kay frowned. They should at least be curious when a user went off the radar. 'Did she come in regularly, this friend of – what was her name, Paige?'

'They're not all homeless. Some of them – Neil says this – some of them use it like a sort of youth club, you know.'

Which was probably true. Bridlington, like too many places, had nothing for young people and if Neil Cowper, the drop-in manager, was expanding his remit to provide a place for the under-occupied youth of Bridlington, then she wasn't going to argue with him. 'OK. Now, you listen to me. You've been there three weeks, you get on with one member of staff, at least one of the kids trusts you enough to talk to you – what's the problem, Becca?'

21

There was a long silence, then a sigh. 'I get it. I'll give it a go.'

'Good for you. That's the right thing to do.'

'So why didn't you say so in the first place? When I said I was going to leave?'

'And you'd listen to me?'

'I might. Just for once you could tell me what to do, stop all of this listening. All of this *It's up to you, Becca.*'

'And if I did? You'd be out of there so fast we wouldn't see you go. Come on, Becca.'

She heard Becca's unfamiliar laugh. 'Yeah, OK. Thanks.'

Kay was left with the dialling tone. She put down the phone and leaned back in her chair as Milo climbed back onto her knee and settled down. 'You're too big to be a lapdog,' she told him, patting his head absently.

This was the second time she'd heard from one of her foster-children in the past couple of weeks. About ten days ago she'd had a call from Maireid – their last foster-child. They hadn't planned on fostering again, but Maireid needed a home, there was no one else – the usual story. She'd come to them a few months before they realised the extent of Matt's illness. When Matt became too ill to cope, they'd had to send Maireid back into care. No matter how valid the reasons, Kay knew she had broken her unspoken promise to the child.

Can I come and see you? Maireid had asked, her voice tentative. It was the first time they'd spoken since Matt's death.

Course you can, Kay said.

OK. I might ...

But Maireid never followed up on the call. She still wasn't prepared to trust Kay. It was going to take time.

You never really retired from fostering.

The tea was cold and beyond redemption, but she couldn't be bothered to make any more. It wasn't Becca who needed to sort her life out, it was Kay. Special Kay, her foster-kids used to call her. She couldn't remember who came up with the name, but it had stuck.

The wind rattled the window frame and the chimney puffed smoke, filling the room with the smell of ashes. Kay leaned back in her chair, running her hands over the dog's back, and listened to the storm building up outside – wind and rain, and a foul day promised tomorrow.

Count your blessings, she said to herself, and felt like some kind of geriatric Pollyanna. She got up and poured a large gin.

That was a blessing worth counting.

Chapter 5

In the light of Jared's torch, the roof of the tunnel vanished into darkness. It was like the arched nave of a church – an old, abandoned church that had been left to the mercy of time and the weather. The evidence of water incursion was everywhere. The bricks were patterned with mineral deposits, and the pointing was worn away. He could see places where the bricks had moved, coming loose and falling out of line, but the structure looked stable enough for now.

Groundwater trickled from the roof and the vent shafts. Crystals glittered from the arched ceiling, and in the distance, the tunnel curved away. Apart from the constant drip of water, it was silent.

He moved on into the darkness. The air smelt of wet earth and ashes, and the clay underfoot gleamed and then vanished as his light travelled across it.

His torch picked up a deeper shadow low in the wall. He let the light play over it. A brick arch opened onto a side tunnel. In the darkness, he could easily have missed it. Beneath the arch, the entrance was square, shored up with timber.

It was lower than head height. He stooped and tried to see further along in the wavering light of his torch. It was probably a side shaft to dump spoil down the cliff side. He could smell damp timber with an undercurrent of sourness. Water lay almost a foot deep on the floor, like a thick brown soup. The walls were held up by planks, and pit props supported the roof.

He crouched down to take a closer look and his back locked in a spasm. He swore and eased himself upright, gritting his teeth against the pain. He used the moves a genius physio had shown him and slowly the cramped muscle relaxed. If his back spasmed while he was in a narrow space, he'd be in deep shit.

Gingerly, he crouched down again and let his torch illuminate the side tunnel. He could make out more detail now. The props were crude, the planks holding the walls back were bulging. Almost beyond the limits of the light, he could see a ladder that must lead to an upper gallery. Was this a mine? He ran his light up and down the ladder.

He was going up there. He knew he was.

The tunnel was dangerous. The old argument that the side tunnel had stood for decades and wasn't going to collapse now was specious. Some of the props were twisted, showing the ground had moved. His actions could be the thing that caused the final shift, the thing that would make the supports move that critical milli-metre and bring the roof down. He'd be buried under

25

tons of mud. It would be crazy to go along there, especially equipped as he was now, without ropes and a head torch.

He grinned as the rat stirred inside him, and, testing his footing, he moved forwards.

Water and rotting wood soaked up oxygen. He remembered the narrow passage under the Derbyshire moors, waiting, listening to the sound of water dripping, dripping, every sense alert for what was coming.

Not now! He forced himself to concentrate.

He needed to watch out for foul air. He took out the lighter that he kept in his pocket for just this purpose and clicked it. It ignited at once and burned steadily. There was no flicker, and no trace of blue, which meant there was enough oxygen in this part of the tunnel. He wanted to keep it lit as he went forward, but the roof was too low for him to stand. His back wouldn't allow him to stoop, or not for any distance, so he had to move in a clumsy crouch. He used one hand to hold the torch, the other to help him keep his balance against the spongy timbers.

He stopped to test the air every couple of feet. Foul air could make you lose consciousness in seconds, and then it would kill you.

The water flooding the tunnel was thick and muddy. As he moved through it, it released a sour smell. His back gave a twinge. It didn't like this unsupported crouch.

Closer to the ladder, the light from his torch revealed

the walls were starting to cave in. They looked almost as if someone had been digging there. An amateur jet miner? Digging in this collapsing tunnel? How crazy was that?

The light of his torch wavered and danced as his awkward stance sent him off balance. He put a hand out to support himself against the wall and felt the timber crumble away.

In front of him, the ladder led upwards into darkness. It wasn't something that had been put there recently. This wood too looked old and rotten. What was it – some kind of escape route? To where? He *had* to know where it led. He gripped the rungs and the ladder held steady.

No excuses left.

Using the ladder for support, he eased himself upright, groaning with relief as the muscles in his back straightened. He shone the torch upwards, but all he could see was an opening and, dimly above it, the glitter of crystals.

Slowly, moving as cautiously as he could, he put a foot on the first rung, part of him expecting it to snap under his weight ... He brought his mind back to the present and focused on what he was doing as he pulled himself up – no slips, no sudden jerks to break the fragile wood – then onto the next rung, and the next. He shone the torch at the opening again.

He could see more detail now. It looked as though there was another tunnel above running crosswise to this one. Something bulky lay across the opening, partly blocking it. It looked like a bundle of ... what? Rags? Sacking? And there was something hanging down from the bundle, touching the top of the ladder – a piece of cloth or something. He gave it a gentle tug.

And the ladder shifted. He gripped it with both hands, trying to keep his hold on the torch as well. He felt the precursor of the collapse as soil scattered onto his head and shoulders. Moving by instinct, he freed his feet from the rungs and slid down the ladder, rubble from the roof cascading with him. His feet hit the ground, sending a shaft of agony through him. He had to move fast, to get out of there before the roof came down on his head, but his arm, his legs, felt numb. The torch dropped from his suddenly nerveless fingers and he slumped to his knees in total blackness as the rush of debris cascaded down.

Oh, fuck, oh shit, oh Christ, he was being buried alive, he ... the fall from above slowed and stopped. He waited frozen in the moment for the fall to start again, but the roof seemed to be holding. Carefully, carefully, he tested his arms and legs. It all hurt, but movement was coming back. He felt around for the torch, but it was gone. The darkness pressed against his face. He slipped his hand into his pocket, tugged the lighter free. He clicked it once, twice, then held it up. The flickering, bluish flame created a small circle of illumination. He moved it towards the ladder and looked up.

A face leaped out of the darkness, the mouth open in a snaggle-toothed snarl, the eyes covered by some kind of mask.

His grip on the lighter failed and it snapped shut, plunging him back into darkness. His hand grabbed for it. Without light, he was dead. The shock made him pant for breath. His head hurt as if someone was tightening a band round it.

God almighty, what had he seen? He tried the lighter again. His hands were shaking so much it took several tries to get it lit.

There was something hanging above the ladder like a – the image came into his mind without prompting – like a statue you might see carved high into the arches of a church. In the dim light, he couldn't tell if he was looking at a face or at a crudely painted drawing.

And there was a smell – heavy, sweet, cloying. A smell like decay . . . His mind searched for links, and he was in a church, listening to the voice of a priest talking about some stranger, someone he'd never known; not about Charlie, his best mate since forever, Charlie who . . . wasn't even there.

Only it wasn't a funeral, it was a wedding.

Now he was going crazy for sure because the figure half-hanging from the collapsing roof was a bride in a white robe with a veil of lace around her face that was mercifully shadowed in the intermittent light.

The blue light.

His mind snapped to attention. The flame was flickering blue, orange tipped. Foul air. The pounding in his head and the tightness in his chest weren't caused by shock. He was short of oxygen.

He had to get out.

29

He used the lighter once to get his direction, then started crawling back along the tunnel, dragging himself through the thick, scummy water. And as he pulled himself forward, he thought he could see, in the darkness in front of him, another figure struggling with the claustrophobic narrowness of the passage. *They just had to get through here, and they would be back in the main cave, then . . .*

He shook his head to clear it. He wasn't in the Derbyshire cave. He was in a side shaft off the Kettleness tunnel. He just had to get back a few hundred metres. He couldn't afford to lose concentration. Put one hand forward, draw up his knee. Ignore the pain. Now the other hand. Now the other knee. Again. Forward.

The chill of the rock was drawing him back, the struggle and stop, struggle and stop as the passage narrowed and narrowed again . . .

Don't lose it. You're in the side tunnel. Just keep moving. Think about something. Think!

His mind was clearing. He could see a lesser dimness in the blackness around him. He flicked the lighter and this time it ignited at once and the flame burned orange. He could feel the oxygen flooding through his body, even though his head still pounded.

The image of the face leaping out of the darkness was vivid, and now he didn't know what to believe. He had been seeing things, he knew that, because in his memory of the scene, among the stuff that had fallen on him, the brief cascade of rubble making him think the roof was coming down . . . he couldn't have seen a bride, or an angel. He couldn't have seen flowers.

Shimmering lacy flowers, gleaming in the flickering light.

Chapter 6

It took Jared forever to get free from the side tunnel. By the time he reached the wall blocking the portal, he seriously doubted his ability to get back over it. The only thing that stopped him from collapsing onto the tunnel floor was the cold and the knowledge that if he fell asleep here he might not wake up.

The climb over the wall was a nightmare. His arms were like wet string, his back a column of agony, every part of his body aching with exertion and fatigue. The effort took almost all of his remaining energy, but he still had to get to the car and he still had to drive back.

He followed the dim glow from his lighter along the path, one step after another – *keep going, keep going* – barely feeling the cold that was eating through to his bones. His crawl through the water had soaked him to the skin. He stumbled his way to the car, his mind focused on one thing – staying alive.

He could hear the sound of the waves as he stood in the car park. Despite the cold, he stripped off his jacket, his fleece, everything, standing naked in the night air. Cold was a killer, and wet clothes only exacerbated the effect. He pulled on dry trousers, T-shirt, heavy jumper, socks and shoes, but the shivering wouldn't stop.

He'd almost panicked. He'd almost got himself stuck in the fucking tunnel. Every time he'd tried to move, the twist sent his back into a spasm, and each time that happened, he'd waited as it eased, knowing if it didn't, he would be stuck until hypothermia took its fatal toll.

But he'd made it.

By the time he was on the road the rain had stopped, but fog was rolling in from the sea. He was driving through a semi-opaque barrier that reflected his head-lights back at him and made the road almost impossible to see. He didn't care. He was past that. He just needed to drive. The caravan was a haven he had to reach.

As he came into Bridlington, the level crossing bar-rier was down. He rested his head against the steering wheel, waiting for the train to pass. He could feel sleep trying to claim him, feel the deadly cold numbing his feet and his hands.

Keep going . . .

Then he was at the turning into the caravan site. Out of season, the owner didn't bother with lighting up the park – cheapskates like Jared who took advantage of winter prices could find their own way about. His car rocked as the wheels crossed the deep ruts in the path. The static vans were darker shadows in the darkness, his headlights briefly illuminating the faded colours, the peeling paint. Someone was shouting and in the distance, at the far side of the park, he could see lights as if some kind of activity was going on.

Parties in the night. His fuddled brain couldn't bring itself to care.

He pushed the car door open, letting its weight pull it back against its hinges. Every bone, every muscle ached. Worse than anything was the exhaustion. He could feel his body starting to take over, to fool him into sleep, and out here in the cold, even so close to home, sleep could be fatal.

There was one more thing he had to do. He didn't want to, but ... The figure hanging from the ladder. How long before someone else would go in there and find her? He took out his phone and made the emergency call. He didn't wait to be put through to the police, just gave his message and hung up.

Then he grabbed his wet clothes from the back of the car, remembered to lock it – though who was likely to steal it? – and dragged himself to the caravan. He could feel his consciousness fading into dreams. Making a massive effort, he focused on the key in the lock, turned it and tumbled through the door, managing to pull it closed behind him.

The last thing he remembered was falling across the bed.

He dreamed of masked faces in the darkness, a tunnel closing in on him, water inexorably rising as he struggled to breathe and the pounding music of a party somewhere nearby, that went on and on into the night.

Chapter 7

Becca Armitage had been in Bridlington for a month and she was not impressed. It was a dump. She didn't like the town and she didn't like the coast. She was used to the stimulus of college, money in her pocket, the urban buzz of Leeds, the busy streets, a city where there was always something to do, a place full of people and activity. Here, the town was empty. The land was too flat, the sky was too big. There was nothing to do and nowhere to go, just the empty streets and the deserted seafront.

The people looked as grey and hopeless as she felt herself. Neil, her boss, said they shipped people in for the cheap winter accommodation but it didn't seem to do much for the town. The few cafés that were open were mostly empty. The only places that seemed to be thriving were the amusement arcades that lined the front, spilling out loud music and flashing lights from their dark interiors.

She'd had a life in Leeds; a college student with friends, an income, places to go. A future. She knew

Leeds. Bridlington felt dangerous, as if the rules she'd understood in the city weren't the rules here. In Bridlington, as she walked the streets, she looked over her shoulder often.

The alarm dragged her out of sleep. She sat up, resisting the impulse to dive back under the covers as the cold hit her. It was Friday, the end of her first month. When she started, she hadn't expected to make it to the end of the first week, so lasting out a month ... she tried to find something good in that, but as far as she could see, it just meant she was a big loser with nowhere else to go.

The room she rented was called a studio flat, but actually it was a bedsit with a cooker in the room and a shower and toilet on the landing that she shared with the shop downstairs. It was heated by an ancient gas fire, squat and ugly against the chimney breast. The fire made the windows drip with condensation and it ate the tokens she fed into the meter at a speed that meant she couldn't afford to keep on using it.

But she was cold now. She wrapped the quilt round her and dived across the room to switch the fire on, huddling close to it until it began to glow and warmth began to seep through the chill.

She should get a move on. It was seven, and she was supposed to be at the drop-in by eight, opening up the café to serve tea and bacon rolls to the first kids through the door, and then to a slow procession through the morning.

'The first ones in will be the ones who've been

36

sleeping rough,' Neil, the centre manager had told her. 'Then we get the sofa surfers and the ones who are living in B & Bs. They get chucked out after breakfast.' The kids should have tokens, he explained, which entitled them to a certain number of free meals a week. The B & B kids didn't get those – they were supposed to be fed in the hotels – but the others did if they signed up. She couldn't hand out food to kids without tokens, but she could give them a cup of tea.

One morning – it was in her first week – she'd seen a small, pale lad spooning sugar into his free cup of tea with the desperation of real hunger. She'd slipped him some toast, just as Neil came in. Neil must have seen, but he hadn't said anything, or not until later when it was quiet. 'Just a quick word, Becca.'

'What?' Her chin lifted as her defences locked in place.

'When you gave Martin some toast.'

She would have explained but he hadn't given her a chance. 'If you see something like that again, tell one of us. We can give them emergency help, but it's got to be done through the system, or they'll all be wanting free food and we'll get swamped. We'll get into trouble, and that will affect our funding. So if you think a kid needs feeding, tell me, or Hannah, or one of the support workers. Don't just act on your own.'

What did Neil know? He'd never gone hungry. He didn't know what it was like to go to sleep so empty it felt like your guts were being torn out. *Tell one of us.* Like she was too stupid to spot a hungry child when she saw one. If she saw a kid as hungry as that again she was giving him something and Neil could fuck off. 'Yeah, whatever.'

It was 7.20 by the time it was warm enough to brave the small bathroom on the landing. The shower gave a meagre spray and was never more than tepid. Breakfast would have to wait until she got to work.

She got out her make-up bag and painted out the unevenness in her skin, especially the white line of the scar that ran from the side of her nose to her lip, but didn't bother with anything else. Her hair, which had reverted to its natural light ginger, she left hanging round her face. She'd been colouring it black when she was in Leeds, liking the effect of the dark hair against her pale skin. She'd cut it all off when the Bexgirl thing blew up – but she didn't want to think about that.

The important thing was, no one really noticed her with her hair like this.

She pulled on jeans, a sweatshirt and another sweatshirt on top of that for warmth. Her clothes had all been bought in the summer in Leeds when she had money in the bank and the expectation of more. They weren't made for winter on the east coast.

She zipped up her jacket and let herself out of the flat. The rain was still falling, a fine, penetrating drizzle. Cars buzzed past, sending up spray, their headlights reflecting off the wet road. The weather was so foul she thought about taking her own car, but she couldn't afford the fuel. She pulled her hood up and headed for the bus stop.

She hated her new life, hated it. It was the weekend.

She should be thinking about shopping, texting friends, discussing the hot clubs and the Saturday night parties. Instead, here she was shivering at the bus stop, a few coins in her purse, heading towards a dead-end job in a dead-end place. How had it all gone so wrong?

Act like a loser, be a loser. She lifted her chin and glared at the bus as it made its bumpy way down the road towards her.

Chapter 8

The rain had stopped and mist was drifting in from the sea as Becca got off the bus. It stung her face where it touched her bare skin. She walked fast up the side street to where the drop-in was located in what used to be a church hall, its dark, barred windows looking cold and unwelcoming. The doors were locked but she could see one or two kids hanging round, huddled into hoodies.

'Let us in, Becca, come on.' She was getting to know the regular users. This one, Paige, was a small, skinny girl who wasn't usually among the first arrivals. According to Neil, she was supposed to be in a B & B with her mother and the younger kids, but mostly she sofa-surfed and her mother seemed too far gone to care.

'You're early,' Becca said. From the look of it, Paige hadn't been home that night. She was dressed for clubbing – short skirt, crop top, bare legs, feet in ballet slippers.

'Yeah. It's freezing. Come on, let us in.'

'I'll go round and hurry them up.' There was a staff entrance off the gennel that ran behind the row of buildings. Becca knocked on the door and Alek, the caretaker, let her in.

'It is a cold day today,' he observed. He had a bit of an accent – probably Polish or something, she didn't know. She was a bit wary of him – he seemed friendly enough, but he was a big man and he rarely smiled. The users didn't mess around with him.

'Yeah. There's some of them, you know . . .'

'They want their breakfast. That's OK, Becca. I let them in.'

Which meant she'd better get moving. The main room was warm enough, though the dirty cream walls, which must have been painted about a million years ago, and the old grey drapes that hung on the windows made the place look dark and depressing. It was where the kids spent most of their time; playing snooker, using the computers, or talking to the youth workers. The café where Becca worked was in a smaller room just off the main one.

Cafés in Leeds were smart places with a bit of style, but this was just a dingy room lit by a couple of fluorescent tubes, with old, cracked lino, some battered tables and chairs and a serving counter at one end.

It could have been made nice. At the first meeting she went to – Neil liked everyone to come to the meetings, including Alek, who almost never did, and a representative of the users, who never did at all – she'd suggested painting the walls, and using some of that coloured stuff to stick over the table tops – something bright and light, red tables, green tables and yellow tables, then the café could be OK. It could be quite cool and it would give the kids something to do. 'They'd, like, have a stake in it, you know?' Using the stuff she'd learned at college.

But Neil just did that sort of laugh that meant she didn't know anything and said they had better things to do with their money. She didn't bother making suggestions after that.

Becca knew the routine now. She locked her bag away in a cupboard under the work top, put on the tabard that she hated – *a loser in an overall*, she'd said to Kay – and began setting up for the morning. Behind the counter was a door leading into a small kitchen with an urn, a hob, a fridge and some cupboards. Someone – probably Alek – had already switched on the urn so there would be plenty of water for tea. She put a frying pan on the hob, got a big tub of spread out of the fridge, put bread in the toaster and opened a bag of rolls.

This reminded her she was starving, and she was just cramming the last of a buttered roll in her mouth as Alek unlocked the doors. For the next couple of hours, she was too busy to think about anything, running between the serving counter and the kitchen, frying bacon, making toast, pouring tea. It was after ten before she had time for a cup of tea and a slice of toast herself.

She sat down at one of the tables, feeling hot and greasy. She had been on her feet for about two hours, she probably smelt like a bacon roll and she was tired. She drank her tea, playing a game idly on her phone.

'Hey. You Becca?'

She looked up. A young lad – he looked very young – was leaning across from the next table. She knew who he was. His name was Liam, and despite his appearance, he was seventeen, and a familiar face at the drop-in with his friend, Terry. Terry was a big, silent lad who followed the lively Liam around.

'Yeah,' she said cautiously. She hadn't had much to do with Liam. He didn't often come into the café but spent most of his time on the computers or playing snooker in the main hall, where he was usually surrounded by a group of followers. The other users treated him with a wary respect and Becca took her cue from them.

'You're from Leeds, right?'

'Yeah.' Becca lined up a bird on her screen and shot it towards the pigs' fortress, which crumbled satisfyingly.

'OK place, Leeds.'

It was an OK place and Becca missed it more than she often admitted to herself. 'Yeah. It is. Do you know it?' She lined up another bird.

'Kind of. I know a mate of yours.'

Becca's hand froze on the screen. She could see him assessing her response and tried to make herself relax. 'Who's that then?'

'Tell you later ... *Bex*.' He jumped up and headed out of the room, followed by the silent Terry.

Becca felt as though someone had punched her in the gut. Then she told herself it was nothing, she was imagining things. Lots of people said Bex for Becca.

43

And he hadn't really emphasised the name, had he? That was just her being paranoid.

'What you doing?' Paige sat down next to Becca and leaned over to look at her phone. 'Cool. You got *Candy Crush*?' She got out her own phone and tapped it, showing the game to Becca.

'Cool phone.' Becca was surprised to see Paige had the latest iPhone, which was an expensive bit of gear.

'Yeah. Look, see, you gotta …' Paige showed her the intricacies of the game. Becca knew it, but she let Paige take her through some of the moves. They sat companionably for a while, Becca playing games, Paige texting. After a while, Paige spoke again. 'So where do you go in the evenings?'

'I don't go anywhere much.' It sounded pathetic to Becca and she wasn't going to be pathetic for anyone. 'Round here, I mean. I go back to Leeds mostly.' She hadn't been near Leeds for months, not since the Bexgirl thing had happened, but Paige didn't have to know about that, or that Becca spent her evenings playing games on her phone and trying to keep the darkness at bay.

'So why don't you come out with us?'

'Where do you go?

'Parties. There's good parties here,' Paige said.

A bunch of kids popping pills and getting high didn't sound that attractive, but Paige was being friendly and it reminded Becca of times sitting in the coffee bar at college with her friend Ashley, chatting, texting, as people came and joined them, left, came back – just best friends in a circle of friends. She'd never had that before. At school, the kids had been wary. Becca was a known troublemaker and ready with her fists. She hadn't really had friends, not even when she calmed down. But college had been a new start, and . . .

'. . . Saturday nights.' Paige had been talking about parties again.

'Sounds cool.'

'So I'll text you, then?'

'Yeah, co—'

'You. Paige. Come on – what you waiting for?'

Becca looked up. Liam was at the door of the café watching them. He started to come across as Paige got to her feet. 'Yeah, yeah,' she said. 'I'm coming.' She smiled at Becca. 'See you.'

They both disappeared into the hall.

Becca didn't like the look of that. There had been a bullying note in Liam's voice, and though Paige hadn't seemed concerned, she'd looked back as Liam led her out. Becca stood up, not sure what she planned to do, but as she reached the café door, Neil came out of his office and saw her. 'There you are.' As if he'd been looking for her for hours. 'Have you got a minute?'

'I just want to . . .' But Liam and Paige had vanished. 'Yeah. OK.'

She followed Neil into his office, wondering what she'd done wrong now. He gestured her towards a chair and sat down himself. 'Just a quick chat, Becca. Are you settling down? Is your flat OK?' He threw the questions at her as if he didn't really want an answer.

'Yes. Fine. I'm fine.' How could she start to explain? She wouldn't talk about anything to Neil anyway. She'd had it up to here with social workers like him.

'Well, now you're at the end of your four-week trial, I just wanted to tell you that we're happy with you, so if you're happy with us ...?'

'I'm ... yeah. Great.' Her smile felt a bit forced. It was nice to be told she was doing something right, but ... if they'd been unhappy with her, if they'd asked her to leave, then she'd have had no choice. She could go. Now she'd have to stay.

And suddenly there was this thing with Liam.

He couldn't have meant anything ...

'Kay told me you were training in health and social care before you came to us. I don't know what happened –' he held up his hand – 'none of my business, Becca, I know. But if you want to do a bit of on-the-job training here – you're good with the kids, Becca. They talk to you.'

Tell you later ... Bex.

'Yeah. Right. That'd be ... yeah. Great.'

'I'll have to go ahead with your CRB check now. We should have done it sooner but there was a bit of an emergency. I'll deal with that ... is that OK? You haven't got a police record or anything have you?' He laughed as he said it to show it was a joke, and Becca shook her head.

'No. No police record.'

And that was true.

Wasn't it?

Chapter 9

Jared opened his eyes. It was freezing. He tried to move. Agony spiked up his leg and through his back. He collapsed onto the mattress, keeping his breathing shallow, his hand fumbling for the morphine pump.

Then he woke up properly. He wasn't in hospital. He was in a caravan on the deserted site near Flamborough Head. The rain was drumming against the roof. The mattress under him was hard and unforgiving, and the pain had him pinned down. The dark tunnel rushed into his mind, the debris falling, the mask, the thick, stinking water as he dragged himself through it . . .

Shit! God al–fucking–*mighty!* What had he been thinking of? He'd never have taken that kind of risk, never have gone into that side tunnel on his own without the right equipment, not before his accident. What was he trying to prove? What a dick he was? If that roof had caved in, he could still be lying there, still alive, still conscious, still trapped, waiting for the rest to come down and suffocate him slowly in mud . . .

A face, masked and snarling, jumping out of the darkness.

And the silky flowers, gleaming in the flickering light.

He jerked awake again, gasping for breath. *Shit!* What had he seen down that tunnel? It was already vanishing from his mind. He couldn't tell what was real and what was part of a delusion induced by oxygen starvation.

It can't have been a body in the tunnel, not just hanging there . . . it was . . . a mask, an effigy . . . a sculpture? That was it. That had to be what it was. Most people who went into the tunnels left no trace of themselves, but some explorers, a few, left transient works of art in strange, inaccessible places, then posted photographs online. If you wanted to see the artwork for real, it was up to you to find it. He could remember coming across a sculpture in some woods near Sheffield once, a reclining woman made out of cling film, suspended between two trees.

So there had been artists around the tunnel – that odd painting of a woman outside, that must have been left by the same person.

He felt himself relaxing.

The sooner he put the whole thing out of his mind the better.

He tried to sit up. White-hot pain stabbed up his leg and into his back. His teeth snapped together and his neck arched. *Fucking Jesus*. It was like the days immediately after his accident. What had he done to himself?

He managed to roll onto his side and grab the bottle

of painkillers – the painkillers he'd cut right down to a couple at night. He tipped two into his hand but they dropped to the floor and rolled away – *fuck* – he tipped out two more and got them into his mouth. The bottle of whisky was by the side of the bed. He managed to get the top off and washed the pills down with two gulps that sent the liquid spilling across the mattress and his sleeping bag. He reached for a half-smoked joint that lay beside the pill bottle, lit it and took a long drag.

Five minutes. He'd give them five minutes to work and then . . .

He was drifting in a glaze of pain, fatigue and drugs. He struggled to keep himself awake, but every time he thought he was standing up, he realised he was half dreaming and was still flat on the hard mattress struggling against the stupor of the analgesics.

How did you get it so wrong, son?

He shouldn't have taken the pills. He should have gritted his fucking teeth and manned up. He should . . . he should . . . *The cave acted like an echo chamber. After he'd eeled his way out of the passage, his breath was ragged with relief and the sound of it filled the space. Only it wasn't his breathing. It was the struggle of someone still in the passage, still squeezing through the narrow space and the last pinch point where the rock had gripped his pelvis and held him trapped for long, tense minutes.*

. . . and the water kept on rising . . .

Someone was knocking on the door. It was a sharp, peremptory knock that jerked him out of his dream.

49

He realised he was still lying flat on the mattress. The fucking drug had got to him again and he must have slept for a while because light was streaming through the window and reflecting off the walls.

The knocking came again. He sat up slowly, wiping his wet face. The pain had receded. It was still there, but it no longer bit deeply into him. He could move. He felt oddly detached, spaced out, the price he had to pay for his mobility.

He had dumped his dirty clothes on the floor and the caravan stank of the filthy water from the tunnel. He slid his legs off the bed and eased himself upright, reaching for his jeans on the seat where he'd left them the night before, and almost fell.

The knock came again, more sharply this time. 'Just a minute.' He pulled on his jeans and a T-shirt, dug a heavy sweater out of his bag and pulled that on as well. His feet were blocks of ice, but he couldn't negotiate his socks and boots, not just yet. He supported himself with his stick as he went to the door and opened it.

Daylight bounced against the backs of his eyeballs, making him wince. It wasn't, as his hallucinating brain had half expected, his father. Two police constables, a man and a woman, stood there, the man with his hand poised to knock again. They stood side by side and looked at him with carefully blank faces. Tweedledum and Tweedledee.

Jared leaned against the doorway, squinting against the bright light. 'Yes?' He remembered, with a sinking feeling, the phone call he'd made the night before.

'We're investigating an incident from last night. We need to ask you some questions. Can we come in?'

The pills scattered around were all legal, all on prescription, but he didn't want the hassle of finding the proof, and the hash certainly wasn't. 'We can talk here.' He lowered himself carefully onto the step, envying them their thick uniforms and gloves.

'Heavy night?' The man grinned at him, bonding.

Jared shrugged but didn't comment. The man pulled up an old milk crate that had been dumped outside the caravan at some time and sat down. 'Not the best time of year for a holiday,' he observed. 'Could you give me your name, please, sir?'

'Sir' was what you said to your superior, your boss. In the mouth of the policeman it sounded like 'scum'. They could find out easily enough. 'Godwin. Jared Godwin.'

'OK, Jared. Now, where were you last night?'

Jared took a gamble on the possibility of someone having seen his car on the road. 'Here.'

'Just – here? Doing what?'

Jared shrugged. 'Nothing much.'

'You didn't go up the coast?'

'No.'

'Someone made an emergency call from this location late last night. Was that you?'

If he'd been thinking straight, he'd have waited, made the call from a phone box – except he'd been in no state to think about anything much. His phone wasn't registered to him – it was just a pay as you go.

They must have tracked it but they had no way of knowing whose it was. He shook his head.

They came at him from both sides. 'A man – sounded like he'd had a few. He said there was a body in the Kettleness tunnel, in one of the side tunnels.'

'The call came from this site. It was you, wasn't it? No one else here.' That was the woman, who was watching him with a mixture of incredulity and distaste. 'The call handler said the caller sounded drunk – might have been a bit of fun to make that call, but people had to go into that tunnel, check it out. They sent a caving team in, Jared. That's expensive. Can we see your phone?'

'No. Why don't you ask the people who were having the party?' He regretted the words as soon as they were out of his mouth. Never offer an explanation. That was their job, not his. Now they'd want to know all about that.

'What party? Who was having a party?'

'I don't know,' he said wearily. 'Someone around here. They kept me awake, that's all. Music, shouting. Just a party.'

They were both studying him closely, seeing, in the daylight, the evidence of long-term illness and injury. 'You're hurt, Jared,' the woman said. 'What happened?'

'The ground. I fell fifty metres and I broke just about every bone in my fucking body. A year ago. I'm getting better, but I need to lie down and I need you two to go away.'

He'd expected them to arrest him on suspicion of

wasting police time. Instead, a close look at what a physical wreck he was must have convinced them, or convinced them enough, that it wasn't him who'd called.

But at least he knew now that his second thoughts of this morning were right. They hadn't found anything. If they'd found a body they'd be here mob-handed with search warrants. He felt a wash of embarrassment. And the glittering flowers? He sent up a silent prayer of thanks that he hadn't mentioned them in the phone call last night.

He felt stupid enough as it was.

Chapter 10

Saturday was Becca's day off, and days off were a drag. Weekends were worst, because at weekends you were supposed to be out having a good time. When Neil said they were short-staffed Saturday evening, she'd volunteered to go in, because what else would she do? And she needed the money. She was close to broke.

It was two o'clock, Saturday afternoon. She'd cleaned the flat, gone to the shops and stocked up on what she could afford – bread, beans, tea, sugar. She'd taken her clothes to the launderette, and by the time she got home, it was just midday. She'd made herself beans on toast, which she didn't really want but it was something to do, then she switched on the TV – small, with a jumpy picture – and lay down on the bed, where she dozed off briefly.

A pathetic loser living a loser's life.

The weekend stretched ahead of her like a featureless wilderness. She didn't know anyone in Brid, she had no money to go anywhere and there wasn't anywhere for her to go anyway.

She could still see Clare's face – Clare had been her tutor, and Becca liked her. Had liked her. Kind of. But Clare was just like all the rest of them – she didn't want to listen, she just wanted Becca out of there. 'You must know I can't let you go on with the course after this. You'd never— What were you thinking of?'

It had been such an easy way to make a bit of money, camming. There was her, the chat room, her webcam and her followers. The crazy thing was, she'd been good at it. You couldn't just sit there and take your clothes off and do things. That was OK for a while, but the guys soon got bored. You had to chat, smile, be flirty, be friendly, make a bit of a joke about it sometimes, play games, be like their girlfriend. And if you got it right, the tips came in.

It wasn't a fortune, but it meant she could run a car, have a bit of money in her pocket, pay her rent. For the first time in her life, she'd been truly independent. Online, she was Bexgirl, and Bexgirl had a very different life from Becca Armitage, college student and future child welfare officer.

Bexgirl looked at the camera with the gleam of promise in her eyes, she drank champagne – well, on camera it was mostly lemonade, but once someone had actually sent her champagne – she played with sex toys and told sexy stories.

Becca Armitage studied hard, didn't have a boyfriend, went round with a group of friends to clubs and places but didn't drink, not really, and never touched hard drugs. As for the rest of it, what Becca

Armitage did in place of the sex toys, mind your own business, right?

And then her worlds collided.

There were just two pictures. One was a screenshot from Twitter, and showed Bexgirl on a bed below a poster of urban graffiti, a riot of primary colours and the word WOW! in the centre. Her skin was dusted with sparkles. She was wearing a thong and a camisole, two fingers tugging teasingly at the top of the thong. The bed was piled with stuffed toys. She was smiling at the camera, her tongue extended a bit to show the stud piercing it. The tweet was from Bexgirl, and it said: *online and camming guys!*

This wasn't the picture that caused the trouble.

It was the second image, which showed Becca sitting on the same bed, in front of the same poster, but this time with a little girl who looked maybe six years old. They were hugging each other and were sticking their tongues out at the camera. They were both wearing shorts and sun tops with the legend *Grrrl Power!* across the front – Becca had bought the tops for them from the market that day.

The girl was Ruby, Ashley's little sister. Ashley was on Becca's course and they were – they had been – best friends. Becca had come across a fed-up Ashley dragging a screaming kid behind her. The kid was howling and Ashley was yelling at her. Becca hadn't had much to do with little kids, but Ashley was her mate, and there was something about the kid's crying that tugged at her.

She'd taken them both for ice cream – *My treat*, she'd said when Ashley grumbled about the expense. Ruby was OK after the ice cream, but Ashley kept moaning she was a pain, and she had to look after her all day, so Becca took them to a movie and then they'd gone back to Becca's flat to have takeaway pizza. To Becca's surprise, she'd really enjoyed it, but Ashley got a bit funny with her when Ruby started saying things like 'I wish *you* were my sister.'

Just before they left, Ashley had taken the photo of the two of them sitting on the bed.

Becca saved it in her cloud file. She didn't think anything about it, but she got hacked. First her Twitter account, then, before she realised what was happening, her cloud stuff was gone, and someone sent pictures to all her friends – and whoever did it put the camming image and the picture of Becca and Ruby together.

The same setting, the spaghetti straps on the sun tops, the tongues sticking out – it was enough. The first she knew about it was when she went into college that morning.

Her gang was huddled in a group when she saw them. She went over to join them, and Ashley turned on her. 'You stay away from my sister, you cow, you . . .'

Becca hadn't understood. She thought Ashley was still upset about the sisters thing. She looked at the others for some support, but they wouldn't meet her gaze. 'I only—' she began.

'You slag!' Ashley kept screaming. 'You slag!' The others had pulled her away still yelling abuse at Becca.

Her friends. She'd gone after them, ready to smile, telling herself it was a joke, this was how friends joked, it had to be ... she could see herself following them saying things like, 'Hey ... What's ... I don't get what ...' How pathetic was that?

And then the summons to Clare's office had come.

And that was it. Her life in Leeds – gone.

Becca lifted her chin. She didn't have to take that kind of shit. Fuck them. She hadn't done anything wrong. She wasn't ashamed of camming – why should she be? If guys wanted to pay, why shouldn't she do it? She was good at it, and they gave her money.

And now Liam at the drop-in had called her Bex. *Tell you later ... Bex.*

It didn't mean anything. Liam did that. Terry was Tez, Darren was Daz. Neil was probably Nez for all she knew. Calling her Bex didn't mean anything.

Nothing at all.

It was good she was working that night. Otherwise she would have been stuck in her flat, staring at the walls, no one to talk to, nothing to do – or nothing she could afford to do – until work on Monday, and she thought, seriously thought, she might go crazy.

Chapter 11

Jared's plans – not for the first time – were pretty much fucked up. Plan A had been to pack up his stuff, load his car and head up the coast towards Kettleness, but as he wasn't fit to drive, it had to be Plan B.

Plan B, as usual, didn't exist.

For the first day after his exploration of the tunnel, he really thought he might need to go back to the hospital – only there was no one to tell and no one to take him. A text arrived from his mother – the usual stuff – *How are you, keep in touch,* yada yada yada, trying to pretend everything was OK.

But Jared could still hear his father's voice. *What happened, mate? How did you get it so wrong?* Jared had been the leader, the experienced caver, and he'd walked away without a scratch, while Charlie . . .

That wasn't the way his father had taught him.

He swallowed a fistful of pills and washed them down with whisky. Pills were for pain, right? He texted back – *Fine. Call soon* – then collapsed onto the bed and stayed there, taking painkillers when he surfaced, washing them down with whisky. He just wanted to be out of it.

After a couple of days, his own stink drove him outside and he managed to clean himself – and the caravan – up a bit and take stock. He wasn't right back where he'd started from, but he couldn't walk without his stick, if you wanted to call it walking. His back kept going into spasm, when all he could do was stand there and let the pain grip him, teeth clenched, breathing shallow, *JesusJesusJesusJesus* until it was gone.

Driving wasn't an option. He survived on dry Weetabix and increasingly dubious milk swigged straight from the bottle. After the first couple of days he cut down on the pills – a bit – and did the exercises his physio had given him. Gradually, his back improved. He managed to go for short walks – very short walks – along the road towards the Flamborough cliffs, but he spent the evenings in a daze of drugs and alcohol.

He was sick of it. Sick down deep in his soul.

On Saturday morning, he hauled himself out of bed, determined to make some kind of move. He was sorting through the piles of his stuff that had accumulated on the floor when he was interrupted by a loud banging on the caravan door.

The police? Back again?

Shit! His gaze skimmed the place looking for any visible evidence of . . . stuff. Things he shouldn't have. Things he shouldn't have been doing.

The knock came again, heavier and more impatient. He opened the door a cautious sliver. 'Yeah?', relaxing and adding 'mate' when he saw it was the site owner. Jared's philosophy was always to try and find the good side of the people he encountered – why get into unnecessary fights? – but as far as he could tell, GBH only had a bad side and a worse side.

The man was equally abrupt. 'You had the cops here. What was that about?'

Jared hesitated, wanting to tell the guy to mind his own business. But fair enough, it was his business if there was trouble on the site. 'Nothing much. They were tracking a phone call. Came from somewhere round here'

'Yeah. What did you tell them?'

'Told them I didn't know anything about it. Why?'

'Never mind why. What else?'

Jared thought back. They were now definitely on *mind your own business* territory, but if the police had been hassling the guy, then Jared had no problems helping him out. 'I told them to ask the people having the parties.'

The reaction surprised him. The man's face went dark with anger. 'What are you talking about?'

Jared shrugged. 'The bunch of headbangers who've been playing music over that way.' He indicated the far side of the field where the late-night partying had been going on.

The man stared at him in silence, then said, 'Yeah? You listen to me. There's been no parties on this site, right?'

'OK, if you say so.'

'This site's closed for the winter now. I want to you out of here. Tomorrow.'

'You're closing down what, exactly?' He looked around the empty site and the rows of battered, deteriorating caravans. Down the rutted track, a broken gate was pushed back against the tangle of winter undergrowth. 'Locking the gates to keep all the tourists out?'

'Don't get funny with me, *mate*. I'm switching the water off. Start packing.'

As GBH strode away, Jared watched until he was out of sight, then went across to where his car was parked. He rummaged inside, pulling out handfuls of junk, until he found what he was looking for – a dispenser's paper bag with his latest prescription painkillers. He was just limping his way back to the caravan when a bike went past at high speed, almost hitting him and making him stagger back from the path. As he stared after it, another one passed him. He caught a glimpse of a boyish, freckled face as a voice shouted, 'Move it, mong!' and they vanished along the path.

Jared steadied himself, but didn't waste the effort in yelling an obscenity after the disappearing rider. Having just avoided being manhandled off the site by the manager, he didn't want to be beaten up by a couple of pill-headed yobs. His own weakness depressed him. He used to be able to stand his ground. Now he seemed to be taking endless shit from just about anyone.

As he closed the caravan door, he decided it was time he stopped messing around. If he wanted to get fit again, he needed to get out and do things. He had to stop letting a bit of pain ground him. For fuck's sake, of course it hurt. He'd broken his fucking back, and then he'd fallen down a ladder in a tunnel. It wouldn't get better unless he started using it.

OK. A timetable. In a way, GBH was doing him a favour. Sort out his stuff today, leave tomorrow. He could manage the drive up the coast if he took it slowly, lots of stops. He had his tent and all his gear. Camping at Kettleness would be better than this – it certainly couldn't be worse.

He cleared the minuscule bit of floor space the caravan offered, and, gritting his teeth, he put himself through another physio routine. After half an hour, it felt as though every muscle in his body was on fire. He crawled onto the bed, making himself ignore the whisky and the painkillers lying temptingly within reach. He'd give himself an hour to recover, then he'd start the whole routine again.

And it worked. By the evening he was knackered, but he felt better. So much better, he almost had to pinch himself to make sure he wasn't dreaming. His head felt clear and for the first time since he'd almost killed himself in the side tunnel, he was feeling properly hungry.

A fry-up – eggs, bacon, sausage, fried bread – then a good night's sleep and he'd be ready for anything ... but that would mean a drive into Brid, a drive back here, cooking it all on the inadequate two-ring burner, leaving the caravan full of condensation and the smell of frying.

Or ... he could go to the pub. Pie and peas. He could

almost feel the crust break under his knife, and see the gravy flooding the plate across the fat crispness of the chips and the green mush of the peas ...

And a pint of beer, get back for about ten, just a couple of pills to make him sleep like a baby until morning ...

He grinned, feeling his spirits lift. Pie and peas was as good a cure for soul sickness as any other he knew. With beer. He finished organising his stuff, pulled on the closest thing he had to clean clothes and put the rest into a black bag for the launderette when he got into Whitby tomorrow, then grabbed his keys and set out.

There was a decent pub about a mile away. He'd earned a good evening.

Chapter 12

The first person Becca saw when she got into the drop-in was Hannah, one of the youth workers who often used the café as a kind of informal counselling booth. Hannah was small and solid, given to dungarees and boots. Liam called her an old dyke – but not to her face, Becca was interested to note. She was always friendly, and managed to offer advice without sounding as if she thought Becca was an idiot. 'Hi Becca. I've switched on the urn. Nothing to report. Just the usual suspects in tonight.'

'Thanks.' Becca had no idea who the usual suspects were, but Hannah always said that. 'See you tomorrow.' Hannah gave her a wave as she headed towards the door, pulling on her coat as she went.

Once she'd gone, the café was all Becca's. In the evenings, the job was simple. There was no cooking. The café served hot drinks for free, and sold canned drinks, sweets and biscuits.

Hannah had left everything ready. All Becca needed to do was keep checking the urn and wait for business. The main room was quiet and the café was empty. Saturday nights, most of the kids managed to find some entertainment in the town. Somewhere, someone was whistling, a sad tune that tugged at her memory ... yeah. Matt used to whistle it when he was working on something, some kind of song about love, and whisky, and stuff like that.

She missed him.

She sat on a stool by the counter and watched two lads who were playing idly on the snooker table and talking earnestly between shots.

It was Liam with, as always, Terry. *Tez*. Wherever Liam went, Terry was not far behind. No one was going to mess with Liam when Terry was there. Terry was big. Though come to think of it, no one messed with Liam anyway.

He looked up and saw her watching him.

'Hi, Bex. Come to make us a drink? Get a move on, then.' He gave Terry a push and the two of them scuffled their way towards the counter where she was standing.

'And two Cokes,' he said, reaching over the counter and helping himself to a biscuit. They were both laughing. As one stopped, the other nudged, and they started again. She wasn't sure if she was the target of the joke or not.

'Fifty pence for Cokes,' she said, heading towards the hatch so she could serve them.

Liam turned his smile on her. 'Come on, Bex. Dyke-lady lets us have it for free.'

'Yeah, right. Fifty.'

'They sell it for half that down the supermarket.'

'This look like a supermarket to you?'

He smiled and held her gaze. While she was distracted, Terry ducked under the hatch, helped himself to two cans of Coke and was away. 'You see?' Liam said cheerfully. 'Self-service.'

'That's going on a tab.'

Liam held up the can as if he was drinking to her, and said, 'Any more at home like you, Bex *girl*. Kid sister, maybe?' Becca froze. He waggled his tongue, and Terry sniggered. The two of them left the room, scuffling and laughing.

Becca felt the wash of rage that preceded the room-wreckings of her teenage years. No one spoke to her like that. No one. Her hand gripped a cup, already seeing the arc it would make through the air, and hearing the satisfying smash. Seeing it smash into Liam's sneer, and seeing . . .

The whistling she'd heard earlier helped her. It made her think of Matt and what he said to her when she went into a meltdown. *Anger is useful, Becca. Don't waste it. Use it the right way.*

Yeah, useful like the power it would give her arm when she hurled the cup into . . . When she did exactly what Liam wanted, and got into serious trouble.

Forget it, she told herself. *Forget it. He's not worth it.* But she didn't believe that, not really.

As the slow evening dragged on, the whole thing went round and round in her head as she served drinks, cleared tables, washed up.

Liam was making it clear, he didn't have to spell it out – if she did anything he didn't like ... Just like Him, her stepfather. *Don't tell, Becca. They won't believe you. They'll send you away.* He'd kept her powerless by the fear of consequences and no one was going to do that to her again.

Maybe she should tell Neil about Bexgirl now, and then... She tried to picture a scene in which Neil listened, nodded understandingly and said it would be OK, she wasn't to worry.

Yeah, right.

The café was empty. She locked up the cash drawer, went into the small kitchen behind the counter and sat down on a box. She needed some time on her own. What to do?

Liam was a creep. He made people do what he wanted – Paige did what he said, Terry did what he said and now he was going to start on Becca. She knew what would happen – if she didn't do what he wanted, he'd make sure everyone knew about Bexgirl.

And she'd lose her job.

Well, wasn't that what she wanted? Hadn't she spent the last month moaning at herself and anyone who would listen how much she hated it.

And she did.

Except ...

She liked it when Paige sought her out. She liked it when Hannah treated her like a ... like a colleague, not some know-nothing kid. She'd even liked it when Neil – who was still a patronising git – said she was doing well. If she left, it was going to be her decision, not something Liam forced her into.

And if she got the push, what would she do for money?

Right. She might not know what to do about Liam, but she wasn't going to let him know that. Her head came up and she stalked back into the café. *Don't try it, creep!*

There was no sign of either Liam or Terry. Paige was sitting in one of the chairs, smoking some kind of roll-up. Her gaze met Becca's.

'Want some?' she asked, holding it up.

Becca couldn't be arsed with the rules tonight. She was going to get the push – what did she care. 'Ta.' She sat down at the table with Paige and took a drag. The hit was amazing – an instant high. This wasn't weed, it was … 'What *is* it?'

Paige, who was watching her closely, grinned. 'Good, isn't it? I can get you some if you want.'

Becca could feel the high fading, and she wanted it back. Now. She wanted to go on feeling like this and already she could sense the down that was coming.

'Becca?' Paige was looking at her expectantly.

'No. I don't want it. And you'd better put that thing out before someone sees you.'

To her surprise, Paige nipped the end of the roll-up and slipped it into her bag with no more than an eloquent rolling of the eyes.

They sat in silence, Paige watching Becca, her gaze dropping or moving away when Becca looked at her.

She fidgeted with her bag and looked at the clock on the wall.

'You OK?' Becca asked eventually.

Paige shrugged. 'Makes me jumpy. That stuff.' She met Becca's gaze. 'I don't get you.'

'What don't you get?'

'What you're doing here. Why did you come to a dump like this? If I had a place in Leeds, I wouldn't.'

Why was everyone so hooked on Leeds? Liam with his *I know a mate of yours*, Paige with her *Leeds is so cool* shit. The trouble was, it was a question Becca asked herself all the time, though the answer was simple. Because she'd fucked up big time. 'I needed a job.'

'Yeah. But . . .' She met Becca's gaze. 'OK. Whatever. Listen, do you know someone called Kay? Kay McKinnon?'

Surprise kept Becca silent for a minute, then she said, 'Yeah. Do you?'

'Kind of. Is she, you know, OK? I mean, can you . . .' Whatever Paige wanted to say, she didn't finish. Her gaze moved beyond Becca to the door.

Liam stood there, jerking a peremptory head. 'You ready or what?' He ignored Becca.

'I'm talking to Becca.'

'Yeah, well, time to stop, isn't it?'

Paige sighed. 'It's only nine thirty. There's plenty of time.'

Liam beckoned her over to the door and they talked, keeping their voices low. Liam looked angry. 'What are you playing at?' Becca heard him say.

'I don't like it,' Paige shot back. 'I want to know what ...' Her gaze slid round to Becca, and Liam looked as well. His gaze challenged her as he put his hand on Paige's arm and tried to draw her away.

Paige shook him off and Becca jumped to her feet just as Alek came into the café. He looked at the three of them, frowning. To Becca's surprise, Liam dropped Paige's arm and she came back to the table rubbing her wrist. Becca took her chance. 'Liam was just going,' she said. 'But he owes us for drinks.' *I'm not scared of you!*

Just for a second, she caught a flash of real hostility in Liam's eyes, then he fished in his pocket and held out a handful of cash. 'Keep the change,' he said. Then his gaze locked on hers. 'Not bad for a quid. Does that include the kid sister?'

Becca met his gaze. 'Get lost, Liam.'

Alek walked with Liam and Terry to the exit, not saying anything – he wasn't big on chat. Becca was pretty sure he was checking they were safely off the premises. It was close to closing time – she could start packing up herself. Then she realised that Paige was still there, watching her.

'Have you finished?' Paige asked.

'Not yet. I've still got to clear up.'

Paige pulled a face. 'What do you want to do this for?' Her gesture encompassed the shabby café, the litter on the floor and the tables, sticky with spilled drinks.

It was another question Becca was asking herself. 'I need the money.' But a different answer was close to the surface.

'Yeah, but ... there's lots of ways to get money. You going to do that now?'

Becca hesitated. It looked like Paige wanted to talk. Hannah had advised her about this – *They can trust you, Becca. You're near their age. No one will get upset with you if you leave your work to talk to one of the users who wants something.*

She wasn't sure if Neil would agree, but it made sense to her. There wasn't much clearing up to do anyway – she could finish off tomorrow morning if she came in a bit early. 'It can wait,' she said.

Paige was still watching her, chewing her lip as if she was unsure about something. Her long fair hair hung round her face and tonight she was wearing a denim jacket and a micro skirt over stylishly ripped leggings. Her feet were thrust into ballet slippers. It was Saturday-night clubbing gear, not walking-the-streets dress.

'Any parties tonight?' Becca asked, to break the silence.

'Why? You want to come?'

'Not really.' And not to any party in this dump. 'Where are you going?'

Paige shrugged. 'Mate's. So, you got your car?'

'Not tonight. I'm walking.'

'I'll walk with you,' Paige said.

Becca was surprised, but didn't say anything as she collected her jacket and her bag. As they were leaving, Alek called her back. 'I find this,' he said. 'Is it yours?' He was holding up a phone. Becca's hand flew to her pocket. Her phone was gone.

'It's – yeah. I must have ... Where did you find it?'

'In the coffee bar. Behind the counter.'

She must have left it there, but she couldn't remember doing it. All that shit with Liam – it was making her confused. 'OK. Thanks,' she said as she took it.

Paige had walked ahead, ignoring Alek, but as Becca went past him he said so quietly she barely heard him, 'Look after her. Make sure she is safe, all right?'

She looked back at him. 'What do you ...?' But the door was already closing.

Chapter 13

Paige slipped her arm through Becca's as they walked along the road, her weight a slight drag against their progress. Becca and Ashley used to walk through Leeds city centre like this on a Saturday night, talking, laughing, a bit high and giddy, part of the street life and part of the city vibe.

Here, there was just the empty streets and the darkness.

Paige fished in her bag and pulled out the roll-up. 'Want some?'

Becca shook her head. She didn't trust herself with that stuff. Whatever it gave you was fake, but already, after one drag, part of her was missing it. Paige stopped in the shelter of the wall to light up, then they walked on towards the front. The lights from the arcade still flashed out across the harbour.

As they passed by, Becca could see the machines and hear the jangling tunes, the whooshes, the sharp cracks as the lights flashed and rippled. It made the arcade seem busy and full but in the shadows between the consoles, there was just emptiness.

'Hey, Bex! Paige!'

Becca looked round. It was Liam, standing with a group outside the arcade. A small, dark girl was clinging to his arm, looking at him with wary devotion. He shook her off and moved to stand in their path.

'What you doing, Paige?' he said.

'What's it to you? Or that slag over there.' She directed her anger towards the girl. 'I told you to keep away, bitch!'

'Yeah, right, it weren't me who—'

'Shut up.' Liam barely raised his voice, but both the girls fell silent. He grinned at Becca. 'Brought my mates, see? Thought you might like a game, Saturday night an all. Threesomes. Jurassic Park? You might get, you know ... eaten.' He grinned. 'You like that, don't you?'

Becca could see the group he'd been with watching them, waiting to see how the exchange would go. She could make out Terry's bulk – she really, really didn't want a face-off with Terry. 'Yeah, right, very funny. Come on, Paige.'

'Wait.' Paige's arm dragged her back. Becca felt a stab of something that was part anger, and part something else. Liam frightened her. Out here in his own domain, he wasn't just a yob. He was dangerous. She knew that. She waited as Paige and Liam had a quick, low-voiced exchange, then, to her relief, Paige turned away.

'Come on,' she said again and after a moment, Paige moved on with her. Becca looked back over her shoulder at Liam, who was talking on his phone. She didn't look back again after that first glance, but her whole body tensed, expecting Liam to come after them.

To her surprise, he didn't, and they continued along the road until they reached the fingerpost where the road forked and Becca's route took her towards the train station. She stopped. 'I go this way. You want to keep away from him.'

'He's OK.' Paige shrugged, taking a final drag.

'Maybe. For a scumbag.'

Paige laughed. 'Can I come back with you?' she said. 'My mate's ... it's too far. We can, you know, if you want ...?' Her fingers moved caressingly up Becca's back.

'I don't want,' Becca said sharply. 'But you can come back if you like.' She tried to imagine what Liam would make of it if he heard Paige had spent the night at hers. Or what Neil would say – he'd been very clear about 'professional distance'. They talked about it at college all the time, keeping your 'professional distance'. Well, fuck that, she wasn't a professional and she wasn't going to be, not now. She couldn't leave Paige on the streets. The 'mate' didn't sound either safe or convincing.

'It's this way,' she said.

It was raining more heavily now and the road was dark. Paige was more of a drag on her arm, and Becca slowed down slightly. 'Are you OK?'

'It's cold,' Paige complained. 'And my feet hurt.'

That was hardly surprising. The ballet slippers weren't exactly designed for walking in bad weather. Becca could remember her own evenings, when she and

Ashley propped each other up on shoes that were so ridiculous but so much fun . . .

A car was coming along the road behind them, making their shadows stretch out along the pavement. It was slowing, then it was past them and pulling up onto the pavement just as they came alongside.

There were two people inside, she could just make out their shapes – one in the passenger seat and a driver sitting silently behind the wheel, looking away. She tried to pull Paige past, aware of the passenger-side window winding down. 'Want a lift?' A male voice. She couldn't see his face.

'No.'

'Nasty night. We'll take you where you want to go.'

'Come on!' She tugged Paige's arm urgently.

'Wait.' Paige had stopped.

'Come on, Paige.'

Paige pulled back. 'You're not the boss of me.'

Becca, frozen, saw the back door of the car move. Just a bit. There was someone in the back seat and they were going to be trapped between the two open doors. Her hand closed round the keys in her pocket, letting the sharp ends protrude. 'We don't want a lift. Paige, we're nearly there. We don't need a lift. Come on.'

But the friendly Paige, the girl who had been chatting and confiding in her, was gone. She looked at the man leaning out of the car. She looked at Becca. 'I've changed my mind. I'm going to the party,' she said, and before Becca could do anything, she hopped into the back of the car. The door closed smartly behind her and the car pulled away with a squeal of tyres. Becca, still trying to process what she was seeing, saw a face looking out of the front passenger-side window checking the street, checking her. Male or female? She couldn't tell. She whipped out her phone and took a picture.

The light cast a shadow across the eyes, like a mask.

Chapter 14

The car reached the end of the road, indicated left and vanished, heading towards the coast road. Becca was frozen with indecision, not knowing what to do – go after the car? Go and get help? It had all happened so quickly, she was still trying to process what she had seen. There had been no threat – Paige had got in the car willingly – but she was in trouble, Becca was sure of that.

She looked at the image on her phone – it was just a silhouette against the light, no detail, nothing. Useless. Someone might recognise the make of the car, but as far as that went, Becca didn't have a clue.

And what could she have done? Stopped Paige getting in? Paige had made it clear she wasn't going to listen.

If it had happened a bit closer to the drop-in, she could have gone back and told someone. Alek had asked her to keep an eye on Paige – what did he know about what just happened? Great job she'd done there. But he would have locked up and gone by now.

It was up to her. She could call the police but she

knew what they were like with girls like Paige – girls like she had been. Her stepfather had been a policeman.

Tomorrow she could tell someone. But that was tomorrow. Hours away. Right now, Paige could be . . . Becca had to do something.

She looked at her watch. To her surprise, it was only a couple of minutes since Paige had been driven off. The car couldn't be that far away. If Becca got her own car she could follow the route the other car had taken out along the coast road. And if they'd turned off? Why would they go out towards the coast? There was nothing there.

But it was better than just going back to her flat and doing nothing. If the car hadn't gone far, she might spot it, might find out where Paige had been taken. She was watching Paige's back, and that's what she was here for.

And then . . .?

She shook her head impatiently. She'd sort that out if she needed to.

The rain was falling again, heavier than before, reflecting from the pavements, making it harder to see. It stung her face as she hurried along the street, her feet splashing in the puddles. The night was silent apart from the falling rain and a distant foghorn. The rain played tricks with the sound so it was hard to tell where it was coming from. Someone laughed – ahead of her? No, behind her. She heard the muffled sound of glass breaking, then more laughter, and then the street was quiet again.

She reached the side street and felt herself relax as she

saw the shape of her car. She'd feel safer once she was inside it. She took out her keys and went to unlock the driver's door before she realised.

The windows were shattered and one of the tyres was slashed.

Chapter 15

The pub just down the road from the caravan site was busy. Even in winter, Flamborough attracted serious walkers and birdwatchers. Jared found a table, then ordered food and a pint at the bar. The beer went down so well that the pint became two, then three.

He got back into his car with a sense of wellbeing he'd half expected never to feel again.

It didn't last. It hadn't been such a good idea after all – not all at once. He had to pull in on the lane and drag himself out, just managing to get clear before he lost the lot – the food, the beer – in a sudden upheaval into the hedgerow that left him cold and dizzy.

After a few minutes, he felt better and got back behind the wheel, rummaging in the pockets for some water to rinse his mouth out. The rocking motion of the car as he drove onto the track through the site made him want to heave again but he managed to keep it under control.

He stopped outside the caravan and climbed heavily out of his car. Immediately, the familiar noise from the other side of the site – shouts, screams, pounding music – almost overwhelmed him. *Fuck!* Who were these guys?

He'd felt so good earlier, and now he felt like shit, but at least he knew why. He was drunk, hammered, rat-arsed for the first time since … when? He told himself it was OK. He'd feel better soon. It was familiar territory.

As he stood outside the caravan, digging in his pocket for his keys, something flashed past him on the track, almost knocking him off his feet. Bikers. Again. Two guys on mountain bikes vanished into the darkness. *Fucking idiots.* Were there any more around?

He couldn't find his fucking keys. Had he dropped them when the bikers made him jump back? Or when he got out of the car earlier? Maybe down the pub? Oh, Jesus, he really wasn't up for this. His head was starting to ache and his stomach was acid and churning.

You're in a bad way, mate. It was his own voice, his own internal commentator chipping in far too late in the day to tell him something he already knew, thanks; that he couldn't fix himself long-term with booze and painkillers. If he wanted to be well again, something needed to change.

Tomorrow. He'd think about it tomorrow.

The noise from across the site showed no signs of abating. Great – no sleep tonight. It reminded him of his return from the tunnel when, mazed by cold and shock, he'd struggled to get himself safely into shelter; in pain, exhausted, while other people were blazing it up a few hundred metres away. How long was it since he'd enjoyed a party?

Not since Charlie ... *Ah,* screw *that. Fuck it. Sideways.*

The voices of memory chattered away into silence. He stood there breathing slowly, letting the landscape absorb him.

The moon hung bright in a clear sky, turning the rutted tracks into patterns of deep shadow and light, the caravans making blocks of darkness against the night sky. He realised the noise from the party had stopped, then there was a sudden burst of sound, someone screamed, a door banged and a car engine revved up.

Fucking hell.

Key. He needed his key. If he'd dropped it ... He sat on the upturned crate and began searching his pockets in earnest. After a couple of minutes' fumbling he found it. For some reason he'd put it in his top pocket. Holding it with exaggerated care, he stood up and attempted to line it up with the keyhole.

And someone came flying out of the darkness towards him. She – it was a girl – skidded to a halt in front of him. 'Let me in! They're coming.'

He stared at her, fuddled, trying to make sense of what she was saying. She grabbed his arm and shook it. 'Let me in!'

Her face hung in the shadows in front of him, barely illuminated by the moonlight. She was wearing a mask – no, the flesh round her eyes was bruised, discoloured – his mind struggled to interpret what he was seeing. Her mouth was moving and something dark was flowing from it – she was saying something but the words were slurred and indistinct.

'My key,' he said. 'I can't ...' He snapped awake to the urgency of the situation. She needed help. He pushed the key into the lock, juggling with it, cursing its awkwardness. He could feel the girl's hand clutching at his arm. He could hear her voice muttering something frantically as she looked back over her shoulder.

Somewhere quite close a car engine roared. His fingers were clumsy with panic.

Her hands gripped at him and now she was making a sound halfway between a choke and a sob.

Then the door swung open and he fell in, turned and grabbed for her to pull her inside.

But she had gone.

In front of him, like a still from a movie, lights illuminated the side of the van. He stared from the darkness as the girl, caught in the glare, flattened herself against it, her eyes wide. And then she turned and ran.

He saw her vanish into the darkness across the field. The engine roared as the car swung round. Someone jumped out and ran after her, the car following along the lane.

Jared cursed his drunken, crippled state – he had to follow, but he could barely walk, never mind run. He grabbed a torch and set off after the girl and her pursuers. His feet slipped in the mud. He fell, smacking his head against something – then he was pulling himself to his feet, running again.

You cunts, leave her alone, you cunts, you cunts . . .

Then the screaming started. Across the site, the far end of the field? He couldn't tell, but she was screaming.

Oh, Jesus, what could he. . .

Police. He could call them, get them here.

He had to stop to pull his phone out, jabbing 999 into the keypad, then he was running again, the phone held to his ear.

Emergency, which services?

He wanted to shout and swear, but he knew he had to give them the information as fast as he could. 'Police. Quick! Someone's getting . . .' He ran between the caravans, trying to locate the sound, but her scream suddenly cut off with an abruptness that was terrifying.

He heard the car engine roar again.

Shit! She was somewhere on the site and he was floundering around in the mud. 'This girl, she – she was running away from someone. She was hurt. Bleeding. She asked me to help her.' His breath was giving out. 'I . . . I could hear her . . . screaming, but . . .' He listened. Silence.

'And what's happening now?' The voice was infuriatingly calm.

'She needs someone, fast. You've got to get someone here!'

'Yes, sir, I've dispatched a car, but I need more information.'

'Nothing. Nothing's happening. It's quiet. I can't find her. They've got a car; they might have her in the car.' His breath was coming in ragged gasps. Maybe there was someone else here, from the party, someone else who could – no, the party had to be where she came from.

Keep away from the party.

He was back on the track now. He'd come in a wide circle almost back to his starting point. The site gate was just ahead of him. Somehow, somewhere in the darkness, he'd lost her.

He limped on through the gate and onto the road. He was pretty sure the car must have gone this way. How long would it take the police to get here – would they come from Bridlington? Or would it be from Scarborough? He couldn't leave it – he had to keep looking.

Clouds had covered the moon. The road was a black emptiness. He staggered forwards, shining his torch onto the surface, into the darkness ahead. Nothing. There was nothing there.

Maybe she got away. Maybe she was hiding.

The bushes.

He shone his torch at the undergrowth, around the lane, nothing, nothing.

And then he heard a sound. It was faint, almost like a breath, like someone trying to moan, only they couldn't manage even that.

He turned, and his torch shone straight at the pile of bramble-covered rubble and junk by the gatepost.

The shimmer of cloth.

The gleam of flesh – an arm, he could see her arm.

She was lying there, not moving, just that strange breath, so faint he could barely hear it.

'It's OK,' he said as he eased himself down next to her. The light of his torch played across her. 'There's help on its way. Here.' He pulled off his jacket to put over her, crouching awkwardly, barely noticing the jab of pain from his back. 'Here.'

I didn't help you before but I'm here now.

His torch moved up her body. He could see dark stains on her arms. Her face – he couldn't interpret what he was seeing. It made no sense. She was smiling, grinning, like she was going to jump up and shout 'Boo!' only … it wasn't a smile, it was like a skeleton face, but skeletons didn't have eyes that stared, unblinking, fixed, and something hanging down in front … and the blood.

She made that noise again and he saw bubbles around the exposed teeth.

Then he realised what he was seeing. He closed his eyes and sat on the ground beside her. He took her hand and said, 'There's help coming. I'm here till they come. I won't leave you. They'll be here any minute.'

And she kept making that sound, like Charlie trying to breathe, trapped in the tunnel as the water kept rising.

It can't have been long, but it felt like an hour before he heard the sound of the police siren on the road.

Chapter 16

When Kay woke up, it was still dark. The cold seeped through the glass from the frozen silence of the moors. Her hand moved automatically to Matt's side of the bed, and she felt the bleak emptiness of the smooth sheet beside her.

She sat up and checked the time. It was just after five thirty – she never seemed to sleep much later these days. If she went down and refuelled the stove, the house would start to warm up while she made tea.

Milo raised a sleepy head and looked at her before flopping down again. While Matt was alive, he slept in his basket downstairs. That didn't last. After Matt's death, Milo had fretted and pined so she'd put a basket in her room. It wasn't long before he moved onto the bed, and now the arrangement was routine.

Shivering in the cold, she pushed back the quilt and stood up, pulling on her warm dressing gown. She could remember Matt saying happily, 'We won't need central heating. That stove's enough to warm the entire cottage.' He'd enjoyed the whole process – storing the wood, setting the fire, tending to it. Kay didn't. She liked heat that came to life at the touch of a switch. But she'd never told him that – at the time, it seemed unimportant, like the isolation and the hard east-coast weather that battered the cottage for much of the year.

And each winter morning when she woke up, the chill was just another thing that reminded her Matt wasn't there anymore. She didn't feel like getting up, going downstairs, starting the day. What was there for her to do? All her adult life, her house had been filled with the demands of difficult, damaged children, but now ... just silence.

Putting on her slippers, she made her way down the narrow staircase past the electric heater on the landing, which she plugged in to take the chill off the upstairs.

'I know, I know.' She spoke to Matt, who used to chide her when she did something dangerous. *Someone will trip on the flex, Kay.* But she was always careful.

The stove downstairs was out. She raked through the embers and stacked in fresh kindling. Once she was sure the stove was burning, she went through to the kitchen.

It was tiny. She would have found it frustratingly cramped in the days when they had a fluctuating family of foster-kids to feed, but it was about the right size for one person. She closed her eyes, remembering the kitchen they'd had in Leeds, the space, the huge battered table where the family – because her foster-kids were her family – could assemble for meals. Kay had been strict about that. *I don't care if you don't eat it, but for tea, we all sit down together.*

Rain rattled against the window as she looked out across the grey winter fields. Without Matt, her new life ... their new life ...

She heard the clatter and scratch of Milo's claws on the staircase and felt her spirits lift, just a bit. It was impossible to feel depressed with Milo around.

Tea. What she needed was a cup of tea. She put the kettle on and turned on the radio to catch the local news.

She let the tea brew while she opened the back door for Milo to go out. He pottered round the small garden, oblivious to the rain, checking out the smells that had accumulated during the night, searching hopefully for any discarded thing that might be edible, looking back at her to see if he could entice her out for an early walk. She leaned in the doorway ignoring the freezing weather, watching him.

Eventually, he came back in and she fed him, then poured herself a cup of tea. She listened to the radio against the percussion of Milo's dish thumping against skirting as he licked it to a bright shine.

The radio was chattering on about traffic problems, weather updates, tide times, interspersed with irritating jingles. Why did they think she needed silly tunes to keep her entertained?

In the summer, she'd taken a tray outside and had breakfast in the early morning sun on the small terrace that looked out across the fields. In her memory, Matt had been with her.

Memory. It couldn't be trusted. It created idylls.

They'd never had breakfast together here. In fact, for most of their lives they'd rarely managed to sit down together in the morning. They were too busy, and breakfast was a clamour of children, teenage girls to winkle out of the bathroom, teenage boys to winkle off their mattresses, a quick cup of tea and a slice of toast, or nothing at all as they raced to get the children to their different schools and themselves off on their different commutes. Breakfasts in the sunshine could only have happened during the retirement Matt never had.

Tears made her eyes blur and she shook her head to clear them.

The radio burbled on. She was only half listening, watching the moon set over the fields. In the distance, the sea glittered, cold and still.

This was why they had bought the cottage. The sea.

'*Radio Humberside for you ... News and weathe-e-e-r ...*'

She was reaching out to change station when she caught what the newscaster was saying:

'*A young woman was assaulted on the road to Flamborough early this morning. She was taken to Scarborough Hospital where her condition is said to be critical. Police describe this as a horrific attack. Our reporter Clare Hammick is on the scene. Clare ...*'

Kay's attention focused sharply as the woman, with carefully maintained gravity, spoke of an assault victim found on the road out in the countryside, miles from anywhere. '*Police are asking for anyone who was in the area last night to come forward,*' she concluded.

The news report switched to an upbeat account of some local team's success. There was no more information about the victim, nothing apart from the fact she was female, and 'young'.

Kay immediately thought of Becca, then told herself she was being daft.

Why would it be Becca? What possible reason would Becca have for being out along the road to the coast? Would she have accepted an invitation – a drink, a drive, a party? Becca was impulsive but she was streetwise – she had to be to have survived.

On the other hand, when had Becca ever needed a reason for risky behaviour?

She picked up the phone.

Chapter 17

Becca woke up with apprehension clutching at her stomach. The image of Paige sliding into the car had preyed on her mind through the night, creeping into her dreams so she kept waking up with a jolt to find that the night was still only half gone. At least it was morning now, but that brought little comfort.

She hadn't done anything, or nothing useful.

After she found her car, she'd run back to the arcade – Liam might be a scumbag but he knew Paige, he might help – but there was no one there, just the arcade lights flashing and the sound of the games machines, like an invisible party deep in the shadows.

In the end, against all her better instincts, she'd called the police and told them what had happened. It was exactly the way she expected – a load of questions and almost no help: Who was she? How did she know Paige? Had Paige got into the car voluntarily? How old was Paige? Where did she live?

As she talked to them, it had begun to rain in earnest. Her shoes – not really designed for walking – filled with water and the cheap leather soon shredded her feet. By the time she got back to her flat, she was soaked to the skin, frozen to her bones and beyond either fear or anger.

She wanted to crawl into a hole and pull the entrance in behind her.

As the memories from last night flooded back, she felt the familiar dark mood start to overwhelm her. Get moving – keep ahead of it. That was the only thing that worked. She swung her legs out of bed and pulled on her dressing gown. It was freezing. She switched on the fire, but nothing happened. The meter was empty, and so was her purse. Last night she'd used up the rest of her money feeding the meter in an attempt to dry herself out and get warm.

How much did she have left in the bank? Hardly anything. Once she'd paid to get her car fixed, there'd be nothing.

Wrapping her quilt round her shoulders, she sat on the bed, shivering. Useless fucking quilt. Useless fucking flat. Useless fucking place. She stopped fighting and let the greyness engulf her.

Useless fucking life.

She was making a mess of everything. She'd made a mess of her friendship with Ashley, she'd made a mess of college and now she was making a mess of work. But most of all, there was Paige. Paige needed help and Becca hadn't given it. Instead, Paige had run out on her, and then . . .

Useless. She'd been useless.

And – dragging, practical detail – she needed to do something about her car. It was there on the street with broken windows and a slashed tyre.

She hated Brid, just hated it. She was going to leave. She was going to keep moving until she left it all – all of it – behind. She'd sell the car to the first person who offered her a bit of cash and then she was going.

Somewhere.

Anywhere.

She was trying to summon up the energy to get dressed when her phone rang. She picked it up listlessly and looked at the screen. It was Kay, and she wasn't in the mood for another of Kay's lectures.

'Before you start. I don't care what you say, I'm not staying. I . . .'

'Becca. You're OK!'

They both spoke at once.

'Why wouldn't I be?'

'There was . . .' Kay took in what she had just said. 'You're not . . .? Not again, Becca. What's wrong now?'

'Oh . . .' She didn't want to talk about it, but neither did she want to sit in her room staring into blank space. 'Why wouldn't I be OK?'

'It was something I heard on the news. A young woman was attacked near one of the caravan parks on the way to the coast. I wanted to make sure . . .'

And Becca was back in the road, watching Paige scramble into the car that had kerb-crawled them, then headed off in the direction of the coast, the face in the window looking back at her, shadowed, like a mask. 'Who? Did it say who?'

'No, nothing. They just said police were investigating ... Becca, do you think it might be someone you know?'

'I don't know. Listen, I need to get to work. I'll call you, OK?'

Kay looked at the silent phone and grimaced. It was typical of Becca to begin her conversation with an announcement she was giving up her job and end it abruptly as she raced off to work to find out what was happening. But she was safe, that was the main thing.

Kay returned to the news. There was more information about the girl now. It was an assault, and the girl had been hurt – badly hurt. Police described the attack as 'sickening', strong language for people who were all too familiar with the worst one person could do to another. There was nothing about her identity – either the police didn't know or they weren't releasing it.

It wasn't Becca. But it could easily be another girl like Becca; there were too many out there on the streets, with indifferent or hostile homes, lonely and vulnerable. Becca had been doing well – until something had stopped her in her tracks. Maybe she'd remember she trusted Kay and tell her, but until then ... Well, at least Becca was safe, or as safe as she ever was, but one girl was not.

The sad truth was there were too many candidates in the Bridlington area to be the victim of this particular crime. Too many vulnerable girls. Violence was inevitable if you had a policy of flooding the poorer coastal towns with the troubled, the homeless and the dispossessed.

If you populate an area with prey, the predators will not be far behind.

Chapter 18

Jared barely slept that night. He'd sat with the girl as the paramedics came, the lights flashing around him, on and off, on and off, and they were carefully easing him out of the way as one of them bent over the girl and the other started talking urgently into his radio. She was still alive, the girl without a face, as they strapped her to a stretcher and took her away.

They'd wanted to take him in as well, but he refused. At first, he thought they were arresting him, then he realised they were concerned about his condition. *Shock*, the paramedic said. The police came and he'd answered their questions as best he could, promising to go into town the next day to sign a statement. After they'd all gone, he crawled back into the caravan.

He sank down onto the bed and pulled the blanket round his shoulders. He was shaking. He couldn't remember ever being so cold. Round and round. It kept going round and round in his head as he tried to tell himself a different story – this time, the girl came running out of the night, and he was ready – he wasn't pissed, he wasn't arsing around with his key. He was alert and on the case, getting the door open, letting her in and closing it, turning everything off, so when the car engine roared and the lights hit the side of the van, it was just another empty caravan, no girl frozen in the sudden brilliance.

Round and round.

In the end, he swallowed a couple of pills, then a couple more, washing them down with whisky on the assumption he'd puked up most of the booze from earlier. He was sober enough now, and he didn't want to be.

But the pills didn't put him to sleep. They added colour and brilliance to the memories that were scrolling relentlessly in his head.

Go back.

Go back . . .

He was eleven. He was climbing a rock face in Derbyshire. The sun was beating down on his bare torso. The climb was tough – tougher than anything he'd tried before. Below, he could hear Charlie panting slightly as he followed Jared's route up the wall.

'To your left, just up . . . bit more . . .' His father, up on the top, taking in the slack on the rope. Jared's reaching hand touched the grip high above him and he launched himself, one hand secure, his body swinging round and then he was up there, above the overhang, grinning in triumph.

'That was one tough overhang, mate. Well done.' His father's hand gripped his shoulder briefly, then he helped Charlie up over the last scramble. 'And you. Good climb!'

Jared knew that though his dad treated Charlie almost like a second son – the child of a friend who had died in the Gulf War, the boy Jared had grown up with, gone to school with – his dad was proud that his own son was always the one who was first, the one who led the hard climb, the one who broke trail on the tough routes. A leader, like his dad.

The rain was beating down on the caravan roof, and here he was on the bleak Yorkshire coast, a wreck who couldn't stay sober long enough to save a girl from . . .

. . . *making that sound, like Charlie trying to breathe, Charlie, trapped* . . .

He'd walked out of that cave with a blanket round his shoulders and hot tea inside him, while Charlie . . . He could still see the contempt in his father's eyes as he looked at the son he had been so proud of.

The son who'd left his mate to drown slowly in a tunnel.

Jared jerked upright. He was on the bed in the caravan. He was years away from the cave.

And just hours away from the girl. He wrapped a blanket round himself in a futile attempt to keep warm and huddled up on the bed, listening to the relentless drumming of the rain on the caravan roof – didn't it do anything but fucking rain here? – and tried not to think too much about what had happened. But the events kept playing over and over on a loop in his head: the screaming, the cave, the unspoken accusation in his father's eyes, and then the girl lying injured by the side of the road as if someone had just dumped her there like a piece of rubbish.

He could have helped her, but he didn't.

He scrabbled around on the small table by the bed until he found his stash, then rolled himself a joint and lay on the bed smoking as the night hours moved slowly past. What was the point of going in to Brid to make a statement? He'd already told them everything he knew. Come morning, he'd pack up his car and leave, get away from all this, just forget about it.

What happened, mate? How did you get it so wrong?

His father had asked him that, and Jared hadn't been able to answer.

And now he was the man who'd let a frightened girl run off into the dark, to get trashed by a bunch of cunts who—

'Fuck it!' he said to no one in particular as he waited out the long night.

Chapter 19

One of the things Kay had learned over the years was that official channels were for officials. If real people wanted to get things done, they used the back door, where there would usually be someone who was able – and willing – to bypass a mountain of red tape to get some action. She might not be a foster-mum anymore, but she still had her contacts.

It wasn't just the attack. Alarm bells were going off in her head, and she remembered the feeling she'd had up on Kettleness. So what had she seen, what had happened to alert her like this? She went to her computer and searched the local newspaper archives.

There was one case. Before Christmas, a body had been washed up on the shore at Ravenscar. The body was female, and 'young'. If there was a follow-up story she couldn't find it. Without a name and without evidence of foul play, the press had quickly lost interest.

Something was nagging at her. What had Becca said? Something about a girl going missing from the drop-in – a friend of one of the users who seemed to have fallen off the radar.

It wasn't much, just the faintest stirring in the undergrowth to warn you that something might be out there, hunting.

Her phone rang just as she was checking through her address book, wondering who to call.

'Is that Kay McKinnon?'

'Speaking.' The voice was familiar, but she couldn't place it.

'It's Shaun Turner. I used to work with your husband.' Now she recognised it. It was the strong, confident voice from the voicemail just a few days ago.

'Yes, I got your message. I'm afraid I don't . . .'

'Remember me? I didn't think you would. It must be almost three years ago now. Matt did a report for us on a children's unit we were – well, that's all finished now.'

Of course. The last project Matt worked on before he became ill. He'd written a report for a police unit set up to deal with homeless children on the east coast. 'Yes, I do remember that. You were the senior officer? Matt spoke very highly of—'

'The unit. And we thought very highly of him.'

A sentence finisher. Well, she could live with that for a few minutes. She realised he was speaking again. '. . . did actually meet once. I don't know if you remember. We had Christmas drinks.'

It was coming back to her now, a slightly uncomfortable evening in a Wetherspoon's in York. She could remember talking to various people from the police team – men in suits, women in smart business clothes – all pleasant enough, sociable enough, and all speaking warmly of Matt. 'Yes – I remember that,' she said, purposely vague.

'It was a real shock to hear about Matt. I had no idea—'

That wasn't something Kay was ready to discuss with a stranger. She cut in quickly, 'What are you doing now? Are you still in York?'

'No. I've retired. You know they closed the unit down, don't you? Cuts. Anyway, we moved to Whitby, but it's a bit ... My wife, Sylvia, died a couple of years ago. Feel as though I'm rattling round a bit, to be honest.'

Kay understood that. She heard the automatic 'we' that still slipped from her occasionally – after all, she was still living the life she and Matt had planned together, even though it wasn't working out as a life for one. It sounded as though Shaun was stuck in the same place as she was. 'I know what you mean,' she said.

Her gaze fell on the open address book. Shaun was ex-police. He'd know something about the attack at Flamborough, if she could think of a way of getting him to tell her. 'I did hear about the unit. That was shocking. Talk about short-term thinking. All that—'

'Money. You don't have to tell me, Kay. There's just a couple of drop-in centres left, and I can't see them—'

She cut in quickly. 'I didn't know those were part of your unit. I know someone who works in the drop-in centre in Bridlington. It sounds a bit tough.'

'How do you mean? The money's always—'

'No, I meant that attack near—'

'Flamborough? You think that's got something to do with the Bridlington drop-in?'

'Wasn't she one of the users, the girl who was attacked?'

There was a moment of silence. 'Who told you that?'

Becca. But what Becca had told her probably came under the heading of confidential information. 'I just assumed. Homeless girls – I know how vulnerable they are.'

He didn't reply at once and she got the impression he was thinking something over. 'Kay, can I sound you out about something? You know this territory – better than I do. The investigating team did talk to me because of my work on the unit. They wanted some background. You understand, this is confidential?'

'Of course.'

'Well, this girl – she was badly hurt. All the usual stuff – I don't want to go into details, but they damaged her face so badly that they can't ask for any visual ID. Whoever did it . . .'

Didn't want their victim identified. She was right. There was something going on. As to whether it involved the drop-in . . . Occam's Razor said it did. 'That's – terrible. Where is she? The girl?'

'She's in hospital. They're not too hopeful, to be honest with you. But she's young, you never know. Kay, what I wanted to know – when you got a new kid come to you, a girl, what made you think, This one will be

OK, this one will make it and what made you think, We might not get there with this one?'

'It doesn't really work that way. You just do the best you can for each of them. Sometimes it works, sometimes it doesn't.'

'But there must be something ... sorry, I'm badgering you. I just keep thinking if there was some way we could spot them, some way of—'

'I think it's called clairvoyance.'

'Clare— Oh, I see what you mean. Yes. I suppose you're right. My problem is – and your Matt told me this often enough – I'm all theory. I've never had much to do with teenage girls.'

Who would probably run rings round him. But the admission made her like him a bit more. 'They keep on surprising me,' she said, and he laughed. 'Well, I have things I need to ...'

'Wait ... before you go.' He sounded hesitant. 'The reason I called – I found something in my old work folders – something Matt wrote. I think you ought to have it. How can I get it to you? I don't want to put it in the post.'

She didn't like mementos. They weren't Matt – they were just the remains from a life that had ended. But it was nice of him to think about it. 'Why don't you ...' She was going to suggest he called round, then realised she didn't want a stranger coming to the house. 'I'm in Whitby most days,' she amended. 'Let me know when you're free and we can have coffee or something.'

'How about tomorrow?'

'Tomorrow?' The speed of it surprised her, but on the other hand, why not? Face to face, she might be able to get a bit more information from him about Flamborough – it was clear he knew more than he was saying. 'Yes. OK. Tomorrow is fine.'

They agreed to meet at a café near the harbour towards midday.

After she'd put down the phone, Kay stayed in the chair, staring out of the window. She was thinking about Matt, but she couldn't keep her mind away from what Shaun had just told her. He hadn't gone into any detail, but Kay could read between the lines. *The usual stuff* – that probably meant raped – and then, apparently, they had destroyed her face – taken away her autonomy, her identity and probably, soon, her life.

Not so long ago, she had been walking on the cliffs above Kettleness, haunted by the feeling that something bad was on its way. Was this it, this vicious attack? What had the girl done to get on the wrong side of . . . what kind of people?

The predators were here.

Chapter 20

When she woke up, Becca had had no intention of going into work. She was leaving. But after Kay's phone call – or more to the point, the news Kay gave her about the attack on Paige – it had to be Paige – everything looked different.

It was late – almost eight – and she was supposed to start at eight. She splashed some water on her face, pulled on her clothes and, grabbing her bag, clattered down into the street. She was lucky. A bus was coming and she had enough change – just – for her fare. After that, she was cleaned out.

The smell of frying bacon greeted her as she walked through the door of the drop-in. She wasn't that late, but someone had opened up for her. Her heart sank at the thought of another row. Neil had made it clear right at the start that she needed to be on time. We have hungry kids at the door every morning, he'd said. We can't make them wait.

She went through to the café to face the music, her feet dragging. But it wasn't Neil. It was Hannah behind the counter, deftly wielding a spatula as a small queue formed of all the early drop-ins. She must have done last night's clearing up as well. Becca braced herself, but all Hannah said was, 'Hi, Becca.'

'I'm sorry I'm late. Someone trashed my car.' She felt bad making it sound like this was why she was late coming in. 'Did you hear about the girl at, you know . . .'

'Flamborough?' Hannah was already slipping off the tabard she'd put on over the dungarees she habitually wore. She put the spatula in Becca's hand and turned her towards the griddle, where rashers of bacon were frying crisp. 'Yes. Neil called – he isn't in yet. He'll talk to all of us about it later. As far as the kids are concerned, you don't know anything and you're not going to talk about it, right? Now, all of these lot have got tokens.' She gestured towards the queue. 'I'm sorry to hear about your car – we can talk about it later if you want.'

And Hannah was gone, leaving Becca in charge, with the reassurance that Neil didn't know she'd been late, and a kind of subtext assurance that Hannah wasn't going to tell.

Hannah was all right.

Becca checked round the room as she handed out sandwiches, toast and cups of tea and collected tokens. There was no sign of Paige, but then she rarely came to the drop-in this early.

Liam and Terry were sitting at a table in the corner, plates in front of them, their heads close together as they talked. Or rather, Liam was talking and Terry was listening, nodding from time to time. Liam seemed to sense Becca's gaze and looked across at her. 'Have a good time last night, then, Bex?'

'Not really. You?'

'Yeah. Smashing, weren't it, Tez?' They grinned at each other.

So now she knew who had trashed her car. His smirk was a challenge, but she managed to ignore him and went on serving until the first rush was over and she had a chance to make herself some toast and a cup of tea. She was just finishing when Neil came into the café and made his way towards her.

She pushed her plate aside. 'Hi.'

'You've heard the news, I assume, about . . .'

'Yes. Do you know . . .? Is it Paige?'

Neil's face was sober. 'You did the right thing last night, Becca, calling the police and telling them about what happened. By the way, how come you were with Paige that late?'

That was Neil. He'd tell her she'd done something right, then follow it up with a snide comment. 'We left at the same time. Is it her?'

'I don't know any more, I'm afraid.'

Becca nodded. Unexpectedly, her eyes filled. She turned away quickly, busying herself with wiping down the counter and tidying up the rows of cups. Her voice sounded funny and she knew Neil had noticed something. It wasn't any of his business how she felt. 'Yeah, well, it could be. Paige, I mean.'

'It could be,' Neil agreed. He frowned. 'Your story – it's got the police thinking. They're wondering if there's a link between what happened and this place. They want to come in and talk to the kids, show them some pictures of people who might be involved in some dodgy stuff. I can't stop them, but the kids aren't going to like it. They don't like the police coming here.'

So she hadn't done the right thing after all.

'Anyway, I've asked if the staff can go down there to start off with. If we can make the links, then there's no reason for them to come here. You're the one who saw what happened last night, so I'd like you to do that. This morning.'

'Talk to the police?'

'Yes. You know the station at Ashville Street, don't you?'

'Now?'

'Yes. As soon as possible. Can you do that?'

He didn't know what he was asking. She couldn't. She just couldn't.

'You may be the most important witness. I'm not expecting many users in today – they've come in for breakfast but they're all disappearing after that. Word's got round about the police.' He frowned. 'This couldn't have happened at a worse time. We've got the funding people in today and tomorrow. If they see the place deserted like this . . .'

'I don't know anything. What can I tell them?'

'Just tell them what you saw last night – I know it wasn't much, but everything will help.'

112

'But if it isn't Paige . . .'

He sounded exasperated. 'They still need to talk to you. Now, will you do that please, Becca?'

She had to. For Paige. Muttering an ungracious 'Suppose so', she picked up her coat.

They wouldn't lock her up, not just for talking to them. She knew she was stupid to be scared of that, but . . . she could still hear the sound of the cell door closing behind her. She couldn't stand to be locked in.

It's for your own safety, Becca.

As she came out of the café, she saw that the drop-in was almost empty. The whole place was deserted. Even Liam and Terry had vanished.

Outside, she saw Alek. He was sitting on a bench, tinkering with something small he held in his hand, whistling between his teeth as he worked. When he saw her, he beckoned to her and she went across. 'Are you going to talk to the police? You know, last night, what you did was the right thing.'

Did everyone know about it? Was everyone talking about her?

Alek looked at her more closely. 'Are you OK, Becca?'

'Yeah. Thanks. I should have done more.'

'You did. You reported it.'

'I should have stopped her. Have you seen her today?'

Alek shook his head. 'She doesn't come in every day, you know that.' The silence held until it was almost uncomfortable. 'Let me show you something.' He reached inside his jacket and pulled out a battered wallet. 'Here.'

She took the photograph he was holding out and studied it. A girl – probably about Becca's age, it was hard to tell. She was in a wheelchair, and her head was lolling to one side as if she couldn't control it properly. Her chair was pushed up against a desk with a keyboard in front of her. She was smiling.

'Is she . . .?'

'My daughter. Ariana.'

'She's . . .' Becca stumbled over what to say. That Ariana was pretty? She was, but she was also badly disabled – that was clear from the picture. 'What's she doing?'

'Studying. She's at Lancaster doing computer-aided engineering. She will have her degree next year, then she will do postgraduate. Then . . .' He stretched out his arms to indicate the future that would open up in front of her. 'Very proud.' He smiled – the first time she'd seen him do that.

'That's . . . great. Yeah. Great.' She wasn't sure why he'd told her, but it was – yeah, it was OK that he had. Ariana. A girl stuck in a wheelchair with a good life opening up, and Paige . . .

'I need to get to Ashville Street.' She looked up at the darkening sky.

'You didn't bring your car today?'

Alek was someone who kept his mouth shut so she told him what had happened. 'I can't afford to get it fixed. Maybe when I get paid.' Except once she'd paid her rent and everything she'd have almost nothing left.

'What is it? Broken windows and cut tyres? I fix it for you. It won't look pretty but you will be able to drive it.'

'I told you. I can't afford it.'

'So? Where I come from ...' He stopped. 'These days – we do each other favours if we can.'

Becca thought about it, looking for the catches in the offer. She didn't like being obligated. Alek didn't seem offended by her hesitation, he just waited for her to make up her mind.

'OK,' she said, then realised this was a bit ungracious. 'Thanks.'

'Then I fix it for you today.'

'Today? You can do it today?' Becca felt her spirits lift at the thought of the car problem being solved.

He didn't reply. He just held out his hand, and after looking at it blankly, Becca realised what he wanted, fished out her keys and gave them to him. 'It's on that back lane near the station.'

'I know it,' he said.

As she walked away, she turned back to wave at him, but he wasn't there. At first, she thought he must have gone back into the building, but then she saw him further up the road, walking fast before vanishing round the corner.

Chapter 21

Becca stood on Ashville Street, looking at the police cars parked outside. The building looked back at her, the windows like blank eyes.

She didn't want to go inside.

She never wanted to have anything to do with the police again. They'd locked her up when she hadn't done anything. She could remember the woman looking at her, her fake smile hiding disbelief. We know you didn't mean to do any harm, but you could have hurt someone badly. *Someone* meant Him, her stepfather. Becca was sorry she hadn't started the fire like they said. If she had, maybe it *would* have hurt Him. Maybe it would have killed Him.

Kay kept saying it was different now, but Kay – Kay might be good with kids but she didn't live in their world. She didn't get it, not really.

OK, time to do this. She took a few deep breaths, then she went in through the main entrance.

Inside, she was confronted by a small room with a screened desk at one end and a random collection of plastic chairs along one wall, two of which were occupied. The man at the desk told her to wait, so she sat down, giving herself a chair's width between the other two people who were waiting there. She took out her phone and pretended to be engaged with something on the screen, trying not to make eye contact.

The man to her left was moving as if he was uncomfortable, and his stick fell across her feet with a clatter. 'Sorry,' he said, leaning forward trying to reach it.

She picked it up for him, glancing sideways at him as she did. The stick made her expect someone old, but he was young with untidy, curly hair. He had a look of the streets about him – his clothes were rumpled and his thin face was unshaven. She could smell cigarettes – he must have had one before he came in. She wished she'd thought of that.

'Thanks,' he said. He shifted in his seat again as if he was in pain. 'Do you know how long they keep you waiting here?'

'No idea.'

He shifted again and muttered, 'Shit.'

'Are you OK?'

'Yeah. I just ... bad back. These seats don't help.'

A door next to the reception desk opened and a man stuck his head out. 'Jared Godwin?'

'Yeah. That's me.' The man heaved himself to his feet, leaning on his stick, and limped his way towards the door. He looked more like someone who had been hit by a train than someone with a bad back. He glanced back at Becca with a grin. 'Wish me a comfortable chair.'

It was twenty minutes before Becca was called through. She spent the time telling herself it was fine, she was fine. She felt a sharp pain in her finger. When she looked at it, she saw she had bitten the nail so far down it was bleeding.

A young police officer took her into a small room and pointed to a chair by a table. It was the same kind of plastic stacking chair that had been in the waiting room. Becca thought about the man with the bad back – so much for his wish. She perched on the edge of the indicated seat, feeling its hard plastic biting into her thighs. The door clicked shut behind her, and she stiffened.

'I'm Ryan,' the man said. 'Detective Constable Ryan Lovell, if you want the whole thing. And you're Rebecca Armitage? Shall I call you Rebecca? Or would you rather be Miss Armitage?' He said it with mock seriousness and grinned at her. He was coming on to her – just a bit. It was a pity he was a pig because he was quite fit.

'Becca.' Her stepfather called her Rebecca.

'Becca. Thank you for coming down. You know there was an incident last night . . .'

'Yes. Can I see a picture? I might . . .'

'You might know her? Let's talk a bit, tell me about what happened.'

Becca looked at him in frustration. If he'd just show her a photo, then she could say, 'Yes, that's Paige' or 'Never seen her', and go. She didn't want to talk. She sat up straight. There were things she wanted to know before any 'talk'. 'How is she?'

'I don't know as of this morning. She was pretty poorly last night.'

He had a ring binder in front of him. He pushed it across to her. 'OK, Becca, I'm going to show you some photographs. I just want you to tell me if you've seen any of these kids at the drop-in.'

All her defences came back. It didn't make sense. They were after something. 'Why don't you just show me her picture?'

'I can't do that, Becca. If you'd look at these and let me—'

'Why not?'

'The doctors say she's too ill for photographs. It would help a lot if you'd look at these.'

Too ill. Becca knew the kinds of threats men made. Acid? Beaten so badly they couldn't photograph her face – or get a photograph they could show to people?

She made a non-committal noise. He took it for assent, and put a slim book down in front of her. He was about to open the first page when Becca put her hand on the cover. 'What colour is her hair? The girl who . . .?'

'Dark.'

Becca noted the hesitation. Paige's hair was fair, but blood might . . .

'What does it look like? Is it long?'

'I don't know, Becca. They don't tell me stuff like that. Could you just . . .'

She wasn't falling for any of that 'you and me, we're just the people no one tells anything to' bullshit.

Exactly how stupid did he think she was? Becca eyed him narrowly as he turned the pages, still not certain what she was going to do. She didn't recognise any of the faces in the photographs. 'I don't know any of these.'

'Any of them been to the drop-in?'

'I haven't been there long, but I've never seen them.'

'Thanks, Becca. OK, one more thing. You reported an incident at the drop-in last night. Can you go over that again for me?'

'You mean – about the car? It wasn't at the drop-in. It was on the way home.'

'OK. Tell me what happened.'

After a second of hesitation, she told him about Paige, about walking back together, and Paige's sudden request to come back to Becca's. She didn't tell him about Paige's offer to party – that wasn't any of his business. She told him about meeting Liam, and about the car pulling up next to them. 'I didn't know what she was going to do. And then . . .'

He nodded. 'Can you remember – did it seem like she knew these men?'

Becca thought back. At the time, it had seemed like the usual creeps, but . . . had one of them said something to Paige? She wasn't sure. 'Not really. I don't think so. But she said something about going to a party.'

'Did you get a look at them?'

'Not really.' She showed him the image on her phone.

'Can I get a copy of this?' He took her phone away, and she fidgeted nervously until he brought it back.

'OK, Becca. Thank you. You've been very helpful. If you think of anything else, call this number. If I'm not around, someone else will be who knows about the case.'

She didn't see how she'd been helpful. All she'd said was, 'I don't know, I don't know.' He gave her a card with the police logo on. Becca took it gingerly and slipped it into her pocket. He showed her out into the now empty waiting room.

Chapter 22

On the street outside the police station, Becca fished her cigarettes out of her pocket and lit one. It was a damp, grey day. The wind was carrying the bite of real winter cold. She zipped her jacket up to her chin and wondered about getting a sandwich before she went back. Except she didn't have any money. She'd be out of ciggies after she finished this packet as well.

The interview hadn't helped. If anything, she was even more worried now. All she had was questions. Had she done the right thing, talking to them? What had happened? Too ill for photographs ... what was that supposed to mean?

As she approached the corner, she saw the man from the waiting room. He was leaning against the wall. As she got closer, she saw his face was tense and his eyes were closed. They opened as she approached. He nodded in recognition and gave her what was probably meant to be a smile. He looked awful. His face was grey.

'Hi ...' It wasn't her business, but he looked properly ill. 'Are you OK?'

'I will be. I get these . . . spasms in my back. Shit!' He clenched his teeth. 'Left my fucking— Sorry – left my painkillers. In the car.'

Becca was sick of owing people. She wanted someone to owe her. 'Is it far?'

He shook his head. 'I'll be fine in a minute. I can— Oh, Jesus!' His head fell forwards and he seemed to stop breathing. Despite the cold, he was sweating.

'You should have stayed at home.' Becca could remember his obvious discomfort in the waiting room, and his comment about the chairs.

He attempted a grin. 'I'll remember that.'

So much for trying to help. 'OK. Fine.'

'They'd probably be dragging me in in handcuffs right now if I hadn't turned up.'

Becca's phone rang before she could reply. She checked the screen. It was the drop-in. They must be wondering where she was. Maybe more people had turned up than they expected. 'Yeah, hi,' she said, still watching the man who was leaning against the wall.

It was Hannah. 'Becca, you left something behind the counter – in case I'm not here when you get back, I've given it to Neil.'

'Oh. OK.' What had she left? It didn't matter. 'I'm nearly done.'

'No need to rush. It's like the grave here.'

The grave. That was Bridlington. Still, no one seemed to be expecting her back too soon. She looked at the man, who still seemed to be pinned to the wall. 'I'll walk you to your car if you want. Where is it?'

'Yeah. That'd help. It's just on the main road. Thanks,' he added, like an afterthought.

His car was parked on the street just around the corner but it took a bit of time to get there because he moved so slowly, using her shoulder for support as well as his stick. They made difficult, hobbling progress, hindered by people who pushed carelessly past them. 'Watch out!' Becca snapped at a youth who caught her companion with his backpack.

'Fuck off, bitch.'

'You fuck off, dickhead,' Becca snarled back.

'Look, don't get into a punch-up outside the nick, not on my account,' the man said. Becca's gaze swivelled sideways, but she couldn't catch his expression. 'It's just along there,' he went on. 'In that car park across from the butcher's.'

His car was a dark-blue Volvo estate that looked as battered as its owner. He propped himself up with one arm on the roof and looked at her with interest. 'Thanks. I'm Jared, by the way.'

'It's OK. I mean – no trouble. I'm Becca.'

'Nice to meet you, Becca.' He looked better, as if the walk had loosened him up a bit, but he still held himself with the wariness of someone who was expecting the pain to return at any moment. 'I can probably manage from here ...' His teeth snapped shut and he held himself rigid against the car, the colour draining out of his face. 'Fuck's sake ... Jesus ...'

After a couple of minutes, he relaxed. 'Sorry. I'm OK now.'

124

'Yeah, right, you look OK. How did you ...? I mean ... hurt yourself. You must have ...'

'Extreme yoga. It's a bitch. I'll take a couple of pills, give it ten minutes and I'll be fine to drive.'

OK, that was her warned off. 'Where are they? Your pills?' She took the keys off him, unlocked the car and rummaged in the front pocket where he'd indicated. She found a box marked 'Tramadol, 50mg'. Just for a second, she thought about slipping a sheet into her pocket – she'd heard you could get between one and two pounds a pill, which would keep her going for a day or two.

But the box was empty.

She showed it to him, and he swore between clenched teeth.

'You shouldn't leave them in your car – someone might lift them.'

He shook his head. 'They're not worth much. Could have made a fortune when I was on Fentanyl, but the doctors stopped playing.' He was standing with his arms propped against the car, looking at her across the roof. 'They'll be back at the caravan. I'll have to—'

She had to ask. 'They gave you Fentanyl? For a bad back?'

He shrugged. 'I'm very persuasive.'

That was the second time he'd cut her off by making fun of her. She lifted her chin. 'OK. I get it. I'll be off then.'

'Don't go. I'm sorry. I make jokes about it because ... you know.'

She did know. You didn't talk about the things that hurt you.

'I had a bad fall. Year ago now. I smashed myself up. I'm OK – more or less. I just – last night – I thought I was a bit better than I really am and got myself into trouble. I'll be all right.'

He didn't look all right. He didn't look much better than he had outside the police station. 'You can't drive like that. I'll take you.'

'Thanks, but I don't want to leave my car here.'

'No, I meant I'll take you in your car.' He looked doubtful. He'd probably say no, and she probably shouldn't do it anyway – it would be against the 'rules' somehow – but fuck that. Everyone had been pushing her around – today she was going to do what she wanted.

The man – Jared – was assessing her offer. 'In my car? It's a bit tricky. The steering can be a bitch. Heavy, you know?'

She'd learned to drive in Leeds, borrowing friends' cars and forking out for a couple of lessons right at the end so she could take her test in an official vehicle. A car was a car, right? 'I'll be OK.'

'I'm out near Flamborough Head. How will you get back?'

'Bus. It'll drop me off in town.' She had no idea about the buses, but it would work out. Probably.

'The buses will be shit out there. You can't—'

'Course I can. You can't drive, can you?'

She saw his mouth tighten, then he relaxed and shrugged. 'No. I was OK when I left. Getting here just about finished me. OK. Thanks. But don't worry about the bus. I'll be fine once I've taken those pills. I'll drive you back. Deal?'

'Deal.' Becca helped him into the car, then got in herself, checking the unfamiliar display, feeling her confidence wobble a bit. It was huge compared to her Micra.

It's just a car, she told herself. She could drive it.

She wasn't so sure about that by the time she'd wrestled it out of the car park – the first time she turned the wheel, the car just kept moving straight on. 'A few more scrapes aren't going to hurt it,' Jared said consolingly. 'You need to turn the wheel hard.'

'I'm doing that.' Stupid car.

She hauled the wheel round and lurched onto the main road. The engine howled. Jared shifted in his seat but didn't say anything. They jerked along in first gear as she wrestled with the clutch, then she managed to change up, and change up again.

After a few hundred yards of kangaroo hops and stop-start progress, she began to get the hang of it. She put her foot down cautiously, raising a finger to the car behind her that had sounded its horn when she'd stalled and stopped abruptly in the middle of the road.

The car gathered speed smoothly. She felt her confidence return. It might be old and battered, but she could feel the power of the engine. As they reached the edge of town, the road opened up in front of her.

This was OK.

This was better than OK. She was starting to enjoy herself.

By the time they were through Sewerby, she was ruling the road, pulling away effortlessly from a van that tried to tailgate her, watching the speedometer going up – sixty, sixty-five, seventy. She had to have a car like this. She had to.

Then the understanding came out of the blue.

A caravan site. He lived on a caravan site on the way to Flamborough and he'd been in to talk to the police.

Paige – the girl, maybe not Paige – had been found in the road near a caravan site.

He knew something about last night.

The car jerked and stalled as her foot slipped off the clutch. There was a horrible grinding noise as it skidded to a halt, ending up almost across the road. The van that had been chasing her veered round with a squeal of tyres, the horn sounding and the driver's hand gesticulating.

Becca sat there, holding the wheel, her heart hammering.

Jared cleared his throat. 'OK, the eejit was too close, but maybe next time just let him get past?'

'What do you know about last night? Why were the police talking to you?'

He stared at her blankly. 'What?'

'The girl. Who was attacked. What do you know?'

He shook his head, still looking confused. 'Fuck all, just about. Why?'

'Because . . .' She struggled with her words. Because it might be my fault? 'I might know her.'

'Know her? She's a friend of yours?'

'Not a friend. I'm not even sure – it might be some-one I know. A bit.'

A horn sounded and he looked behind him. 'Do you think this is the best place to have this conversation?'

'OK, OK.' Becca struggled with the ignition and the clutch, clumsy because she was flustered, and the car lurched into forward motion. Another car swerved past them. 'If you don't know anything, why were you there?'

'I think we'd better not talk while you're driving.'

'I'm doing you a favour,' Becca snapped.

'Right. I really need to be wrapped round a lamp post or rear-ended. I quite like my car as it is, thanks. Look, just pay attention. Either drive or ask me questions. Don't do both. How long have you been driving?'

'A few weeks,' Becca admitted.

He groaned. 'Then definitely pay attention, OK? We can talk at the site.'

Becca drove on in silence. After a few minutes, she put her foot down again and speeded up, waiting for his objections, but he didn't say anything. They crossed the railway line, then the road narrowed to a country lane running between flat fields with sparse hedges and stunted trees. They passed a gateway, and then Jared said, 'Next turning. The road's a bit rough', and she was hauling the car round a left turn – she'd got the hang of the steering now – skidding just a bit on the loose gravel and bumping along what was little more than a farm track. She couldn't help grinning at her success as she switched off the ignition and pulled on the hand brake. Then she opened the car door and got a proper look at her surroundings, turning to Jared in surprise. 'I thought caravan sites were, you know, a bit more classy.'

'Yeah. Some are. This one isn't. But it's cheap.'

Becca looked round the bleak field. When she was very young, too young to have any proper recall of it, she must have been on holiday to a caravan park. From somewhere, she had a memory of bright colours and caravans all shiny and white, with little fences and gardens and stuff. And smooth, green grass and neat paths with lines of little white stones, and everywhere, the smell of the sea.

Here, the vans were just lined up any old how, as if someone had dumped them on the cliff to just ... fall apart. They looked battered; the paint chipped, the windows cracked and dirty. Who'd come here for a holiday? The ground was muddy and there was rubbish strewn around that looked as though it had been there since last summer – empty cans, trays from takeaways trampled into the ground. A plastic bag was tangled in a nearby tree and flapped in the breeze. The rain was starting again, drumming on the caravans and spattering up from the ground.

She shivered as the wind, icy cold from the sea, blew through her jacket. The gate behind her creaked as the wind caught it. Somewhere she could hear the monotonous sound of a door banging.

It was a horrible place to live.

And a horrible place to die.

Chapter 23

The first thing Jared did when Becca helped him out of the car was to haul himself into the caravan to find the painkillers. He gave himself a double dose – he'd taken so many in the past few days the standard dose wasn't working anymore – and reached for the whisky. But he'd promised to drive her back. His hand hovered, then he picked up a half-finished can of Coke. It was warm and flat, but it was enough to wash the pills down.

'You OK?' She was standing in the doorway, clearly unnerved by the smallness of the caravan. He went back outside. 'Give me a few minutes and I'll make you a drink or something.'

The sky had cleared. He could see dots of birds high up in the immense deep blue. He couldn't imagine a life that kept you confined inside, working in an office in the middle of a city, breathing aircon with people all around you that you couldn't escape. If his fall had left him in a wheelchair, he might just have topped himself.

He eased himself onto the crate and watched Becca

as she inspected her surroundings. She reminded him of a cat put down in a strange place: edgy, suspicious and alert. 'Tell me what happened last night,' she said.

The pills were starting to kick in. Jared could feel the familiar sensation of distance, of watching himself doing whatever it was he was doing with a mild detachment settling across his mind. Becca was looking at him expectantly.

'There isn't much to tell. I went to the pub and drank a bit too much. Didn't mean to, but these days it doesn't take a lot ... Anyway, when I got back, I could barely stand up. There was some kind of party going on over on the other side.' He gestured to the other side of the caravan site. Seeing it through her eyes was almost like seeing it for the first time. The site lay in a slight dip in the land, which meant you had to walk to the cliff if you wanted to look at the sea. One or two caravans were up there in the dead gorse and bracken. They were closed up, windows covered by blinds, sunk down into the ground as though they would never move again. Instead of the sea, the air smelt of rotting vegetation and backed-up drains.

This was no place for summer visitors – so what the fuck was it for?

Becca was looking at him, puzzled. 'What?' she said.

He brought himself back to the present. 'She came from over there. I think.' He pointed towards the cliff edge. 'It was dark. She was running. I couldn't find my key – she was asking me for help, and I couldn't find my fucking key. There was a car – she heard it, and she started running. I got the door open, but she'd gone. She was here.' He stood up and went to the side of the caravan. 'Just here. The car lights – they shone the lights right at her, and she ran that way.' He pointed back along the path, the way she'd come. He was getting a clearer picture himself now. Why hadn't she run for the gate? It was visible down the path straight ahead. But the car lights must have blinded her.

'So – did you go after her?'

Jared nodded. 'Yeah. I went after her. I called the police and I went after her. I found her,' he said, 'in the end. Outside the gate. They'd already . . .' He didn't want to tell Becca what they'd done. She didn't need that in her head. Nobody did. '. . . done what they were going to do. I waited with her for the ambulance.'

'Did she say anything?'

Jared shook his head. She probably wouldn't have been able to speak – he hoped she hadn't been conscious enough to speak, but he could still hear the gurgling breath and the soft, almost silent moans.

'What?' Becca was watching closely.

'Nothing. Look, I need to move around or I'll stiffen up.' He didn't want to talk about it. He didn't want to think about it. Buried under the barrier of the drugs was anger – anger at the people who'd done it, anger at himself.

'Did they tell you how she was?'

He shook his head. 'I didn't ask.'

'Don't you care?' Now Becca sounded accusing.

'Yes. I care. OK?'

'Yeah, right.' She shrugged.

Fuck's sake. 'I saw her. I already know how she is. I can't think about it now – the drugs are doing their stuff so I'm not feeling much pain. I'm not feeling much of anything to tell you the truth. If it makes you any happier, you're right. I let her down.'

She seemed about to continue her attack, but her shoulders slumped. 'Me too. I let her get in that car.'

'You don't know it's the same girl.'

'Who else is it going to be? Did she have long hair?'

There was just the face, coming out of the darkness. 'I don't know.'

He was moving better now. The pain was receding, and this slow walk was stretching his cramped muscles. He was aware of Becca watching him. 'Don't you get – you know – hooked on that stuff?'

'No. I take it when I need it. When I don't, I'll stop.' Whenever that would be. The pills took the edge off – not just the pain, but everything else, and right now, there was more edge than he wanted to cope with.

He and Becca had reached the far side of the site, where there was just a fence looking out over flat, dead fields. A police car was pulled up at the end of the path. Jared turned away. He didn't want to get mixed up in this any more than he already was.

'Do you think they'll find anything?'

'No idea. Leave it up to them. The rain's getting heavy. Come on, I'll make you that cup of tea and then I'll be OK to drive you back.'

He led the way back to the caravan. When they

got there, the owner, Greaseball Harry, was standing by Jared's car, watching them. As Jared and Becca reached the door of the caravan, he pointed a finger at Jared's chest. 'You. I told you. I want you off here. Today.'

Jared unlocked the door. 'And I told you. I'm leaving as soon as I can.'

'Yeah. Today.'

Jared could feel Becca winding up beside him. 'Fine by me. You can explain to the police why you've thrown their witness out.'

He pulled the door open and jerked his head at Becca, indicating she should go in. To his relief, she did. 'Tomorrow,' he said, holding the other man's gaze.

The owner looked away first. 'That's what you said yesterday. Tomorrow. I'm here to make sure, right?' He got into his car. 'I'll be back to check,' he threw out of the window. Jared heard the car pull away as he shut the door, wondering why he'd got into that fight. He was going, as soon as he could. Would getting thumped by GBH make him feel better or something?

The caravan was so small he and Becca had to shuffle around each other to avoid physical contact. He edged his way carefully past her and pointed at the bed, which, thank Christ, was moderately respectable. 'Best sit on there.'

She ignored him and stayed where she was, in the space in front of the kitchen area. 'It's too small,' she said. 'And it smells funny.' She was right. It was a mixture of condensation, mildew and the decaying fabric of the caravan. He pushed the door open despite the cold and the air began to clear.

Becca looked round, then sat on the bed, very stiff and upright while he waited for the kettle to boil. 'What's these?' she said after a minute. She'd found the pictures of the tunnels he'd printed off before he came up here.

He hesitated, then said, 'Old railway tunnels. Up beyond Whitby. I found those online and they looked, you know, interesting.'

'Oh.' She frowned. 'What are they for?'

'They aren't for anything now. They're blocked off.'

'And you go in there?'

He hadn't told her that's what he did, but . . . 'Yeah. Places like that.'

'And that's why you fell?'

'Yeah.' He sniffed the milk. It seemed OK. More or less. 'Milk?'

She'd been watching him with the carton, and made a face. 'No thanks. Just sugar.' He gave her the least cracked mug and she wrapped her hands round it, then pulled her legs up and positioned herself in the centre of the bed, leaving Jared wedged up against the hob. She looked at him with puzzled interest. 'You fell in a tunnel?'

'No. We were having a look round an old blast furnace. They have these ladders up the side. One of them broke, and . . .' He shrugged. The outcome was obvious.

She was looking at the photo of the low tunnel in the wall, the one where he'd nearly killed himself. 'Looks . . . scary.'

He grinned. 'That's why I do it. It's fun.'

And that was a lie. It wasn't fun. It was terrifying. The more frightened he was, the more compelling it was and the greater the high of the adrenaline rush.

All the time she'd been here, he'd been testing himself, and now he was sure – well, pretty sure – he'd be OK to head north today. What was the point in hanging round, just to annoy Greaseball Harry? He emptied his cup. 'OK, I think I can manage the car now. Shall I take you back? Becca, thanks for your help. I'd have been stuck without it.'

She flushed slightly. It was as if she wasn't used to being thanked. 'That's OK. Sorry I scraped your car.'

'I don't think anyone's going to notice. I don't want to rush you, but I need to get going. I'm not spending the day here with that cunt – sorry – that ... *shit* breathing down my neck. And the police. I need to find somewhere to stay. I'm going up the coast. I'll drop you off in Brid.'

'So where are you going?'

'Whitby. North of Whitby.'

'What about here?'

'What about here?'

'You saw something. You can help.'

'Becca, I've told the police what I know. I'll tell them where I'm going. What else can I do?'

'They don't care – the police. They never do anything. Don't you read the papers?'

'What can I do if I stay?'

'Nothing. Same as you did last night. It's OK. You

don't have to give me a lift back. I don't need one. I can get back myself.' She jumped to her feet. He stood back as she pushed past him to the caravan door, stumbling as the gap between the door and the ground took her by surprise.

Jared watched her as she stalked off down the path and out of the caravan site. What the fuck just happened? And how was she going to get back? There was a bus stop some way down the road, but he had no idea if she knew where it was, and no idea if there was a bus due for hours – or even if there was a bus at all.

And it was starting to rain again.

The trouble was, there was enough truth in what she had said to sting. OK, he'd gone in and made a statement, but he had thought seriously about running away – and leaving now still felt a little bit like that. He swore under his breath and went to get his car.

Chapter 24

Becca had made it a fair way along the road in the direction of Bridlington by the time Jared pulled up beside her. 'Get in,' he said.

She looked at him and turned away.

'Stop being such a fucking princess. You heard what the guy said. I can't stay here. Look. Get in. Tell me what you think I can do.'

She hesitated, then climbed into the passenger seat, dripping water all over the inside of his car, which, fair enough, was a bit beyond damage, and sat with a kind of slumped defiance. He pulled away and they drove in silence until he said, 'OK. I'm listening.'

She kept her face turned away from him. 'I should have stopped her and I didn't. You should have helped her and you didn't. Everyone says they're doing something, but no one is. They don't even say that it's Paige, but it has to be.'

'Yeah, well, I feel pretty bad myself.'

'It's easy to be sorry about something.'

Her words stung. *How did you get it so wrong?*

His father's face as he looked at the son who hadn't had the guts to go back.

Becca remained silent. He realised he was going to tell her. Why? She was touchy and unpredictable and would probably insist he left her by the side of the road so she could walk back – but he thought she would listen before she did that. 'I do that. I let people down ...'

'How do you mean?'

'What I said. The stuff I do, you have to depend on your mates.'

'Like going into tunnels?'

'Not so much. I do that on my own.' And then I only kill myself. 'Some things, like climbing or ... or potholing. You go in pairs, or a group, and you look after each other ... only I didn't.'

He'd been twenty. He was starting his final year at uni in Sheffield. He went there for the climbing and the caving. Sheffield was a climbers' city.

'You can do climbing at uni?'

It sounded like a genuine question, so he treated it as such. 'No. Not as a subject. I was reading geology. But I chose Sheffield because it's close to the Peak District and there's some of the best rock climbing and caving in the country there. That's where my dad taught me to climb. When I was a kid.'

And Charlie.

The rat hadn't been an issue then. His father had taught him to enjoy a challenge, the adrenaline high of attempting a climb that was at the edge of his ability.

You want to give it a try? Good lad! That's what his father said, each time he aimed for a route that was tougher than the one before. But the explorations where one wrong step could kill him? They'd never done that.

'Yeah?' Becca was fiddling with her phone, but she seemed to be listening. He wasn't going to tell her the whole story, but as he picked out the bare bones, it ran through his head like a familiar movie, one that might, just might, change its ending if he watched it often enough.

'There used to be mining across the whole area and there's deep shafts and tunnels – there's a whole world under there that's still not mapped, not fully.'

He and Charlie had set out that morning to explore a mine shaft near Sparrowpit. It was a fine day – he still couldn't look up at a clear blue sky without a sense of foreboding. They were doing it by the book; they'd got the landowner's permission and they had the best equipment they could afford. What they didn't have was a phone that would work underground, but they could communicate with each other well enough by shouting. They had no communication with the sur-face, but why would they need it?

It probably wouldn't have made any difference.

The shaft was capped by a metal grill, with a trap-door to allow access. The shaft itself fell away below them, vanishing into the deep ground. They fixed the ropes, and Jared led the way out of the daylight and into the darkness, lit by their head torches and the diminishing daylight above them. Loose crystals fell from the walls, hitting the water far below them with a boom that echoed up the shaft.

Jared called up to Charlie. 'It's flooded.'

'Yeah.' Charlie sounded excited. This was only his second experience of caving – rock climbing was his thing. 'But there's a way off the shaft before you get to the bottom.'

The slit was in the shaft wall, vertical and narrow. They'd read up on the caves and they knew it led to a chamber, followed by a series of pitches and squeezes that would lead, eventually, to the main cave system and the way out. It would be good practice for Charlie before they tried something more challenging. Jared found the slit and waited for Charlie to reach him.

He didn't mind squeezes. The trick was to relax, breathe steadily, let your body flow. Charlie held the equipment while Jared went through, then Charlie passed it to Jared and followed.

The chamber barely deserved the name. There was no floor, just an edge to skirt round and a low opening that was the continuation of the route. Another pitch, steep, about ten metres, and then another squeeze.

But Charlie wasn't liking the squeezes. It was OK at first, but then they came to one that was like a zigzag, a claustrophobe's nightmare where the passage enclosed the body, the rock grazed your face and it was like being buried alive. *Like water*, Jared could remember the mantra that ran through his head. *Flow like water.*

He went through legs first, and it was a struggle to get his chest through, but he made it. Charlie, slighter, should have found it easier, but he stuck, struggled, started to panic and Jared had to shout to calm him down and get through.

That was when it all went wrong. The book said they were through the worst of the squeezes, but they still had maybe a couple of hours of rough going to reach the main system and out. After Charlie's panic, Jared suggested they give up: 'Look, mate, this is more than we bargained for. We can go back through, get back up the shaft, no problem.'

But Charlie wouldn't return through the zigzag squeeze, so they went on. The going was tough, there were a couple of narrow bits – nothing too bad, but Charlie tensed up before each one. The air felt heavy, and beyond the limits of their torches, darkness concealed emptiness and the unknown. All sense of adventure and excitement was gone. All they wanted to do was get out. This was far tougher than the book had said.

It was Jared's job to get them through safely. He was acutely aware of the sound of water as he moved on, keeping his hand on the wall, checking all the time for the opening that would lead to the last passage. These caves and tunnels were notoriously wet, full of underground streams. In some places, the only way through was with diving equipment.

He tried to reassure himself as the dripping became a trickle and the trickle grew stronger and steadier.

143

The water was up to their ankles now and it was still running into the passage. The book hadn't said these passages could flood. He checked the walls for a high-water mark.

There wasn't one.

He started whistling to keep his spirits up and called back to Charlie to get a move on, claiming he was getting cold. He didn't know if Charlie understood the significance of the rising water, but Jared did. He drove himself forwards, shouting instructions to keep Charlie moving and keep him moving fast. The compulsion was overwhelming: *get out, get out, get out.*

He was looking for an opening in the passage wall – the way out. The book said it was there, but he'd stopped trusting the book. And then he saw it in the light of his head torch: a narrow slit in the rock. He didn't like the look of it, but it was all they had. He stopped and waited until Charlie caught him up.

'OK, mate,' Jared said. 'It's the way out.'

'Are you sure?' Charlie sounded close to panic. The water was almost up to their knees and rising fast.

'It's the way out,' Jared said, with a confidence he didn't feel. 'It shouldn't be too bad. We've been through the roughest bit.'

Charlie managed a grin, but he refused point blank when Jared suggested Charlie go first. 'Look,' Jared said, 'I'm bigger than you. If anyone's going to get stuck it'll be me. Fuck's sake, mate; it'll be a doddle.'

But Charlie was adamant. He didn't want to break trail. He wanted the reassurance of Jared having got through. In the end, Jared agreed. The water was above his knees now. They didn't have time to hang around. He pulled himself through the slit, which widened slightly into a narrow chamber. He had to crawl on his hands and knees to get through.

But then the passage narrowed, and narrowed again. Shit! Fuck! It must be a dead end and he was going to drown in there. Panic yammered in the back of his mind, demanding a way in. Jared felt himself tense up, and as the passage narrowed even more, he stuck. Jesus. *Jesus.* He took some deep breaths and forced himself to calm down. *Breathe slowly. Flow. Like water.* The roof came down closer and closer until he could barely lift his head. At least the passage was there. At least he hadn't come to a stop against solid rock.

Then there was a zigzag. He tried to go through, and couldn't. It was tight, and with his torso gripped by the narrow passage, he couldn't bend his back enough. He wriggled his way back until there was just enough space to turn over, and approached the zigzag again, his face scraping the roof. He had to eel his way down the first turn, then almost corkscrew his way round the next one. For a heart-stopping moment, his hips stuck, then he was through, then a short climb and he was pulling himself out into a spacious chamber.

He lay on the ground, panting. But he didn't have time for this.

He looked back at the gap he had crawled though. It didn't look possible that he'd fitted through there. He put his mouth to it and called down. 'Come through, Charlie! Stay on your back! It's a bit tight at the end! Yell when you get there, and I'll talk you through. It's OK. We're nearly out.' He held his breath until he heard a faint call of acknowledgement, then sat back against the wall to wait.

He checked his watch. It had taken him ten minutes to navigate that passage. It had felt like hours, but it was only ten minutes. The tension that had been inside him since Charlie panicked in the first zigzag squeeze began to dissipate.

The sound of water was louder now, and the stream running through the chamber looked swollen. He wasn't worried – he knew where he was and this part of the system didn't flood, but it was a good job he and Charlie had got out of that other bit while they could.

He listened as the scuffling that marked Charlie's progress came closer, then closer.

Then stopped.

He shouted into the gap, 'Get a move on, mate! Come on!'

'I'm stuck.' It was Charlie's voice, muffled as if his face was pressed against something solid.

And that was the start of the real nightmare. The surface was an hour away, he had no phone. All he could do was encourage, hector, bully, try to get Charlie to stop panicking, to make the twist that would get his body through, but the more Charlie tried, the more he panicked, and the faster he stuck.

And then he started screaming.

146

Water began to run out of the narrow passage, just a trickle at first, and then a flow, faster and faster, into the stream that ran through the cave.

And after that, Charlie was silent.

Chapter 25

Jared didn't tell all of this to Becca. He told her they'd gone caving, he'd led, Charlie got stuck and drowned. It was the memories that engulfed him and he surfaced to Becca's panicked 'Watch out!' He'd drifted across the road and a van was coming towards them, fast. He swerved and the van skidded past them with a blaring horn.

He was driving on autopilot. Also driving like an idiot. He pulled in to the side of the road and made himself breathe slowly until he began to relax a bit and his heart slowed down. He'd only told her the bare bones, but the telling had taken him right back into it. 'Charlie was my best mate,' he said. 'He was only nineteen. I left him to drown in a cave that I got out of.'

Becca was watching him, a frown creasing her forehead. 'You didn't though. Not really. I mean – what could you have done different?'

She didn't say it as though she was trying to re-assure him. She was asking an honest question, and one he'd asked himself enough times. What could he have done? Made Charlie go through first? They'd both have drowned. Would that make him feel better? 'Later, I found out it was the wrong tunnel. If we'd just kept going a few metres further on we could have strolled out. I got it wrong.'

'Yeah, but you didn't know that at the time, though, did you?'

But he should have known. His father got it. *What went wrong, mate?* And unspoken: *What stopped you going back?*

'What else could you have done?' Becca persisted.

'I dunno. Stayed out of that fucking shaft in the first place.'

'Makes sense to me.' Becca played with her phone a bit more then said, 'So where are you going?'

'Just up the coast. Past Whitby.'

'Is that where the tunnel is – the one where you got hurt?'

'Yes – more or less.'

'And you're going back in?'

He was, but he didn't want to admit it. 'It wasn't the tunnel. There was a sort of side shaft where ...' He wasn't going to start telling her about weird masked faces under the ground. He didn't want her to think he was completely crazy. 'I thought I'd look for the place where the side tunnel comes out.' Then one of those impulses – exactly like the ones that drove him forward when the rat was biting – made him say, 'You can come with me, if you want.'

She looked at him for a long time. 'Come with you?'

'Why not?'

She chewed her lip. 'Why would I . . . yeah, I . . . No. I can't. I've got to get to work. But thanks.'

They drove into Brid in silence, but it was no longer a hostile silence. He thought she was mulling his suggestion over, and half expected her to accept at the last minute. When she didn't, he wasn't sure if he was relieved or disappointed. He was sick to death of himself.

Following her directions, he stopped near the bus station. 'Thanks,' she said.

'No, it's me should be thanking you. Look, sorry about hitting you with all that cave stuff; it was years ago.'

'Yeah. Shit happens,' she agreed. He saw the faint line of a scar running from the side of her nose to her upper lip, giving it a slight quirk, like a half smile.

'I hope your friend's OK,' he said. 'Take my number – you can call me if there's any news.'

'OK.' She keyed it into her phone, then sent through a quick call to check it.

'I'll be in touch,' he said as she slid out of the door. He'd like to see her again, but he probably wouldn't.

She stood watching him as he turned the car round, and waved as he drove off. He raised a hand in acknowledgement. When he glanced in his mirror as he reached the junction, she'd gone.

Under a grey sky with towering banks of cloud, he turned the car round and headed east towards Flamborough Head to pack up his stuff.

Then he was going north, towards Kettleness.

Towards the tunnel.

Chapter 26

It was after midday by the time Becca reached the drop-in. She wondered if she should have called anyone – but they knew where she was. More or less. After a morning spent talking to someone who didn't bang on about jobs and responsibilities and obligations, the thought of the drop-in was dreary and depressing. More and more, she wished she'd taken Jared up on his mad offer. He needed someone to look out for him.

That was the way Kay thought about her. She was always looking out for Becca, and sometimes ...

When Kay had told her about the job, it had been a lifeline – somewhere she could get away, somewhere where no one knew her, somewhere she could make a bit of money and keep herself going while she decided what to do next. How to move on from Bexgirl. To Kay, it was a way of getting experience in social care that would put Becca back on track. But Kay didn't understand how impossible that was. Becca wasn't even sure any longer if she wanted to be on that track and anyway, no matter how long, no matter where she went, the Bexgirl image might surface at any time.

But despite the dreariness, things about the drop-in were starting to matter. When Becca was twelve, she'd run away and survived for three months on the streets. You learned to sense danger – if you survived, you learned how to spot when something was off. And more and more, here in Bridlington, she was getting the feeling something bad was going on.

And it was her job – never mind the bacon sand-wiches and the coffee and the *listening* – it was her job to keep people safe. Paige had been going to tell her something, and then she'd changed her mind. And now Paige wasn't going to tell anyone anything.

The drop-in worried Becca.

It looked like a safe place, but maybe it wasn't. Maybe it was a cleverly baited trap.

She wanted to tell Alek what had happened at the police station. She went round to the back to see if he was in the yard. He was there, but he was talking to someone, another man. The two of them were engaged in one of those low-voiced conversations that looked angry. The man he was talking to looked big and bulky – bigger than Alek, even.

Alek looked up suddenly over the other man's shoulder. When he saw her, he scowled and waved his hand at her in a shooing motion, indicating she should go. She backed away, unnerved by the anger on his face. It was only a couple of hours ago he'd been telling her about his daughter, Ariana, about Ariana's disability, about how proud he was.

Fuck that. She didn't have time to worry about it – she had to get to work. It was busier than it had been earlier, though nothing like as busy as it usually was around lunch time. She put her bag in her locker and pulled on the hated tabard – *loser in an overall*. She was just heading towards the coffee bar when Neil's office door opened. 'Becca. Where have you been?'

'At Ashville Street,' she said, surprised. He knew that.

'All this time?'

'Not exactly. I . . .' She wasn't going to explain about Jared – it would sound too crazy. 'Is there any news about Paige?'

'No. The police are checking. Becca, we need to have a talk.'

'Where's Paige staying? Where does she sleep? Has anyone—'

'The police have all the information they need. We've told them—'

'Where? Neil, I could go and talk to some of them, her mates, you know? I've been in places like that. They'll talk to me.' He wasn't listening. 'Ask Alek. He knows Paige talked to me. He was . . .' How to explain that Alek knew how she was with the users, and that he trusted her? 'He told me about his daughter,' she said. She could hear the pleading in her voice and hated it.

Neil looked at her. 'What?'

'Alek. He told me about his daughter, Ariana . . .'

'Alek hasn't got a daughter.'

Not got ...? 'But—'

Neil spoke over her. 'Becca, you must understand that I'm not going to give you confidential information. This discussion is over.'

OK. Fuck him, she'd get it from one of the other users.

'Come in.' Neil stood aside and gestured her into the room. He closed the door behind him. 'Sit down.'

Becca sat on the indicated chair and watched Neil as he fiddled with the papers on his desk, not meeting her eye. She began to feel the coldness of apprehension. Something bad was coming. 'Is it Paige?'

'No, nothing like that. Becca, I've had some very disturbing information. It seems you were involved in ... well ... participated in ... an illegal act.'

Bexgirl. Becca felt her chin lift. 'No I didn't.'

'Becca, I'd prefer it if you told me the truth. I have the photos. Are you saying someone faked them? They look genuine enough to me.'

The thought of Neil looking at stills from her camming felt perverted, the way the camming never had. She knew her face had gone red and was angry with herself. She didn't want him to see she cared. 'I know which photo you mean. It's me with my friend's sister. That my friend took. It's just a photo. There's nothing wrong with it.'

'Come on, Becca. I wasn't born yesterday. I have checked this. I don't act on malicious gossip – it was taken in a sex chat room.'

'It was taken in my flat. We'd been into town, to a movie, and we came back to my flat and had pizza and then Ashley took the photograph.'

154

'I'm not interested in how the little girl was persuaded, Becca, I'm interested in the outcome.'

The unfairness of it almost took her breath away. 'She wasn't persuaded to do anything. There was nothing wrong with the photo.'

'Then how did it end up in a sex chat room?'

'It didn't. It's . . . I used to make a bit of money camming. I did it at my flat. There wasn't anything funny about it. I just took my clothes off and did things, OK?' Neil looked away and Becca was glad to see he looked embarrassed. 'I wasn't camming when we took the picture. I'd never do that – I . . .' She couldn't talk about her past to Neil. That was hers. That was private. 'I got doxed.'

'Doxed?'

'It means they find out who you are. They know where to find you. They hacked all my accounts. I had the photo in my stuff on Facebook. Private stuff, you know?' *Friends and Family.* Yeah, right. 'They sent it to all my friends along with some of the camming shots. It was . . .'

Neil sighed. 'Becca, I'm prepared to accept your word that you intended no harm. But it caused harm, and it was your actions, and your lack of care that did it. We have vulnerable people here, as you know. Since you started work here, the girls – they trust you. Some of them look up to you. And now we've had an incident of one of them going off in a car – with a kerb-crawler by the sound of it – you must see how that looks.'

'It doesn't look like anything! *I* told you about that.

155

You wouldn't know if I hadn't told you. How do you know it's since I started? It's probably been going on for months and you were all too stupid to see it.'

'Shouting isn't going to help, Becca. I can't have someone here who has worked in the sex industry. You must see that. You'll have to leave. You can go without any unpleasantness, but I want you to leave today. We'll pay you up to the end of the month.'

He thought he was being generous. She was supposed to be grateful that he didn't pitch her out on her ear with no money. Well, fuck that. She wasn't grateful. He'd talked nicely, kept his voice down, made it all sound so sensible – *you must see that* – but what he'd said in the nice, quiet voice was hateful: *persuaded ... how the little girl was persuaded ... since you started work here ...*

'One thing. How did you find out?'

'I don't think that matters, Becca.'

'Of course it matters! If someone's got it in for me, I need to know'

'Becca, no one has "got it in" for you. Being paranoid won't help. You have to take responsibility for your actions. Someone concerned about the welfare of these young people very rightly alerted me to an important issue relating to a member of my staff.'

'But they didn't give you a name.' She could tell from his expression that she was right. 'Someone who won't even tell you who they are ... and you just believe them without asking me my side.'

His voice didn't change. He spoke with that

unnatural calm that social workers used when they were trashing your life and didn't just expect you to accept it; they expected you to be grateful and obedient and all that shit.

'I got an email,' he said. 'The person who sent it was worried about the users. Somewhere like this, Becca, people will be concerned about these issues. It isn't personal. You can get another job. Why don't you try one of the pubs? Or a supermarket? No one's going to worry about it if you're working in a place that doesn't deal with vulnerable people like we do.'

Pub, supermarket; that's all you're worth, Becca. She was on her feet and her arm swept everything off the surface of his desk. There was a thump as his books hit the floor, followed by the splat of papers landing every-where. 'Don't you ever – *ever* – talk to me like that!'

He'd jumped to his feet as she attacked his desk, but his voice still had that fake calm that she hated. 'Getting abusive won't help anything, Becca. I want you to go. Alek will come with you to collect your things and he'll see you off the premises.'

'You have no idea what's going on in this place! You think it's so amazing and you don't have a fucking clue.'

'Becca, don't make me ask Alek to force you to leave. This isn't helping.'

In her head, Becca was back at Matt and Kay's; she'd lost her temper and the lovely bedroom Matt had shown her into was a mess of strewn sheets, pillows, covers, the drawers pulled out and thrown across the room, the curtains hanging off the windows, a vase shattered on the floor. Matt was talking to her, his voice just starting to penetrate the red mist of her rage. She knew this was just part of where he told her she'd have to go but how it wasn't her fault. She didn't care. One foster home, another foster home ... but she was tired. After the secure unit, the big soft bed looked – had looked – inviting, and there was a smell of cooking coming up the stairs ...

Matt had checked his watch. 'Tell you what. Kay's making pizza. We've got a bit of time. Let's put your room back together then get something to eat.'

So that's what they'd done. And he'd shown her lots of ways not to go into meltdown when she lost her temper.

Anger is useful. It's energy. Don't waste it.

And right now, she needed that energy. She needed it to keep herself afloat, but more than that, she needed it to help Paige. But she wasn't letting Neil get away with it. She looked at all his stuff on the floor and forced her breathing to slow down. 'I'm sorry, but you shouldn't have said that. You know you shouldn't. Don't worry, I'll go. You know I didn't do anything wrong so don't pretend you're doing me any favours. We both know you aren't.'

'You can see it any way you like, Becca.' He waited a long moment, watching her warily, then said, 'Oh, before you go ...' He reached onto a shelf behind him and handed her a small tablet computer. 'You shouldn't leave these things lying around. Hannah found it behind the bar this morning.'

She'd never seen it in her life before and was about to say so when she saw that someone had written 'BECKA' on it in marker. She took it from Neil without a word.

Alek appeared at the door and she stalked past him, still angry at his earlier dismissal. They didn't speak as they went to the room where the storage lockers were and he waited while she got out her stuff. There was very little – her bag, her coat and a pair of trainers she wore if her feet got too tired – loser shoes.

'I am sorry,' he said suddenly. 'About before. That is not a nice man. I didn't want him to ... You tell the police? About Paige?'

Becca wanted to hang on to her anger. She wanted to be angry with all of them, with Neil, with Hannah, with Alek, with Jared ... but she felt too tired. 'It's OK,' she muttered as she shoved her things into a carrier bag.

'I fix your car,' he said, handing her an envelope. 'Here. Your windscreen – it has a crack but it will be OK. For a bit. The windows – I had to use tape, I'm sorry. You can drive the car, just ... not open or close. The tyres – all fine.'

Becca nodded. 'Thanks.' She wanted to ask him about the man he'd been talking to, about what Neil had said. She wanted to thank him for being on her side but she couldn't trust her voice. She dumped her tabard on a table, pulled on her jacket, stuffing the envelope into her pocket, and was ready to go. Alek walked to the door with her. Making a sudden decision, she looked up at him. 'Neil said you haven't got a daughter.'

'Why should I tell Neil about my life? He is nothing. Take care, Becca.' He closed the door behind her.

And that was that. No more drop-in. No more job. She walked down the street, wondering where to go and what to do.

Shoving her hands into her pockets, she found Alek's envelope. It was bulky and irregular. She opened it, and her keys fell out, along with a ten-quid note.

She wasn't taking that. She wasn't a charity case. He could just . . .

She could just . . .

She could accept it. It was a nice thing to do, almost like they were friends. *Why should I tell Neil?* But he'd told her, Becca.

OK.

'Thanks, Alek,' she said out loud.

But there was no one to hear her.

Chapter 27

Becca walked along the road, following the signs to the beach. There were cafés along here that were always open and she was starving. She huddled herself into her coat. It was freezing, with a cutting wind that was blowing straight off the sea.

The front was lined with fish restaurants, but most of them were shut in the winter. She passed one that was open, but it was deserted. It looked depressing and she was miserable enough already.

The cobbled road leading to the harbour forked off the main road and she followed it down. There was a line of low, red-brick buildings, one with the sign 'Harbour Café'. There were a few more people at the tables. That looked OK. That would do. Becca pushed open the door and went into the welcome warmth of steam and the smell of hot fat.

A couple of women sat in a corner, their heads close together, talking. They stopped and watched Becca in silence as she came through the door. Becca took a table by the window. Almost before she had sat down, a waitress appeared. Becca ordered chips and tea. 'And some bread and butter,' she said.

The waitress scribbled something down. 'Small or large? Tea?'

'Large.'

She hung her coat round the back of the chair. She could get a job in a place like this – Bridlington was full of cafés – she could work for a week or two while she decided what to do.

Her flat was paid for up to the end of the month. There was no way she was going to get that money back from the skinflint landlord. Her car was fixed and was parked round the back at the drop-in.

She could pack up, move somewhere else. Back to Leeds? Too many people knew about the Bexgirl story, and anyway, where would she live? If she couldn't afford a flat in Brid, she couldn't afford one in Leeds. Another city? But it looked as though someone was making sure the story followed her wherever she went.

Could she find a way of hiding?

Bridlington had seemed like a hiding place, but it wasn't.

'There you go, love.' The woman dumped a plate of chips in front of Becca, and a mug of tea.

'Thanks.' The smell of the chips made Becca's spirits lift, just a bit. Alek's tenner was a lifesaver, but she had no idea what she was going to do next. She wasn't even sure how much money she had left. Bexgirl had paid quite well, but Becca had never really thought about saving. She probably had about £300 in the bank, and she'd get the week's money Neil had promised her – another hundred quid.

It was better than nothing, but most of that would go on rent this month, and then ... next month, she wouldn't be able to pay. She fished into her bag to find her phone – something else she wouldn't be able to afford – and her fingers touched an unfamiliar shape.

The tablet. She licked her fingers clean, took it out and looked at it. It was a small one – seven-inch; a make she didn't know. And why had someone written BECKA on the case? How weird was that? Neil thought it was hers, thought she had left it behind the coffee-bar counter. She'd never seen it in her life. Who had left it there?

Suddenly, she remembered Paige ducking down behind the bar, helping herself to a drink from the fridge and putting a coin on the counter. Hannah had found the tablet this morning. Last night, Becca hadn't cleared up properly – she'd been too focused on Paige – so she hadn't gone back behind the counter.

Had it been Paige's? Had she left it there, expecting Becca to find it at once?

She pressed the button and the tablet lit up. A video. Someone had left her a tab playing a video, and she felt the familiar sick twist in her stomach. She should have guessed. Liam had been behind the bar as well. With a sense of inevitability, she tapped it, and the video began to play.

But it wasn't what she was expecting.

The camera was unsteady, moving across a grey,

gravelly surface that was covered in places by a sparse green growth. To one side, the sea came into view, then the camera swung away. There was a low wall – not quite a wall, really, just a line of stones. The landscape was odd, with strange mounds, like something was buried there that might come back to life.

The camera seemed to be following some kind of path. The grey surface sloped away and downwards, the camera jerking and jolting as the person carrying it scrambled over the rough terrain. She could hear breathing, and a tune, whistled almost under the breath, as if the person doing the filming was walking about on uneven, dangerous ground, trying to concentrate, like Matt when he was doing a fiddly repair, trying to line up a tiny screw and a tiny hole . . .

The image moved up a slope, and then the camera was looking down into a gully. There was an opening half concealed in the shadows of the gully bottom, dark and featureless. She thought about Jared and his flooded tunnel.

Now the camera was moving towards the opening, just a grey blur as the person holding it slithered down the slope, then it steadied, and focused.

The whistling stopped. Now there was only the breathing.

It was just a rough-edged gap dug into the cliff side, supported by bricks set in an almost flat arch above. Becca tensed. She didn't want to go in there, but the camera moved inexorably on.

The light faded and the screen darkened until all she

could see was something vague bobbing in the shadows. The breathing quickened and there was a grunt of effort, then a dim light filled the scene.

She had no idea what she was looking at.

Water gleamed in front of her, cloudy and yellowish with the vague outline of shapes beneath the surface. The camera moved again and panned across a low, flat ceiling, the same bricks, the same shallow arch. The bricks seemed loose – she couldn't see any mortar. They were stained rust-red in places, green in others with some kind of growth.

What kind of place was this? It was like a tunnel, a shallow tunnel. A series of pools crossed by low walls – clearly man-made – stretched away from her. In the middle, two iron pillars rose towards the ceiling, fungal with growths of rust.

The breathing was irregular, catching in the filmmaker's throat; *breathe* – uh! – *breathe* – uh! The picture froze, but the sound continued, someone whistling that strange, familiar tune.

A hand came into the picture. She had no scale to judge it against. It reached into the water, scooped something out and held it for the camera to record.

A piece of cloth . . . stained fabric and wire . . .

The fingers reshaped and suddenly she knew what it was.

A flower. A white silk flower.

165

Chapter 28

It had taken Jared longer to extricate himself from the Bridlington caravan park than he expected. He wished he'd thought to pack up and put everything in the car before taking Becca into Brid – then he'd never have to see this place again. It had all gone wrong here – going up the coast meant another chance. He'd start taking care of himself, stop relying on the pills and the whisky, work himself back to something like good health.

He'd been getting there, before the tunnel. Before the girl.

His laptop, his phone, his camera and all his camping equipment were already secure in the boot. He dumped the black bags full of dirty clothes – launderette as soon as – onto the back seat, along with a couple of books, his wash stuff and his medicines. A quick recce of the caravan didn't reveal anything and he was just locking the door when Greaseball Harry's car pulled up at the entrance to the site, probably here to see Jared off the premises.

Jared ignored him and gave his road map a quick once over, looking for the best route between Scarborough and Whitby. The plan was to head for Whitby, find somewhere with a decent internet connection and catch up on his website, which provided what passed for his income since the accident. Then he'd find a launderette and get himself sorted. Maybe a night in a B & B – a bit of comfort wouldn't go amiss – then, stoked up by a good night's sleep and a full English, he could drive up to Kettleness, where he should be able to locate a site to pitch his tent.

As he packed the last of his stuff into the back, he saw that Greaseball's car was rolling slowly towards him. Shit. Jared wanted nothing to do with him. Getting out of Greaseball's way was one of the big incentives for moving on.

He slid behind the wheel of his Volvo as Greaseball wound down his window. 'Where are you going?'

'I'm leaving,' Jared said.

'Yeah, I can see that. I said, where are you going?'

'Out of here. That's all you need to know.'

'Don't get funny with me, sunshine. What if there's any damage? I haven't checked it, you know.'

Jared looked over his shoulder at the battered caravan. 'Look, mate, the only way I could have damaged that caravan is if I'd fixed it up for you. You've got my email.' He pressed the button and his window slid closed. He wasn't wasting his time with this moron. As GBH climbed out of his car, Jared pulled round him and headed for the entrance. He could see Greaseball watching him and as Jared went through the gate, he was already talking into his phone.

Arse. Jared wondered what the problem was. The man had tried to throw him out earlier that day and had been a sore loser when Jared said he was staying. Now he seemed mad that Jared was going. Jared's mood lifted and he grinned as he remembered Becca's simmering indignation with Greaseball. Maybe he should have let her get on with it. She was only small but he suspected she packed a hefty punch. She would have been good company on his trip up the coast . . . but from what he'd seen, she had her own issues. She didn't need his as well.

The road surface was terrible and the car bounced and jolted towards the end of the lane. He eased his foot off the gas. If GBH decided to follow him, it would be the slowest car chase in history.

His phone rang. He was on a quiet road so he picked up. 'Yeah?'

'Is that you?'

Becca. He recognised her voice, and found himself smiling. 'Who else would it be?'

'Very funny. It's me. Becca,' she clarified, before he could say anything.

'I kind of thought it might be. Hi, Becca.'

'Look, I've changed my mind. I want to come with you.'

He glanced in his mirror. A car was coming along the road behind him. He recognised it. It was GBH. Shit, shit, and . . . shit on a plate. 'I'm driving. Call me back later, OK?'

'Yeah, but—'

He had to cut her off. He might have been joking to himself about the slow-motion car chase, but he really didn't want this guy on his tail. Jared had him labelled as a nasty piece of work, and he'd run into a few in his time. He was in no condition to deal with the guy at the moment. It was possible – probable – GBH was just driving into Brid, but Jared wanted to be out of his way.

He must have a reason for seeing Jared off the site, for wanting to know where he was going. He'd never shown any interest at all until after the night when the girl was attacked, then he'd wanted Jared gone. Jared didn't want to start speculating about why. With a bit of luck, all he was doing was making sure.

But he didn't want Greaseball to know where he was going. When he got to the junction, instead of turning north, he stayed on the road heading south towards the M62 and the M18, gaining speed now he was driving on a better surface. He kept his eye on the rear-view mirror. The car was still behind him.

He kept going, taking the turning south at the next junction. His car was powerful enough to leave the guy behind, but Jared wanted Greaseball to back off of his own volition, not because Jared managed to outrun him. He was following a route that would take him away from the east and onto the southbound motorways, right out of the area and away. He was pretty sure that all GBH wanted to know was that Jared was going to be out of his hair. The next turning was signposted M62 and, dutifully, Jared took it. If this went on much longer, he'd end up on the fucking motorway and then he might as well continue south. The Kettleness tunnels weren't *that* interesting, and there seemed to be a pile of trouble building up here. He'd head south, get right away from it, concentrate on getting well. It was a shame about the girl – what had happened to her was seriously bad, but what else could he do?

What went wrong, mate? What stopped you going back?

I'm sorry . . .

It's easy to be sorry . . .

Becca, stalking away down the path, off to find a bus she didn't even know existed. Becca, squaring up to tackle GBH at the caravan site. Becca who stood up for someone she'd just met . . .

A dull ache started low down in his back. He'd let everyone else down. He didn't have to let Becca down as well. OK. However far GBH followed him, he wasn't going to let it chase him off. He didn't know what he could do, but maybe just being around was enough. The green car was at the junction now. It pulled out – and took the road heading north-west. Back into Brid.

Jared kept going, watching for the next turn off that would take him back north. As he drove, he thought about Becca's call.

What had made her change her mind? She'd probably kicked one of her charges in his disadvantaged teeth and got thrown out. Becca was trouble on legs – he'd seen enough of her to know that.

He wondered whether to call her now, but decided to keep going. There was no point in losing the advantage and letting GBH see him back in Brid. He'd call Becca from Whitby.

Chapter 29

Becca looked at her phone in disgust. So much for Jared. He'd already left, and by the time he called back – if he called back – he'd be in that Kettle place or wherever it was he said he was going. Anyway, it had been a lame decision; she didn't want to go with him, she just wanted him to look at the video on the tab – Paige's tab, Paige's video, she was pretty sure.

She felt better after she'd eaten. Ignoring the pointed table-wiping from the waitress who collected her empty plate and mug, she stared out of the window. The sea beyond the harbour wall was grey and restless. Sea should be blue with little waves and kids playing in the water and stuff like that. This sea looked like something that would drown you and then spit you out again.

So what should she do now?

Kay. She should phone Kay and let her know ... let her know what? She wasn't going to tell Kay about Bexgirl and the photo, but she'd have to tell her something – she'd just say she'd lost the job. Becca sometimes

172

wondered how far she'd have to go before Kay finally gave up on her.

And then ... wait and see what Kay said? There wasn't much Kay could do. The days and weeks ahead stretched out in front of her – no job, no money, no home.

She didn't need to think about that right now.

She paid her bill and left the café. There was no protection from the wind on the harbour wall. It cut through her clothes, spun her hair into a tangle and made her eyes water. She struggled against it up to the main road and headed back towards her flat. A taxi went past. She remembered the night before, the night Paige had got into a similar car – and found her gaze moving round warily, checking the street behind her, in front, for another cruising vehicle, but all she could see was empty streets. Bridlington – the dull town, the dump she'd talked to Kay about – suddenly felt edgy and dangerous, like ... like a loaf of bread spiked with razor blades.

She didn't go along the back alley to her flat – she used the entrance through the shop. The landlord had made it clear he didn't want her doing this, but screw him. The shop was busy, and no one seemed to notice.

The door of the landing bathroom was open, and someone had used it and not flushed. Becca ignored it – let the next person from the shop who needed to pee deal with that. She let herself into the room, dumped her coat on the bed and slumped into the chair.

Then she started crying. It was like she had held it

in since this morning – no, since the night before when Paige had got in the car – and once she started, she couldn't stop.

It had all been working out. First there had been college, there had been friends like Ashley, there had been her tutors telling her she was doing well – and she *had* done well, she'd worked, she hadn't screwed up . . .

And then she had.

Just a photograph taken by a friend – and it was all gone.

And now, the drop-in. It had been a nothing job in a going-nowhere place – but she'd been doing well at it. The kids liked her, they talked to her – look at Paige, Paige had trusted her. And where had that got her? She'd let Paige down, and now Bexgirl had followed her here – no, not Bexgirl. A photograph. It was just a photograph. She hadn't done anything wrong, but no one would believe her. No one would even listen.

She sat up and rubbed her hands across her face. Her nose was running so she wiped it on her sleeve. What was she doing, sitting here like a crybaby? Since when did that get you anywhere? She went to the small sink and splashed water on her face. This was all a waste of time. She had more important things to worry about.

The first thing she needed to do was find a job. Her breath was still catching in her throat, and her eyes kept filling but she ignored her tears and got out her phone. An internet search didn't show much for jobs in Bridlington, just dead-end, nothing stuff. There were a couple of minimum-wage supermarket jobs. They were only part-time – sixteen hours a week – but they wanted people working early, late and weekends, so no chance of topping up her wage with pub work. She did some adding up. Her flat was one of the cheapest she could find at £70 a week. The supermarket job paid £90 – there might be a bit of overtime, but she wouldn't be able to rely on it. She'd have twenty pounds left for everything – food, heat, travel, clothes ...

Shit.

Anger was starting to take over now and anger was better than tears. She'd find a sodding job and she'd manage to live and she'd stick around too so there was someone here who cared about Paige, and fuck the lot of them.

Her phone rang. She saw Jared's name on the display and almost didn't answer it after the way he'd brushed her off before, but she was running out of options. She picked it up.

'Yeah?' She knew she didn't sound friendly and she didn't intend to.

Chapter 30

It was easy enough for Jared to find somewhere to stay near Kettleness. He gave up the idea of a B & B. A local farmer was happy to offer camping space with access to some basic facilities. Sleeping in a tent wasn't ideal for his back, but he was short of money and over the years he'd collected some decent equipment. He'd manage.

The good news was his back was improving. He'd pushed it, got himself into a bad state, almost like it had been at the beginning, but now it was ... not better, but OK. He was on the mend and soon he'd be able to put the legacy of the fall behind him and get back to ...

It didn't matter now. He could think about that later.

The bad news was he was close to broke. Previously, he'd kept himself going with casual work – people were always wanting someone who could climb in construction work. It paid well, and he lived cheaply. Since his accident, that income stream was closed to him, at least for now, and his savings were just about gone. Apart from that, there was his website, and he'd been neglecting that for a while. These past few months he hadn't had much to post, unless people wanted directions to his hospital bed.

And there was the money his mother kept putting in his account. He wasn't touching that.

So he needed to start earning. Soon.

He popped a couple of pills and started sorting out his tent. By six, everything was set up, then he went and had a cold shower – necessity rather than choice; the facilities on offer didn't run to hot water – in the out-house the farmer had directed him to. He was frozen when he came out, but his small heater turned the tent into a warm refuge, so by the time he was dressed and ready to head down into Whitby, he told himself he was feeling pretty good.

There was an internet café on Flowergate. He ordered pie and chips and settled down at a table that looked out onto the narrow street. He was setting up his laptop when his phone pinged with a message. He opened it, half his attention on his laptop, which was slowly booting up.

An image filled his screen. He looked at it in blank surprise. It was a picture of Becca, sitting on a bed. She was naked. She was holding an outsize vibrator and looking straight into the camera. But instead of the fake sexy pout women in images like this usually had, she was laughing – something, presumably the ludicrous sex toy, had really struck her as funny. Her free hand was upturned in a kind of 'What the fuck?' gesture.

She looked . . . amazing.

He felt his jaw drop. His first reaction after his

initial surprise was a kind of wordless Holy shit! but then his rational brain kicked in. Why would Becca send him this?

His phone pinged, pinged again and again. Six more texts, all from the same number. Why would she ...? Was it a way of saying: look what you're missing out on if you don't call me?

He couldn't imagine the girl he'd met – the one who'd almost got into a fight on his account on the front steps of the nick, and who'd made a good attempt at killing them both trying to drive an unfamiliar car – sending sex pictures as a kind of hidden message to someone she barely knew.

He thought about it for a few minutes, then moved to touch 'call' on the screen. That was when he realised the pictures had been sent from a withheld number. What the fuck was going on? He went to his contacts list and checked – yes, Becca's name was there.

He wanted some answers.

The phone rang for so long he thought she wasn't going to reply, then suddenly she was there. 'Yeah?'

It wasn't the most welcoming response. 'I thought you were going to call me,' he reminded her mildly.

'Yeah, well ...'

She'd obviously changed her mind again. Fair enough, and that made the texted images even more unlikely. 'I'm in Whitby. I've got a place to camp a bit further north. You know, where I said.'

'Kettlewhatsit?'

'Kettleness. There's old mines and railway tunnels

and things. It's interesting.' It sounded lame and it was lame, but it seemed to grab her attention.

'Old mines? Like in the cliffs?'

'Yeah, kind of.'

'Can you show me? Are there pictures?'

Pictures. 'There's loads. Look, before we talk about this, did you just text me?

'No.'

'I got some pictures. Just now. I thought they might be from you.'

'I didn't send any pictures. Shit, I . . .'

'They weren't from you?'

'No. They weren't.' The silence lengthened, then she said, 'What were they? Were they . . . kind of . . . sex . . . pictures?'

'I only opened one. Yeah, it was . . . you know, photos.'

'But . . . *just* a sex picture?'

Odd use of *just*. 'I only opened one. It was you . . .' He floundered. 'Look, it was a good picture, you were laughing like it was a bit of fun, it wasn't . . .' It wasn't sleazy, it wasn't fake, he wanted to say. It was like a picture she might send to her boyfriend. Was that it? Had some slimeball posted private photographs on the internet?

'You'd better know. I used to do camming, OK? I had a good site. But I don't do it anymore. And I don't send pictures like that. To anyone. OK?'

'OK. Becca, it's not my business. You don't have to explain. I just wondered – why would someone send it to me? How would they even know . . .?'

Because Greaseball saw them together? So how would Greaseball know who Becca was? Then he remembered Greaseball standing outside the caravan as Jared left, his phone jammed to his ear. Greaseball may not know, but someone did.

'It's me they're after, not you. You don't have to worry.'

Why did she have to be so touchy? 'That's not what I meant. I meant – why is someone after you like this?'

'I got doxed. I made a stupid mistake and they sent pictures to people I knew. And ... there was one picture – it wasn't anything, but ... You deleted the others?'

He selected the unopened texts and pressed the delete key. 'They're gone. I didn't look at them.'

There was the same long silence. When she spoke again, her voice wobbled, just for a second, then she was back to normal. 'They sent them to work. I lost my job.'

'When?'

'Just now. Today.'

'For those pictures?'

'There was one – I bet it's in the ones you deleted. You probably wouldn't be calling me if you'd seen it.'

He wondered what it was. Dogs? Donkeys? 'Do you want to tell me about it?'

'Yeah. OK. You'll see it and you'll only think bad things about me.'

'Look, Becca, you can tell me if you want to, that's up to you, but those pictures are gone. If any more arrive, I'm not looking at them unless you say I can. OK?'

180

'OK.' She sounded subdued. He listened to the story of the friend's sister, the movie, the pizza and the ice cream, and the picture at the end, Becca and a little girl – on a cam-girl's bed.

Shit.

'So what happened?'

'They put it with the other pictures and sent it to my friends. And my course tutor. I thought it was all done with but now they've sent them to my boss at the drop-in.'

'And they sacked you? For that?'

'Yeah.'

'What a load of . . .' He was about to cut the epithet, then remembered that Becca wasn't exactly into censorship. '. . . bullshit. Stupid cunts. Did you explain?'

'What's the point?'

There probably wasn't any point. 'You can come up to Kettleness now, can't you?'

'I . . . look, those pictures . . . they don't mean we can . . .'

'No strings,' he said quickly.

'Yeah. OK. I want to see those mines you were saying about.' The phone went dead.

This was getting fucked up. He thought about the girl in the caravan site the night before and his weird experience in the tunnel. And now these messages, out of the blue. He was glad to be out of Bridlington, but it looked as though Bridlington might be following him up here.

Chapter 31

Kay sat in front of the fire with Milo in her lap, watching the grey day turn into grey twilight. She'd been trying to read, but her attention kept drifting. At this time of year, the sun barely rose at all. It felt like forever before the long days would be here and she could walk along the cliff path in the evening light watching the setting sun glint off the sea.

She heard the *ping* from her laptop that told her she had mail, but she couldn't be bothered to go and check. Milo was restless. He jumped down from her lap and started wandering round the room, growling at the window, then sniffing round the door and growling again. 'Stop it, Milo.' A spooked dog. That was all she needed. Milo looked up and gave her a vague wag, then applied his nose to the front door again, the growl deep in his throat.

She was in a fair way to a self-pitying wallow. Making a conscious effort, she turned her thoughts to the day before when she'd met Shaun Turner for coffee.

He'd been there waiting when she arrived. She didn't remember him, but he'd clearly remembered her, standing up to greet her with a broad smile. He was a big man, tall and heavyset, with fair hair that was fading to grey. She was glad she'd made a bit of an effort with her own appearance. She'd put her hair up, clicking her tongue over the way she'd let the grey streak through it. Hairdresser. Soon. And she'd worn smart trousers rather than the usual jeans. And, OK, the green shirt that she'd bought in the summer sales.

She'd enjoyed herself. Her plan had been a cup of coffee; find out what, if anything more, Shaun knew about the Flamborough attack, then she'd be off to get her shopping done. Instead, she found herself accepting his suggestion that they might as well have lunch given the time, and lingering over a final cup of coffee before they went their separate ways.

He'd brought up Flamborough himself without her asking, giving her the latest news about the girl's condition – 'I know you're worried' – telling her the police were working on the theory the girl might be an illegal immigrant. 'Might have fallen foul of traffickers,' he'd added, with a grimace.

They'd talked about living alone after so many years of living with someone else, they'd talked about the cliff edge of retirement, they'd talked about the pros and cons of living on the east coast. And he'd managed to stop himself finishing too many of her sentences when he saw her frown the first time he did it.

He'd mentioned the drop-in as well. 'All that's left of our initiative, sad to say. Do you know it?'

'Yes. I—'

'Of course you do. You keep your finger on the pulse more than I do.'

'Well, it's more that someone I know, a friend of mine, works there.' He didn't pursue it, and she was glad. She didn't want to discuss Becca with him – it was all too easy to misunderstand Becca, especially if you were looking at her life with a policeman's eye.

The rest of their time had been marked by a pleasantly light-hearted flirtation that left her feeling a bit frivolous, in a mood for fun. As they'd parted, he'd said, 'Would you like to do this again? Maybe dinner next time?'

Her youth had been marked by seriousness and responsibility. Maybe it was time to misspend her old age, or some of it. So she found herself saying yes, and they agreed to keep in touch.

Her reverie was interrupted by Milo leaping up and barking furiously, knocking a stool over as he raced to the door and threw himself at it. Kay jumped. 'Milo!' she said, but he paid no attention, jumping and barking for all he was worth.

'All right, all right.' She looked out of the window. A car – a rather battered old Micra – was pulled up outside her gate. Milo's barking intensified.

'Shut up, Milo,' Kay said, more for form's sake than because she expected him to obey. A young woman with fair, reddish hair got out of the car and studied the phone she was holding. Then she hitched the backpack she was carrying up onto her shoulders with a gesture Kay recognised.

Becca.

But a very different Becca from the one she'd last seen. That Becca had multi-coloured hair, dramatic make-up, a nose jewel and a pierced eyebrow. Kay didn't even want to speculate about where else she might have piercings.

This Becca had let her hair return to its natural colour, the piercings were gone and she wore no make-up.

Kay hadn't seen Becca for eight months, not since they'd met in Leeds before Becca started college. This unexpected visit didn't bode well. What had brought her up here, an hour's drive from Bridlington? And on a weekday, when she should be at work. She grabbed Milo's collar and opened the door just as Becca approached it. 'Becca! What are you doing here?'

Becca looked offended. 'I've come to see you. What's wrong with that? Shut up, Milo.'

'I'm surprised, that's all. Is something wrong?' Milo had stopped barking, but he was circling Becca, frantically sniffing at her shoes and legs, gathering all the information he could.

'Why should something be wrong? Can't I visit without something being wrong?'

Kay sighed. It was too easy to get off on the wrong foot with Becca. 'It's good to see you, Becca love.'

She held out her arms, and after a brief hesitation, Becca let Kay hug her, then hugged her back. 'I'm freezing.'

'Come in. Go through there. There's a fire. Get warm and I'll make us a brew. Then we can catch up.' Becca went into the front room, followed by the attentive Milo.

In the kitchen, filling the kettle, getting out cups, looking in the cupboard for some cake, Kay's mind was working overtime. She didn't believe Becca's reassurances for a moment – she knew Becca of old, and she could see the telltale signs of distress. But there was no point in pushing – Becca would just clam up all the more.

She put everything on a tray, carried it through to the front room and put it on a table in front of the fire. Becca was curled up in the big chair, her arms round Milo, who was in her lap. She looked small and lost.

Kay poured the tea. 'Cake?' she said.

'Chocolate cake? Did you make it?' Becca perked up and took the proffered plate. 'I'm starving,' she added with her mouth full.

Kay sat back in her chair and watched as Becca ate the slice of cake hungrily. She was reminded of the skinny, dirty thirteen-year-old who had first come to her and Matt after several fostering attempts failed because of her violent, destructive rages.

Things had been going so right for Becca, and now ... now they weren't.

'So, how are you? Do you want to stop over tonight?'

Becca shook her head. 'I'm OK. Thanks.'

'Well, if you change your mind ...'

Becca was looking round. It was the first time she'd visited Kay since Kay had moved. 'Why didn't you go back to Leeds?' she said. 'I mean, after Matt?' Becca had lived in cities all her life. Bridlington was as close to a village as she had ever got. Like Kay, she preferred a place with supermarkets and clubs and bars within easy access.

'Matt always liked it here,' Kay said, and chatted on vaguely about walks, about scenery, about places where Milo could have a run, all the time observing Becca slumped in the chair, stroking Milo and staring blankly into the fire.

Becca finally seemed to come to a decision. 'I've left. The drop-in.'

It was what Kay had been half expecting. 'Have you? But Becca, you said that this morning, then you changed your mind. You've really left?'

'Yeah.'

Kay told herself to take this carefully. If she challenged Becca, Becca would probably just storm out. 'Do you mean you've handed in your notice?'

'No. I've left.'

'You just walked out?'

Becca's chin lifted. 'It wasn't like that. They asked me to leave.'

Fired? Becca had been fired? 'Why? What happened?' Becca had a wicked temper but she'd learned to control it over the years. It was a long time since she'd had a full-blown meltdown.

'Nothing happened. They just decided.'

'But something—'

'Nothing happened.'

Kay knew when she was being warned off. She could ask Neil Cowper. No, she couldn't. It was Becca's business, not hers. 'I'm sorry.'

'It's easy to be sorry about things. It doesn't change anything. Anyway, you haven't done anything.'

'I'm sorry you lost the job.'

'I'm not. I never liked it. I told you.'

'OK. You did. Becca, first it was college, now it's the job. What's wrong? Is there anything I can do?'

'No. I'm fine. Look, let's stop talking about it, OK? I just wanted you to know.'

'You can't go on like this, Becca. You know that. You have to decide on what you want to do and—'

'I have decided. Not the fucking drop-in, right?'

They were teetering on the brink of a full-blown row. It wouldn't be the first – or the last, Kay was sure – but she didn't want tonight to end up with Becca storming out. Matt was always the one who could get through to her, and, shamelessly, Kay used this now. 'It was the anniversary last week,' she said. 'Matt's . . . a year since he died. I went walking on the cliff path at Kettleness. I went down to the railway tunnel, and – I know it was just a coincidence, but there was someone on the path behind me, and he was whistling – you'll never guess. Here, listen to this.'

She picked up the CD remote and found the track she wanted. 'Listen.'

The harsh voice filled the room. *I wish, I wish, I wish in vain* ... Kay looked at Becca. 'Do you remember?'

But Becca was looking at the CD player with a blank, shocked expression. Was it the sudden memory of Matt? Kay cursed herself for being insensitive. The music still tugged at her – and she had sprung it on Becca without warning.

'You heard someone ... Where? Where was it?'

'Kettleness.'

'You said the railway tunnel. Which tunnel? What's it like? Is it like, sort of buried in the ground?'

Kay blinked at the barrage of questions. 'It's a railway tunnel – look, up there.' There was a print of the old railway in its glory days, a steam engine travelling along the line, trailing a plume of smoke.

Becca studied it. 'Oh. There's trains.'

'That's an old photograph. The line has been closed for years. The tunnel's sealed off, but people do go in there. Sometimes.'

'And that's where you heard ...?'

'Yes.'

Becca was gathering her stuff together as she spoke. 'I've got to go. I'm late. Thanks for the tea,' she added as an afterthought.

'Are you sure you won't stay? It's getting dark.'

'No, I'm OK. Thanks.'

Kay saw her to the door. 'Where are you going?'

She saw Becca mull the question over,

testing it for ulterior motives. 'Just, you know, up the coast,' she said.

Kay bit her tongue on all the questions she wanted to ask. Having just avoided one row, she didn't want to start another. 'Have you got somewhere to stay?'

Becca bent down to pat Milo. Whatever she was doing, she wasn't going to tell Kay. 'Yeah. I'll be fine.'

Kay reached for her handbag. She hadn't been to the bank and she didn't have a lot of cash, but what she did have ... 'Here.' She thrust a couple of twenties and a ten into Becca's hand. 'Don't start arguing. Take it. And give me a call. Let me know you're all right.'

Becca looked as if she was going to object, then her hand closed over the cash. She wouldn't meet Kay's gaze. 'Right. OK. Thanks. Really. See you! Ta-ta Milo!' And with a wave, she was gone, out the door, heading towards her battered car.

Kay sighed. All the anger, all the loss of control, was supposed to be behind Becca, but suppose they weren't. Kay had never got to the bottom of Becca's decision to leave college, a topic Becca simply refused to discuss. And now an unexpected sacking from a job she was doing well at ...

It was getting on for ten, and she was tired. Early night. She went to turn off her laptop, then remembered the email alert she'd heard earlier. Leave it until tomorrow? No, it would nag at her.

She sat down at her desk. Two emails had arrived. One was routine business and could wait. The other – she didn't recognise the address, but the subject line said *From Becca*. She knew Becca's email address – this wasn't it. With a real sense of trepidation, she opened it.

Two photographs filled her screen.

Oh, Becca! Just what have you got yourself mixed up in now?

Chapter 32

The rain was still falling as Becca followed the narrow road towards the coast. Alek had replaced the slashed tyre, but all he'd managed to do with the windows was piece them together with heavy-duty tape. The inside of the car was freezing and her windscreen wipers weren't working properly. She had to drive with her nose almost against the glass, trying to see ahead.

This was supposed to be the main road, though it was more like a country lane. According to Jared, there should be a right turn coming up soon, signposted . . .

Goldsborough. There it was, on cue. She wasn't lost. The turning took her onto an even narrower road, heading towards the coast.

It couldn't be far now.

The rain was falling heavily and the light was gone. She could barely see a few feet ahead of her and when the road took a tight turn to the left, she almost ended up in a field. Jared hadn't mentioned that. Her faith in his directions began to fade. Why didn't she just head back to Kay's? She could find whatever field Jared had parked himself in much easier in the morning.

But a sense of urgency drove her on. The video on the tablet couldn't wait. Paige had left that for her – she was sure of it now – and it was already over twenty-four hours since Paige had got in the car and vanished. She should have found it that night – Paige might have been relying on that. Time was running away and she couldn't wait any longer.

And there was the tune.

It was the tune someone was whistling on the video. And now Kay had heard it, up near the tunnel Jared talked about. There was a tunnel in the video, but not the same tunnel . . . or was it?

Jared was the only person Becca could think of who might know what it was the video showed. She had to find him tonight and let him watch it, then they could decide what to do.

But the road seemed endless. She was lost.

Her phone was on the dashboard with the satnav open, but out here the signal was unreliable. *Follow the road to Goldsborough*, Jared had said. *Then take the right turn along the road marked 'dead end'. You can't miss it.*

Dead end. That sounded about right.

It was like Matt used to say – *You're impulsive, Becca. That's why you get into bother sometimes. Don't just jump – try and think things through.*

And now, too late, she *was* thinking. She was trying to find out what had happened to Paige, but Jared had no reasons to be concerned about Paige. Jared was a pill-head who wasn't really concerned about anyone else. When Becca called him, said she had something she wanted him to see, he'd been all *Yeah, great, come up here*, but he probably thought she meant more camming photos and had his own ideas about how they'd spend the time. He *said* he'd deleted the photos someone had sent him, but that was no guarantee he wasn't perving over them right now.

Why should she rely on him? He'd messed up on helping Paige at the caravan site, he'd run out on his friend in the caves – he'd said as much – and he'd run out on her back in Brid, so what use was he going to be now?

The more she thought about it, the more she was sure he wouldn't help. He'd turn out just like the rest of them. And now someone was trashing her life again and she couldn't do anything to stop them. Like her pervy policeman stepfather who'd just – without her permission, without asking, he'd just . . .

Lights dazzled her in her rear-view mirror and she hit the steering wheel with her fist in angry frustration. Un-*fucking*-believable! Out here in the middle of nowhere, out here at the end of the world, in the fucking boon-docks, she'd got someone sitting on her tail.

What the fuck was he doing? She couldn't pull over – the road was too narrow for passing. The headlights were blinding her now and she put her foot down to get away.

But the bastard was still hassling her, coming right

up behind her, tailgating her, forcing her to drive faster than she wanted to when she couldn't see and didn't know where she was going.

Her speed was going up and up – forty-five, fifty, fifty-five – she wrestled with the steering wheel, trying to clear bends she only saw when she was on top of them, and he was still behind her, not sounding his horn, just close on her tail, pushing and pushing her – shit! Anything could be coming the other way. At this speed if she hit anything, she would be . . .

A wall loomed out of the darkness and she hauled the wheel round, hearing the squeal of tyres and the tooth-clenching screech of metal against stone. The car jolted, skidded round, throwing her against the wheel and whipping her head back.

And then the road was gone and she was bumping over rough ground as the car rocked from side to side, rocked again – she was going over, she was going over – then rocked back. She banged her head against the door pillar and the car bounced to a stop.

The engine cut out, leaving her to the silence and the falling rain.

Chapter 33

Becca didn't know how long she sat there. Seconds, minutes, hours?

Oh, God.

Then the shaking started. Her hands were out of her control as she fumbled with the seat belt that wouldn't shift, and with the door lock. Somewhere trapped in her head a voice was telling her to get out of the car, to get away.

The car that had driven her off the road – it was out there somewhere.

She tried to look behind her, but a stab of pain in her neck as she twisted round made her sink back into the seat.

She was out in the middle of the countryside on her own, she had no idea where she was, she'd probably wrecked her car, it was raining and she was hurt.

And somewhere in the night was the other car.

Drive away. Get the car started and drive away.

She was reaching for the ignition when the passenger door was wrenched open and a bright light shone in her face. Becca's scream cracked in her dry throat. She turned the key and turned it again as the engine whinnied and failed. Her shaking hands fumbled with the seat belt and she pushed against the door, as the pain in her neck and shoulder stabbed at her.

She couldn't do it.

She couldn't get out.

Paige had been so badly beaten they couldn't identify her. Couldn't even photograph her.

Then someone spoke. 'I kind of thought it must be you. Are you OK?'

She lashed out at the voice. 'Don't! Touch me! Don't …'

'Becca. Hey, come on, take it easy. It's me. Jared.'

Jared. It was Jared. Her heart was hammering in her throat and she couldn't speak. She sat in the car reaching for air that seemed to have vanished.

'What happened? Are you hurt?'

'I …' She steadied her breathing. 'I'm … someone ran me off the road. I …' She could just make out Jared's shape behind the torch he was holding. 'The light. They'll see the light.'

'The other car? It's gone. Someone went down the lane at about seventy. They're in for a nasty surprise if they don't slow down.'

'What if he comes back?'

His attention was suddenly focused. 'Someone was after you?'

Becca shook her head. She wanted to cry so she summoned her anger instead. 'I don't know. Stupid arse.

He nearly killed me.' Now the seat belt undid easily. Moving gingerly, she eased herself out of the front seat. Her neck was painful, but she could move it OK. Her stomach was sore and when she touched it she flinched at the pain. A bruise – the seat belt.

She felt Jared put something round her shoulders and realised the rain was coming down in buckets and she was wet. He looked across the field to where the road must be. It was too dark to see anything, but his face, in the light of his torch, looked worried. 'Best get out of sight,' he said. 'You're cold. Let's get you warmed up.'

Suddenly her legs were shaking and she could barely stand. Gritting her teeth, she ignored his proffered arm and limped across the field.

She heard the sound of a car in the distance. It was heading towards them. Jared switched the torch off, leaving them in darkness. The car was closer now, moving slowly, somewhere to their left where the road must be. Jared tugged on her arm. 'Down!' He spoke into her ear as he pulled her onto the ground.

About 100 metres away, she could see the glow of the headlights moving on the other side of the wall. Then they blazed out, and she realised the car had reached the gate. She gripped Jared's arm. Her guts were tight, she needed to pee – a sudden, urgent spasm – and there was something in her that wanted to shout out *We're here!* – just to get it over with.

She heard a car door – someone was getting out, going to look at her car. They'd see she wasn't there and then – she and Jared were on their own. She was hurt and couldn't run fast, and Jared – he was hurt too.

A light started to play across the field, towards her car, swinging wider, towards the place where they were hiding . . .

The girl in the hospital, damaged so badly, no one could recognise her.

Pools of water and someone whistling a familiar tune.

OK, OK, I'm here, I give up, come and find me . . . No!

Then in the distance she heard the sound of a siren, a police car, an ambulance, she didn't know. She grasped the sound like a comfort blanket. Maybe the driver of the car had called for an ambulance, maybe that was why he'd come back, maybe . . .

The car door again. The car engine and the headlights swinging round the field. Jared pushing her head down and then the sound of the car as it headed away down the road, back towards Kay's, back towards Whitby.

The siren wailed and wailed, moving closer, then moving away, then fading into silence.

Chapter 34

Half an hour later, Becca was wearing dry clothes – a pair of Jared's jeans and one of his warm sweaters – with her hands wrapped round a cup of hot soup. She still looked pale, and from time to time her teeth clattered against the side of the mug as the shivering came back, but she looked a lot better than she had.

Once he got her comfortable, Jared divested himself of his all-enveloping waterproof and dumped it in the outer part of the tent. He didn't know what to do, and he didn't know what was going on. Becca had arrived with an anonymous car on her heels and a cascade of malicious texts dogging her tracks. Who the fuck had she got on the wrong side of? And how? He shook his head.

'What?' Becca was watching him closely over the rim of her mug.

'Just . . . trying to work out what to do.'

Her chin lifted. 'You don't have to do anything. I'll be fine.'

'I know. But I'm doing it, right?' He'd kept the stove

lit for the shortest time possible – getting something warm into Becca seemed important, but he didn't want to draw any more attention to their location. He knew how to keep them both out of sight. Years ago, his father had taken him camping in the wild, taught him to survive with just a compass and a map. He'd already closed the entrance up tight and dimmed the light. If someone wanted to find them, they were going to have to do some hard searching in the dark.

Becca was curled up against a rolled-up sleeping bag. She looked round the tent. 'This is cool. I've never been camping before.'

He grinned. She wasn't going to admit she'd been scared. 'It's not bad, is it? Better than the caravan.' He listened to the sounds of the night. Just the rain still falling. No vehicles, nothing moving in the field, or nothing that had no right to be there.

She shifted uneasily. 'What do you do if you want . . . you know.'

He grimaced. For him, this field was fine, but the sanitary arrangements left a lot to be desired. In this weather, he'd probably use a bottle, but he couldn't expect Becca to do that. 'It's not brilliant. There's a shed across the field with a shower and stuff. In this rain, I just nip out if it's only – you need to go?'

She looked towards the closed entrance and shivered. Just for a moment, her armour slipped, and she looked scared.

'They've gone. They wouldn't hang around if the police were on their way. I think we're OK.'

201

She pointed at the waterproof. 'OK, give me that.'

Jared unlaced the tent flaps and she squeezed out, coming back ten minutes later making faces and shaking the wet off her like a discontented cat.

While she was gone, Jared had been thinking. 'That car – did it follow you from Brid?'

'I don't know. No. There wasn't anyone really. I stopped at a friend's house in some kind of, you know, village kind of thing. Lythe. Then –' her eyes closed as she thought back – 'it wasn't until I got off that hill – they call it a main road if you want to believe that. One minute the road was empty, next minute . . .'

'I was just wondering how they knew it was you if they hadn't followed you.'

'But why? I mean, yeah, if you're that kind of moron, a girl drives past, you tailgate her and all that, but – why would they be looking for me?'

'That's what I'm trying to work out. You said someone had vandalised your car. And someone sent me those pictures, right?'

'And then they try to drive me off the road. That's . . .' She frowned as the implications sank in.

'They probably didn't mean for you to crash. They were trying to get you to stop. Then . . .' He remembered the feel of the girl's hand in his, how she'd gripped it, and the faint moans as she lay there in the darkness.

Becca was watching him. 'What?' she said.

'Look, it might be a coincidence. I don't know why anyone would be going after you – well, you'd know better than me, but I do know there's something pretty bad going on down near Brid. It was me who found that girl – there was something I didn't tell you. They really trashed her.'

Becca looked stricken. 'Paige ...'

'You know who it is now? You know it's your friend?' When he met her at Ashville Street, after the police interview, she hadn't been sure.

'It must be. Who else?'

So she still wasn't certain.

'Listen. There's something I need to show you. It's important.'

'OK.' He suspected she'd deliberately changed the subject.

She rummaged in her bag and pulled out a small tablet. 'You know you said you went in a small side tunnel ...'

'Near here. Yes.'

'Look at this.'

The screen displayed a video. He clicked play and watched as the wobbly camera moved across a moonscape of serpentine mounds, listening to the breathy, fragmented tune. He did that himself in tough places, whistled to keep his mind focused, to stop it from going places he didn't want it to. The camera took him inexorably into darkness and then looked out across a strange, luminescent pool. He watched the hand dip into the water, then form the stained, dripping fragment of fabric into a flower.

'Shit.' He was staring at the dark screen. And again. 'Shit.'

'It gets worse.' Becca sounded almost buoyant at his response. She'd been alone with this and she must have expected him to dismiss it as some kind of joke. She told him about the woman in Lythe – her foster-mother, an elderly woman, who, for reasons Becca didn't explain, had been messing about near the tunnels around the time he'd gone in.

'The same tune? Are you sure?'

'And I've heard it – a couple of times. Someone at the drop-in . . .'

He leaned back on the cushions and closed his eyes. The significance of what she had just shown him, and what she was telling him, was just beginning to sink in. He could remember the debris falling around him, remember thinking it was a roof fall and he was going to die. But there hadn't been a body. The police had said.

But . . . if the flower was real, then what about the rest of it? Maybe there *had* been a body. And between his fall, and the police arriving a few hours later, some-one – somehow – had hidden it.

He could still see the face that had leaped out at him in the flickering blue light. What had seemed like a snarl could have been the exposed teeth of a skull. And the mask across the eyes, the shadows of empty sockets, a face skeletonised before its time. 'Jesus.'

'What?'

'I thought it was all in my head. I saw some things in the tunnel. The air was bad. I thought I was seeing things. If it was real . . .'

'If what was real? What are you talking about?'

'I thought I saw a body. A dead woman. And . . .' He really didn't want to admit this because it just sounded crazy, but . . . 'And a flower, you know, sort of silk . . . like that one. It looked like that in the . . .' In the same blue, flickering light.

They both sat in silence, then Becca said, 'The video?'

'I don't know, but I think it must be one of the old mines or tunnels round here. We need to go and find it.'

Chapter 35

The cry of a gull woke Jared. It was still too dark to see much. He stretched and was about to greet the day with a prolonged fart when he remembered he had a guest. No living like a slob now. Becca was just a mound in the tent's shadows. He tested his back, his shoulders, his leg – a few twinges, nothing to worry about. Moving carefully so as not to disturb her, he slid out of his sleeping bag and edged his way carefully out of the tent.

The temperature had dropped during the night and the air felt crisp and sharp. The frozen grass glimmered white in the light of the setting moon. He could hear the sea, a restless surging as it washed against the cliffs. The field edge was marked by low scrubland that he knew fell away down the crumbling coast to end in a sheer drop. Beyond the edge, there was just darkness.

He walked back across the field to where they'd left Becca's car the night before, the ground crunching under his feet, loud in the silence. Using his torch, he carried out a quick external check. There was no obvious damage. He got down to look at the undercarriage, wincing as his back delivered a stab of pain. He needed a pill. No, he didn't. What he needed was a clear head.

He could manage.

The car looked sound as far as he could tell – everything looked intact.

He remained crouched down, thinking. Last night, the people who had driven Becca off the road had come back to look for her. It might have been altruism – some idiot boy racer wanting to make sure she wasn't hurt – but Jared didn't find that explanation very convincing. For some reason, someone had it in for Becca, and until they could work out why, it made sense not to stick around and find out the hard way.

He stood up, releasing the strain on his back. Why 'they'? From Becca's dramatic arrival late last night, her car skidding across the field and lurching to a halt, he'd thought about this as 'their' problem. But it wasn't. It was Becca someone was after, Becca who was being trolled, Becca who had been run off the road.

A dull ache began low down in his back and the first stirrings of nausea started in his gut. *Shit!* He dug in his pocket, feeling a surge of relief as his fingers encountered the pill box. He didn't have his flask – a slug of whisky helped the pills to work – but a couple of pills on their own would do the trick. He swallowed two dry, hesitated, then took two more.

As he did it, he made his decision. He hadn't asked for this, but neither had Becca. Nor had the girl at the caravan site. All she'd asked for was help. And so had Becca, in her own spiky way. He could walk away, tell himself it was OK if anything bad happened because he was *sorry*. Or he could do something before it was too late.

Becca might be tough and resourceful, but the people in the car had been able to take her off the road without any difficulty. If he hadn't been here, she would have been left to face them on her own, hurt, with no way to hide.

They'd be back, but he knew how to keep them both out of the way and he knew how to survive. Wasn't that what his father had taught him?

Until he fucked up.

That didn't matter now. What mattered was keeping Becca safe until they could work out what was happening.

When he got back to the tent, Becca was sitting up, rubbing her eyes. 'It's freezing,' she complained when he crawled back in through the tent flap.

'It's January,' he said. 'And there's a frost. Go and stand out there for ten minutes, then it'll feel warm in here.'

She didn't bother replying, but burrowed down inside the sleeping bag again.

Jared lit the lamp, opened the front of the tent a bit and lit the stove. As he sat there, waiting for the water to boil, he could feel the pills start to soothe the ache in his back. The knot of anxiety in his stomach began to loosen, and he leaned back and let the sounds of the early dawn wash over him. If only it could always be like this.

He poured the water into the mugs and prodded the hump that was Becca. 'Tea?'

She crawled out again and took the proffered drink. 'Thanks.' She spooned some sugar in and sat up, wrapping her hands round it for warmth, her face unreadable. 'What time is it?'

'Six thirty. We need to get moving. I had a look at your car. I think it's OK, but you'll need to try it.'

'Yeah.'

'You want some breakfast? Weetabix? Toast?'

She made a face but didn't respond. Clearly not a morning person. 'Up to you. Look, we need to get out of here. Those guys could be back. Most of my stuff's packed up anyway. Yours . . .' He felt the jeans and top she'd been wearing the night before. 'These are still wet. We need to get moving.'

Her chin lifted. 'You don't have to worry. I'm not going to hang around and make trouble. If I can get the car started, I'll go back to Brid.'

'Jesus Christ, Becca. You come flying in here last night with the Black Riders on your heels and stories of videos and bodies in tunnels and now you're all "I'm going back to Brid." What's that about?' He was angry with himself as much as with her. It would be so easy just to let her go, let her take all the trouble away with her.

'Yeah. And you're all like, "Got to get a move on, got to go, your bag's packed, your car's ready when you are." I don't need you to tell me what to do.'

209

He threw himself back onto the sleeping mat. He didn't know whether to laugh or to yell at her. He was trying to be one of the good guys, for fuck's sake. 'I just went across the field and looked at your fucking car. I thought it was going to be a tow job and I didn't know how we were going to manage that. You'll need to try it, but it looks fine. That's a good news story, right? How you get from there to *Get lost* I have no idea and I don't care, but don't start giving me a hard time about it, right?'

She glared at her mug of tea. After a few moments, she said, 'Have you got cornflakes?'

'Where does it say five-star hotel?'

'Just asking. Can I have some toast then?'

OK, she might jump down your throat for a dodgy intonation on a 'Good morning', but at least she didn't sulk.

As she ate her toast, he tried to focus through his pill-induced brain-fuzz. 'What I said before was right. We need to move on from here. I think they'll be back, but not until it gets light. We need to lose your car – for the moment,' he added as she opened her mouth to object. 'They know it. We might be able to leave it here – there's a place up beyond the car park where it'll be OK for a while.' There was something wrong here, something he was missing, but the more he tried to pin it down, the more elusive it became.

She chewed her lip, thinking it over, then gave a reluctant nod. 'OK. What about the rest?'

'We could go to the police. Show them what we've got.'

'No! I don't trust them.' Her face was closed. 'Paige left the video for me, not for the police.'

Maybe she was right. What would the police do? The video didn't show much – an entrance in the cliff side and the flower. Becca was certain the video was connected to the attack on her friend, but where was the link? It was just weird events happening together. And the thing he'd seen in the tunnel. Don't forget that. But he had no proof, and the police had found nothing.

Becca's friend had gone off in a car with a couple of dodgy-sounding men who'd talked about a 'party'. One of the caravan site parties that had been going on night after night? Was that the 'party' they'd been talking about, and did that mean there was a link between the drop-in where Becca worked and the caravan site? Even if there was, why the attack? Why trash a young girl so comprehensively?

'Your foster-mum. When was she at the tunnel?'

Becca frowned, thinking back. 'She said ... it was like Matt's tune. Like she thought it might be him, you know?'

'Matt?'

'Her husband. He died. It was the anniversary of his death.'

'Can you remember the date?' Jared kept his opinions about whistling ghosts to himself, but something must have showed on his face because her eyes narrowed.

'Course I can. He was my foster-dad.'

'Oh, for ... yeah, OK, I'm sorry. So what date was it?'

'The tenth. And it would have been— She said it was after three. It was getting dark.'

The tenth. That had been the day he'd almost killed himself in that same tunnel. But where did that get them? It was light enough now to manage without the lamp so he reached out and turned it off. Then he realised.

Daylight. Shit! He'd let her story distract him. Get a grip! 'We need to get moving. We can talk about this later.'

To his relief, she didn't argue. She stood up and reached for the clothes he'd lent her the night before. He turned his back to give her some privacy, and started clearing up his own stuff. He used to be organisation guy when he camped – the way his father had taught him. It had made sense then, and it made sense now. He wasn't a natural slob. It was just since ...

Since ...

What happened, mate? How did you get it so wrong?

Once she was ready, he pulled the stuff out of the tent and collapsed it. 'Come on. Let's get your car moved first.' He headed across the rough ground as fast as he could, Becca stumbling behind him in unsuitable shoes. The car was a silhouette against the pre-dawn light. The sky was glowing over the sea, the clouds a fanfare of colour to welcome the day. How early would they come? And they would come, he was more and more certain.

He waited for Becca to catch up. 'Give me your keys. I'll go over. If there's anyone there, then I'm just some dozy walker going for a stroll. If it's safe, you can come and we can get the car out of sight.'

Again, he had that feeling he was missing something. Too bad. He couldn't wait.

He walked across to the car and circled it, looking round. The road was empty in both directions, and there was no sign of movement in the still dawn. But he could feel it: a prickle of apprehension running down his spine, the hairs starting to rise on his neck. If they weren't here, they weren't far away.

He waved Becca across. 'Come on. We need to get moving. Let me drive – I know this road.' He unlocked the door and slid into the driver's seat. It was cramped for him and he lost a minute working out how to adjust the seat. She hadn't been able to get it started the night before, but with luck, all she'd done was flood the engine. The car was old enough. To his relief, it started on first try. Becca was opening the passenger door, and he was off before she'd fully closed it.

He bumped the car across the field, checking the road as they came out of the gate. It was empty, but there was something . . . On impulse, he turned towards the coast.

'It's a dead end,' Becca protested.

'We can't go that way. They're on the road behind us.'

'How do you know?'

He shrugged. He could be wrong, but the sixth sense that had always kept him safe – well, reasonably safe – was on full alert. That, at least, was still working.

Past the farm there was the derelict coastguard

cottage, the old railway station, a turning place and a small car park. Jared took the car beyond this point, bumping across rough ground and round more farm buildings, hoping he'd remembered right. They were on a grassy track where a dilapidated cottage stood, empty so far as Jared knew. He drove past it, then pulled the car round onto rough ground so that it was concealed behind the building.

If they came looking, they'd find it, but with luck, they wouldn't look this far.

Now they had to get back. 'Let's just keep this side of the wall,' he said as he started to lead the way back to the farm. Becca followed, but her shoes were slipping in the mud. He was being over-cautious. They'd be fine on the path for a couple of minutes. He was just about to suggest it when he heard the sound his ears had been alert for: a car. He pushed Becca down and listened, but he couldn't locate the direction it was coming from.

Close by – he couldn't tell exactly where, but past the field, near the farm. He touched her arm and could feel the tension. 'Stay down. I'll go and check,' he whispered. He wanted them to see the car had gone, wanted them to think Becca had left last night and was far away by now.

She nodded reluctantly. Jared took the path towards the cliff and followed it round to the field where his tent had been pitched. He picked up his stuff and went to find his car, which was parked behind the farm buildings. He was just packing everything into the boot when he heard the sound of an engine, and a car bumping along the rough track towards him.

Jared stiffened. Natural. Act natural. He looked up and as the car rolled to a halt next to him, he breathed again. It was the farmer's mud-spattered Land Rover. Two border collies panted eagerly from a trailer. 'Morning,' Jared said.

The farmer wound down the window. 'Morning. You off, then?'

'Yeah. I was coming up to the house to tell you. Just for a couple of days. OK if I come back?' The tunnels and the old mines in the cliffs were still there.

'Aye. You paid for a week. Just let me know, right?' He frowned. 'Before you go – did you hear anything last night?'

'No. Nothing.'

'The wife said she thought a car come off the road. I just went to take a look. There must have been a car – right mess it's made of the ground – but it's gone. Mind you, they see the sign, they see the road and they still come along it like fucking Brands Hatch. Someone's going to get killed one day.'

'Yeah. Well, I'd best be off then,' he said.

The farmer nodded and wound up the window.

Had he covered everything? There was still that nagging feeling of something forgotten, but it was too late now.

Chapter 36

Kay was surprised and – OK – a bit flattered when Shaun Turner arrived on her doorstep the following morning with a bunch of early daffodils and a sheepish expression. 'Kay. I was just passing, and I, well, I thought you might like these.' He handed her the flowers.

'Thank you.' Kay took them, mentally noting that Lythe wasn't really on the way to anywhere, and that if he was just passing, it was fortunate he happened to have a bunch of flowers with him. Shaun's diffidence was more attractive than the bluff self-assurance she had seen before. 'Would you like coffee?'

'I wondered . . .' He stepped around Milo, who was sniffing his shoes and trouser legs with focused intent. 'I wondered if you'd like to come out for a drive and have lunch with me? Today? I know it's short notice but it's a beautiful day as I was just—'

'That's a lovely thought but I can't today. I have to go to Bridlington.'

His eyebrows shot up. 'Bridlington? Why are you—'

He saw her frown. 'Sorry. None of my business. OK, serves me right. I should have called first.'

He looked so crestfallen, Kay said, 'Why don't we have coffee at least? I've got half an hour.'

The offer of coffee cheered Shaun up. She got him ensconced in the chair by the stove and left him looking nervously at Milo, who was scouting for routes up onto Shaun's lap as she went into the kitchen.

There was a small mirror on the kitchen wall and she checked her hair and make-up. She had dressed smartly for her Bridlington trip, and had to admit she felt relieved Shaun hadn't caught her in her tatty dog-walking trousers, her old woolly hat and no make-up. Never too old for vanity.

She put the coffee on a tray and took it through with some of the chocolate cake she'd given to Becca the evening before. Shaun was thumbing through a book about the local coast Kay had been reading. 'Wonderful smell,' he said as she poured the coffee.

'Cake?'

'No, I— It looks very good. Did you make it?'

Kay nodded. 'Yes. I've always liked baking.' Baking was her way of distracting herself. Matt used to say he could tell if she was stressed by the number of cakes in the cupboard.

'Then I will have some. Thank you.'

Briefly, the silence was awkward, then Shaun started talking about the project he and Matt had worked on together. 'It got me thinking, what we talked about the other day,' he said. 'It's a crying shame all that work got cut. I know there's nothing I can do to reinstate it, but I'm wondering if I can make a case for more funding.'

Kay gave an encouraging murmur. She felt sceptical about his chances, but it was a good idea.

'Take this drop-in in Bridlington,' Shaun went on. 'That's why I was surprised – here I am thinking about Bridlington, and you're on your way there. Now, I happen to know that Neil Cowper is up against it financially all the time. They're always looking for reasons to cut his budget. It's not right, Kay.'

'You're in touch with Neil?' Maybe she should discuss Becca with him. If he could get Neil Cowper to see things a bit differently ... but it wasn't her story to share.

'No. I get to hear because I ask questions. I'll be honest with you, Kay. I need something to keep myself occupied. I can't get on with this *retirement* stuff. It was different when Sylvia was alive, but now, well, I don't know what to do with myself. You seem to cope really well, but me – I'm struggling.'

Was she so different? What did her life hold? Walks with Milo, memories of Matt, *baking* – and trying to support Becca. That was worth something, but she couldn't live the rest of her life through her foster-children. 'It can be tough,' she said, non-committally.

Shaun seemed to expand with enthusiasm. 'Exactly, Kay. Exactly. You and me, we're not the kind of people who can sit at home and do nothing. I was hoping – could we do this together? What I was thinking – start small, set up a fund, try and support the Bridlington place. That's best because we both know it, but if it works, it'll give us a starting point for expanding to set up other centres. What do you think?' He was looking at her hopefully.

She let the idea run through her mind, not trying to conceal her doubts. It was a good idea, but Shaun was someone you'd have to be on your guard with. He was a take-charge person – so was she. They'd clash. But he'd be a good fundraiser. And – *honesty now, Kay* – she'd enjoy seeing more of him. And wasn't it true that she, too, needed a project, needed something meaningful to do? She nodded. 'I think it's a very good idea. OK, I'm in. I'm not sure what role I could play, though.'

He beamed at her. 'Thank you, Kay. I'll confess, now. I've been having kittens thinking you'd say it was hopeless.' He stood up and started pacing up and down, as far as the small, cluttered room would let him. 'I'm impatient to get started now. Are you sure you need to go to Bridlington? We could have lunch, make some plans ...'

Bridlington. The drop-in. She felt the stab of worry as his words reminded her of Becca's visit the night before. Where was Becca? *How* was she? What was she doing? 'I can't change my plans, Shaun, but we can get together another day.'

'Tomorrow?'

She laughed. She couldn't get upset at his attempts to railroad her – they were so blatant. 'Soon. But now I need to make a move or I'll be late.'

'Of course, of course. I'm sorry, I get carried away.

I'll call you. Listen, this is business, but we can arrange that dinner as well. And I promise I won't talk shop.'

'I don't mind if it's interesting.'

He smiled and held her gaze for a moment, then picked up his coat. 'I'm looking forward to it,' he said. As she closed the door behind him, she realised she was looking forward to it too.

But now, she had to get herself to Bridlington.

Chapter 37

Kay came into Bridlington on the Scarborough Road and started looking for somewhere to park. Her instinct was to march into the drop-in, confront Neil with the evidence of malicious trolling and challenge him to defend his treatment of Becca. Her conversation with Shaun had reminded her of the pressures Neil was under, but that didn't excuse what he had done.

Her first reaction to the photos had been shock – not the sexy still of Becca reclining on the bed, but the photograph of the child. What had Becca been thinking? But as she calmed down, she realised there was no intended link – if they hadn't been presented to her as a pair, she wouldn't have made the connection.

The background was the same, but it took close study to identify it. In the sexy picture, the bed was central, filling the whole picture, ornamented with fluffy throws, sex toys, glitter – a kind of Barbie-world of soft porn. Becca was wearing a flimsy, almost transparent camisole top and knickers. Her tongue – Kay hadn't known until then that Becca had a pierced tongue – touched her glistening lips. The word WOW! leaped out of a poster on the wall that was cropped by the edges of the image.

The other photograph was of a student flat – a desk, books, a laptop, the bed with a slightly rumpled throw – Becca and the child were both dressed in sun tops with spaghetti straps, but these were not the sexy, revealing tops of the other image. Both had *Grrrl Power!* written across the front, and they were laughing and sticking their tongues out at the camera. The poster, and Becca herself, gave away the location to someone who really looked closely, but no one could possibly think the link was intentional.

Neil was a prat, and she was on her way to the drop-in to tell him so.

She found parking near the bus station. In summer, she would have been lucky to find street parking anywhere, but in winter, the town was empty. Kay had always liked Bridlington's raffish air. The narrow streets of the old town, the harbour, the slightly rackety seafront had real charm despite the evidence of poverty and deprivation.

She stood by her car for a few minutes, trying to decide the best way to approach this. It was anger at Neil that had got her into the car, and a desire to challenge him about the spineless decision he'd made, but she needed a strategy. She needed a plan.

As she approached the drop-in, she saw a small group hanging around outside. Most of them drifted away as she approached, but two of them who were standing with bikes outside the entrance remained, watching her with interest.

One of them, a smallish lad with curly hair and an engaging freckled face, grinned at her, and years of fostering put her immediately on the alert. She knew trouble when she saw it. 'Help you?' he said.

'I don't know. Why don't we introduce ourselves?' These two were clearly something to do with the drop-in. 'I'm Mrs McKinnon, and you're ...?'

She expected them to prevaricate and go, but the small lad grinned again and said, 'I'm Liam. He's Tez. You here for Bex, then?'

Kay became even more alert. These lads must know who she was and know about her connection with Becca. How? And their interest suggested the whole story was common knowledge. There was something seriously wrong here. Her anger at Neil increased. 'That's nothing to do with you.' She said it pleasantly but firmly, concealing her alarm. If they wanted to talk to her, then they needed to mind their manners. She wanted to get to the bottom of this, but first, she needed to talk to Neil.

'Liam, Terry,' came a woman's voice, 'either come in, or go away. Don't hang about outside, right?' It was the cheerful voice of authority, and Kay looked towards the door where a small woman in dungarees with short, grey hair was standing.

'Yeah, Hannah. Sorry, Hannah,' the freckled one chanted, and the two of them rode away.

'Little bugger, that one,' the woman, Hannah, said,

but she said it with a kind of residual affection that suggested the lads were just lovable rogues.

'He looks like a bit of a handful,' Kay said neutrally. 'I'm Kay McKinnon. I've come to see Neil Cowper.'

'Neil? Is he expecting you?'

'He should be,' Kay said, both grimly and untruthfully.

She followed Hannah through a hall that looked a bit like the youth clubs she remembered from her teen years, where she and her friends used to go to hops with live bands, the boys all standing round the dance floor looking self-conscious and young, the girls, more sophisticated, dolled up to the nines, dancing round their handbags.

It was a bare, utilitarian room, stacking chairs pushed back against the walls, scratched lino on the floor. There was a snooker table occupying one end of the space, and a small stage at the other. The paintwork looked grubby, and the windows were hung with limp, threadbare drapes. It cried out for some colour – bright curtains at the windows, posters on the walls. She knew Neil's budget was tight to the point of vanishing, but surely some of the kids could have been persuaded to do some work on the place to make it more welcoming, more comfortable.

Hannah tapped on a closed door, then pushed it open without waiting for a response. 'Neil. Kay McKinnon's here.'

The door opened onto a small office. Neil was sitting at a desk that filled most of the room. He stood as they came in. 'Kay! I wasn't expecting anyone. You should have called. I'm very busy.'

'I'm sure you can find me ten minutes,' Kay said, shifting a pile of papers from a chair and sitting down. She smiled at Neil brightly.

'I'll get back to work,' Hannah said. 'Maybe see you later.' She winked at Kay and left.

Neil looked furious. 'I assume you're here about Becca. There's no point in having this discussion. As far as I'm concerned, the matter is closed.'

'I don't agree. I saw the pictures,' Kay said. 'All you need to tell me is why you took them so seriously.'

'Why I— Kay, there was a child. What else could I do?'

'Oh, for heaven's sake. Did you actually *look* at the pictures?'

'No. Of course not. Well. Only to check they were what . . . what they looked like.'

'And what's that? What do they look like? To you?' He flushed and she knew she'd scored a point, but the best way to get what she wanted was to let him off the hook. 'You didn't look too closely, I can understand that. But it doesn't take a minute to see that the one with the child is perfectly innocent. It's only the fact they were sent together that made the connection between them, you know.'

'Kay, it's more than that. They came with an email that said – accurately – that Becca had been sex-camming online, and one of the images involved a child. I did look at the images enough to work out that the second photograph, the one with the child, was not taken during a camming session, but the link is there. It's unmistakeable. I'm not accusing Becca of doing anything deliberate, but we have to be vigilant, you know that.'

'Of course you do. But there's vigilance, and there's ...' *Kay*, Matt-in-her-head cautioned, and she caught herself. 'The way to look at it is this: if you'd seen the picture of Becca and the little girl on its own, what would you have thought?'

Neil smiled. 'Ah, but, Kay, I didn't see it on its own, so that's irrelevant, isn't it now?'

'Not at all. You saw it in a fabricated context – not the context Becca intended. You know she wasn't the photographer, don't you? The image was part of her friends and family collection on Facebook, which had no connection whatsoever with her chat room – which, if you want to check it out, is Bexgirl.' That crack about checking it out was probably unhelpful, but Neil had got right up her nose.

'I'm not interested in the chat room.'

'Of course not – but maybe you should be. You see, Becca wasn't doing anything wrong there. She did what a lot of young girls do today – she made a bit of money out of web camming. And she used her own place to do it because she didn't have anywhere else. It's all ...' The word that came into her mind was 'innocent'. 'I expect there are loads of pictures from that flat that have nothing to do with the camming – it's only because someone wanted to cause trouble that you were sent those two and made the connection.'

'I can make up my own mind, be very certain of that, Kay.'

'Then look again and do that.' She showed him the photograph with Becca and the little girl – best not remind him of the sexy one again. 'It's just a snapshot,' Kay said. And it was true; there were no prurient elements – except for the prurience in the viewer's mind. 'There's no connection,' she finished. 'This is a photo. The other one's a camera still.'

'Yes, I see all that, but the connection is there. The college thought the same.'

Kay was temporarily silenced. She hadn't thought about that. So *this* was why Becca had left college. Oh, Becca, why didn't you tell me ...?

'We've got our funding review coming up – I can't take any risks, Kay. There's more than just Becca to think of.'

'And you think that giving in to mean-spirited bullying is the way to make this place work? Someone's been chasing Becca with these, you must see that.'

'I do, Kay. I told you – I'm not making accusations against Becca, but she behaved recklessly. She put a child at risk.'

'Oh, rubbish. Tell me, if Becca had shown you this picture –' she slapped it down on the desk in front of him – 'would you have sacked her?'

'I don't know. That didn't happen.'

'This picture. Would you have sacked her? Come on, Neil. It's a simple question.'

'No it isn't. You know and I know that one person's

innocent picture of a child can be another person's pornography. Becca put this child in the position of appearing in an image that could be used as pornography.'

'Becca is not responsible for other people's minds, Neil.'

'Kay, I understand you want to protect her, but you must know how attractive the sex industry can be made to seem for some of the girls here. It offers money, relationships, attention – I know it's not like that, but if one of our workers makes it look like an alternative to a steady job, then that's not good.'

He wasn't going to shift. His argument about the sex industry was a hard one to counter. But she wasn't giving up. 'You realise any of your employees might be vulnerable to this kind of malice. If you let it succeed now, with Becca . . .' She trailed off.

Neil sighed. 'I didn't want to lose Becca, to be honest. She was good at the job and the kids liked her. She was also responsible – she reported it at once when one of them got involved in something a bit dodgy.'

'The car episode? The attack?'

He nodded. 'We still don't know if that was one of ours, but Becca did everything right.'

'Then give her another chance.'

'I can't. Or not yet. The Head of Youth Services is asking questions – someone sent the pictures to him as well.' Kay felt a sinking sensation in her stomach and had a vision of herself barging through doors higher and higher up the social services building in defence of Becca. 'I could talk to him again I suppose. But not right away. Tell Becca to contact me in a couple of weeks, but I can't make any promises.'

Kay was retired. She didn't have an official position she could take, not anymore. She couldn't act as an intermediary. '*You* need to tell her yourself, Neil,' she said. 'Anyway, I'm not sure where Becca is.'

He looked surprised. 'I thought she was staying with you.'

'You did? Why?'

'Well, you said you'd seen her – I just assumed ...'

'I've no idea where she is.'

He sighed. 'It isn't just Becca. I've lost my caretaker. Turns out he was here illegally, working on false papers – he did a runner as soon as he realised the police might be on their way. If we get fined it could put us in real trouble.' He shook his head. 'I'm short-staffed, I need someone for the café, I need someone to look after this place and I've got the funding people in for the next few days. I don't have time to worry about Becca, Kay.'

He had a point. Kay wasn't prepared to let him off the hook, but she left the office with the hostility between them slightly reduced. As she walked towards the exit, Hannah stopped her. 'Is Becca all right?'

'I don't know, Hannah. I really don't. I'm worried, if you want to know.'

Hannah nodded sympathetically. 'Neil's in a difficult position,' she said.

'I know.' But he could have had a bit more loyalty towards a vulnerable member of his team.

'Ask Becca to call me, keep me posted about what she's doing. It'll all die down once this funding thing's off his back.'

'When I see her, I will.' Kay said her farewells to Hannah, and headed back towards the bus station and her car. A bike drew up beside her, and the lad, Liam, greeted her. 'Hey, miss.' He treated her to the boyish grin again.

'Hello, Liam.' He'd pulled the bike across the pavement, making it difficult to get past. The bigger lad was behind her. They were effectively blocking her path. There was no overt threat, but the subtle menace was there. She knew it, and they knew it. 'OK, what's this about?'

'Nothing, miss. We was just wondering – you know where Becca is?'

'I don't, and I'm not sure it's anything to do with you. Why do you want to know?'

He shrugged. 'Nothing. Much. Hey, is it right she did some sex pics? Kiddie porn?'

The lad behind her sniggered.

Kay wasn't giving in to bullying. 'If there's anything you want to talk to me about, I'll listen, but you'll talk to me properly. You'll move your bikes and you'll show me some respect.'

Liam was eyeing her, mulling over his options. After a tense moment of waiting, he moved his bike out of her way. 'You're that Special Kay lady, right?' he asked.

'Some people call me that.'

'So, what's up with Bex?'

'What's up with Becca, *Mrs McKinnon*.'

He grinned suddenly. 'Mrs McKinnon. Can you tell me what's wrong with Bex ... *Becca*?'

Was he responsible for the emails? 'Becca is fine. Why do you want to know?'

He grinned. 'Nothing to do with you. Come on, Tez.' The two of them stepped on their pedals and rode away.

Chapter 38

Becca shoved the bags from her car into the boot of Jared's Volvo. 'Do you really think they'll come back?'

Jared stood by the car, his gaze fixed on the road where it vanished among some bare trees. He didn't turn when Becca spoke, but shrugged to show he'd heard. 'I dunno. But we need to get moving. I've got a bad feeling.'

Becca nodded. She knew about trusting bad feelings. She'd always known when He was on his way back. Her sense of dread began long before He arrived, so when she finally heard Him at the door, it was never a surprise. 'OK. Can I drive?'

For a moment, it looked as though he was going to agree, then he shook his head. 'If they're around, we don't want them seeing you. Look, if we pass another car on the road, don't wait, get right down. Here.' He tossed her a black woolly hat, which she inspected without much enthusiasm. It was the kind of thing Kay might wear, but she pulled it down over her hair and looked at him. He grinned. 'That makes you less recognisable.'

Once she was in the car, he did a quick check then sat behind the wheel, twisting his body round to reverse out of the gateway. She heard him swear under his breath, and remembered the way his back had crippled him the first time they met. 'You should have let me drive,' she said.

He didn't respond, just said, 'We need to get off this road. They'll know we've come from Kettleness if they see us here.'

'But if it's just you . . .'

She saw his face change as if he'd just remembered something. 'Shit for brains,' he muttered. 'Sorry, Not you. Me.'

'Where are we going?'

'Whitby, for starters. You can get some boots there.'

'I can't afford boots.'

'You'll need some if we're going to find where that video was taken. Look, we can pick up a cheap pair and you can pay me back.'

Pay him back how? It wasn't that she didn't trust him, it was more . . . sometimes trusting anyone, even Kay, seemed like a loser's game. 'No. I'll get them.'

'OK. You don't have to— Hang on. Get down!'

She ducked down until her head was below the level of the windows. Jared threw something over her – his jacket, she realised as she slid down into the footwell. The fabric smelt of rain and grass and, faintly, a smell she was starting to recognise, of him. 'What's happening?'

'There's a car coming along the road. Shit! We were so fucking close to the turn. Hang on.'

She felt herself pitched towards the door as Jared swung the car round a tight bend. She waited for the push of acceleration as he pulled away, but he kept up the same steady pace. 'Move it!' she hissed.

'That's really going to work, right? They see us, we shoot round the nearest corner and hit the gas? Might as well stick a big sign on the car saying "Here we are!"'

The air tasted stale and she was starting to feel too warm and shut in. 'Did it work? Can I come out?'

'Wait ... they might ... Shit! They're following us. I should've ... Fuck. *Fuck!*'

Becca felt her throat close. It was like being under the covers at her mother's house – pulling them over her head and feeling the same sense of being pinned down, being trapped, as a heavy weight descended on the bed and His voice said, *How's our Rebecca, then?* She'd never answer, and He'd laugh and go downstairs again, but later – not always, but sometimes – she would hear the footsteps again, slower, quieter, and the voice that came through the darkness would not be the warm, light-hearted voice of before.

It whispered.

It menaced.

It promised terrible things.

Becca, you know that's not true ... not true ... not true ...

'What's wrong?'

She was back in the car with Jared and her head was spinning. She felt sick. 'I can't ... it's hot. There's no air down here.'

'Sorry. I'm sorry.' The cloth covering her face was pulled away, and the world came back. 'I was just playing safe. They went past. I think they wanted to check us out. They've gone.'

Slowly Becca sat up. She was aware of Jared's glance. Had she said anything? What had she said?

'You don't look too good. Do you want to stop for a bit?'

'I'm fine.'

'We can stop if you—'

'I said I'm fine. Right?'

'OK, OK. I'm going to stop anyway. First off, you look like you're going to throw up and I don't want to spend the next half hour cleaning puke out of the car. Second, if we stop and take a break, that car will be miles away by the time we get back on the road. I don't know if they were anything to do with us, but I'd rather not run into them again.'

The sick feeling was getting worse. She couldn't throw up all over his car, but ... 'I don't mind. Stop if you want to.'

He pulled in by the side of the road and wound down a window, then started rummaging in the side pocket. The air was freezing, but as it blew into her face, she felt the dampness of her skin start to dry, the nausea in the back of her throat start to fade.

She'd never told anyone, not after the police. Not Kay. Not even Matt.

She got out of the car and let the breeze blow over her, welcoming, for the first time, the bone-numbing chill. The road was bordered by low hedges and the land stretched all around them, flat until it dropped away to the sea in the far distance. Her mother's house was miles away. Bridlington was two hours behind them, Leeds was weeks away, but all those places had followed her here.

Jared came and stood beside her, taking a swig of water. He stood with one hand in the small of his back, stretching to ease it. He was washing down some pills, she realised, and remembered their conversation in the car park in Brid. 'I thought you didn't need that stuff.'

His mouth tightened. 'They're painkillers, right? What I don't need is you going on about it.'

She shrugged. It wasn't her business, but she didn't like drugs, didn't like pill-heads.

They stood in silence for a few minutes, then he said, 'Feeling better?'

'I was fine!' she snapped. He grinned, and her annoyance – and her worry – faded. He was helping her, and he had a point – the pills were nothing to do with her. 'Yeah. I'm feeling better.' She was about to explain about the jacket and being too warm, then realised she didn't need to. 'Thanks.'

'No problem. I needed a break too. You still want to drive?'

This surprised her. Last time she'd driven his car – the only time she'd driven his car – she'd scraped it and almost got rear-ended by a van. 'Yes. You still want to go to Whitby?'

'Works for me. You?'
'I don't mind.'

Despite Becca's tendency to floor the accelerator on any stretch of road longer than about three metres, Jared was happy to let her take over. He needed to think. He'd fucked up. Royally. If the people following Becca were anything to do with the caravan site, then Greaseball Harry knew him, and knew his car. They'd seen Becca arrive at Kettleness, and now they'd seen him driving away. They weren't stupid. Wherever they were now, they knew that he and Becca were together.

If he'd just stopped to think, if he'd just taken time to chase that memory down, if he hadn't taken the fucking pills … they would have got out sooner. Or they could have hidden his car as well as Becca's, lain low. Either way, they would have been clear of it by now.

As soon as he'd realised what he'd done, he'd felt sick, and an ache had started low down in his back, deep in the muscle where the spasms began. He couldn't afford to be ill, not now. He'd taken more pills. It was the only thing to do. They were a quick fix, and he needed a quick fix right now.

But already he was starting to feel spaced out and far away, as though nothing much mattered.

And it did fucking matter.

'Yeah,' he said absently in response to some comment she made. She looked at him from the corner of her eye and he scrambled to retrieve what she'd said. *Have they gone?*

'I don't know. I don't think so.'

OK. A good way to kill yourself is to spend your time brooding over past mistakes. When you were climbing, it wasn't the stupid mistake that had nearly made you fall that was important, it was the stupid mistake you were going to make if you couldn't stop thinking about the last stupid mistake.

They needed to drop out of sight for a while. Whitby was still the best place for that round here. Could they dump the car, hire another for a few days? Yeah, and he'd get the money for that how? It was this car or nothing. It was best to be mobile, but it would be good if they could find a place to lie low for a couple of days.

If they couldn't run, then they'd have to hide.

Chapter 39

Becca didn't have any great expectations of Whitby. Jared directed her across the river to a maze of small streets that formed an estate of run-down houses. 'It's mind-your-own-business territory here,' he said as she parked behind a car that was almost as battered as Jared's. 'Don't leave anything you don't want to lose,' he added.

It was cold, it kept drizzling and there was a persistent wind coming off the sea that cut through her as soon as she got out of the car. Another dump like Brid. Great.

'What are we going to do?' She huddled into her jacket, but she might as well have wrapped herself in tissue paper for all the good it did.

'Not stand here getting wet?' Jared pulled some stuff out of the back of the car. 'They'll be a bit big,' he said, 'but they'll keep you dry. And warm.' He was holding out a fleece and a waterproof. She looked at them. Did he really think she was going to walk around dressed like some big loser? 'No thanks.'

'Up to you,' he said. 'But it's cold, and it's going to get colder.'

Becca glared at him, then grabbed the clothes and pulled them on. She wasn't going to admit it, but once she was wearing them it was as if the icy wind had been switched off. She yanked the hood over her hair and wouldn't look at him. But he wasn't someone you could strop at, not really.

He led them off the estate to the top of a steep hill. In front of them she could see the town, which looked like someone had tipped a load of houses down the cliff, a pile of red roofs in a sort of jumble below. As they walked down the slope, her feet sliding in her shoes – Jared was right about the boots – she could see rows and rows of masts sticking up high. And then they were on the level, walking along beside a river, and there were people – lots of people even on this cold rainy day. The cafés in Bridlington were either closed or empty – here they were full, and the smell of coffee and cooking wafted out into the street. She and Jared were just two people among the crowd. No one knew them, no one would be able to pick them out.

She decided she liked Whitby.

'It's OK, isn't it?' Jared said.

She shrugged. 'It's all right.'

He grinned. 'Come on. Let's get across the river and down to the beach. Rain's stopped.'

It had, and the sun had come out. He led the way down a little cobbled lane that took them onto a bridge. There were boats on the river – lots of small, sleek ones that must belong to rich people. But there were older, scruffy boats as well that looked like they were used every day by people who worked, people like her.

'What do you do, if you work on a boat?'

'Fishing, mostly. There's a fishing fleet here. Some of them take visitors out.' He nodded towards signs up by the riverside offering boat trips. It was a bit like the seafront at Brid, only nicer. There were stalls advertising fish and chips, and prawns and mussels and that sort of shit. The pubs were all called things like 'The Ship' or 'The Jolly Sailor'. There was a dark house-kind-of-thing with a sign that said 'The Dracula Experience'.

'What's that?'

'That? It's Dracula.'

'Yeah. But why? Why've they got . . .?'

'This is where Dracula came ashore when he first arrived in England. If you look up there –' he pointed across the river. On the cliff, over the sea, there was a sort of castle – 'that's St Mary's church. Dracula attacked his first victim in the graveyard there.'

She gave him a side-look. He was having her on. 'Dracula's not real.'

'He is in Whitby.' They walked along the narrow street, and he pointed out places where Dracula had been. 'That's where his ship was wrecked – he came ashore here.'

'Yeah, but not really.'

'That's what they want you to think.'

She knew it was just a story, but it was kind of fun to half believe it. Jared insisted that a tattooed guy walking through the cold in jeans and a T-shirt was a vampire. 'Stands to reason,' he said. 'They must have sorted out the sun thing by now. Factor fifty and all that.'

They wandered down onto the beach and walked along the water's edge. The tide was turning and ripples started to trickle round their feet. 'When I was a kid, I used to build castles and let the tide flood them.' Jared dug a pit in the sand with his foot and watched as it filled with water, then he turned away abruptly.

'So where do you come from?' Becca asked, when the silence stretched out. She was wary about asking questions – she didn't like it when people did it to her.

'Manchester. That's where I was born. We moved around a lot – my dad was in the army. Then I went away to school. So I'm not really from anywhere.'

Like her. She hadn't moved around like he had – she'd never left Yorkshire – but she wasn't *from* anywhere. She was from Kay and Matt's house in Leeds if it came to it.

'So what about your mum and dad?'

'Yeah, well, they don't really ... I don't see them much.'

She could tell from the way he stopped looking at her that he didn't want to talk about it. He picked up some stones from the sand and started skimming them across the water. 'So how do you, you know, live?' He'd never mentioned work or a job, but he must do something.

'I'm a good climber.' He made a face. 'Yeah, I know, I fell. But there's loads of companies want people who

242

can climb, and they pay well – there's a group of us, we pass the jobs round as we hear about them. Give me a bit more time and I'll get back to that. And I make a bit of money out of my website – I get plenty of hits so I pick up some money from companies that advertise on my page.'

She didn't really get it, but it sounded cool.

Despite the loser clothes, she was starting to feel cold, so they left the beach. Jared bought them fish and chips and they sat on the harbour wall eating, watching the boats at their moorings. Becca found herself telling him a bit about her life. He didn't ask questions, he just listened. 'It was OK after I went to Kay and Matt,' she said.

'She lives near here, right?'

Becca nodded, wondering if they were going to talk about what was happening, but all he said was, 'Nice part of the world.'

'This bit's OK,' Becca conceded.

Seabirds screamed in the sky above them. When Becca had finished she scattered her remaining chips on the ground, and the birds came down and fought over them, tugging the chips between them and flapping up into the air, squabbling over the paper.

'Thanks,' she said, licking the salt and grease off her fingers.

'That's OK. You've got to have fish and chips if you come to Whitby. What do you want to do now?'

'Let's go and look at that church – you know, the Dracula one.'

They crossed the river and climbed up about a thousand steps. The church was old and it was weird – full of pillars in fancy metal and carved seats with sort of wooden screens around them. Becca thought about Dracula again, but somehow, up here, it wasn't funny.

Outside, the graves were all this way and that. They wandered round, reading the inscriptions, or the ones that hadn't been blown away by the weather. 'They were young,' Jared said, almost as if he was talking to himself.

The wind blew in from the sea, making her shiver. There were no crowds up here. She looked back the way they had come, and saw a man standing at the top of the steps. He was looking at them.

Watching them.

She was taking a breath to alert Jared when there was a shout, and a small boy came running up the steps behind the man, who scooped him up and twirled him round.

Becca's heart pounded. 'Let's go,' she said. 'Back down.' She didn't like this solitary place.

It was dark by the time they got back into the town centre, and she realised she was hungry. 'What are we going to do now?'

He looked at his watch. 'Go and get something to eat. I'm starving.'

Her hand went to her purse instinctively.

'Don't worry. My treat.'

But she wasn't going to accept that. He'd bought lunch. She should buy tea.

'I'll tell you what,' he said after they'd wrangled for a while. 'I know a pub just across the river. The servings are so big you could feed your family and your dog. We'll get one plate, two knives and forks and I buy the drinks. Deal?'

She chewed her lip. 'OK. Deal.'

They walked along the narrow road in the intermittent street lighting, towards the river. He reached out his hand, and after a moment's hesitation, she took it. For the first time since the Bexgirl incident in Leeds, she felt happy.

Chapter 40

Kay hated the drive back from Bridlington. It was awful. It was raining hard, a sleety rain that made the road surface mushy and built up on the windscreen, restricting her vision. She wasn't so good at night driving now – the lights of the oncoming cars shattered into radiating lines, turning the road ahead of her pitch black. Milo, in the back, picked up on her unease and shifted in his basket, whining occasionally. 'Good boy,' she reassured him – or maybe the reassurance was for her. By the time she was driving up the hill from Whitby, her head was pounding and she ached all over from the stress of intense concentration.

She negotiated the car into the small lean-to garage – made even smaller by Matt's motorbike, his pride and joy that she hadn't yet had the heart to get rid of – and let herself in. The cottage felt cold and dank. She fed Milo, then lit the stove, huddling in front of it in her coat. All the things that had seemed so good about the place when they bought it grated on her now – the stove, the small windows, the thick stone walls, the isolation . . .

OK, self-pity time over. Come the spring, she'd put the place on the market and move – maybe get a flat in Whitby if she could afford it, or Scarborough, or ... Milo came and nosed at her. She sat down and he jumped up onto her lap. She stared at the fire, burying her fingers in his fur, wondering how useful the day had been.

Neil hadn't changed his mind about Becca, but he had listened and he would probably think about what she had said. The trouble was, she could see why he was so sensitive about what had happened.

Becca had made a bad decision. Kay knew that young women of Becca's age didn't view displays like camming with the instinctive distaste women of Kay's age did. Somehow it had become self-affirming to bend down in front of some swivel-hipped male and simulate submissive sex on stage and video – so where was the harm in Becca's rather less decadent activities?

Kay sighed. What Becca apparently didn't get was that you couldn't work with vulnerable kids and be involved in the sex industry in any way. Recent scandals meant that organisations lived in fear of the moral outrage of a press that was always a bit selective about which issues upset it.

Becca's photo by the phone scowled at her. Where was she? She'd driven off in a half strop for some unnamed destination and wasn't answering her phone. All Kay could do was wait.

There was another photo beside the phone – Maireid, the thirteen-year-old they had been fostering when Matt got so ill. In the eight months she'd been with them, her face had lost that pale, pinched look, filled out, become healthier and happier, and then it all started. It hadn't seemed right to have Maireid there, have her go through the trauma of Matt's illness.

No, that wasn't it. Kay had made the decision selfishly. She didn't want to have the worry of Maireid while she was caring for Matt, so Maireid had had to go. It had been the wrong decision. Kay knew that now. No matter what was happening, she should have kept Maireid with her – that was how families worked.

Kay had let her down. Badly. She'd been waiting, hoping Maireid would call again, but so far, nothing. On impulse, she tried the number on her phone, but it was unavailable.

Tomorrow. Finding Maireid was tomorrow's task. Right now she was too tired to think about it any more. She'd get something to eat and go to bed. Scrambled eggs on toast would be fine – no need for anything more elaborate. She went into the kitchen and started cutting bread and whisking eggs. Nibbling a crust, she put some bread in the toaster and melted some butter in a pan.

Milo usually positioned himself under her feet when she was cooking in the hopes of benefitting from anything that got dropped, but he seemed more intent on a close exploration of the kitchen, snuffling his way round the room until he reached the back door. He tried to stuff his nose under the threshold, sniffing eagerly and whining a bit.

'It's foxes, Milo. Leave it!'

He looked up at her and came away reluctantly, whining under his breath.

Kay piled the eggs onto the warm toast and went back to her chair in front of the stove, where she ate them and poured herself a glass of red wine. Milo seemed to lose interest in whatever it was that had attracted him and sat at her feet waiting for any crumbs or other offerings. She finished, held out her fingers for Milo to lick and checked the time.

It was only nine, but she was wiped out. 'Early night, Milo,' she said. She put him on his lead before she let him out – he was more than capable of racing off into the dark after whatever had been interesting him before – but he went out quite happily and peed obediently on his – and unfortunately her – favourite bush.

She tucked him under her arm and carried him upstairs. She planned to read herself to sleep, but as soon as she was lying down, her eyes felt heavy and her thoughts began to break down into a drowsy muddle.

She closed her eyes.

Chapter 41

Kay's sleep was troubled. Milo was restless, barking a couple of times, turning round and round, jumping on and off the bed, growling, then she was dreaming, some long, complicated dream that she knew was a dream but couldn't seem to break out of. She was walking on a path down the cliff. It was a sunny day – in her dream she was sure of that – but down here, it was dark and getting darker. Matt had come this way – she'd heard him calling and now she was following him, but she couldn't hear him anymore as the roar of the sea was so loud.

The air grew hot and heavy and it was hard to breathe. She wanted to turn back, but her feet moved relentlessly onwards and the pressure on her chest got heavier and heavier. Something was trying to dig into her, and she couldn't see the path – she had to get down there because Matt was getting further and further ahead and she'd lost sight of him.

Then she was rising from sleep, feeling Milo moving on the bed, and her relief at being out of the dream vanished as the hot, heavy air came with her and she opened her eyes into thick darkness.

Milo pawed at her and she sat up, reaching for the light.

Nothing happened.

Something gripped at her throat and she was coughing so hard she couldn't stop to draw breath. It was as if there wasn't any air to breathe.

Acting instinctively, she rolled off the bed onto the floor, dragging Milo with her. He vanished under the bed, looking for somewhere to hide.

Milo ... No ... She couldn't speak.

Smoke.

Fire.

There was a fire. She could hear the flames and the thick smoke was gripping her throat, making it impossible to breathe. She'd die, they'd both die, her and Milo trapped inside the cottage, in this room.

She forced the panic away. *Think!* Keep down. Keep near the floor. That's what they said. Damp towels, breathe through a damp towel – how could she find a towel and wet it in this smoke? Her hand touched something soft, some kind of fabric on the floor. She held it over her mouth and nose, reached up and fumbled for the water glass at the side of her bed, catching it as it tipped. She managed to soak part of whatever it was she was carrying, and her breathing eased, just a bit.

OK. Now ... The panic was yammering in her head, demanding entrance. She had to keep it out. To survive, she had to keep it out.

OK.

OK. Think!

Now, call the emergency services – but her phone was downstairs. In her mind, she could see it on the table by the stove. The stove must have ... or the electrics. It didn't matter.

She had to concentrate on getting out.

Milo! She reached under the bed, grabbed the first bit of him she touched and yanked. He slid out, a limp weight that didn't respond.

Milo!

She was near the door. Right. Push it open, down the stairs, out the front door, run through whatever is there, just ...

The door was hot to the touch. The fire must be just on the other side. If she opened it, the air would ignite.

Not the door. That left the window.

The window was on the other side of the bed. She knew what she would find. The small metal panes, and the window itself – painted shut. She could remember struggling to get it open in the summer and failing, but she was going to have the windows replaced anyway ... or was she ... she ...

... had to stay awake. Had to breathe.

OK.

Get onto the bed. Her improvised smoke mask had almost dried out. Get to the window, knock out a pane of glass. She might be able to squeeze Milo through. She might be able to attract someone's attention.

Her legs felt like lead, her body was screaming out

for air, her concentration was fading and she kept losing focus. She could see the outline of the window, a faint square of grey in the blackness. She was on the bed now. She crawled across and tried to drive her fist through the glass, but her arm was too feeble. It was almost too heavy to lift. Her head was pounding, her lungs were bursting.

She pulled Milo against her, and collapsed onto the bed.

Chapter 42

When Becca checked the time, it was almost ten. 'We need a place to stay. What are we going to do?' Jared might be able to afford a B & B, but she couldn't.

'It's late. We can find somewhere around here – I've got the tent.'

'Why not Kettlewhatsit?'

'To look for that mine?' It was the first time either of them had referred to what was happening. He frowned. 'We'd probably be OK but I'm pretty sure they recognised us this morning – best not go back. I want them thinking we've moved on.'

Becca thought about the car on the road driving Paige away, about Liam's strange aggression outside the arcade, about the girl in hospital, too badly hurt to be identified. If the people following her had anything to do with that – and why else had they come after her? – then she didn't want to meet them again in a lonely place after dark.

'I know what we can do. We can go to my friend's, to Kay's. She'll give us a bed for the night, and she'll lend me some boots as well.' They hadn't managed to find a cheap enough pair and her feet were starting to ache with the walking they'd done.

'OK. I can drop you off.'

The idea of him just driving off felt … wrong. 'I didn't mean that. She'll give you a bed too.'

'It's too late. She doesn't know me. She won't want a stranger spending the night. It's OK, I've got the tent. Plenty of places I can stop.'

'Kay won't mind – I'll tell her you're OK.'

He grinned. 'Don't get too extravagant with the compliments or she'll never believe you. Look, I'll take you there and we can see what's what. Right?'

'OK.'

When they got back to the road where they'd parked the car, Jared gave it a quick once over. 'We've still got wheels and the windows aren't broken. We're ahead.' It looked to her as though someone had keyed it down the side, but he either didn't notice or didn't care.

She fished the keys out of her bag, expecting him to want to drive. But he seemed happy for her to do it and she managed to get the car out of the narrow space without scraping anything.

Well, almost.

She was aware of Jared watching out as they drove through Whitby. He swore under his breath once, then relaxed.

'What?' she said.

'Nothing.' She saw him reach into the side pocket and

get the pills out again. OK. They were just painkillers. He hadn't taken any while they were walking around.

As far as she knew.

It was a few miles to Kay's along the coast road. The sea glittered in the cold night air. The road was straight and empty, and she put her foot down, enjoying the power of the engine and the instant response. Jared glanced at the display and said, 'We'll be in Sandsend in a minute and there's a tight turn on the bridge. Best not end up in the river.' Becca glared at him. 'Just saying,' he added.

Reluctantly, she eased up on the gas, but he was right; the turn was sudden: sharp left, narrow bridge then sharp right. And then they were at the start of the steep hill she remembered from before that went up to the village where Kay lived.

In fact, she could see the village ahead – a few lights in the night and a sort of glow that reminded her of . . . 'Looks like they've got a club or something.'

Jared sat up. 'Not in Lythe. It's . . . hang on. There's something on fire.'

Even as he said it, they heard the sounds of the sirens. Becca stared into the darkness, looking at the source of the light, the blaze. It was . . . it couldn't be, but it was. She slammed on the brakes. The car jumped and stalled.

'*Kay.*'

Her voice came out as a whisper, but she could see it now, on the far side of the village, the small cottage where she'd parked just the day before. She shoved the gears into neutral and reached for the ignition, but Jared put his hand over hers to stop her. 'Steady.'

'Fuck steady! That's Kay's house! I've got to—'

His hand clamped down. 'Right. It's your friend's house. Use your brain, Becca. The fire service is there. If you go racing over, you'll just get in their way. Give them some space.'

'You don't tell me what to do, you fucking pill-head!' She was so angry she wanted to hit him. It wasn't just anger – it was that head-spinning storm that made her want to slam her fist down on the horn, scream, kick him – a kick that would really hurt him – rip the fittings from the car, how *dare* he try and stop her, how dare he come in here without so much as . . .

You're caught in a loop, Becca. It was Matt's voice, speaking in her head, Matt as he carefully pieced together a broken picture frame, concentrating on what he was doing, then looking across at her with a smile as it came together. *Anger is useful, Becca . . . don't waste it. Use it the right way . . .* She closed her eyes and breathed deeply and slowly. It wasn't anger she was feeling – she knew that now. It was terror.

Matt was already gone. If Kay died, she'd be alone.

Jared's face looked tense and angry. 'OK. If that's what you want, turn into the side road – where the sign says Kettleness – you can walk across the field.'

She scrambled out of the car as soon as she got it parked, and ran towards Kay's cottage in the distance.

Jared didn't follow.

Chapter 43

It was after midnight. Jared sat at the wheel of his car. The scene at the cottage was one of dereliction – the wet, charred carpet, the broken furniture, all just dumped on the ground by the firefighters trying to extinguish the flames. It was like the aftermath of a violent eviction. The chemical smell of burning plastic was lodged in his nose. He wondered if he'd ever stop smelling it.

When Becca had scrambled out of the car, his plan had been to leave her to it – *little cow!* – get the fuck out of there and get on with his life. Let this Kay sort it all out. He was done.

But as he'd watched her running across the field – no coat, her shoes coming off her feet – he'd got out of the car and followed her. What was it he'd accused her of back at the caravan site? Being a fucking princess? So what did that make him, flouncing off because she'd called him a pill-head? She wasn't so far off the mark.

He'd collected waterproofs and a couple of towels from the boot and set off across the field after her. He'd got there just in time to see her climbing into the back of the ambulance. 'I'm her daughter,' he'd heard her snap at the paramedic.

'Here!' He'd tossed her the waterproof and the shoes he'd picked up on his way. 'I'll call you. We're good.' She'd nodded, then the doors had closed and the ambulance pulled away, the blue lights flashing.

He'd run back to his car to follow it but by the time he got there, the ambulance had vanished and he had no idea where they would be heading. Whitby? The hospital was tiny. They wouldn't take trauma cases there. Scarborough? Or even York? *Fuck!* He was supposed to be taking care of Becca, and now he had no idea where she'd gone.

Everything had moved at high speed from the moment they saw the fire, and now, for the first time, he had a chance to think, with the dawning realisation that once again, he'd got it wrong, wrong, wrong. The night before, a car had driven Becca off the road, and it was sheer luck they hadn't been able to finish the job, or so it seemed to Jared. They'd even talked about it, for fuck's sake:

That car – did it follow you from Brid?

It wasn't until I got off that hill ... One minute the road was empty, next minute ...

He rested his head against the steering wheel. Now he knew exactly how much of a fuck-up he'd made. He hadn't just forgotten that GBH knew him and his car, he'd forgotten what Becca had told him. Told him as clear as daylight.

The car had followed her from here, from this house. Jesus Christ. Shit for brains.

He'd thought he was being so clever, thought he knew all about keeping out of the way. Instead, he'd let her walk right back into it. He had to warn her. Now.

He pulled out his phone and called her number.

Something rang in the back seat behind him.

Oh, Jesus. He reached over and hauled up Becca's backpack. Inside, he found not just her phone but her purse as well. She'd gone off with no money and he had no means of contacting her.

He forced himself to focus through the brain-fuzz. It was up to him. He had to find out where the ambulance had gone. Then ... it all fell apart inside his head. He could feel the pain starting up again in his back, and the nausea churning in his stomach. You could talk about pill-heads and all that shit, but right now, he needed something, just so he could function. Just to make him ...

Yeah, that would really work. He'd made all these fuck-ups while he was out of it on the fucking pills. He couldn't do that again. It wasn't his life he was trashing – it could be Becca's. OK. Now.

Think.

He had to find out where she had gone, and then he could get himself over there.

He got out of the car and walked across the field to where the small cottage stood slightly back from the road. There was just one fire engine left and no one in sight.

'Hey. You.'

The voice came from behind him. He spun round, his heart jumping, but it was just one of the firemen, who was crouched down by something on the ground. Jared went across. 'Listen, mate, where did they go? The ambulance?'

'I'm not sure if it's Scarborough or York tonight. You can call—'

'York?' That was fucking miles. It'd take the ambulance – what? – an hour to get there? More.

'Might be Scarborough. Are you family?'

Jared thought quickly, then nodded. It was the way to get information. 'Yeah. I'm, you know, with the daughter.'

'Well, don't worry. They'd have sent the helicopter if they thought she wouldn't make it. Look, there's this dog – he needs looking after.'

The little dog was a sorry puddle of white hair on the ground, panting and whimpering. 'We gave him some oxygen,' the fireman said, 'but he needs a vet. Otherwise I'll have to take him to the shelter.'

'I don't have . . .' Jared wanted to get straight off in pursuit of the ambulance, but he forced himself to calm down. Whichever hospital it was, Becca would be safe there. She'd stay with this Kay woman, because as far as Jared could tell, Kay was the closest thing she had to family. The ambulance would either be just arriving in Scarborough now, or still on the road if they were going to York. He was dead on his feet. If he tried driving across the moors in this state, he'd fall asleep behind the wheel.

261

What he needed to do was wait and let the hospital do the admin, then call and find out which hospital they'd gone to. Once he was through to the right department, he could get a message to Becca saying he was on his way. With a bit of luck, she'd sit tight.

In the meantime . . . He knelt down and touched the dog. It was shivering and its fur felt damp. He checked the name tag on the collar: Milo. He patted the damp fur tentatively. 'Milo. Poor old lad. How you doing, mate?' The tail twitched in a feeble wag. OK, he could do something about this. He checked his watch – it was getting on for one – and looked up at the other man. 'Is there a twenty-four-hour vet?'

There was one down in Whitby, the man said, and gave him directions. Jared scooped the little animal up and walked back to the car, feeling the warmth of the surprisingly solid body against him. He put Milo on the passenger seat, then drove carefully down the hill towards the harbour where the vet was located.

Despite the late hour, the surgery was busy, but they whisked Milo through quickly. He was on the treatment table with an oxygen mask held over his muzzle with the same speed at which they took the details of Jared's credit card.

Jared sent up a silent prayer that this friend of Becca's – or should he call her Becca's mum? It sounded like a complicated relationship – could afford all of this, because he certainly couldn't. His savings were just about gone.

The dog staggered to his feet and tried to jump off

the vet's table. 'Good sign,' the vet said cheerfully. 'He's had a bad shock and he's inhaled some smoke – the problem here is we don't know what was in it. Smoke can be toxic, even in small quantities, depending on what was burning. I want to do some bloods and keep him here overnight for observation. Is that OK?'

Jared nodded, wondering what they'd do if his credit card refused payment. 'I'll call back in the morning, then.'

When he got outside, he found a light drizzle was falling. Here he was, in the middle of Whitby. It was after midnight, it was raining, his credit card was now maxed out and he was so tired he was starting to fall asleep on his feet.

He knew a trick or two about staying awake. A cup of strong coffee, really strong coffee, followed by a ten-minute catnap would keep him going a few more hours. He'd feel like a zombie tomorrow, but he could deal with that then.

So where to get coffee? The streets were empty, the shops and restaurants closed. There might be a café open somewhere, but he had no idea where and he didn't want to linger, a solitary walker on the empty streets.

The cottage. There would be coffee there. He could use his camping stove to heat up some water, make a hell-brew and get himself sorted. Wearily, he got back into the car and set off up the hill. His eyes started closing as he headed out of the town. The car drifted across the road and he jerked himself awake.

Come on! *Fuck's sake!*

As he pulled in on a narrow lane by a field, he drifted off and woke suddenly, slumped in the front seat of his car, from a dream of driving along some endless road, looking for a turning he knew was there, haunted by the urgency of his hunt. *Find it, find it, find it ...*

Christ, how long had he been asleep? But it was OK. A quick check of his watch told him he'd only dropped off for a few minutes, but next time ... He needed that coffee, now. He retrieved his small camping stove from the boot and, torch in hand, he walked towards to the cottage. In the darkness, it looked intact. There was no evidence of fire damage until he got closer and saw the frame pulled out of the upstairs window and the boarded-up door – the firefighters had probably broken that down to get in. The smell of smoke hung heavily in the air, not the celebratory smoke of Guy Fawkes bonfires and summer barbecues, but the sour smell of pollutants and burned chemicals. Jared thought about the small, shivering dog and wondered how he was faring.

The back door was locked. There was a small garage to one side, but it was just a lean-to without a door into the house. The downstairs windows had old sash-cord frames; upstairs they looked like metal-framed windows with small panes, caked shut with layer upon layer of old paint – no way out if the window wouldn't open.

But sash windows – he knew those well and followed the path round the house trying each one as he went.

Sure enough, he found one that wasn't locked, presumably because it, too, was painted shut. A few minutes' work with his pocket knife solved that problem. He eased the window up and climbed over the sill.

He was in a small living room. It was cluttered but neat, a chair pulled up in front of a stove, a table with an open wine bottle, almost full, and a glass. The surfaces – deep windowsills, another table, a dresser – were almost covered with ornaments and framed photographs. Jared noted one of Becca on the table by the stove.

He crossed the small room and opened the door tentatively. The sour smell of smoke hit him full in the face, making him gag. He pulled his scarf up round his mouth and nose and stepped through.

It was like a different place. The fire was evident everywhere. Water lay in dirty pools on the floor. The walls were black with a dark, oily film. The stairs, steep and narrow, led up into darkness.

Another door opened into a kitchen that looked more or less intact in the light of Jared's torch. There was a jar of Nescafé on the worktop. The water was probably turned off, but there'd be enough in the pipes for a brew.

He set up his stove and heated water in a small pan, then tipped a load of coffee granules into a mug. Not waiting for the water to boil, he poured it on top and gave it a good stir. He added sugar for good measure, then drank the lot down. It was disgusting, but with luck, it would do the trick.

Using his torch to light his way, he went back through to the undamaged living room where only the smell of burning remained. He went across to the window and let the light from his torch play over it. There were framed photographs on the sill next to a small white vase. One was of Becca again. She looked about twelve, thirteen, and was standing with a tall, thin man – glasses, bit of a wonk – who was smiling vaguely at the camera. Becca was scowling fiercely.

The next photo was of the same man standing with another girl – this one looked a bit older – dark curls framing a face that was peaky and shadowed around the eyes.

Hang on. He picked it up.

There was something . . .

And he saw the face, the face in the photograph, but this time it was flying out of the darkness towards him. *Let me in! They're coming!* And there were bruises starting around her eyes and her mouth was bleeding . . .

Oh shit.

Oh fucking hell.

His repertoire of obscenities failed him. No wonder they were after Becca. And an accidental fire? Not fucking likely. They were after this Kay woman as well.

He stopped. He'd heard a sound – his imagination? *No.* There it was again. Someone was outside the cottage. He hurriedly put the photograph back down but fumbled it and it fell with a clatter.

Fuck!

Adrenaline flooded through him. He snapped off his torch and the darkness closed around him. After a few seconds, his eyes began adjusting. It was still hard to see, but he could just make out the outline of the window he'd used to get in. Moving carefully, he crossed the room, pausing at each step to avoid tripping or knocking something else over. His hands touched the sill. He felt for the window and eased it up gently, knowing how easily these windows could slip and jam.

When it was wide enough he slid across, ducked under the window and dropped down onto the path.

The weather was changing for the worse. The wind caught him as he straightened up and tried to get his bearings, making him stagger back against the wall. Sleet spattered across his face.

At least it would mask any sounds he was making as he left the house. For a moment he wondered if what he'd heard had been the sound of the wind gusting in from the sea. But as he stood there, he saw a circle of torchlight moving back and forth across the ground. There was something in the stealthy movement that told him to get out. Fast.

He moved quickly towards the gate, then, keeping himself in the shadow of the wall, he headed back towards the car.

That was when Becca's phone, stuck in his pocket, started ringing.

Chapter 44

Becca hated hospitals. They were full of people telling you what to do and asking the same questions over and over again. 'I don't know,' she told the doctor – the third doctor who'd talked to her – when he asked her if Kay was allergic to anything. 'I don't think so.'

'And you're . . .?'

'I'm her daughter.' She said this defiantly, but it was true. If she was anyone's daughter, she was Kay's. 'Can I see her?'

They'd been doing things and they wouldn't let her in earlier, but this time the doctor nodded and led her through A & E, an area that was a maze of curtained-off spaces with a door at the far end that said 'Resus'.

And there was Kay, on a bed in a cubicle. Becca felt cold. Kay looked so small – and old. Her face was pale with an angry red weal on one side. Her hair was frizzled at the ends from the heat – had she come so close to burning? Her eyes were closed, but when Becca came to the side of the bed, she opened them and her lips moved.

'What?' Becca leaned over, struggling with this image of Kay as the one who needed help, Kay who always knew what to do, and now . . .

'Becca . . .' Kay's voice wasn't even a whisper – it was more like a breath.

'Yeah. It's me. I'm . . . we saw the fire.'

Kay's hand closed on her wrist. 'Milo . . .' She had to say it twice before Becca could understand.

'Milo? He's . . .' She had no idea about Milo. 'He's OK. They're looking after him.'

Kay's hand squeezed her wrist and her eyes closed.

What happened? Becca wanted to say. What should I do? I need you to tell me what to do, but Kay, her source of wisdom over the years, was silent.

'We're taking her up to the ward now.' A nurse was standing behind her, and two men began to move the bed, pushing it away from the wall.

'What's wrong with her? Why can't she talk?' Kay's pallor and her laboured speech frightened Becca. She could remember Matt's progressive weakness as the cancer took hold.

'The smoke's hurt her throat, so it's really sore. It sounds worse than it is.'

'So why can't she go home?'

The nurse smiled at her reassuringly. 'She'll be fine, your mum. We just want to keep an eye on her. Smoke can be nasty stuff.'

'But she's burned.'

'Not badly. Those will heal quickly.'

'Can I come up with her?'

269

'Course you can. Just see her settled on the ward, then she'll need to sleep.'

Becca followed the porters through a maze of corridors and then up in a lift. They tried to talk to her, making jokes about mums getting into trouble, and how you had to look after them, until Becca's monosyllabic responses silenced them.

She wasn't in a mood for making jokes about what had happened. It was still there, right in front of her, the sight of Kay's cottage ablaze and the realisation that Kay was inside and might ... Jared had stopped her from driving across and getting in the way of the people who were getting Kay out. She'd been mad at him then. She'd said things she shouldn't have said. He might not want anything more to do with her and he'd be right. He'd been helping her, and she'd just ...

She should contact him at least, let him know what was happening. As she followed the porters through a door and into a bay that contained three other beds, she reached into her bag for her phone.

It wasn't there. Nor, she realised after some frantic rummaging, was her purse.

They were in her backpack, where she'd put them for safekeeping.

In Jared's car.

She felt a moment of blind panic. She was stuck here miles away from her stuff with no phone to contact anyone and no money.

A nurse came over to Becca. 'Do you want to see your mum before you go? She needs to get some sleep now.'

OK, that was clear enough. *Say goodnight and piss off.*

But where. And how? Get to wherever Jared might be? She had no idea where he was and she couldn't contact him – she didn't know his number. A taxi? Yeah, right. Like she had – what? – sixty, seventy quid even if she had her purse. A quick trawl through her pockets produced a fiver and a bit of change – money she'd shoved in her pocket at the pub.

She was stuck.

And where would Jared be? She needed her stuff, they'd been travelling together – they hadn't really talked about what they were going to do next. He might not be in Whitby. He might have got fed up with all the trouble and gone back to Kettlewhatsit. Or just gone. Why would he stick around?

Hang on. He had her phone. She followed the exit signs until she reached a foyer area and sure enough, there was a public phone. She took her fistful of change and keyed in her own number. Just as she thought it wasn't going to work, Jared answered it.

'*Yeah?*' He sounded cautious.

'It's me, Becca. Listen, I haven't got much cash. I'm in York. Where are you?' She had to feed another precious coin into the phone.

'Whitby. Listen, Becca—'

'Kay's OK. I think. I'm going to—'

He interrupted her. 'Becca. Listen. I can't talk now. I need to get out of here. There's things happening.'

'What things?'

271

'Just ... we've got to go to the police. I think I know who the girl is from the caravan site. I'll drive across to York and pick you up.'

'I was going to hitch.' She'd only just thought of that. It was the last thing she wanted to do, but she didn't want him feeling he had to look after her, do things for her. She could take care of herself.

'Yeah. And I'll go and tap dance in that tunnel while I'm waiting for you. Got any other bright ideas?' He sounded really angry.

'Look, I can—' *You're not the boss of me!* Paige's childish gibe echoed in her head.

'Look after yourself? Of course you can. Listen, there's something going on at your friend's house. Your mum's house. We need to go to the police. I'll pick you up in an hour, OK? I ... oh shit. Oh, shit ...'

And he was gone. She wasn't sure if her money had run out or if he'd hung up on her. She slammed the receiver back onto the handset. Who did he think he was, telling her what to do? *Got any other bright ideas?* Yes, Jared Whatever-you're-called. Loads of them. I'll get a lift from this fucking car park and then I'll call you from Whitby and say, *Still tap dancing in the tunnel?* Fuck off! And if he turned up before she got a lift? Then she'd just grab her phone and her backpack and walk away, because no one, *no one* talked to her like that, not again, not any-more, not ...

Anger is useful. It's energy. Don't waste it. Use it the right way.

Right. So she could use her anger to make sure she got a ride across to Whitby so that ... so that ...

The rage that had been boiling up inside her faded, leaving her feeling cold, empty and alone. Her anger had been so intense, she'd forgotten, just for that moment, what Jared had said. What did he mean? He knew who the girl was? How did he know? *Something going on at your friend's house* ... There was something in Kay's house? What was it? What did Kay know?

Why was she angry at Jared? He was worried about her, that's why he'd been shitty to her. And he was driving across to pick her up, which was ... that was an OK thing to do, when you got down to it. It was ... yeah, it was nice of him.

He was coming to pick her up, then they'd go to the police. Her stomach clenched. Why couldn't they just phone, make an anonymous call, they didn't need to go and stick their heads above the parapet. They already knew who she was, now they'd know where she was.

The hospital foyer was stark and bleak. A few people came through the doors, mostly porters and people in overalls and stuff. There was a row of seats bolted to the wall, and she went and sat down.

Shut inside the hospital, watching the night shift going about their business, people coming in and out, a couple of drunks under police escort, Becca made herself small as one of the police glanced her way. Eventually she drifted into a semi-doze, jerked awake from time to time by jangles of sudden noise.

As she surfaced from one of these intermittent

dozes and checked her watch, she saw it was just after three – over an hour since she and Jared had spoken. Stiffly, she straightened herself up and went to the main entrance, a double door that slid open to admit her into the chill of the outside, then a final door that released her into a storm.

The wind caught her as soon as she left the shelter of the building, making her stagger. She braced herself against it, feeling the cold cut into her. Sleety rain spattered across her face, and then the back of her head, drenching her. Within seconds, the rain had started to penetrate her jacket.

The trees were bending in the force of the wind and the buildings around her rattled as the sound of the storm rose to a howl. The car-park lights dazzled her but left patches of deep darkness.

Where was Jared? He said an hour, but in this weather? From Whitby, he'd have to drive across the moors, an exposed, single-lane road where the wind would buffet the car, maybe bring down trees, capsize high-sided lorries ...

He couldn't contact her, but maybe she could contact him. She checked her change, went back to the pay phone and tried her number again, but all she got was a message telling her it was unavailable. She just had to trust him to turn up where he said he would. She found a bench that was more sheltered that the others, and huddled into her coat as best she could. She didn't want to go back into the hospital and risk missing him – he'd said an hour, and it was now twenty past three – he'd be here any minute.

But the night got colder and colder. Becca retreated behind the final door and stood in the small entrance between the two sets of doors, her face pressed against the glass. *With you in an hour ... the police ... I think I know who ...*

Oh, she was going to give him a hard time for thinking he could drive across those moors in an hour in this weather. Jared, Mr Know-it-all, Mr ...

After another hour, she knew he wasn't coming.

Chapter 45

As Jared spoke to Becca on her phone, he moved as fast as he could in the darkness across the field towards his car. The noise of the rising wind might have masked the sound of the phone, if he was lucky, but he wanted to get out of there quickly.

The night was pitch black. If he used his phone as a torch, he'd give himself away. He had to make it back to his car without help. 'Becca. Listen. I can't talk now. I need to get out of here. There's things happening.'

He looked up at the sky. Despite the clouds, the stars were intermittently visible. Right – there was the Plough. He followed the line made by Merak and Dubhe, and found the North Star. Making an improvised sextant with his outstretched fist, he located north and adjusted his bearings.

He didn't have time to explain to Becca what he had found. They needed to go to the police. Together. 'Just … we've got to go to the police. I think I know who the girl is from the caravan site. I'll drive across to York and pick you up,' he said, looking round for any signs of pursuit.

There was an area of rough land and a hedge between him and the road. As he got closer, he felt in his pocket for his keys. His plan was to get over the hedge then freewheel the car towards the main road. Then he could head into Whitby and pick up the road across the moors that would take him through Pickering and Malton to York before anyone could be after him. But, of course, Becca decided to pick a fight. His frustration boiled over into anger. Why couldn't she trust him for once?

He could see the faint outline of his car in the moonlight, and his tension increased. It was like those last moments in a difficult climb when you had to focus, not allow yourself to relax as the end came into view, because one slip, one second's lapse, could end your life.

The hedge was sparse, but it grew around a barred fence. Jared moved along until he came to the gate, which was easy enough to climb over. He dropped down into the lane, and, breathing more freely now, jogged back towards the car, his keys in his hand. He wasn't up for arguing as Becca pissed around.

'. . . I'll pick you up in an hour, OK? I . . . oh shit.'

An engine roared and headlights blazed out.

'Oh shit.'

Jared froze in the middle of the lane, pinned by the light as a car bore down on him at high speed.

Chapter 46

Kay's throat was burning. It was all she could feel of the fire, the searing pain of heat deep in her gullet that made it impossible to call out, to try and get help, to try and reach the world outside that existed just beyond this window with the small metal panes. A phone was ringing, with a maddening electronic *beep ... beep ...* that wouldn't go away. She tried to hammer on the window with her fist, but her arm was too feeble to make any impact.

She tried again but her hand was stuck, as if it was tied down. She struggled to free it, and something closed over it. 'Try and keep still, Kay. You'll pull out the line.'

What were they talking about? She had to get out! She had to find Milo and get out, but something was flooding through her, bringing a wave of darkness, and she slipped away.

And then she surfaced again. She had a sense that time had passed. She was still on the bed ... no, it was a different bed. Her throat burned, but everything else ... Memory seeped back. There'd been brightness, people around her doing things, urgent voices reassuring her, a mask over her face making the air suddenly easier to breathe ...

And Becca. Becca had been there. Among the confusion of faces around her, Becca's face had appeared, white and frightened, a vulnerable Becca who rarely revealed herself.

Where was she? Where had Becca gone?

Kay struggled to sit up, and the confusion of her dream fell away. She was in a hospital bed in a small ward, attached to a drip. A nurse was standing by the bed, carefully detaching the line from the cannula inserted into the back of her hand. 'Good morning, Kay,' the nurse said, loudly and clearly, 'you're in York General Hospital. There was a bit of a fire at yours last night, but you're fine now. Just a bit of smoke inhalation. You'll be right as rain in a couple of days. The doctor will be round to see you later.'

'Becca?' Kay tried to say, but her voice was no more than a high-pitched breath. Her throat ached.

'Don't try and talk, Kay. You need to rest your throat,' the nurse cautioned.

There were questions Kay needed to ask and things she had to say. She held one hand out and made writing gestures with the other, but the nurse didn't seem to understand. She just smiled and said, 'The doctor will be round later. He'll talk to you, OK?'

Not OK. Not OK. Kay wanted to shout out loud, but her voice wouldn't work.

'Don't get yourself worked up, love,' the woman in the bed opposite said. 'They'll not do anything even if you could ask so don't waste your breath. Was it your lass you was worried about? Small girl, red hair?'

Your lass. Your daughter. Becca. Kay nodded.

'Well, she were here last night, went off later, said she were going home, said she'd call.'

Kay's eyes felt as though they were full of grit. Home. Where had Becca gone? Back to the cottage? Unlikely. Back to Bridlington? As far as Kay knew, she still had a flat there. Or had she gone off with this man she was apparently travelling with?

There was something about last night, something that was nagging at Kay's brain. She couldn't bring it to the surface – it was there, maddeningly elusive, slipping out of sight as she tried to focus on it. It was important, and she had a feeling Becca was involved.

She needed to talk to Becca urgently.

And Milo. Had Milo survived? If so, where was he? She had a sudden image of Milo, hurt by the fire, damaged by the smoke, whimpering, crawling off into a ditch to die on his own.

Her eyes filled with tears that she was too weak to fight off. She was angry with herself for being a stupid, maudlin cow, for wallowing in sentimentality about a dog, for God's sake. Things needed taking care of, things needed doing and it was up to her to deal with it, not to waste time snivelling in a hospital bed.

She needed to pin down that elusive memory – the one thing she knew was that it was important. She needed to make sure Becca was all right. Becca could take care of herself but she'd just been through a bad time. Milo had either died in the fire – her eyes stung again and she blinked hard – or the firemen would have taken care of him. All she had to do was ask.

So the first thing she needed to do was talk to the doctor and ask him how quickly she could be out of here. Like, today, for example.

Sorting things out in her mind helped her relax. Her eyes were still painful from the smoke, so she closed them and after a while, she began to drift.

Chapter 47

Becca sat huddled in a chair in the hospital lobby. She was waiting for daylight. The night-time business of the hospital went on around her, people clattering past, a trolley wheeled at high speed by a careless porter. A couple of times someone asked her if she was all right, their gaze suspicious.

The small hours dragged on, an interminable time until a faint, grey dawn began to light up the doors. It was warm in the hospital, but Becca was cold. She felt detached from the bright clarity of the morning. It was like waking after a night of sleeping out on the streets. She was so, so tired. She'd already been exhausted after the day she had spent with Jared. Now, there weren't any words for how tired she felt.

And Jared. Where was he? He'd said, *Oh shit!* and cut her off. Or had her money run out? It was hard to work out exactly what had happened. She tried to tell herself he was fed up with her, angry because she'd said vile things, called him a fucking pill-head. *Oh shit* just meant, *Right, you're on your own.*

282

But he'd also said, *An hour, OK?*

The abrupt end to the call ... something had gone badly wrong.

And she'd just sat there waiting for him while whatever was happening happened. It was like Paige, all over again, just watching, not doing anything.

Her brain felt mushy with fatigue. What had Jared said – *We need to go to the police ...?* She couldn't do that – Jared meant they should go together, not her, on her own. He said he knew who the girl was. What had he found out? Where had he found it?

She stood up and stretched her cramped limbs. There was a toilet along the corridor. She went there, sorted herself out and gave herself a rudimentary wash in the basin. At least she knew how to take care of herself in the most basic circumstances.

Her hair looked bad, as though she'd slept rough. OK. Fair enough. Her face was pale with dark shadows under her eyes, her lips were dry and flaky and the line of the scar stood out more than usual against the pallor of her skin. If she went along to A & E looking like this, they'd probably admit her.

Time to take stock. She had just over five pounds in her pocket and no phone. Her coat was damp from sitting out in the rain waiting for Jared. She had no way of getting anywhere, and nowhere to go if she did. Her only friends were out of commission: Jared had vanished and Kay ... Kay was ill in a hospital bed upstairs and couldn't be expected to bail Becca out of this one.

She had to get back to Whitby, try and find Jared,

try and find out what had happened to him, help him. Something hollow inside her was telling her it was too late – Jared, like Paige, was gone.

No. She wasn't going to accept that. Jared was tough. He could look after himself. He did stupid things sometimes, got himself into trouble, but he'd be OK. He just needed some help.

So maybe she *should* go to the police, tell them what had happened and what she knew. When she told them what Jared had said, and how he'd disappeared after that, they'd go and look for him.

But that was hours ago. And Whitby had cliffs, and the sea. There were tunnels and old mines up the coast. People knew Jared explored them – all his online stuff told you he explored them. If someone found him in a tunnel, unconscious or – or something – they'd just think it was an accident. That Jared had been stupid and had an accident that had ...

Tears were running down her face. She wiped them away angrily. Stupid. Stupid, soft cow. Jared could look after himself, of course he could.

But he might be depending on her to do her bit.

She pulled on her damp jacket and went to the reception desk. Her request sounded odd in her ears: Where's the nearest police station? But the receptionist just showed her on a map and gave her directions.

'How far is it?'

'Ten minutes? Mind you, the traffic's heavy right now.'

'I'm walking,' Becca said.

'Oh, love, it's quite a trek. It'll take you a good half hour,' the woman said, looking concerned. 'There's a bus if you . . .'

'No, it's OK.' Why couldn't people mind their own business?

'Here.' The woman gave her the map – just a sheet of paper with a street map on.

'Thanks.' Becca looked at it and squared her shoulders. It wouldn't be her first walk in the rain.

Chapter 48

The face behind the wheel was illuminated just for a moment, a face Jared recognised. GBH. The caravan site owner from Bridlington. Jared froze, then he threw himself back against the hedge, rolling backwards over the rail and landing on his knees in the field. The car lurched, veered and came straight towards him, fixing Jared in the lights.

But the metal fence concealed in the bushes was just enough to stop it. There was a crunch and a scraping noise. The car skidded to a halt. Jared scrambled to his feet and was away, running across the fields, realising as he fled that he'd turned east, towards the coast, where there were no houses, no roads, nothing – just the cliffs and the sea – and his pursuer was close. Jared could hear the thud of feet on the ground behind him. GBH was a thug, heavier than Jared, stronger. If he caught Jared, he'd kill him. Jared had no illusions about that. The adrenaline of fear flooded through him.

His mind was racing. He couldn't outrun the guy, and from the corner of his eye he could see another light bobbing to the south – the second person, the one he heard at the cottage, running to cut him off if he headed back for the road.

Where to go? There was no time to call for help, even if any help would come.

East. He had no way to go but east. Already, his chest was feeling tight and his legs heavy. He wasn't fit, he wasn't ready for this.

There were trees. He could remember trees. Slightly to the south. He'd seen a clump of them, like the edge of a wood, earlier that day. Trees could conceal him. It was his only chance. Get to the trees and hide. Somehow.

If he could keep ahead, just enough, he could do it. They'd expect him to make for the houses at Sandsend, but Jared knew that wouldn't work. He couldn't keep up this speed for long – already, he was struggling for breath – and if he made it, they'd get him before any help came. No one paid attention to shouts in the night.

The ground was sloping downwards. Jared propelled himself forwards, not checking his path, just putting as much space between him and his pursuers as he could. His foot caught on something and he fell, rolling down a steep hill, his arms curled round his head, a slide, a drop, crashing into a tree, another drop. And then he was at the bottom, lying in the mud and the leaf mould.

He could hear the sounds of people crashing about above him, and shouts. They didn't seem to know he'd come down this way, and looking back up the hill in the faint moonlight, he could see why. The hillside was so steep as to be almost sheer in places. Gingerly, he tested himself. The trees had slowed his fall and the thick leaf mould had made a soft landing. Nothing hurt any more than usual, and everything moved OK.

There was a footpath of a kind at his feet – more a trodden-down track than anything else, one that hadn't been walked recently. Above him, he could hear the sounds of someone coming through the undergrowth and see the intermittent flashing of a torch – just slightly off his path. His fall had changed his direction, but the sooner he got away from here, the better.

He could no longer see the stars, but he knew more or less where he was now. The map was in his head as clearly as if it was in his hand. He could hear the sea behind him. His pursuers were heading in that direction. It was dark – he could barely see the ground. Moving cautiously, he started to head away along the path.

His breath was sticking in his throat, but there was no time for a rest. He moved as fast as he dared along the faint track, trying to see ahead through the darkness. There could be anything – another drop; maybe he'd got the direction wrong and maybe he was heading straight for the cliff edge.

And then . . .

He looked up. In front of him were stone walls protecting a dark arched opening. It was the portal to a tunnel, a bricked-up tunnel, and the path led straight to it. For a moment of complete disorientation, he thought he was back at Kettleness, but then his sense of direction came back and he knew where he was.

This gully was Deepgrove, and he was at the southern entrance to the Sandsend tunnel.

His first thought was to scramble in and hide. He could even make his getaway – he could walk through the tunnel to the northern entrance that came out in wasteland halfway down the cliff, leading straight to the southern portal of the Kettleness tunnel.

... in the dark, no torch, no proper boots ...

The searchers had been heading south. They'd assume he'd made it to Sandsend when they didn't find him, so what would they do then? They'd come back this way – GBH's car was up there near the cottage somewhere.

He needed to think but his head was all over the place. He felt jittery, sweaty, and nausea was making his stomach churn. As if on cue, the familiar dull ache began low down in his back.

He sank down with his back against the tunnel wall, and dug down for the determination that had got him out of tight places before, but there was nothing there, just the knowledge that he'd abandoned Charlie, left the girl, and now he was in the process of abandoning Becca.

He could stay here, sitting against the wall, waiting for daylight. He was pretty well hidden and the people who were after him wouldn't stick around once it got light. Then he could climb back up the gully and go to the police, make it all someone else's responsibility.

He could do that.

A memory surfaced from his childhood. When he

was eight, his father had taken him up into the Scottish Highlands, near Cape Wrath. It was one of the first times they'd gone wild camping – pitching their tent on rough ground, finding their own routes away from official paths in one of the few parts of the country that was genuinely isolated. And he'd got ill – puking his guts up and worse. His dad had put him in the sleeping bag for warmth and fed him rehydration fluid made from boiled water, sugar and salt. 'What do you want to do, mate?' he'd asked Jared. 'Go home? Or we can go on – if you want.'

Cold, sick and scared, Jared had just wanted to go home. Most of him wanted to be warm in his own bed with his mum to look after him, but something, another part of him, made him look at his father and say, 'Let's go on.' His father had grinned and given him a high five.

What do you want to do, mate? Slowly, shakily, he stood up. His knee hurt – he could remember twisting it in the fall – but it took his weight OK. His back ached – so what's new there? The painful joints, the shivering and the hot and cold feeling – he couldn't do anything about that. It would have to wait.

Now he had to decide on the best thing to do. He was worried about Becca. He had no idea what she'd make of his non-appearance in York. He checked her phone. The battery was critically low, and down here in the gully, there was no signal. If she tried to contact him the phone would register as unavailable.

The obvious thing for her to do was to find her way

back to the cottage, and if she did that, she might run smack into the people he'd had trouble with. She had no idea the cottage was dangerous.

He checked his watch with the light from his phone and swore under his breath. Almost an hour had passed since their call. She'd be expecting him to arrive soon and he had no way of contacting her.

Breathe ... just flow ... like water ...

How did you get it so wrong, mate?

One thing at a time. With an effort, he pushed the thought of Becca to the back of his mind. He couldn't do anything about her now.

He needed to get this sorted out in his head. Another thing his father had taught him – know the territory. Right now, he didn't understand what was going on so he couldn't make any sensible decisions. He'd been in dangerous situations before, but they were situations he'd chosen, and situations where he had – to some extent – the expertise and understanding necessary to get himself out. Mostly. The thing was, he'd known what was happening.

Now, he didn't. These fuckers were trying to kill him. He couldn't ever remember being as scared as he'd been just now, running away from the men who were after him. It had started the day of his first trip to the Kettleness tunnel. The police came, and GBH was there to hassle him as soon as they'd left.

At the time, GBH's attitude had seemed like bad temper and bullying. The guy had just wanted to throw his weight about. Then the girl had been attacked on his property and Jared was a witness. The police were all over the site. After that, GBH had seriously wanted Jared gone. That made sense, in a way. But Jared had already been interviewed and had given all the information he had to the police. GBH must know that. So throwing Jared out was a classic case of closing the stable door after the horse had bolted, except . . .

Becca.

That was the difference. Jared had come back to the site with Becca, and GBH had seen her. Becca knew this Kay woman; Kay knew the girl on the site. Someone must have put it all together. That was when Jared had become dangerous in someone's eyes.

Except he wasn't. He knew fuck all about what was going on – he was like some moron who'd stepped onto a railway line he didn't know was there and now the train was about to run him down. He barely knew Becca and hadn't even met Kay.

But the people who were after him didn't know that. And it seemed they were after Becca as well.

OK. The first thing he needed to do was get to his car and then either get himself across to York in the hopes Becca hadn't given up on him and tried to make her own way back, or head into Whitby and talk to the police. He could help them identify the girl from the caravan site, and that was something, but without Becca, he only had half a story.

Shit! Whichever way he looked at it, it was a mess.

The adrenaline of fear had kept him going, but now his body was demanding payback. As he scrambled up the gully, using the tree roots and hanging branches as climbing aids, his mind started playing tricks on him. He almost fell when he caught sight of a figure standing among the trees, a figure that faded away as he jerked out of the exhaustion that was overcoming him.

And then he was climbing up a wall but he knew if he just lay down, he would find a safe, soft place where he could rest, and ...

His foot slipped, almost sending him tumbling back down the slope. He was dreaming on his feet and if he fell into the gully again, he might not be so lucky. He'd be no use to Becca if he broke his back.

How long was it since he'd slept? Fatigue was making him stupid, and stupid meant he was putting himself in danger, but there was nothing he could do about that now. He unzipped his fleece, thinking he could use the cold to keep himself alert. He needed to lie low until he knew where GBH and the people who'd been after him were. He scrambled further up the hill until he was among the trees, then, using the intermittent moonlight, he found a vantage point where he could see the cottage and the line of the path.

The landscape was empty. He was pretty sure he could walk across there, get to his car and be away before anyone saw him, but that was the impulse of an addled brain. The people who'd been after him would need to come back this way and he was pretty sure they hadn't, or not yet.

All he could do was sit it out.

He found a hollow and piled up the fallen leaves

to make a thick layer of insulation between himself and the ground, then, settling his back against a tree, he watched.

If no one came in half an hour, then he was going out there. He couldn't leave it any longer.

Chapter 49

The police station turned out to be a police HQ: large, intimidating and with no obvious place for a visitor to go. Becca almost turned round to go back to the hospital, but Jared was missing and there was only her that knew. Or cared.

An obscure sign directed her towards reception, and she lifted her chin and marched through the door, which opened into a bare entrance with a window at one end. A sign said *All visitors report here.* Becca hesitated, then went across. She had no idea what she was supposed to do. 'I want to talk to someone,' she said to the woman who was sitting there staring at a computer screen.

The woman's gaze didn't shift and Becca said again, more loudly, 'I want to . . .'

'Name,' the woman said, still focused on the screen. 'Becca.'

The woman raised her gaze to look directly at her. 'Second name?'

Becca stared straight back. *I don't have to tell you*

anything. 'I just want to talk to someone.' She refused to say what it was about, or to give any further information. The woman directed her to a chair with an irritated wave.

After a twenty-minute wait, she was shown into a small room by a young man who introduced himself as Dave. A woman joined them, nodded at the man and smiled at Becca. They both seemed friendly, but Becca knew all about that. 'I'm DC Sharpe,' the woman said. 'Call me Mandy.' Becca knew the 'call-me' types. *Call-me-Julie, Call-me-Mike, I'm your friend. I want what's best for you.* Yeah, right. 'OK, Becca – is it all right if I call you Becca?' She didn't wait for Becca's response. 'How can we help you?'

Becca had spent the walk over trying to work out what to say. It was all a muddle. Nothing fitted together. Stumbling badly over the story, she told them about the attack in the caravan park, about being followed at Kettlewhatsit. 'Kettle-something,' she told them.

'Kettleness? Did you report that?' Call-Me-Mandy asked.

Becca shook her head.

'Why not?'

'I just didn't.'

'So what's happened to change your mind?'

Becca turned away from her and spoke directly to the man. She didn't like Call-Me-Mandy with her *Why nots*. She told Dave about the fire and coming to the hospital with Kay and the call to Jared. 'He's got my phone,' she said.

'And he told you he knows who this girl at the caravan site is?'

Becca nodded.

'But he didn't tell you?'

'No, the call ... it just stopped. I think ...' She fought to keep her voice steady. 'I think something might have happened to him.'

'Can I have your number?' Dave asked. He called it, listened, then, glancing up at Call-Me-Mandy, shook his head. 'Unobtainable,' he said. He sat in silence for a moment, then smiled at Becca. 'Right. Becca. We need to check on a couple of things. We'll sort you out with a cup of tea while you're waiting.'

The tea was welcome. It came with some biscuits, which made her realise how hungry she was. She still had no idea what was going to happen next. When she'd finished here, what was she going to do? She'd have to go back to the hospital, talk to Kay – if Kay was OK. Last night Kay had looked so old. What if she didn't make it?

The nurse had said Kay would be all right. They were just keeping her in for observation, wasn't that it? But they didn't keep you in hospital for nothing. Kay might be ...

There was no point in thinking about it right now. Jared was missing. She had to get this interview or whatever it was sorted, then decide what to do next. She hated the way they were dragging their feet, but that was how they worked. *Pigs*. Call-Me-Mandy was a cow, but Dave seemed all right. For a pig.

If she could get back to Kay's cottage, Jared's car

might still be there. She could get her money, and maybe there would be something to show where he'd gone. Maybe he'd be there himself. It went round and round in her head. She didn't know what to do.

Almost half an hour passed before Dave and Call-Me-Mandy came back. By this time, Becca was fidgety with anxiety. Call-Me-Mandy gave her a long, measured look, but Dave's grin was friendly. 'Bit of bother at your foster-mum's last night, then, Becca? It is Becca Armitage, isn't it?'

She looked at him blankly, then understood what they'd been doing. They'd been looking up the Bridlington case, and they'd been looking up the people involved. They knew who she was. Now. 'Yeah. She's in hospital. I want to get back there. When we've done here.'

'OK, Becca. Bear with me because this is all a bit complicated. Let's try and start at the beginning. Now, I've been looking at your record. You've been in a bit of bother before, haven't you?'

Becca's mouth dropped open. 'No, I haven't.'

'They don't put you in a secure unit as a good citizenship prize, Becca. You were in there for six weeks, according to this.' Call-Me-Mandy raised her eyebrows. 'So what was going on?'

'Nothing . . . it's not a prison. It's . . .' *Just for your own safety and protection, Becca. We're trying to keep you safe.*

'Anti-social behaviour,' Dave said. He looked at her thoughtfully. 'And there was something about a fire.

Then you went to live with the McKinnons. New start. Turning over a new leaf, right?'

'I didn't . . .' She wanted to push the table over, kick their files across the room, smack their stupid faces until . . . *Anger . . . Don't waste . . . right way . . .* 'I didn't do anything. They didn't have anywhere else to send me, that's all.'

'That's not what it says, Becca. You see, I don't quite get what you're doing here. Kay McKinnon's house burns down, and you turn up with some story about a missing boyfriend and things he's found out, only you don't know what it is.'

'It's Jared. He isn't my boyfriend. Something's—'

'Let's just go back a bit, OK? Now, you leave the McKinnons' and go to college in Leeds, right? But then you get into a bit of bother there, so Kay McKinnon finds you a job in Bridlington. And then you get into more bother, lose your job.'

Becca felt the colour flood into her face. 'That's got nothing to do with—'

'You're very touchy about it. Why's that?' Call-Me-Mandy sticking her oar in.

'Because I got fired.' *Why do you think, you stupid cow?*

'It was over some pictures you posted, wasn't it?' Dave was looking through some papers on the table in front of him.

'I didn't post anything.'

'Oh, come on, Becca.' Call-Me-Mandy. 'We know about the chat room.'

'Nothing wrong with that,' Dave said. 'But your boss didn't like it?'

'It wasn't ...' Becca was left floundering by her frustration. She'd come here to get help for Jared, and they were just mouthing on about the past, about the pictures. 'What about Jared?'

'Yes. let's get back to Jared Godwin. Just help me out here, Becca. You drove from Bridlington to meet up with him.'

She didn't know Jared's name was Godwin. They must have looked him up as well. At least they were doing something. 'Yeah.'

'And you stopped off at Kay McKinnon's. Why did you do that?'

'Because I wanted to see her.'

'OK. You maybe wanted to tell her about your job, is that right?'

'I might have done. Yeah.'

'Was she upset? She helped you get that job, didn't she?'

'Yes.'

'*Yes* she was upset or *yes* she got you the job?'

'She helped me get the job. She wasn't upset.'

'Wasn't she? We've found out she bent quite a few rules to get you in there, Becca. My problem here is I think she would have been upset. I mean, first off, you give up your college course, and then you get sacked from the job she helped you with – my mum would go mental. Or didn't she care?'

'She ... Yeah, she minded, but she didn't ... we didn't ... It wasn't, like, a row, we just, you know ...'

'Had a bit of a disagreement. I understand Becca. Here. I'd like you to look at this.' Dave showed her a small tablet he was holding. She looked at the screen, not really seeing it at first. And then it resolved into recognisable images. There were photos of her from her Bexgirl chat room, some of the images she used to sell after camming sessions. For the first time, looking at them with Dave and Call-Me-Mandy, she felt grubby, tainted by their gaze on her.

Becca wanted to smash the tablet out of Dave's hand, tell them both to close it down if they thought it was so ... so ... Call-Me-Mandy was looking at Becca as if she thought Becca was dirt. Well, no one would want to look at *her* pictures. They'd pay her to put her clothes back on.

'Your friend, Mrs McKinnon, looked these up yesterday ...' Dave explained, and Becca felt her stomach lurch. Kay knew. Kay had seen this. 'You had a bit of a row about it, didn't you?'

'It wasn't that,' Becca protested, and then saw the trap she'd stepped right into.

'So you did have a row that evening?'

'No. I just – I told her I'd lost my job.'

'And left.'

'Yes.'

'And then you came back.' Call-Me-Mandy. 'With Jared Godwin.'

Now, too late, Becca could see where they were going. 'We were driving back from Whitby. We went there ...'

'OK. You get run off the road and you think people are following you, so you go for a day out by the sea? Come on, Becca. How stupid do you think I am?' Dave sounded genuinely angry.

Call-Me-Mandy leaned forward. They were both in her face. 'Did you just mean to give her a fright? Get back at her for pissing you off earlier?'

'I don't know what you're talking about. We saw the fire. We drove back and we saw the fire, that's why I was—'

Call-Me-Mandy's face was openly disbelieving now. 'So you're so scared of the people following you, you come back to the place where you were the day before, just for what? A bed for the night?'

'Yes. Kay would have put us up.'

'I'll tell you why I think you came here, Becca. You lost your rag with Kay McKinnon. You went back to her house and you set the fire. Now you're sorry and you're scared. You do things when you lose your temper – it's on the record. You get into fights, don't you? And this isn't the first fire that's happened when you're around.'

Becca was shocked into silence. She'd come here about Jared, about the girl on the caravan site, not about this. What were they thinking? How could they? She'd done the right thing by coming here, and this was how they treated her?

'So you come over here – you're worried about Mrs McKinnon, I get that, but now you're coming to us with some story about a phone call and a girl's name, but mostly to tell us that Jared Godwin was at the cottage. Only he's conveniently vanished.'

'I called him. He said he knew who the girl was – the girl who'd been attacked. He said he was on his way to York, and then he didn't get here. That's what happened.'

'You called him? I thought you'd lost your phone.'

'I called my phone. He's got it.'

'Convenient.' A murmur from Call-Me-Mandy.

'Just go back a bit. He said he knew who this girl is and you should go to the police. So who is she?' Dave said.

Becca shook her head. 'He didn't say.'

'He asked you to come and talk to us, but he didn't tell you this girl's name?'

'He didn't have time.'

Dave shook his head. 'Stop treating me like I'm stupid, Becca. I'm getting a bit tired of this. Listen to me. You want to give your foster-mum a fright. Godwin may or may not have helped you. It all goes wrong, you stick around to make sure she's OK – you did the right thing there, Becca, but Godwin does a runner, doesn't want to know anymore.'

'He was coming here to pick me up.' She had to convince them.

Dave's voice was relentless. 'No he wasn't. There's some things you need to know, Becca. Godwin's not your friend, he never was. He makes his money on the internet. He's got sites on the dark web – we can't access those at the moment. He keeps them well protected and maybe you should ask yourself why. But he puts stuff out on the regular web – he's got to do that to get people onto his site.' He held up the tablet. Her own face smiled at her from the glossy images. 'This is from his open site, Becca. You might want to think about what he puts on the hidden site. This is what Jared Godwin does.'

Becca shook her head. She'd come here knowing she shouldn't, and now everything was shifting under her feet. Who to trust? She didn't know anymore.

Those pictures. She only had Jared's word he hadn't looked at them. She only had his promise that they'd been texted to him. Maybe that was all part of . . . part of what? Was she trusting these pigs against Jared? Jared was OK. He . . .

In an unwanted memory, a snatch of conversation came back to her, Jared saying he'd been neglecting his website and needed to post something to get his visitors back.

Pictures. Photos. Bexgirl's photos.

That would do it.

She wasn't going to let Dave and Call-Me-Mandy see they'd got to her. Jared might not be the person she thought, but she knew who they were. They were pigs and they were just like the rest. She stood up. 'I'm going.'

'We haven't finished talking to you, Becca. Sit down.'

But she'd been down this road before. They thought she'd set the fire at Kay's but they didn't have any evidence. They couldn't have, or they would have arrested her. She'd done nothing wrong and more to the point, they couldn't prove she had. 'You can't make me stay.'

'Best to get this sorted out, Becca. It won't look good if you leave now.' That was Call-Me-Mandy, and Becca fired her anger directly at the other woman.

'For who? It looks fine to me. I'm not some sad kid who doesn't know anything, not anymore. For a start, I know what you can do and what you can't do, so what you *can* do is arrest me or piss off, both of you. I'm going.'

And in a strange way, telling them like that was just as satisfying as smashing up the room and smacking their smug faces. Better, really, because they couldn't touch her for it.

There was a moment of tense silence, then Dave stood up. 'OK, Becca, but don't forget. Jared Godwin is trouble. Keep out of his way, or you may find yourself back here. Next time, we might not be on your side.'

'And that'll be different how?'

'You don't want to know, Becca.' A last shot from Call-Me-Mandy.

Expecting to be stopped at any moment and maybe locked up in a cell, Becca walked out into a day of grey skies, icy cold and nowhere to go.

Chapter 50

Jared waited, shivering and sweating in the darkness, his stomach a pit of nausea. Flu? He hadn't had flu, or even a cold, for years, but his resistance must be rock bottom right now.

His head pounded and he groaned against his sleeve to muffle the sound. If he had his pills now would be the time to take them, but they were in his fucking car, as useful as if they'd been on the other side of the world.

But the pills had stopped working properly weeks ago. He'd solved the problem by taking more, and then by washing them down with whisky or whatever alcohol was to hand. And it was now over twenty-four hours since he'd taken any. Time to get real. The pills wouldn't help because the pills were the problem. This wasn't flu. This was withdrawal.

He closed his eyes. If he really wanted to get straight, he'd just have to suck it up.

Suddenly, he was alert. His survival instincts acted like a reflex and he kept his head low to the ground. What was it?

The sky was just starting to lighten, the faint grey of early dawn appearing. The moon was past its apex, brilliant and remote. He could see lights moving through the trees above him, the steady glow that suggested someone was walking rather than running. Two people moving along the path near the top of the gully. Voices drifted down, fading in and out among the trees.

'. . . doesn't know anything. What the fuck did you go and . . .'

'. . . expect me to do? I told you, for fuck's sake!'

'Pull a stunt like that again . . .'

'Don't take that . . .'

'Or what? I pay you enough and you've fucked . . .'

'. . . worked out didn't it? No one's been . . .'

'. . . thing at Kettleness. You'd better . . . and get it right this . . .'

They were passing just a couple of metres above him now. Jared lifted his head slightly. The line of the path ran along the top of the gully and he could see the walkers. They were silhouetted against the sky, two of them. Jared thought he could make out the bulk of Greaseball, but the other . . . for a moment, the light of the setting moon caught the face, but it was no one he recognised.

As Jared watched, he saw a third figure behind the other two, too far back to be involved in the conversation. This figure was mounted on a bike that he was riding slowly up the steep rise. As Jared watched, this figure turned away and vanished. He couldn't tell if the biker was with the other two or just an early morning rider on the path.

He was too tired to begin to make sense of what he'd just heard, but it sounded as though they were going to Kettleness. They might go to the cottage first – as Jared knew all too well, GBH's car was in the lane, and he didn't want to go anywhere near the place while that insane cunt was around.

He had no choice. Becca was out there somewhere, broke and with no way of contacting him, apart from ... He checked her phone. The battery was dead. Now there was no way to contact her at all. He told himself he didn't need to worry. What she'd probably do was stick around in York with her friend Kay, and Kay would help her get back.

But Becca was a fighter, and he suspected that as far as she was concerned, he'd gone missing. Was she charging across the moors right now to his rescue? That sounded much more like her than sitting in a hospital ward waiting for help. So if she was doing that, where would she go first? Probably to the cottage. Could she be there right now? Jared was scrambling to his feet as the thought occurred to him.

No. She couldn't. It was almost two in the morning when they'd talked. Becca would have waited for him at the hospital, and she wouldn't be sure he wasn't coming until three fifteen, three thirty. She'd probably give him a bit more time than that. OK. Suppose she'd followed that crazy plan to hitch, and suppose she'd got a lift at once, and suppose the driver was mad enough to take her to the cottage: it would still be after five at the very earliest before she got there.

He checked his phone. It was almost five now – he needed to move.

On the other hand, she might go to Kettleness. It would make a lot of sense because then she could pick up her car. It was a difficult place to get to if you didn't have transport, but he'd put his money on Becca getting there somehow.

His whole body ached. Despite the cold, he was sweating. All he wanted to do was lie down somewhere and sleep. He tried to force his exhausted brain into some kind of action. He needed to be at the cottage in case Becca turned up there – that was the most likely place. But he needed to be at Kettleness as well, in case she went there. And from what he'd just heard, that was where the danger was likely to be.

Shit, shit, shit. He had to make a decision. OK. First, the cottage. Leave a message for Becca, pick up his car, head to Kettleness. That was the one place he was certain she would go to. Her car was there.

Jared hesitated, looking for the flaw. His whole plan was full of them, but he couldn't think of anything else. Limping slightly, he set out across the fields, moving carefully and keeping off the skyline. GBH and his friend might still be around somewhere. They'd go back to the cottage to pick up the car, but Jared doubted they'd stick around, not with daylight close.

He kept low as he came to the open fields, moving from shadow to shadow. The cottage stood at the edge of the village. It was in darkness, and he couldn't see any cars close by. He went past, to the lane where his car was parked, and watched for ten minutes. There was no movement, no sound, and the other car – GBH's car – was gone.

This would be where they would expect him to come back. If they were lying in wait, this was where they'd be.

He moved closer, warily, every hair on his body standing upright.

His hand was feeling in his pocket and closed round his keys.

If he could get into the car and away before they could catch him, then they'd follow him, leaving the cottage clear for Becca.

He slid over the fence, the hedge snagging at his clothes, and slipped round to the car door. He was moving quickly now because if there was anyone there, they would have seen him for sure. Bracing himself for the sudden glare of headlights, the sound of a racing engine, he slipped the key into the door – and then he realised.

There was no reason to be bothering with stealth anymore. It was too late for that. The car was sunk low onto the ground. The tyres were slashed to ribbons and the windscreen was shattered. This car wasn't going anywhere.

Jared stood, waiting. If they were here, they'd seen him. *Come on, then!*

Nothing.

It looked as though they'd gone. It must have been sheer bad luck last night that he'd walked into them. But he was still stuck. If he was going to get to Kettleness, he needed transport. And . . .

He opened the boot. Someone had been through everything and his laptop was gone. *Shit!* But he'd worry about that later. His camping gear was still there, still packed in his rucksack. It was pulled about, but nothing seemed to be missing. He swung the rucksack onto his back, then reached in through the driver's window and felt around in the side pocket. Relief filled him as his shaking hand closed around the pill packet. Now was not the time to go through withdrawal. He could just pop a couple, get himself sorted for the moment, then . . .

What the fuck was he doing? He'd screwed up because of the pills and now he was thinking of taking more? He could function through the withdrawal, but the pills? They were worse. He moved to shove the pack into his pocket – a safety net, in case he needed them later – then realised that if he had them, he'd take them. He held them in his shaking, sweating hand for a long moment, considering them, then wound his arm back and threw them as far as he could into the undergrowth.

Might be a few high rabbits around tonight.

But he couldn't raise a smile. He needed to get out of here and his car was fucked.

There was a garage at the cottage – this Kay woman must have a car. That would do it, if he could get it started. He followed the road down to the cottage – no point in climbing fences if he didn't have to. The garage was to one side, and the door, an up and over, wasn't locked.

There was a small VW, and – better and better – a motorbike. Over the years, Jared had learned a range of useful skills, and hot-wiring a bike was one of the simpler ones. A quick rummage through some of the boxes stored there soon produced the requisite small piece of wire.

He checked the bike over. It looked fine, as long as there was fuel. If there wasn't, he could freewheel it into Whitby, get some there. He found the ignition wire, followed it down to the connector, pulled it apart and inserted the short wire. There was a faint pop, and the engine came smoothly to life.

At last, something was going his way. Under the aches and the sweating, he felt the first touch of hope.

The bike had enough fuel to get him where he wanted – these things could go forever on half a tank.

OK, transport: check. Now he needed to leave something for Becca. At his car? If they came back, they'd see it. The house then. He left his rucksack by the bike and went back to the cottage. The window he'd used before slid open more easily this time. Grimacing at the sour smell of burning, he slipped across the sill and back into the cottage.

How to let her know where he was? A note? Genius, Jared. They wouldn't see that, would they? As he thought about it, his gaze was moving across the table, the windowsill, the phone table, looking for the photograph he'd seen earlier, the one that had sent him off half-cock, blathering on to Becca about what he'd found instead of . . .

It had been on the windowsill; he'd knocked it over but that's where it had fallen. And now it was gone. They must have worked it out, Greaseball and his mate, and taken it. It didn't matter. Jared knew what he'd seen.

And now he knew what he could leave for Becca. There was a laptop on the table and the usual spaghetti of chargers, headphones and other detritus that tended to gather around computers. No one would notice a phone among that lot. He rummaged through it and found a standard charger with a USB connector. He attached Becca's phone to the laptop – the power to the cottage was switched off, but the laptop should be charged and if it was, it would give her phone enough of a boost to put some life into it.

Then he texted her: *K whatsit*. And her phone gave a *ping* of acknowledgement.

He hesitated. Leaving the phone was leaving behind her best opportunity of contacting him, but he had to provide for two places. He'd be at Kettleness where her car was. If she came to the cottage first, then with luck she'd find the phone and know he'd been here, and the message would tell her where he'd gone.

Belt and braces. She might be set up to collect her voicemail remotely. He called her number again and said, 'It's me. I'm going to pick up your car. I'll stay up there tonight.' He left his number – she wouldn't know that without her phone, and that was the best he could do. He left the window slightly open for her to find – she probably wouldn't have a key and anyway, the front door was boarded up.

He wheeled the bike out of the garage and straddled it, getting the feel of the weight and the balance. It was a good bike, a serious bike, not one of these blinged-up hairdryers kids went round on. This Kay was starting to reveal unexpected depths. He ran a quick check over the controls, freewheeled to the road, then, with a light twist on the throttle, he opened up the engine and headed north towards Kettleness.

Chapter 51

When Kay woke again, she felt better. The sun was shining, the ward was bright with daylight and she was surrounded by the bustle of the early morning. Cautiously, she sat herself up, waiting for the pounding in her head to start again, but it didn't.

She took stock. Her eyes still felt sore and swollen, as if she'd spent the night in tears. Her hands and arms were bruised, but other than that, she was in reasonable shape.

A quick check of her locker showed she had nothing with her – no purse, no phone, no keys. Nothing. For the moment, she was dependent on the hospital to get her what she needed. And what she needed more than anything was a phone. She needed to find out what had happened to her cottage and what had happened to Milo.

A more immediate problem was the need for a pee. She pressed the call button but, after waiting ten minutes, decided no one was going to come. Kay swung her legs out of bed and sat up. She was wearing a hospital gown that tied inadequately up the back and she would give the rest of the ward – and any other observers – a bad fright if she walked off down the corridor dressed like this.

Moving carefully, she pulled the curtains round her bed, took off the gown and put it on back to front, creating a makeshift dressing gown that wasn't exactly elegant, but was decent. Feeling a bit more protected and freed from the trappings of medicine, Kay made for the bathroom.

She managed an all-over wash, drying herself with paper towels. Her image in the mirror was not reassuring. Swollen, bloodshot eyes, no make-up and dirty, unbrushed hair was not a good look, but there was nothing she could do about that until she got back home

Feeling better, she made her way back to her bed. A nurse was waiting for her. 'Kay, you shouldn't go off like that. You should have asked one of us to take you, first time. You might have fallen.'

'I'm fine.' She wasn't going to admit it to the nurse, but the short walk had exhausted her. She lay back on the bed, trying not to show what a relief it was.

'Well, press the call button next time.'

'When can I go home?' Kay's voice was silenced by a bout of coughing.

The nurse looked at her pointedly. 'You're doing very well. Let's not spoil it by overdoing it. The doctors will be round after breakfast.'

Kay wasn't hungry, but she knew she had to eat. Speaking carefully so as not to start the coughing off again, she said, 'I really need to contact some people, let them know I'm safe, but I don't have my phone, or any money. I don't even know how I'm going to get home.'

'I'll talk to the charge nurse. We can see what we can do to help. But there's someone here to see you. We don't usually let visitors on the ward this early, but this is the police, so ... do you feel well enough to talk to them?'

The police? 'Why? What's happened?' Becca. It must be Becca.

'I think they need some information about the fire,' the nurse said.

It wasn't Becca. Kay breathed again. She really didn't feel up to talking to the police, but if they had questions, the sooner she answered them, the sooner they'd go away. 'Yes, I'm fine.'

'I put them in the relatives' room. Do you want to go along there? Hang on, I'll just ...' The nurse found her a better dressing gown and some slippers, then took Kay to a small room off the main corridor, Kay surreptitiously making use of the nurse's supporting arm. This experience had turned her into an old woman overnight.

Two men were waiting for her. As she came in, they stood up. One of them was a stranger, but the other was Shaun Turner.

Her first reaction was surprise, the second, anger. Shaun couldn't just barge into the hospital outside visiting hours and demand to see her. They were just getting to know each other, and here she was, vulnerable in a faded hospital dressing gown, her feet shoved into granny slippers and her hair greasy with smoke from the fire. He should know enough to respect her privacy.

'What are you doing here?' She couldn't keep the coldness out of her voice.

He came towards her so his back was to the other man and spoke quietly. 'I know. I'm truly sorry, Kay, but there's— Listen. Be careful what you say. I'm here to help.' His face carried an urgent warning, but she wasn't sure what he was trying to tell her.

She nodded abruptly to show that she'd heard him. What was going on? She turned to the other man, who looked a bit awkward as he waited for their exchange to finish. 'I'm Kay McKinnon,' she said, holding out her hand, then withdrawing it as she started to cough.

'I'm DC Norton, Keith Norton. How are you, Mrs McKinnon? Are you sure you're up to a chat?'

Kay nodded, unable to speak but waving aside his concern. Shaun guided her to a chair and put a bottle of water on the table next to her. She nodded her thanks, accepting, for the moment, his over-punctilious care. Shaun was playing some kind of game, and until she knew what it was, it might be best to go along with it.

'I've been better,' Kay said cautiously, testing her voice. 'But not too bad, thanks. Before we start – is there any news about my dog?' She felt the irritation in her throat again and picked up the water.

'Yes.' DC Norton didn't seem surprised by the question. He told her someone – he wasn't sure who – had dropped Milo off at the vet's. He didn't know any more than that, but she felt the relief of knowing that at least Milo was in a safe place – if he'd survived, he was being looked after.

Kay could tell him very little about the fire. Until the moment she woke up in a burning house, there was nothing much to remember. 'No,' she said in response to a question about the electric fire. 'I do use it sometimes, but I didn't turn it on last night.' Far too late, she realised the significance of what he was saying. The smoke must have addled her brain. 'Are you telling me someone started the fire deliberately?'

'That's what it looks like, Mrs McKinnon.'

'But why? Why would anyone do that?'

'I was hoping you might be able to help us find out.'

Kay shook her head. She glanced at Shaun to see if he had anything to add, but he was studying his hands, frowning slightly as he listened. There was something wrong, something he wanted her to know, but she couldn't work out what it was.

She looked back at DC Norton. 'I can't help you,' she said. She had no idea why anyone would try to burn her house down. If they had. Which she wasn't convinced of. And then that elusive memory came back. 'Actually –' she was aware of Shaun coming alert next to her – 'there was someone at the house last night. There was something making Milo – that's my dog – uneasy. I thought it was foxes or something – but he just barks at them. Last night, he was different. I think there was someone out there.'

'Can you remember what time? About?'

Kay thought back. 'Early evening. I was making tea.'

'OK.' The young DC flipped open a pad and made some notes, then he glanced up at her again. 'I heard you were at Bridlington yesterday. At the drop-in.'

'Yes. But I don't see ...' *Oh.* 'I had a run-in with a couple of lads.' She told them about her encounter with Liam and Terry. 'But ... how would they know where I live?'

'They'll know your foster-daughter, Becca, won't they?'

'Yes, they probably ...' Again, too late, the alarm bells sounded and she realised what Shaun's warning had been about. Becca had never been charged, but one of the things that got her placed in that secure unit was a fire at the house where she lived with her mother and stepfather.

And Becca had been at the cottage last night. Kay could remember her white, scared face. The police would know that by now.

'And Becca was there, wasn't she? Yesterday, at your cottage?'

She was, and she'd been angry when she left, but then Becca was often angry. Kay wanted to snap back, *Do your kids ever drop in on you?* but that would look defensive, and that was the last impression she wanted to give. 'She came by.'

'What time?'

'I don't remember. It's all a bit vague.'

'We need to talk to her, Mrs McKinnon.'

'Then I'll ask her to get in touch with you.'

DC Norton opened his mouth to speak, but Shaun said quickly, 'Mrs McKinnon has already told you what she'll do, Constable.'

'Do you know where—'

'That's enough, DC Norton. Mrs McKinnon doesn't look well. Kay, do you need to lie down?'

Normally, she would have been furious that he was taking over, speaking for her, but right now, she was glad of his help. Norton's comments about Becca had shaken her up and she needed time to think about this. 'Yes, I do.'

DC Norton looked pissed off, but he didn't have much choice. He stood up. 'Well, thank you for your help, Mrs McKinnon. We can talk again when you're feeling better. In the meantime, if you think of anything else, give me a ring. I hope you recover soon.'

As the door closed behind the detective, Shaun looked at her. 'I'm really sorry I burst in on you like this. I didn't want Norton to ambush you, but I was too late. He was already here.'

'Thanks for the warning – and for getting rid of him.' Kay felt her face flush and took refuge in a faked cough that quickly developed into the real thing. Her anger at Shaun had gone, replaced by anger at the police for going after the easy target instead of doing their jobs properly. She knew Becca had nothing to do with the fire, but she couldn't account for her presence last night and until they'd had a chance to talk, she wasn't going to try. 'Why are the police so sure it's arson?'

'Because the heater was set up to look like the cause.'

'But as soon as they talked to me—'

'Kay. The arsonist used accelerant. The fire had you trapped in the bedroom, and that window doesn't open. Whoever set that fire meant to kill you.'

She felt something cold wash over her and was glad she was sitting down. Kill her? Someone had tried to kill her. Why? Shaun was still talking and she made herself pay attention.

'. . . have to ask you this. Is there any chance . . .?'

'That it was Becca? No.'

'OK. But it might be an idea to have some legal representation standing by for this girl. I can organise that, if you want me to.'

'Is it really necessary?'

His face was serious. 'It's necessary. They think they've got a good case. It doesn't help that she's taken up with this young man, Jared Godwin. He doesn't have a record, but if you ask me, it's because he's too clever to get caught. He's a pretty dodgy character.'

Kay could remember Becca heading off up the coast at night, apparently in pursuit of this man. What had she got herself involved in? 'You'd better tell me what you know.'

'I only know what Norton told me – Godwin doesn't have a job, no fixed abode and he has a couple of dodgy websites – porn sites, Norton says – and some on the dark web they can't access. For what it's worth, it looks as though he's dumped your Becca. Apparently, she turned up at the HQ here – in York – with some story about her boyfriend going missing. They tried to ask her about the fire, and she ran off.'

Kay sighed. It was possible Becca could have sorted it all out in that visit, but she was never going to be reasonable around the police. The police had locked her up, and Becca couldn't take that. 'Becca can be her own worst enemy. The important thing is they don't get her on her own. Can you make sure you get legal support to her if they do pick her up?'

'I'll do my best, Kay, but if you can get in touch with Becca, get her to give a voluntary statement, that's the best thing she could do.'

Kay nodded. Shaun had no idea what a big ask that one was, but she could see the wisdom of his advice. 'Thank you for all your help.'

He smiled. 'It's what friends do. By the way, I hope you don't mind but I stopped off at the cottage on the way and picked this up.' He was holding out her handbag. 'The police found it and they let me have it. I picked up a charger for the phone as well – it's in there.'

'Thank you,' she said again. She already knew from previous contacts with him that he was a 'take charge' person. That made her wary, but she had to admit his help right now had been invaluable. 'What state is the cottage in?'

'I won't lie to you, Kay. It's a mess. You can't go back there. Do you know when they're letting you out?'

'Today or tomorrow.'

'Give me a ring and I'll come and pick you up. I can sort out a place for you ...'

Woah, woah, woah. Slow down. 'It's OK, Shaun. I have a friend in Scarborough who'll be happy to put me up.'

'Of course, of course. But let me take you back. You'll wait forever for an ambulance.'

He was right. 'Yes. I'll call you. And – Shaun? Thank you for all your help. I do appreciate it.'

'My pleasure.' He hesitated, then leaned forward and kissed her cheek.

'I must smell like a barbecue,' she said.

He grinned. 'Good job I like barbecues. Don't forget to call me.' He left, taking the smell of the outdoors and fresh air with him. Kay made her way back to her bed and lay down. She hadn't wanted to admit it to Shaun – or to anyone – but that brief period of being up and about had exhausted her.

She plugged her phone into the charger and tried Becca's number. Unobtainable. Where was Becca? Kay had to warn her. She had the feeling of everything slipping beyond her control.

Shaun said someone had tried to kill her. Why would anyone want to kill her?

If they did, they hadn't succeeded. Which meant . . . would they try again?

Chapter 52

Becca headed for the bus station. She was starving, but she only had five quid and a bit of change in her pocket – she didn't dare spend anything until she'd had a chance to check the buses. Her plan had been to go to the hospital and find out how Kay was, but after her interview with Dave and Call-Me-Mandy, she knew she had to get away, get out of York and disappear again as quickly as possible.

They thought she'd tried to kill Kay.

It took her almost half an hour to walk to the bus station, but for once, her luck was in. There was a bus that went right into Whitby, and the next one left in about twenty minutes. She didn't have enough money for a ticket all the way there, but she had enough to get on the bus. With luck, the driver would forget her. There should be plenty of other travellers. There were only three buses a day.

As she made her way towards the stand, which was at the other side of the station, she felt light-headed and sick. Dark shadows kept creeping in at the sides of her vision. She couldn't faint – she had to get out of here before anyone else came after her.

The bus was already in and there was a queue of people waiting to board. Next to the stand was a small newspaper kiosk. Becca browsed through the magazines until another customer attracted the attention of the woman behind the counter, then she slipped an energy bar into her pocket. She checked her watch and walked slowly towards the bus, feeling as though everyone was staring at her and was about to denounce her, but no one paid her any attention at all.

The bus was an ordinary double-decker, which made things easier. Becca stood in line and paid her fare, just another passenger among many, and made her way upstairs. She took herself to the back of the bus out of the line of the driver's periscope, and settled down as comfortably as she could. Her plan was to look out of the window for the first hour until she was sure no one had spotted her as a free rider, then doze for the rest of the journey. Once she was in Whitby, she could decide what to do next.

The bus set off, turning and jolting along the pot-holed roads. The movement made Becca feel sick, but she made herself eat the energy bar slowly, and gradually the nausea dwindled, leaving her feeling cold and tired. She watched the city go past, fade into endless suburbs, and then they were out into the countryside. Stop, start. Stop, start. With each mile they travelled, it was a mile off the distance she would have to cover if she got thrown off. Once they were on the road across the moors, she tried to sleep, but the bump and rattle of the bus kept waking her.

She was walking across a strange, undulating landscape, empty and cold like the moon. She was looking for something. For someone. But she couldn't remember where she was or where she was going. She was vaguely aware of people moving about, of the bus stopping and starting, and then she was back in the barren landscape and her restless search. In this state of half sleep, she endured the two-hour journey.

And then finally, stiff and weary, she was climbing down the stairs and off the bus in the centre of Whitby.

She could smell the sea. The air was filled with the cry of gulls as they wheeled over the town. The sky was leaden. The weather had changed from relentlessly wet to grey and cold. Becca wrapped her arms around herself. It was freezing. Her jacket had dried out, but there was no warmth in it.

She knew what she had to do – get to Kay's and see if Jared had left anything for her there, and maybe get some food, a change of clothes, some walking shoes. She was still in her old ballet slippers; her feet were already sore from trekking through York earlier, and hadn't recovered from her walking the day before, or the day before that.

But instead of setting off, she slumped down on a low wall and took stock of her situation. There was a cold, shivery feeling deep inside her and an ache in her throat. All she wanted to do was curl up somewhere warm and sleep. It was like her time on the streets, a time she thought she'd left behind forever, a time when her days were a blur of hunger and tiredness. It was like being in the stripped-down cell in the secure unit when they left her in the cold with nothing more than a blanket, and any sleep she managed was disrupted by the clatter of the peep hole being yanked open and then closed again.

All those years at Kay and Matt's, all those exams, college, even the job at the drop-in, and here she was, right at the bottom again, below Liam, below Terry, below Paige, because who knew where Paige was?

Her head jerked and her eyes snapped open. She'd fallen asleep and almost slipped off the wall. There was no point in sitting here like a big loser. She tried to remember the route to Kay's, tried to tell herself it really wasn't that far, but she knew it was going to take her well over an hour to get there on foot. She lifted her chin and made herself stumble to her feet. If she had to walk for an hour to get to Kay's, then now was a good time to get started.

Chapter 53

It took Becca more than an hour to walk. By the time she got there, her feet were almost too painful for her to stand, her hands were numb with cold and the rest of her felt as bruised and battered as if she'd been beaten up. But she'd made it. She was here, standing outside Kay's cottage in the grey afternoon light.

From the front, it barely looked touched, but as she walked round the house, she could see the smoke-blackened walls framing an upstairs window that had been just about pulled out.

They must have got Kay out from up there. She must have been trapped behind that window in the fire. It had been that close.

The front door was boarded up; the back door was locked. All the windows were closed. Becca sank down onto the step. She was here, but so far, she was no better off. It was hard to think with the shivery feeling and the way her throat ached.

And where was Jared?

She'd got the impression he was at the cottage when

she phoned him, so where had he gone? He might have come back here and if he had done, he'd probably park in the lane where his car was out of sight. She stood up, not bothering to stifle the groan her painful feet elicited, and limped the short way across the field to the side road where they'd left the car before.

And . . .

Her heart started beating fast and her spirits leaped like an instant candy flip. His car was there, right where they'd parked before. He was here, waiting for her! Her eyes flooded with tears of relief and she forgot the pain in her feet as she ran towards the side road. 'Jared! What happened? Where . . .'

And then she saw the smashed windscreen and the cut tyres. All the elation dropped away, like she'd been punched in the gut. The car wasn't here because Jared had come back. It was here because he'd never left.

For the second time in almost as many days, she found the tears pouring down her face, her nose filling up with snot, but she was fucked if she was going to stand here and cry like, like some big loser who . . .

She wiped the tears away angrily, swatting her face with her fingers again and again, but they wouldn't stop so in the end she just ignored them. Jared might not be here but his car was. The car might tell her what had happened, and it might give her what she needed – some shelter and some food.

The car doors were locked. She wiped her face again and reached in through the broken windscreen

330

to open the passenger side, then slipped into the seat. It was no warmer, but it was more comfortable. She could put something over the windscreen to keep out the cold and she might be able to sleep. As far as she could tell, Jared's stuff was still in the back of the car so there'd be a sleeping bag to climb into. Then, hardly daring to hope, she felt under the front seat and there it was, her bag.

Her phone was gone – well, Jared had taken that, she'd talked to him on it, but her purse was still there. She opened it and found her money intact. Whoever had trashed the car hadn't bothered taking anything. So why had they done it? Was Jared here when it happened? And where was he now?

A horrible sense of familiarity was starting to grow inside her. Her memory took her back to Bridlington, to the street lights wavering through the mist, to the sound of breaking glass and laughter, and her own car in the side road with its windows smashed and the tyres cut.

And Paige. Gone.

Like Jared.

Have a good time last night, then, Bex?

Not really. You?

Yeah. Smashing, weren't it, Tez?

Jared's car, which had seemed like a haven with its familiar contents and that smell she was beginning to associate with him – a mixture of smoke, spices, the outdoors – was suddenly a trap.

Moving quickly and looking round all the time, she

opened the back. She needed a sleeping bag, a blanket, anything, but someone had been there before her. All Jared's neat bundles had been pulled apart. Whoever searched the car hadn't taken her bag with her money and cards. They weren't looking for money. They were looking for something else.

There was nothing she could do here. She bundled a blanket under her arm and limped back across the field towards Kay's. She had to rest for a while, get something to eat, try and think, and the only possible place for her to do any of that was the cottage. There was nowhere else to go. There had to be a way to break in.

She moved round the cottage again, and this time she saw that one sash window was open, just slightly. She tried it; it moved and, after a bit of a struggle, came up. Collecting her stuff, she climbed over the sill and closed the window behind her.

Half an hour later, she was feeling better. She'd made herself a cheese and ketchup sandwich and was curled up in Kay's big chair, wrapped in Jared's blanket. It was almost possible to forget about the fire in this room, apart from the smell of smoke. She'd pulled the chair round so if anyone looked in, they'd just see the high back, not her, asleep, because she was going to be asleep, any minute now.

The light was fading. She took a last look around the room, and she saw it.

Her phone. She sat up abruptly, the drowsiness vanishing. Her phone was on Kay's desk, plugged into Kay's laptop.

Jared. He was the only person who could have left it here.

Relief overwhelmed her. Jared was OK. He'd been here, and he'd left her phone, left it charging from Kay's laptop. She pressed the start button, and the screen lit up. And ... yes, there was a message.

--K whatsit

She grinned, the fatigue falling away like magic. Jared. He'd gone to that Kettle place. Of course he had. Her car was there; the video had been made there. Kettlewhatsit was where they were going to find answers, so Kettlewhatsit was where she was going too. She texted back *on my way*, then stopped.

On my way was fine, but how was she going to get there? Jared's car was wrecked, her car was up there already and it would take her— she couldn't do it, couldn't walk all that way, not now, not when she hadn't slept and had been travelling all day.

Kay's car. She could borrow Kay's car. Kay wouldn't mind.

With a bit of luck, she wouldn't even know.

So where were the keys? Kay had always kept her keys on a board just inside the front door when they lived in Leeds. First place thieves would look, Matt used to say.

Then they won't smash the house up searching for them, Kay would respond.

Holding her breath, Becca went to the front door, and there it was – a board with a row of keys neatly dangling from it. Good old Kay. You could tell her a hundred times, but she'd never listen. The car keys were there.

It was time to go. All she wanted to do was find Jared. She hurried back to the living room, scooped up her bag, the keys and her phone in one armful, and then dropped everything. The keys skittered off under one of the small tables that Kay always seemed to scatter round rooms.

She crawled under it. Where were they? There was a photo frame up against the skirting. It had smashed, and the photo was on the floor. That was when she remembered what Jared had said, before the phone cut out. *I think I know who the girl is from the caravan site*, and just before he got cut off, he said, *your friend's house.*

The photograph. Jared had been here. This might be what he meant.

She turned it over.

A girl with dark hair and olive skin looked back at her, smiling cautiously at the camera. Who was this? No one Becca had ever seen ... except she had.

Her first times at the drop-in – had she seen this girl there? Was this the girl who used to come in with Paige? Was this who Jared meant, the caravan-site girl – not Paige, but this girl? Jared had sounded so sure, but would he be? Really? She studied the photograph intently. One of Kay's foster-kids, one she'd never met. In the photograph, Matt looked thin, his smile was tired – he was already ill when this was taken, so ... when? A year ago? No, more like two years.

She stuffed the photo into her bag – she didn't want to think about it now.

She didn't want to think about it ever.

Her hand closed over the keys. She picked them up, grabbed her bag and her phone and went outside into the rain and the cold. The garage wasn't locked, though the door was stiff and she had to dump all her stuff on the wet ground and wrestle with the handle.

Kay's car was a small VW. Becca had never driven it, but if she could drive Jared's car, she could drive a tiny thing like this. She got behind the wheel, and after a bit of a struggle finding reverse – something crunched against the wall when she shot forward unexpectedly – she got it out of the garage and onto the road.

It was dark and she couldn't stop herself thinking about her last drive to meet Jared, the car coming up behind her, its headlights menacing her in the rear-view mirror, getting closer, dazzling her, speeding up as she speeded up, until ...

Each time a car appeared behind her, she had to fight an impulse to put her foot down and push the VW to its limits.

There was one now. She watched the lights loom larger, then had to correct suddenly as the road curved. The other car stayed behind her and she felt herself growing tense. Then she saw the sign to Goldsborough. Should she take it, let them know where she was going? The other car was sitting on her tail.

Without signalling, she turned right, and the other

car shot past the junction, its horn blaring, and vanished into the darkness.

Just another wanker, after all.

She drove slowly along the narrow road that led to the headland. Where would Jared be? Now she was here, her certainty was fading. He hadn't replied to her text.

Someone else could have left the phone. Jared had been near the cottage when they talked. Someone else could have left the message to bring her here.

She drove past the field she'd been forced into by the black car just a few nights ago, and on past the farm house. There was a car park, she could remember that, and they'd left her car up along a rough path, sort of hidden behind an old, derelict building.

There was no sign of anyone.

She drove into the car park and stopped, reaching into her bag for her phone, but before she could find it, in her headlights she saw a familiar figure running along the path to the car park entrance.

Jared.

She dumped her bag and scrambled out of the door.

'I thought it must be you,' he said.

'Where were you? Are you all right? What happened?'

'Why didn't you call? Don't you check your voice-mail? What—?'

'I didn't know where—'

The flurry of questions faded into silence. 'I left a voicemail,' Jared said. 'To call me when you were on the road past Goldsborough.'

'I sent a text.'

'Yeah. I ... Oh, shit, what the hell. Becca.' He held out his arms and she stepped into the warmth as he wrapped his waterproof round both of them. 'Come on,' he said. 'The tent's all set up.'

Just then, she felt certain of where they were going.

Chapter 54

Kay was discharged the next morning, but by the time all the formalities had been completed, it was almost eleven. Shaun had come back to the hospital later the previous day, unasked, carrying a large bag. He'd bought her a change of clothes – *Some stuff of Sylvia's. I hope that's OK* – and a hairbrush and toiletries, including some shower gel and body lotion. He might be a bit domineering, but he was thoughtful, she'd give him that. And she'd accepted his offer of a lift – it would be ridiculous of her to make the NHS supply an ambulance when she had the offer of transport.

Her throat was still sore and the smell of smoke seemed to be lodged in her sinuses, but she felt a thousand times better. When she'd looked at herself in the mirror the day before, an old lady had looked back. Now, she saw a more familiar face. A bit of lipstick would have helped, but otherwise she was fine.

Once she had all her discharge formalities complete, she called Shaun.

'Kay! I'd just about given you up for lost. How are you?'

'Fine, no damage done. I'm ready to go home.'

'Then I'll be with you soon.'

She wasn't used to this level of care and protectiveness. Matt had always operated on the assumption she could look after herself. At the moment, she was rather enjoying Shaun's attention, but she suspected she might find it a bit claustrophobic after a while. Matt had never crowded her. He just let her get on with things.

But she had to admit to herself that it was nice to see Shaun as he breezed in, carrying the freshness of the outside into the sterile atmosphere of the hospital. She liked his confidence, his air of get up and go. He looked at her and smiled. 'You look a lot better, Kay. Right, where to? Have you decided where you want to stay?'

'I'd like to go home.'

'You can't stay in the cottage, Kay. Trust me on this one.'

'I know. But I need to go there. I want to see it. And I have to collect some things, then go to the vet's to pick Milo up – I called them, someone left him there the night of the fire.'

'Who did that? The fire service?'

'I don't know. I'm just glad someone took care of him.' She didn't tell him she'd been haunted by the image of going back to the cottage and finding Milo, abandoned, lying in a small white heap in the garden.

'And then ...? You've got somewhere to stay?'

'I've booked myself into a B & B in Scarborough

that's run by a friend of mine. She knows me, she knows Milo. I can pick up my car at the cottage and drive myself to Scarborough. Then you won't have Milo shedding hairs all over yours.' She raised her hand to silence him as he started to object. 'You did very well, Shaun, but your face – don't ever become a politician. They'd be onto you at once.'

He gave a reluctant grin. 'I admit it. I'm not the number-one fan of dogs.'

She pulled on the fleece he'd brought for her. 'Right. I'm ready when you are.'

It was good to be out of the overheated hospital. The day was grey and chilly but she relished the wind that blew spatters of rain in her face. 'You've been a real help, Shaun. Thank you.'

'Glad I could help.' He spoke a bit gruffly, as if being thanked embarrassed him. 'Here's the car.' He held the door open for her. It was a deep-blue Audi, powerful and expensive. Kay sank into the softness of the leather-smelling interior and prepared to enjoy the journey.

It took a bit of time to get out of the centre of York, but once they were on the moors, Shaun put his foot down and the car accelerated smoothly. She was barely aware of the speed. Secretly, deep down, she was a bit of a petrolhead, something she'd never admitted to Matt. A car like this, a top-of-the-range Audi, was something he'd never have aspired to – *It's just a machine for getting you around, Kay.* But she longed to get her hands on the wheel. 'Beautiful car,' she said.

He grinned. 'My baby. I promised myself one treat when I retired. It was going to be a round the world trip, but when Sylvia died . . . well, I got the car instead.'

'Yes. Your plans change, don't they.' She would never have isolated herself on the coast if she'd known it would be without Matt. But that was the way life went.

She yawned again. 'Sorry. There's something about hospitals . . .'

'Do you fancy a coffee?'

'I'd rather get back as soon as possible.' She didn't want to leave Milo any longer than necessary.

'No, I meant I've got some. In the car. I thought we might need it.'

Kay loved the idea of coffee, but she didn't want to be making loo stops across the moors. 'Later?'

'When we get to Whitby,' he agreed.

They drove in silence, and more quickly than she would have thought possible, they were pulling into the side of the road outside the cottage.

All the other thoughts were pushed out of her head as Kay looked at her home. At first glance, there was no obvious damage, but then she saw the boarded-up door and the ruined upstairs window. 'How do I get in?'

'I had a look round when I picked up your bag. The door's intact round the back. Was your key in your bag?'

Kay nodded, and climbed slowly out of the car. She had never felt settled at the cottage, but it had been her home for over a year and now it was close to derelict. The tasks ahead were starting to weigh on her – the

341

cottage would have to be repaired, cleaned, redecorated. All her stuff – what could be retrieved and what was damaged beyond saving?

And the implications of arson had other consequences. Would her insurance company pay out, or would she have to wait for a court case, or a full police investigation? Was her home covered? She had no idea. The house was her most valuable asset – all her money was tied up in it. If she lost it . . .

She followed Shaun to the back of the house and let herself in. The acrid smell of smoke hit her in the face, taking her straight back to that night, trapped in the room, the fire outside the door, the window impassable. She had to step back outside and take a few deep breaths to calm herself down.

'Steady.' Shaun's hand touched her elbow, offering support if she needed it.

'I'm OK.' It was just the shock of first seeing it.

'It's not too bad downstairs. In the front room you wouldn't really know, apart from the smell.' Shaun was being determinedly cheerful.

Kay followed him through, looking round. The kitchen was more or less untouched, and she lingered, putting off the moment when she would have to see the full extent of the damage. She noticed a plate and cutlery in the sink that she hadn't left. Someone had been there. Someone had made themselves a sandwich. She checked the bin. Someone had been eating bread and cheese. And tomato sauce.

Becca. Becca loved cheese and ketchup sandwiches.

She must have come back here – Kay remembered Becca at the hospital, something about her having left her phone and her bag ... her memories of that night were still dark and confused. But Becca must have come back here to collect her things.

'Is everything all right?' Shaun called from the front room.

'Yes. I'm just checking.' She braced herself, and went through.

Everything stank of smoke. The door to the stairs and the wall around it were black with soot. The room was in disarray, as if people had stormed through it – which they probably had. Everything was familiar and everything was strange. Her laptop was still on the desk, her comfortable chair was – actually, it was in a different place, moved, so the high back was to the window. She had a sudden vision of Becca curled up in it, asleep, a plate smeared with tomato sauce on the floor beside her.

The stairs were impassable. All her stuff was up there, and even if she could get through, her clothes would carry the smell of the fire and be unwearable. For tonight, her friend Maggie would supply her. In the end, she packed her laptop and charger into her bag, grabbed some tins of food for Milo, his lead and his blanket, and she was done.

'Is that everything?' Shaun said.

'I just want to talk to the vet.' She made the call, following Shaun out of the door as she did so. Milo was fine, it seemed, and could be collected any time up to six.

One knot of worry untied itself.

343

As they walked up the path, Shaun stopped abruptly. 'What's happened to your car?'

The garage was open, and the car was gone. They'd wrecked her house, and taken her Beetle. Why would they steal her tatty old car? Then she realised what must have happened.

She knew Becca had been here. Who else would let themselves into her house and eat cheese and ketchup sandwiches? Becca knew where Kay had kept her keys in the Leeds house, so it wouldn't be hard to find them here. She had no idea why Becca would take her car, and right now, she couldn't be bothered to work it out, but she didn't want Shaun getting militant on her behalf. 'Do you know, I completely forgot. It's in for servicing. I'd better give them a ring – they'll be wondering what's happened to me.'

'Well, don't worry about it. I can take you down to Scarborough. And stop to pick up the dog. Milo,' he added quickly.

'I could easily—'

'I'm not taking no for an answer. You'll wait hours for a taxi. What's the point?'

He was right. She was being stupid, and anyway, a taxi driver wouldn't be willing to take Milo. Sliding back into the leather comfort of the car was a relief. She waited while he put her things in the boot. Much more of this, and she'd get used to it.

'OK. Let's go and pick up Milo.' She yawned – despite what she'd told the doctor, and Shaun, the fire had taken its toll. Claiming fatigue hadn't been an excuse – she was knackered. 'Do you know where the vet's is?'

'Yes. Do you want that coffee now? There's a thermos in the glove box.'

She laughed. 'Shaun, you're a hero.'

He grinned, looking pleased. 'There's two cups – pour me one as well, will you?'

She took out the flask and poured two cups, putting one in the cup holder on the seat between them. The comforting fragrance filled the car. The coffee was hot and rich, just what she'd been wanting. She could forgive a lot of Shaun's over-protectiveness for coffee as good as this.

Shaun glanced at his watch. 'What time does the vet close?'

'It's an all-night place, but I don't think they do discharges after six.'

'OK. I'm a bit low on fuel – we've got time to get a fill-up before we collect the dog if that's all right with you?'

'That's fine. Drink your coffee.'

She was feeling pleasantly drowsy as they drove through the darkening streets. Where was the best place for him to get petrol in Whitby? There used to be small garages everywhere where you could refuel, but these days you needed a supermarket or a motorway services or . . .

She and Matt used to travel miles on their motorbikes – a bike could go all week without refuelling, could go from John o' Groats to . . .

Everyone said John o' Groats when they talked about long distances. John o' Quotes ... John o'Boats ... John o'Stoats ...

Milo saw a stoat once when she and Matt were ... she couldn't remember. Her mind was all over ...

'Matt ...?' she said.

'It's fine,' he replied. 'Everything's fine.'

Chapter 55

Jared woke shortly after six. The storm had blown all night, rattling the tent, the rain drumming down on the canvas, but now everything was quiet. Becca's head was pillowed on his arm, her hair moving slightly with her breath. Carefully, making sure he didn't disturb her, he eased his arm out from under her and she murmured in her sleep, burrowing herself deeper into the sleeping bag.

He stretched, testing his body. Knees? Sore. Back? Ditto. Aching joints and limbs? All present and correct. General feeling as though he'd been run over by a train? Right here and ready for duty. So why did he feel as if he could run a marathon? Two marathons.

Today, despite everything, he felt good.

It was still dark. He switched on the lamp, keeping the brightness low. Becca's face was a pale circle on the pillow, shadows of exhaustion under her eyes. The scar that ran from the side of her nose to her lip stood out and he wondered, not for the first time, what the story behind that was.

Last night, Becca had been close to collapse. She was cold, exhausted and hungry, and when they got to the tent he'd got her into one of the sleeping bags and given her some hot soup and a couple of doorsteps of bread. She hadn't managed to eat much, but the soup and a mug of tea revived her a bit. 'Do you want to tell me about it?' he asked.

'Not now.' She shook her head, looking puzzled and lost. As he moved across the tent and knelt down beside her, he could feel the tension in her. Very gently, he moved the hair away from her face. 'What's wrong?'

She turned and looked at him. 'I – people aren't always what they seem, you know?'

He did know. He'd learned some hard lessons himself, but maybe not as hard as the ones Becca had faced. 'Listen. You don't ever have to worry with me.'

She held his gaze for a long time before she nodded and held the sleeping bag open by way of invitation. There didn't seem much else to say, then.

An hour later Becca was asleep, her head on Jared's arm, the sleeping bag rumpled up around them. Moving carefully, so as not to disturb her, he straightened it out as best he could and pulled the other sleeping bag over them.

Even though he was tired, he hadn't been able to sleep and had lain awake, watching Becca, thinking about the events of the past twenty-four hours, and trying to anticipate what the next twenty-four would bring. At some stage, he must have fallen asleep as well, and he'd slept deeply and dreamlessly until morning.

Now, sitting in the tent awning with a mug of tea in his hands, he tried to make sense of the past few days. Becca had come into his life with the Furies at her heels and since then she'd lost her job, almost lost the woman she thought of as her mother and made her way back – without transport, communication or money – from York to an isolated place like Kettleness. And she was still standing, still swinging punches.

If he was going to help her, he needed to work out what was going on. He was starting to make sense of it. There was a connection between Becca and Kay, and between Kay and the girl who had been attacked.

Those parties at the caravan site – he should have thought about this before. GBH had jumped down his throat when he'd mentioned them – they had to be something to do with all of this. Drugs? Sex? Both? You could get away with a lot at that site in the winter.

And in the summer, who would go there? Even if they tarted it up a bit, it still wouldn't offer much compared to other sites on the coast. Jared suspected there was some kind of land-sale scam at work – run the value down, then let a dummy company pick it up for a song, get the tax break on the loss – it was how these things worked. But in the meantime, GBH had to make a living.

And there was a marketable asset in the town – the kids who came with homeless families to the B & Bs, or the kids who came on their own – a community of the vulnerable. They were a commodity. You could – what was the word? – monetise them. Offer them cash, offer them drugs – shit, affection was probably enough – and get what you wanted in return.

Sex.

And anyone who stepped out of line – Jared had seen what they did to them.

But why mutilate them like that? A quick slap would do it with most of these girls. And how did Becca and Kay fit in? Why the fire, the dedicated pursuit? His father would have told him to follow the money. But how much would anyone make from sex parties in a caravan on a site near Bridlington? Not enough to risk a murder charge. It didn't make sense.

The pale grey of the clouds began to appear on the horizon and the sky became a deep purple that faded into blue as the light of the rising sun bled into it.

He had to decide what to do. The sensible thing would be to tell the police what he'd found at Kay's, then he and Becca could both get the fuck out, head off somewhere miles away and sort themselves out. He was feeling better already, and in a few days he'd be over the worst of his withdrawal as long as he could keep off the pills. He'd done the right thing, chucking them. If he had any here with him now, though . . .

Or a joint, or his whisky.

All back in the car.

He had to do something to take his mind off it. He thought about the video. Their original plan had been to come back here and try and locate the cave.

Maybe it was time to get started on that.

He looked back into the tent. Becca was still asleep. There was no need to wake her up – she'd probably still be asleep by the time he got back. He had his boots, his helmet and a spare, head torches, some rope and a few bolts. It wasn't much, but it should be enough.

He scribbled a note for Becca – *7.30 Gone for a walk* – then headed off towards the crumbling cliffs of the Ness, the light from his torch illuminating the uneven ground. There were places on the Ness where the remains of the old mine workings could be seen. They weren't readily accessible. The path down the cliff had long since been washed away and there was just a rope to get you onto the beach.

As he walked towards the point, the shadows faded in the dawn and he could see where the land fell away and the low scrub thinned. Soon, his boots were crunching on shale. The cliff dropped away, and he had to lean into the slope and make sure his footing was secure as he moved across the cliff face.

Like something long forgotten, the rat inside him stirred, and Jared welcomed it like an old friend.

Right now, he needed the rat.

There was evidence of workings here – lines of stone, the remains of a wall, then – he was getting close – a buried arch falling off the cliff edge. He closed his eyes, bringing the video back into his mind. The camera went up a slope, and then down into a gully . . .

There was a slope to his left. He scrambled up it and

found himself on a narrow ledge that dropped down a bit, and then . . .

It was there.

There was a low arch hidden by the undulations of the cliff face. It had probably been buried like the other one, but someone had dug it out, opening up what must have been the entrance to a mine. It was invisible from the beach, and from the clifftop. The only way you would find it was sheer luck – or if, like him, you suspected it was here.

Jared slid down the slope and shone his torch into the hole. From the video, he expected to see water, but all he could make out was a tunnel that slanted down, half full of rubble. He shone his torch up at the roof: first question if you see rubble – where did it come from? But the roof was intact. He didn't like the look of it, though. It wouldn't take much to bring it down. But it wasn't roof fall that had blocked the tunnel.

Now he had to decide what to do. His first instinct was to go in and recce, but the memory of what had happened – and what had almost happened – in the side tunnel a few days ago remained strong. And if the whole lot came down on his head, or if he hurt himself and got trapped, Becca would have no idea where he was. From her point of view, he would just have vanished. She might even think he had run out on her. What had he left behind after all? Just a scruffy old tent and some bits and pieces. He'd promised her. *You don't have to worry with me.* He wasn't leaving her to face Greaseball Harry and whoever else was working with him on her own.

This was Becca's story. He had to go back, tell her, see what she wanted to do. He was going in there, no question, but he wasn't doing it until he'd told her what he'd found.

Chapter 56

Becca sat in the entrance to the tent, waiting for Jared to come back. Gone for a walk? Yeah, right. Who did he think she was? Some kind of moron? He'd gone hunting for the place in the video. Part of her wanted to go after him, but another part, a stronger part, was happy to sit here with her hands round a mug of tea, gazing out at the winter landscape.

It was nothing really – just a grey field, a lot of sky and the sea – no sand, no sun, no ice cream or candy floss. The grey of the tent flaps seemed to blend into the surroundings. A motorbike was parked up by the tent – she hadn't seen it in the night. Jared must be using it for transport after his car was damaged. She wondered vaguely where he'd got it from, but it wasn't a big deal. It was peaceful here, and after the struggles of yesterday, peaceful was good. She checked her phone. Not having it had been like being blind in one eye, or deaf in one ear.

There was a text from Kay. She felt the tight band of worry that had been there since she left the hospital loosen. If Kay was texting, then she must be better. Becca looked at the message:

--Out of hospital. Fine. Staying with a friend. Come and see me. I've got something to tell you. xxx.

There was also a Whitby address.

Kay was the only person she knew who texted with punctuation – but she'd sent kisses. That wasn't like Kay. She must still be feeling rough, but at least she was OK. That was one worry off Becca's mind, but now there was another.

Her and Jared.

All her life, after Him, she'd had to be on her guard. In the secure unit, on the streets, in foster care, there were always men who said they were like your dad, or your brother, or your boyfriend, and you had to just . . . Becca saw what happened to the kids who didn't watch out. She had a bad feeling that Paige was one of them, that Paige, for all she seemed to know her way about, had let her guard down.

Last night, Jared had got closer to her than anyone ever had. She realised she trusted him, though she wasn't sure why. Jared was a fuck-up and a pill-head – he admitted as much – and he did stupid things. He was likely to kill himself one day. She didn't want to be so close to him, then lose him.

She'd lost too many people. Her mother. Matt. Kay, almost.

Halloween in Leeds. There was her and Ashley and the rest of the crowd, and they were going clubbing all dressed up in witchy stuff and they were all a bit high.

She and Ashley were walking arm in arm, and they were chanting something – she couldn't remember what it was or what had started it, but she could remember the sense of belonging, the sense of being enclosed within a group.

And now Ashley hated her, the rest of the crowd didn't want to know her. She'd probably never see them again.

She realised she didn't mind too much. Whatever happened, she didn't want to go back to that life, to college, to clubbing, to planning careers and places to live and all of that shit. Despite the discomfort and the difficult times, she was enjoying the random life Jared lived.

She couldn't make her mind up about him. There was something eating Jared the way there was something eating her. It made her wary about trusting anything. Even Kay, sometimes. She just couldn't. And it made Jared do the crazy things that that had almost killed him.

Maybe that's what he wanted.

And what did she want? The same as Jared? To always keep moving?

To die?

She wrapped the blanket round her more closely. It was almost nine o'clock. She emptied her mug onto the grass and stood up. She could see someone walking along the cliff path, coming from the headland. As she watched, the anonymous figure resolved itself into Jared in boots and a fleece, carrying a backpack, which he hitched off and dumped on the ground beside her as he came up to the tent. He tugged her hair gently as he sat down beside her. 'You OK?'

She nodded.

'Any of that left?' he said, pointing at her mug.

'I'll make some more. Did you find it?'

'How did . . .? Never mind.' He sat down and waited as she boiled the kettle again and made some coffee.

She listened as he described the opening into the mine, halfway down the cliff face.

'Why would they build a mine on the cliff face?'

'They didn't. When it was built, there was more land. The entrance would have been at ground level. But the cliff's fallen since then. There used to be a village here – the whole lot fell into the sea, hundred or more years ago. There's just the opening now.'

'So . . . what are we going to do?'

He sighed, running his hand through his hair as he thought. 'I'm not sure. It's hidden – you can't see it until you're on top of it. I don't think it would have been left open like that when the mine closed – it'd have been filled in with shale to block the entrance, you know? Someone's dug it out, and fairly recently by the looks of it.'

'Yeah. OK.' He was going all around the houses with this.

'It won't be safe, is what I'm saying. Look, I can go in there – I've got the equipment, I know what I'm doing . . .'

'Is that how you put yourself in hospital, knowing what you're doing?'

'That's right. I know what I'm doing and I still put myself in hospital. Let me go in and check it out. Then if there's anything there, if it's safe, you can—'

She stood up. 'Bullshit. You're going, I'm going. Paige is my friend. She gave the video to me, not you.'

He looked as if he was going to argue some more, then he shrugged. 'OK. It's up to you. But you're not going in if you haven't got the right equipment. I can fix you up with a helmet and a torch, but you'll need waterproofs, something warm and some decent boots.' She could tell from his face that he thought he'd just won the argument.

It was true, her feet were still killing her, but she'd gone back to Kay's car and found what she expected in the back – Kay's walking gear.

Half an hour later, scrambling across the cliff face, she looked down the uneven slope to the rocks on the beach far below and wondered if this was such a good idea. But it was too late to change her mind now.

Chapter 57

Jared looked at the arch uneasily. It was low with almost no curve, which meant the roof of the tunnel would be shallow. Tunnels were supposed to form a perfect arch that balanced all the different forces working on them. This place had not been constructed with safety in mind. After all, who cared about a few miners getting buried? And it had had no maintenance for decades. The structure wasn't stable, not like the railway tunnels, and the cliff itself was collapsing, which meant that the tunnel was changing constantly.

Déjà vu twisted his stomach into a knot, taking him back to a deep shaft and a side tunnel, a series of pitches and squeezes and an over-confident twat who thought he knew what he was doing, who was supposed to be in charge as he led his mate to his death.

'Are you sure you want to do this?' he said to Becca. She'd been looking uneasy ever since they moved onto the cliff, and her expression was apprehensive as she studied the crumbling face and the half-buried entrance.

She nodded.

'You don't have to come. I can go in on my own.'

'I'm coming in.'

'OK. We go in carefully. If I say we're getting out, we get out. Fast.'

She nodded again, biting her lip. It was good she was scared. She might listen to him. He checked to make sure her helmet was firmly on and her head torch was working. 'Wait until I call,' he said, then switched on his own torch, ducked down to get under the low arch and let himself slide through, controlling his movement with the rope.

He found himself in a small chamber, roughly hewn out of the rock. He had to stoop, the roof was so low. A black stalactite hung almost to the ground. Jared skirted it. The mine went deeper into the cliff.

'How's it going?' Becca was whispering from the entrance.

'Give me a few minutes, and then you can come down.'

There was a tunnel directly opposite. Jared picked his way across the chamber and shone his light down to the end. It didn't look promising – either it was blocked by roof fall, or it was a dead end.

Roof fall. He looked up. Rocks and shale and some brick reinforcement – it didn't inspire a lot of confidence.

There was a second tunnel from the chamber, leading off to the left, south-west by Jared's reckoning. This tunnel looked as if it went somewhere. It was the same height as the chamber to start with, just about, but the roof became lower at the tunnel went on – they'd have to crawl if they wanted to go through. He could see some twisting in the line of the passage that was almost certainly caused by torsion in the unstable cliff – in ten years' time he doubted this place would be here, but it should stand for a few more years. It would stand today.

Probably.

'OK,' he said to Becca. 'Come on, but it's a bit tight in places.'

Charlie. Hating the squeezes.

He held the rope as she slithered into the tunnel, and soon she appeared in the entrance to the chamber. 'You do this for fun?' she asked. But her attempt at bravado failed as her voice cracked on the question.

'Not today.' Jared directed his head torch so that it illuminated the south tunnel. 'We need to go that way. We can stand at the beginning, but the roof comes down so we'll have to crawl eventually. I'm not sure what's through there.'

He led the way past some more stalactites – impossibly slender, maybe a metre long or more. For a moment, he forgot why they were there and stopped to look at one. It was formed from some kind of crystal, the same white and brown that had covered the ceiling over the years. There must be iron in the rocks.

He heard Becca moving behind him. 'OK?' he asked.

'Yeah.'

The roof came low as he moved into the tunnel. He hunkered down, his back aching at the movement, and said, 'We crawl from here. We'll take a rope, let me go first and don't follow until I signal – three sharp tugs on the rope, and it's OK to come through.'

'What if . . . never mind.'

'If anything goes wrong, get out of here and get some help. Got it?'

She nodded, scowling at the passage ahead. She looked scared and he couldn't blame her.

Jared went forwards on his hands and knees, and began his crawl through the tunnel. It went round a corner, then opened up into another low chamber, which opened up into . . . something magical.

The light of his head torch filled the room with a strange, greenish shimmer. For a moment, he didn't understand what he was seeing, then it came together.

Water.

His heart leaped. Flooding. Like the tunnel where he and Charlie . . . but it wasn't flood water. He was looking at a stone pool that almost filled the width of the chamber. The water reflected the roof and walls, still as glass. It was the pool from the video, and it was beautiful. He dropped a pebble in and ripples spread, making the light on the roof dance. The pebble vanished, and thick mud clouded up from the bottom.

He could feel a draught blowing on his face from deeper in the mine, on the other side of the pool, but the air smelt thick and sour. They'd have to be careful. Remembering why he was here, he gave the rope three sharp tugs, and in a minute, Becca was crawling through behind him.

'What is it?' Becca spoke in a whisper that seemed to fill the low, arched space.

'It's part of an old mine.' Jared had heard of these pools, even seen images, but he had no idea there was one here. 'It's a cistern where they washed the stuff they dug up.'

'There was a flower, a kind of silk flower.' Becca was looking round her. 'Remember. On the video. It was in the water.'

The water stretched from wall to wall, the cistern divided by three bars that were raised about a foot above the surface. It was impossible to tell how deep it was. 'What are you doing?' Jared asked.

Becca had pulled her boots off and was about to slide her foot into the pool.

'We've got to go across there, haven't we? I'm going to wade over and—'

'Hang on. It could be over your head.'

'No it's shallow—'

'It isn't. Take my word for it, OK? We agreed – tunnels, my thing. You do it my way.'

'Yeah, well, I thought you were the kind of guy who's all, you know, *let's go*, not *oh no, I might hurt myself.*'

'I'm all *let's get out of here alive.* If you get wet, you're going to get cold really quickly. Next thing you know, you've got hypothermia. We've got more to explore – there's another tunnel the other side of this.'

He squatted at the side of the water, thinking. Someone must have come through here before them. Someone had filmed it, though whoever it was didn't seem to have got beyond this point. But there must be something beyond this – or someone thought there was. Otherwise, what was the point of the film? And the flower – what did the flower mean?

Jared shone his torch around again, aware that Becca was watching him. 'What are you looking for?' she said.

'We need to get across,' he said, more to himself than to Becca. He didn't trust his own judgement. Twice, three times he'd missed things recently, things that had got them into trouble. He couldn't afford to do that here.

He studied the problem. There was a narrow ledge running along the length of the cistern and . . . a rope hugging the wall a few feet above it. Someone had slung a rope along the wall to provide a hand hold. Getting across wouldn't be difficult. The main danger would be the rope pulling away under their grip and sending them plunging into the water. He nodded towards the ledge.

'We can use that. I'll go first – I can test it.' She opened her mouth to object. 'Don't be stupid, Becca. I do this. I know about ropes.'

She nodded.

He pulled himself up onto the ledge and began edging along above the water, checking the anchors as he went. They all looked secure, but he put some extra ones in anyway – he didn't want Becca putting her faith in something that would pull away if she needed it.

When he got to the far end of the cistern, he found a ledge that was wide enough for both of them to stand on, and a low tunnel leading away. Another crawl. He debated checking it out before Becca came across. The sour, heavy smell filled the tunnel. He snapped his lighter on and the flame flickered in the draught, but it burned a clear, bright yellow. The air smelt bad, but it wouldn't kill them.

'Come over,' he called. Five minutes later, Becca stepped off the narrow ledge to stand beside him. Her nose wrinkled. 'Something stinks.'

'Yeah.' He wasn't worried about foul air now. He was worried about the smell and what might be causing it.

The passage was narrow and, in places, the roof came down low. It was a mining tunnel – they didn't dig for space, but they must have brought the rock through here. It had been wider once. The roof must have slipped.

They shouldn't be here.

Adrenaline had cleared the withdrawal fuzz from Jared's head. He felt alert, on edge, watchful, but his sense of direction had gone. Were they heading along the shoreline, or had the tunnel been driven inland? He tried to reorient himself.

And then he was out of the tunnel. He scrambled to his feet. Above him, way beyond the reach of his outstretched arm, was a crumbling ceiling, crystal formations glittering as the light of his torch swept across them. From the ceiling, slender stalactites hung, some no wider than his finger, ready to break at a touch.

The smell was stronger here.

He turned slowly, aware of Becca getting to her feet

beside him. She didn't speak, just turned her head, looking around her. 'What is it?' Then she turned sharply, sending the light from her headlamp in a beam across the darkness. Her hand dug into his arm. 'There's people!' she hissed.

Jared knew there would be. With a sense of inevitability, he turned in the direction she'd been looking and he could see them, two figures slumped against the wall, one half-lying on the ground, one with its head bowed towards drawn-up knees. He kept his light steady on them. They didn't move.

Chapter 58

Two girls alone in the dark. The one against the wall sat with her head resting on her raised knees; the other one lay on her back, her hair a dark mass around her head.

Jared ran his light across the supine body until it reached her face, then he turned away. Becca, coming up behind him, looked towards them, the light of her head torch holding steady. Her fingers still dug into his arm.

The face was decayed almost to the bone, but not quite, not enough. There was enough of it left to tell the story of what had happened to her. The teeth were bared, some dark growth of decay crept across the remains of the eyes, but the face itself had been torn away leaving just this death mask framed by long, dark hair. And twined in that hair he could see the remains of a garland of silk flowers – like a bridal headdress. No, more like the crown of flowers you might weave through your hair at a music festival, or for a brides-maid or a May Queen.

Jared forced himself to look more closely. Both girls had the remains of ropes around them – as if their wrists and ankles had been tied and the ropes cut but not removed before they were left here.

Left here dead, or left here to die? He didn't know.

Becca held her torch on the second body, the one slumped forward, her head resting on her knees, her arms touching the ground. One leg was bent at an awkward angle – broken, he thought, as if she'd been in a fall. 'It isn't Paige.' She sounded oddly calm and distant. And then her voice broke. 'I thought it was Paige.'

He pulled her into his arms and pressed her face against his shoulder. 'We need to get out of here,' he said gently. They'd found what they'd come looking for. The sooner they got out, the better. In this tunnel – in that silent presence – he couldn't think. He could barely speak.

He turned to lead the way out, then checked to make sure Becca was following. They made their way back through the tunnel to the cistern chamber, where they slumped down onto the ledge, knocking loose pebbles into the water as they sat. Becca put her face in her hands, but when she spoke her voice was calm. 'It doesn't make any sense – I don't get it.'

'What's not to get?' Jared felt a rage inside him he had never felt before. What had they done to those girls? Used them, ripped their faces off and dumped them like so much rubbish. The crown of flowers was an obscene joke. His fists were clenched, his nails digging into his palms. He wanted to hit someone, pound his fist into flesh again and again and again.

'We need to get out of here. We've got to let someone know.'

'Wait. I've got to tell you what happened in York.'

He listened with growing alarm as she told him about her visit to the police. 'They were OK, until they went out to look some stuff up. When they came back, it was different. They knew about – some stuff, from when I was a kid, and they knew I'd had a fight with Kay. It didn't mean anything,' she said as he looked surprised. 'I always have fights with Kay. And they knew about you. They showed me your website. They said you had pictures of me on it.'

Jared opened his mouth to respond, then closed it. 'What?'

'Pictures of me. On your site.'

'Like fuck. Like fuck I do. I haven't been on my site for a week. You really think ...?' Oh, Jesus. He remembered his missing laptop. His website was wide open now.

'It wasn't you, I already worked that out. Someone's messing us around and it's someone who can get into places. It's someone the police listen to. If we go to them ... Jared, I'm afraid they'll ...' Her hands picked at her trousers. 'I won't let them lock me up.' For the first time since he'd met her, she couldn't hide the fear she was feeling.

'They won't lock us up. Hang on. Wait here.'

He checked that his camera was still in his pocket,

and made his way back into the tunnel. The police couldn't argue with photographs. He'd go back, get some close-up shots of the bodies in the chamber.

It only took minutes before he was in the chamber again. This time, the figures evoked pity rather than horror. What had happened to them after the attack? How long before they died?

Then, as he moved across the rocky floor, reaching for his camera, he heard sounds.

The scrape of heavy boots on stone. Stertorous breathing from the tunnel, from the cistern chamber.

Someone was coming.

Chapter 59

Jesus Christ! What were the chances? It had to be whoever had put these girls here. Where was Becca? There
hadn't been any sound of trouble. She must have managed to duck out of sight. He looked round – nothing
that would make a weapon, just ... there was a faint
glimmer of light in the darkness.

He extinguished his own light and slid backwards
until he was in the shadow between a rock and the
wall. It was the only concealment he could find.

He could hear feet crunching on loose stone as
someone emerged from the tunnel. Light shone
through the narrow entrance, throwing shadows
across the walls.

The bulky figure of a man, a silhouette behind his
torch, moved slowly into the chamber. He stopped in
the entrance, frowning like someone who wasn't sure of
his way, looking round. He shone his light up towards
the roof where it vanished in the uneven shadows, then
moved it slowly around the chamber focusing on the
dark recesses and hollows.

The light fell onto the two girls, and the man nodded, walking across the chamber as if he was suddenly in familiar surroundings. He stood above them, staring down, and then ...

One of them moved. The girl who had been slumped with her head on her knees – her head lifted, turning blindly towards the new sound.

Still alive. One of them was still alive. Oh, Jesus Christ, how could he not have known?

He heard the man sigh, the impatient, irritated sigh of someone who was being made to wait too long for service. He shoved the torch into his belt, and before Jared could move, grabbed the girl's hair and put a gun against her head. The sound of the shot filled the chamber, and dust, and then a shower of small stones trickled down from the roof. The torch fell to the ground and began to flicker. Jared's ears rang. The man straightened up, letting the girl's body slump back onto the ground, shaking his head in obvious disbelief. 'Fucking mess,' he said.

Then he scooped up the torch and shook it until the flickering stopped. In the jumping light, Jared saw his face.

Greaseball Harry. GBH. The gun was in his hand, ready to be used. Jared, cold with shock, somehow pressed himself back into the shadow. The reverberations of the gunshot had brought down a trickle of shale from the fragile roof. Another one might bury them both alive, and Becca too, in the cistern chamber.

He tried to project a message to Becca. *Get out!*

Now! It was useless, he knew it was useless but it was all he could do.

Then GBH left the chamber, passing so close to Jared's hiding place he could have touched him. He went on down the tunnel, deeper into the mine.

The scraping sound of movement faded away, leaving darkness and silence.

Chapter 60

Kay felt sick, very sick, and her head was aching. She seemed to be coming back from nowhere, from a blackness with no memory to anchor to. Light speared through her closed lids, and she moved her head to try and relieve the pain, but it surged in an agonising pounding.

Oh, God. What had happened? Where was she?

Slowly, slowly, it was starting to come back to her. The fire, the hospital, driving back with Shaun ... then ...

She opened her eyes, squinting against the light. She was lying on a bed in a spacious room. It had a slanted ceiling with a skylight that was shaded by a blind. As her eyes adjusted, she realised the light wasn't really so bright – she was just hypersensitive to it. Everything was pale – the walls, the wood floor, the cushions on the chair by her bed – the kind of impersonal decor you'd find in a hotel, or ...

Supporting her aching head, she rolled over and sat up. There was a glass of water beside the bed and she was suddenly aware of a raging thirst. Her instinct was to gulp the water down, but if she did, she'd just bring it back up, so she sipped it cautiously.

OK, it was time to find out where she was. She was just gathering her resources to stand up – her head-ache was settling and she knew standing up would send it into a frenzy of pounding – when the door opened slowly, there was a gentle tap and Shaun looked into the room.

'Kay. I'm sorry. I thought you'd still be asleep. Can I come in?'

'Yes. I . . .'

'Are you still feeling rough? I should have taken you straight to your friend's last night. I could have collected the dog, got your stuff.'

'What . . .'

'Happened? You passed out on me.' He sketched a grin, but she could see the worry in his eyes. 'Hasn't happened to me since I was twenty. One minute we were talking, next minute you were gone. I brought you here and called my doctor.'

'Here?'

'Sorry. Sorry. My house. You haven't been here before, have you? He's coming back this morning to check you're all right.'

Kay closed her eyes and waited for the pounding in her head to subside. 'Your doctor?' she finally managed.

'I thought you should be back in hospital but he said it was best you not be moved. He said it was just exhaustion and a reaction to the smoke. That you'd come round fine with a good night's sleep. He's calling in a bit later this morning. Why don't you rest until then – I can send up some breakfast if you like?'

Kay made an involuntary gesture of revulsion. 'Nothing. Thank you. Just some more water. And some paracetamol if you've got any.'

'He said paracetamol as well as sleep. Apparently, you can get epic headaches after smoke inhalation. Here.' He put a foil sheet of pills on the table by the bed. 'If you want a shower, there's a bathroom through there.' He pointed to a door next to the one he'd come in by. 'There's everything you need.'

'Maggie? She was expecting me last night.'

'I called her. Don't worry. I had to get her number from your phone – I hope you don't mind.'

'And Milo?'

'I'm afraid he had to spend another night at the vet's. If you're OK, we can get him later today. I'll leave you to come round a bit.'

Kay nodded. She'd barely taken half of this in. It was hard to concentrate – her mind kept drifting away.

The door closed quietly behind him and she was left on her own. She was glad he wasn't badgering her with lots of questions and advice. She'd never enjoyed being coddled. When she was ill, or when Matt had been ill for that matter, they retired into solitude until they were fit for human company again.

She picked up the sheet of pills he'd left. She couldn't think for the pain in her head. The first thing she needed to do was get it under some kind of control, then she'd have a shower, call Maggie and get over there as soon as she could. Shaun was being very kind, but . . .

But what? Something was making her uneasy and she needed to pin down what it was. She popped a couple of pills out of the foil and swallowed them, gagging as they caught in her throat.

Just taking them gave her a boost. She went into the bathroom, pulled off her clothes and stood under the shower. The water seemed to clear some of her confusion. She shampooed her hair, relieved to feel the grime from the fire and the hospital washing away, and stepped out feeling about ten years younger. The headache was still there, and the nausea, but she felt much better.

OK. Plans. Call Maggie and arrange to move there this morning. Shaun's doctor could wait – she'd rather see her own. Arrange to collect Milo. And call Becca. She had no idea where Becca was or how much she knew, but she needed warning about the police, who seemed to be on the lookout for an easy scapegoat.

Wrapping herself in the dressing gown – soft, thick, fleecy and warm – Kay went to find her phone. Her bag was on the pale wood dresser, but her phone wasn't there.

Shaun said he'd taken it to get Maggie's number, but surely he'd . . .

Dizzy. She felt really dizzy. She shook her head to clear it, holding on to the edge of the basin. What was this? Had she hit her head during the fire? Had she got concussion? Was she going to collapse here on the floor where she could be left for a couple of hours before anyone thought to . . .

Just . . .

A wave of drowsiness swept over her, its intensity making her shiver. She fought to keep her mind on track. *This is important!* a voice in her head kept insisting. It was as if part of her had split away and barged in through an office door in her brain and was banging on the desk and shouting at her.

What exactly had happened last night? She'd felt too ill to think about it, really think about it, but it didn't make any sense. They hadn't said anything at the hospital about after-effects of the fire; nothing about passing out, about headaches and sickness and . . .

She'd been fine. She had just been feeling a bit tired, looking forward to picking up Milo, getting to Maggie's and maybe having a glass of wine with an old friend before she went to bed. Getting life back to normal.

They'd been driving into Whitby, to the vet.

No. Shaun wanted to go and get petrol, and they had been heading . . . She screwed her face up trying to remember. Her thoughts kept drifting away from her.

He'd been driving away from the coast, heading inland. And then he'd offered her coffee. *There's two cups – pour me one as well, will you?*

What she was thinking was crazy. It couldn't be. Shaun had drunk the coffee too, he couldn't . . .

No. She hadn't actually *seen* him drink any, but she'd finished hers – the entire cup. And then she'd started feeling weird – and then nothing until she woke up here, at Shaun's, with a massive headache.

The pills! What had she taken just now? She dragged herself across the bathroom to the toilet bowl and stuck her fingers down her throat until she threw up, until her stomach was empty and she was retching nothing. It was too late, but if any of the pills remained in her stomach, they were gone.

Then she staggered to the bed and lay down. She was vaguely aware, before the pills carried her away, of the door opening briefly, and then closing again.

Chapter 61

As soon as the footsteps faded into silence, Jared was across the chamber to the girl, but he already knew he was too late. She was dead.

Jared's head was reeling.

Just like that.

Killed. Like a rat.

And Becca? Was she lying in the cistern chamber, a bullet in her brain? There was a scraping sound from the tunnel, and the first glow of a light. He stood up, bracing himself.

Becca emerged from the passage, jumping to her feet, her arm raised, ready to throw the stone she was holding. Then she saw him, and her hand dropped. 'I heard . . . I thought he'd . . .' Her face was very pale. He felt his throat constrict. Becca, charging to his rescue in this bleak and dangerous place, prepared to fight a gunman with a stone.

'Becca. You're safe. Oh Christ. Did he see you?' It was an inane question. If GBH had seen Becca, she would be dead.

'I heard him coming so I just kind of went into the shadows. He didn't realise there was anyone there. It's him, isn't it, that guy from the caravan site? I heard a – like an explosion. What happened?'

He had to get her out of there. He had to get them both out of there. The photos would have to wait. He couldn't risk the flash from the camera – fuck knew where GBH had gone, but wherever it was, it was too close. 'Yeah. He's the one who's been following us. I think. And he had something to do with the fire at your friend's. I don't know where he's gone, but he'll be coming back. We need to get out.'

Becca looked across at the bodies lying against the wall. She moved towards them, and Jared stopped her. It was bad enough that he'd carry the memory of the girl's murder for the rest of his life. There was no need for Becca to have it too. 'There's nothing you can do. We need to get out of here fast, before he comes back. He's got a gun.'

'Is that what I . . .' She trailed off.

Jared nodded. 'Tell you later. We need to move.'

He sent Becca through in front of him, hustling them through the cistern chamber, moving along the ledge as quickly as he could. He thought about releasing the rope and hauling it in – anything to slow GBH down – but decided against it. He didn't want the man to know anyone had been there.

'This guy,' he said to Becca in a low voice. 'Last time I saw him, he had a sidekick with him. At least one. He might have left someone here, or there might be someone at the entrance to the mine. We've got to be careful.'

She nodded.

Jared switched off his torch and indicated to Becca to do the same. They stood still in the pitch dark as he listened. This is what it must have been like for that girl, abandoned in the mine in a darkness that was so dense it seemed to press against your face.

He had to stop thinking about it. He had to concentrate on getting them both out.

All he could hear was the sound of water, a steady, monotonous *drip* ... *drip* ... *drip* with a slight echo. He could hear the whisper of Becca's breath. Nothing else. He switched his torch on again. 'OK. Let's go.'

They moved into the final chamber. Jared climbed carefully up the slope to the exit. There was no surreptitious way of getting out – he moved as quickly as he could and, in a matter of seconds, was standing on the cliff side. It was deserted. He called down to Becca, and in a minute, she was standing beside him. He put his arm round her, and she leaned into him, just for a moment. 'I think we're OK.'

They'd pick up the car and go to the police. OK, they didn't have the photos, but the police couldn't ignore their story. They'd have to go into the mine, check it out. Then no one could suspect him and Becca of being involved.

As they moved across the cliff face, finding their way back up to the headland, he caught sight of something from the corner of his eye. He twisted around to look but there was nothing there. Something was wrong. He could feel adrenaline rushing through his veins, his body going into high alert.

Something was *very* wrong.

He moved closer to Becca and whispered, urgently. 'Hurry up. We need to get off this cliff.'

'What is it?'

'I don't know. Something.'

She seemed to trust his instinct, and they both moved on quickly, Jared following Becca closely, helping her up the tricky bits, help she accepted without objection.

Once they were on the path, he felt a bit better. But he wanted to get them away from the Ness as fast as possible. 'I've got to take these boots off,' Becca said. She was limping a bit – unfamiliar boots could rub your feet badly.

'OK. Go to the tent and get some shoes. I'll bring the car round. Couple of minutes.'

Becca nodded. 'Just – before you go. What happened? In the cave, when the caravan man came in?'

'What do you mean?'

'Down there. Something happened. That man. He shot at something, didn't he?'

'OK.' The sky was clear, the rain had stopped and the air smelt clean. He had something in his head now that would never go away, and he didn't want to put it into Becca's, but he had no right to keep it secret. 'That girl, the second girl, the one whose face wasn't ...'

'In that little room thing?'

'Yeah. She wasn't dead. Not quite.'

'And we left her there?' Becca stopped in her tracks. 'We've got to go—'

'No. He shot her. Greaseball Harry, the caravan guy. He ... He saw she was alive and he put a bullet in her head. Just like that.'

Becca tipped her head back, her gaze following a seabird as it glided above them and out across the sea. Jared had never wanted more to have those wings, to be able to detach himself from this life and soar away into the heavens. He saw that Becca's eyes were wet.

He didn't bother with the platitudes about how it wasn't their fault, they hadn't done it, there was nothing they could have done.

He knew how she felt. He felt it too. He turned away to get the car.

Chapter 62

Becca sat on the groundsheet tugging off her boots. She'd tried calling Kay on her way back to the tent, but there was no answer. Jared was right, she knew he was right, they needed to get to the police, but in York they hadn't believed her.

Jared wouldn't understand, but she needed to talk to Kay first, before they did anything. Kay might go off on one, but she made people listen. You didn't tell Kay who she could talk to and where she could go – she just pushed doors open and banged on desks and in the end people gave her what she wanted just to make her go away. Becca wanted to see Kay. She needed her.

It would be different if they had the photos, but they didn't.

She took out her phone and texted Kay.

--*Soz cant come this a.m.*

After a minute, her phone buzzed. Kay's reply:

--*Thank you for letting me know. Can you come this afternoon? Xxx Kay*

It made it sound like a job interview. *Can you come*

this afternoon not *Get yourself over here.* And the kisses. Kay was going soft.

Becca rubbed her feet, listening for the car. What was taking Jared so long? The place they'd hidden it by the cottage wasn't that far away. Maybe it wouldn't start. She gathered her stuff together and stood up. Screw waiting. She'd walk up the path and meet him.

'Well, isn't this nice?'

Becca spun round. Sauntering down the path towards her was Liam, looking as if Becca was the person he most wanted to see in all the world. Behind him came Terry, shoving Jared in front of him, Jared's arm twisted up behind his back. There was a cut on Jared's face, and what looked like a bruise forming around his mouth. 'Hi Bex,' Liam greeted her cheerfully. 'Who are you spying on now?'

The jeer in his voice made fury flood through her. How dare he talk to her like that. How dare he, how *dare* he hurt Jared! And she could tell by his grin that he knew exactly what she was feeling. And her rage seemed to *amuse* him. 'What are you doing here?' She was almost too angry to speak.

'Looking for you, Becca. You've managed to get some people seriously pissed off.'

Jared managed to break free, grunting with pain as he twisted away from Terry. Terry made a move, but Liam said sharply, 'Let him go, Tez. She'll get upset if you hurt lover boy.'

Jared glared at Terry, rubbing his arm. 'What the fuck was that about?' He looked just as angry when he turned to Becca. 'Who are they? They've got a van – they jumped me up in the car park. They knew we were here.'

'They're from the drop-in. They're . . .' She turned to Liam. 'What did you do to Paige?'

'He didn't do anything to me, Becca. I'm fine.' A small figure who had come down the path unobserved stepped out from behind Terry's bulk.

Paige.

Paige alive. Paige unhurt.

Paige looking pleased with herself.

Chapter 63

Jared watched Becca's face register astonishment as she stared at the small figure standing on the path.

Then Becca was across the path and just as Jared realised what she was going to do, she drew her arm back and slapped the girl across the face. The girl staggered back, froze in surprise, then she came back at Becca, reaching for Becca's hair. 'Ginger cunt! Bitch!' she yelled.

The smaller lad grinned, but he got hold of the girl's arms and held her back as Jared moved quickly across to Becca, keeping an eye on the big lad who'd hit him when he'd resisted them. He owed that shit one. 'Steady,' Jared said, his eyes on the two lads and the girl. What was this all about?

Becca was shouting at the girl. 'I thought you were dead! I thought they'd killed you. We've been looking for you for days!' She threw off Jared's restraining hand. 'It's Paige,' she yelled at him, trying to get past him, obviously mad enough for a full-out fight. 'Fucking cow! I've been . . . I thought she was hurt.'

'What's up with her?' Paige asked the group, looking genuinely puzzled. She rubbed her reddening cheek and shot Becca a look of resentment, but she didn't try to attack again.

'It's just Bex, going off on one. She does that.' The smaller lad was watching Becca as he spoke, assessing the effect of his words.

Jared saw them hit home, but he also saw Becca struggling to contain her anger, her lips moving silently. With visible effort, she got herself under control and stared furiously at the fair-haired girl.

'You ran out on me,' Becca said, her voice low and angry. 'I thought you were the one who got hurt. How could you just go off with them like that?'

'Yeah. Well. *Liam* looks out for me, not you,' Paige spat.

'Good luck with that,' Becca muttered, but she seemed to be back in control. Jared was looking at the small lad; the one the girl, Paige, had called Liam. There was something familiar about him.

Then he remembered.

'I saw you,' Jared said. 'In the woods. A couple of nights ago. You were following someone.'

'Yeah,' the lad, Liam, said. 'I wanted a word with the guy who owns the caravan site.'

'Greaseball.' Jared hadn't meant to say it, but Liam grinned appreciatively at the nickname, a startling smile that made him look about twelve.

'Yeah.' Liam nodded. 'Greaseball. That's about right. He was walking back with someone I hadn't seen

389

before so I followed a bit to try and get a good look. But it was too dark.'

Jared didn't get it. 'What's he got to do with you?' He was remembering now. They'd been at the caravan site too, this pair. *Move it, mong!* He remembered the bikes flashing past him as he struggled to stay upright.

'We're in business, me and that lot. Supposed to be. We're, you know, supply side.'

'What do you mean, supply side?'

'What do you think?'

Jared looked at the small girl beside him, Paige. She was sitting on the ground now, chewing her hair, looking like a school kid in a boring class. What was she? Fourteen? Fifteen? Jared wanted to run Liam to the cliff edge and kick him over.

Becca, who had been listening in silence, spoke up. 'I knew what you were doing,' she said. 'I *knew* it!'

Liam gave her a mock salute. 'Give the lady a prize. You know all about this kind of thing, don't you, Bexgirl?'

'My name's Becca, and I know what you did. You and him.' She nodded towards the big lad, the one who had hit Jared, who was watching the scene in silence. 'Tez,' She spat the name, making it sound like an obscenity.

Liam grinned, pleased with the effect of his need-ling. 'Top marks for you, *Becca*. This is how it works. Worked. The caravan guy – *Greaseball*.' He looked at Jared and nodded. 'That's cool, that.' He grinned as if he and Jared were big mates. 'He pays for the girls, the punters pay to come to the party. The girls get some money, he gets some money, everyone's happy.' As he was speaking, he wandered across the grass to where Jared had parked the motorbike. 'Hey. Serious bike. Yours?' He looked at Jared with something like respect.

Becca wasn't going to let Liam change the subject. 'Everyone's happy?' she snapped. 'You mean, *you're* happy. You get the girls, you get the money.'

Liam spoke over his shoulder as he inspected the bike. 'Yeah. Why not? We're in the same business, Bex. Sorry. *Becca.* You and me – let's make a deal after this is done, right? I can get you more money than you ever dreamed of.'

'*Fuck off,*' Becca said.

Liam laughed. 'Haven't got any other job though, have you Bex?' He turned back to Jared. 'It was Greaseball on his own at first. But then some others came in on the deal and that's when it got, you know, heavy. When it was just Greaseball, everyone makes a bit so everyone's happy, no one gets hurt. But now they've got it going up and down the coast.'

And probably other places. Jared thought about all the half-empty caravan parks, the holiday lets standing empty through the winter. They could use hundreds of locations. 'Pop-up brothels,' he said, glancing at Becca.

Liam nodded. 'That's right. Only – there weren't enough girls, so they started bringing them in.'

'Bringing them in?'

Liam's look at Jared said *Duh!* as clearly as if he had spoken it aloud. 'Illegals,' he said with exaggerated patience. 'You know? Nothing to do with us. We got girls from the drop-in. Then Paige says it's getting too heavy and she wants to stop. I never make her do what she doesn't want to, right, Paige?'

'Suppose.' Paige plucked the grass at her feet, apparently bored.

Liam's eyes narrowed. 'Suppose?'

She looked at him and, briefly, fear showed on her face as she scrambled for the words. 'I mean, yeah, I only do what, you know, I want. Get some money, whatever. Only . . .' She looked at Liam. 'It's not a laugh anymore.'

Jared caught Becca's eye and shook his head. She looked ready to kill someone. *Christ, don't lose it now, Becca.* Keeping a cautious eye on her, he said, 'I think I get it. It was just small-time when it was Greaseball, bit of dosh, bit of a laugh, but now it's gone big-time, right? People who can cause bad trouble. How bad? Could they get in the way of a police investigation?'

Liam considered Jared's question seriously. 'Yeah. Probably. They might even *be* police for all I know.' His eyes narrowed in sudden resentment. 'It was my piece of action and they pushed me out. Thought we might be able to cut a deal with Greaseball, keep our little op to ourselves, but . . .' Liam shrugged. 'He's not The Man, not now. So we're getting out.'

'So what are you doing up here?'

Liam looked – almost – embarrassed. 'I said. To see Greaseball. He had – business up this way. But he's not interested. So we thought we might drop in on Bex, visit a mate, you know?'

Becca ignored Liam's goading. She seemed to have a grip on her anger now. 'How did you know I was here?'

Liam shrugged, but he spoke to Jared. 'Word gets out. Becca's in Whitby, Becca's at Kettleness. Got a bit of a proposition for her. Like I said, she's got some people seriously pissed off.'

Becca's eyes narrowed. 'A proposition? How's that supposed to work?'

Liam grinned. 'OK, here's the deal. Me and Paige – we're setting up elsewhere. Thought you might like to join us. We need a bit of – some nice girls, and you need to move on.' He held her gaze, and for a moment, his face was serious. 'Trust me. You do.'

Jared stepped in before Becca could speak. He was back at the caravan site that night. He was looking down at the girl, at the bared teeth and the staring eyes, listening to the halting, agonised breath.

Only this time, it wasn't a stranger lying at his feet. This time, it was Becca. 'What the fuck is that supposed to mean? I know what they've been doing! '

'Hey, hey, hey.' Liam held up a conciliatory hand. 'Calm down, lover boy. That shit's new. Nothing to do with us. When it was just your mate Greaseball, it was OK. If a girl tried anything, Greaseball got a couple of guys to, you know, nothing much, just, have a bit of a party with her, let her know who's boss, teach her a lesson.'

'So what happened. What *shit*?' Jared glanced at Becca, who was about to speak. He shook his head. *Keep quiet. Let him talk. We have to know.*

'All that shit with the knife and the –' Liam made a graphic peeling gesture against his face – 'All of that, it started after the new people came in.'

The new people. Human traffickers, selling sex. Like some kind of fucking hedge fund. Jared closed his eyes. He ached for his pills, whisky, whatever it took to wipe the images away, scrub out the thoughts. 'Why?' he said.

'Why do you think?' Liam rubbed his thumb and forefinger together in the sign for money. 'These new girls, they weren't like Paige. They didn't have someone looking out for them.' He looked across to where Paige was sitting. 'You want to remember that sometimes.'

She smiled up at him. 'I know, Lee. I'm sorry.'

'I still don't get it,' Jared said. 'Why would they do that?'

'Well, it's the dosh, isn't it?' Liam explained. 'They pay to bring these girls over. That costs. So the girls gotta do what they're told to pay them back, you know? When a girl gets a bit uppity, tries to get away without paying, makes trouble, they do, like, a special, the thing with the face, and they film it. There's good money in that.'

Jared felt sick, but he kept his face expressionless. 'They film it?'

'Yeah. It's hardcore.' Liam spoke as if he admired the business acumen of the men who were doing this. 'The stuff with lots of guys. The really violent stuff, you know? Then when they're done, one of the heavies gets a knife, and he just – it's like skinning a cat. Loads of dosh in that. Oh, and it keeps the other girls in line.'

Jesus. But Jared could believe it. He knew all too well the kinds of things that lurked on the dark web. 'And then?'

Liam looked across the empty land towards the sea. 'Then someone gets rid of them.'

Chapter 64

Jared followed Liam's gaze out across the grey, restless water. The waves showed nothing of what might lie beneath them. It was the perfect dumping ground if you chose the right time to make sure the bodies washed away, rather than drifting back up on the shore. Not so long ago, he'd stood not far from here, watching the sea surging against the Ness, the waves pounding the cliffs. You could hide a body in the mine, wait for a real high tide, then tumble it down into the water and let the sea take it. If anything did come back it would be battered beyond any possibility of recognition.

'And they told *you* about all this?' No way. No way they would have let a little shit like Liam in on it.

'I don't need to be told. I keep my eyes open.'

Becca had sunk down onto the grass and was sitting with her head bowed, her hair hiding her face. Now, she looked up, looked directly at Paige. 'Did you know?'

'What's it to you?'

'It's everything to me. Your friend. Mari. Did you *know*?'

'No I fucking didn't!' Paige exploded. Suddenly, she wasn't the withdrawn kid sitting out some dull, adult ritual, she was angry and her eyes sparkled with tears. 'She was my mate. We were, you know, besties? The guy who runs the site, he kind of likes her.' She looked down and started pulling up bits of grass, scattering them around. 'Liked her. They used to do it. In his office.'

Becca cut in. 'That's not liking. That's perving.'

'Yeah, well.' Paige dismissed the distinction. 'So sometimes he left her there and she was messing around with his laptop. And she found, you know, one of the movies. One of them that Lee said about.'

'The hardcore shit,' Liam affirmed.

Jared didn't want to hear any more – he wanted to stop them talking, but he had to know.

'So she got scared,' Paige continued, 'and she told me what she saw, and she said – Mari, I mean – she said she knew someone who could do something about it. And then . . .' She trailed off, tore up another blade of grass and threw it away.

'Did she tell this person?'

'I dunno. That's what she went to do, but she didn't come back. She was supposed to meet me at the drop-in, but she never. I told Liam—'

Liam shook his head. 'I was taking care of it.'

'Taking care of it how?'

Liam's eyes narrowed. '*Taking care of it*, right?' He looked at Paige. 'Only she goes and shoots her mouth off – *Where's my mate? Where's my mate?* So they come to get Paige and the stupid cow only goes with them, doesn't she? She's lucky I was looking out for her.'

Jared remembered the bikes flashing past him, the night of the attack. Liam, riding to the rescue. Kind of.

'They let you take Paige?'

'Well, good business, innit? I told them she didn't know about, you know, the stuff. I told them I'd keep her in line, and, you know, I'd give them ... well, doesn't matter.'

Liam was proud of his skill in making deals, Jared realised; that's why he'd been talking so freely. But now, for the first time, he seemed evasive.

'You'd give them what?' Becca broke in, her voice uneven, disbelieving. 'Another girl? Ma—'

'Shut the fuck up!' Liam's shout was sudden and shocking as he moved sharply across to Becca. He grabbed her hair and jammed her face against his crotch. 'Use your mouth for something useful or keep it shut.' He shoved her away and she flung her arms out to stop herself from falling to the ground.

'Get your fucking hands off her!' Jared was beside her in a second. He crouched down next to her. 'Are you OK?' Her face was white and she looked sick.

She nodded. 'Yeah, I just ... Fucking perve!'

Liam seemed to hesitate, then he turned to Paige, holding out his hand. 'Come on. We're out of here.' Paige scrambled to her feet. 'We're moving on, me and Paige, aren't we?'

Paige nodded. 'Going to Leeds,' she said.

'You can't go with him,' Becca said. 'You heard what he did!'

'You can't tell me what to do! Lee's OK. He got me out of there, didn't he? You're just jealous because you haven't got anything like me and Lee have.'

'Yeah, right. Like I'd want that.' Becca had found her anger again.

Paige opened her mouth to respond, but Liam grabbed her arm and pulled her away. 'We're going,' he said. He looked at Jared. 'And you won't be following us, *right*?'

'Fucking right we won't.' Any time Jared saw Liam again would be too soon.

Liam put his arm round Paige and she gave him a playful shove as they headed back up the path towards the car park, Terry walking behind – just kids, messing around.

Chapter 65

Jared put his hand on Becca's arm. She shook him off. 'We've got to stop them! He could really hurt Paige.'

'Wait.' He watched until they were out of sight. 'Listen, that little scrote knew you were up here. *Word gets out* – that's just shit. Has he ever got his hands on your phone?'

'No, he – hang on. I lost it. At the drop-in. It turned up somewhere in the coffee bar. I just thought I must have, you know, put it down.'

'He said he knew where you'd been but he didn't. He said Whitby and up here. He didn't say anything about York. He's got some tracking on your phone.'

Becca's mouth fell open, then she pulled her phone out of her pocket and threw it onto the grass, wiping her hands on her trousers as if she had touched something disgusting.

Jared picked it up.

'I don't want it,' she said.

'Yeah you do. You're going to need it. Look, we can clean it up later. For now, just . . .' He fiddled with the back and took the battery out. 'Here. He can't track you now.'

After a moment's hesitation, she took it gingerly and slipped it into her pocket. 'Come on then. We've got to get after them.'

Jared shook his head. 'We can't. Right now, it's only us that knows what happened. That's got to change. It's got to be the police but we've got to have something to back it up.' After what happened to her in York, he wasn't letting the police anywhere near her, not until they had evidence no one could argue with.

Becca nodded reluctantly. 'I – listen. We have got something. The girl, Mari, the one who was hurt . . . there was a photo at Kay's.'

'That's what I was trying to tell you. You know her?'

'She came into the drop-in. When I first started. They called her Mari, but I think her real name's Maireid. Kay and Matt, they fostered her, just before Matt got ill. I never met her, not then.'

'But the photo's gone.' Jared could have taken it with him the first time he saw it. Why hadn't he? Fucking pills had addled his brain.

'I've got it,' Becca said. 'I found it on the floor. It's in my bag.'

He wanted to kiss her. 'Then this is what we're going to do. That photo – it's not enough, but it's something. We're going back into the mine. This time, we'll get some photographs and then we'll go to the police. And we'll tell them—'

Jared was interrupted by two sharp reports, slightly

muffled. Gunshots? Ordinarily that wouldn't be unusual. Farmers shot rabbits all the time. But there was someone else around here with a gun, someone they really didn't want to meet.

'Come on!' Jared said, grabbing Becca's hand. He ran towards the cliff path, pulling Becca with him. 'Here.' There was a vantage point, behind a large rock, where they could watch the path to the tunnel but keep themselves concealed. The same sound echoed up the cliff a couple more times, followed by a slithering, slumping sound. A few minutes later, GBH emerged along the path leading from the cliff and the mine entrance. Jared could see no sign of a gun, but his face was grim.

Becca's hand tightened on his arm. GBH stood on the clifftop for a few minutes, looking back, his gaze sweeping the beach below, then he turned away and headed up the path towards the car park and the road.

Jared waited until he was out of sight. He felt Becca start to move. 'Not yet,' he whispered. 'He might come back.' They waited ten minutes before they heard the sound of an engine.

'OK,' Jared murmured.

They stood, sore from crouching, and made their way along the path until they were scrambling down the cliff face, Becca forging ahead, moving too fast for the terrain.

'Take it easy—' he began as she vanished from sight. Then he heard her exclamation of dismay. For a brief moment, he thought she had fallen, but it wasn't that.

When Jared had first seen GBH's gun in the cave

402

with the girls, his fear had been what might happen if bullets were fired into the unstable roof. GBH must have had the same thought.

The arch in the cliff was collapsed. The entrance, what remained of it, was blocked with mud and shale.

The evidence they had come back for was buried beyond retrieval.

Chapter 66

When Kay woke, she had no idea what time it was. She opened her eyes, expecting to see the small window of her bedroom – no, the hospital ward – then the events of the morning came flooding back. She closed her eyes and lay back, letting everything become clear in her mind. Her head felt muzzy and she was thirsty, but she didn't feel as bad as she had when she had woken up before. Slowly, she opened her eyes again and sat up, swinging her legs over the side of the bed. When she stood, her legs were a bit shaky, but they supported her. She reached for the water jug by her bed, then stopped. It might be paranoia, but she wasn't going to drink anything that didn't come out of the tap. She took the jug into the bathroom, rinsed it out well and refilled it. Then she drank what must have been close to a pint of water. When she put the jug back on the bedside table, it was almost empty.

What could she do? Her phone was gone, and the only window in the room was a skylight, so she had no way of seeing where she was or what was happening outside. She went across to the door and tried it. Locked.

Shaun was keeping her here. But why?

There was a chair but it was nowhere near high enough for her to reach the skylight if she stood on it. If she could drag the chest of drawers to the middle of the room and stacked the chair on that, then she might be able to get it open, but she still wouldn't be high enough to pull herself up and through, so what good would that do?

Sitting down on the bed, she put her head in her hands and forced herself to think back. What did she know – really know – about Shaun? His first call had come the day after the attack on the girl at Flamborough. There had to be a connection. And then he'd stuck around, meeting her for coffee, inviting her out, bringing her flowers, all of which had appealed to her vanity, as he must have guessed.

Then he'd turned up at the hospital after she had been hurt. It had seemed like genuine concern before he'd drugged and kidnapped her. All this time, he'd been keeping an eye on her. He must think she knew something – but what? She didn't know anything. She couldn't even imagine what he thought she knew.

No, wait, he'd called before the Flamborough attack – on the anniversary of Matt's death. *Sorry to call out of the blue like this.* It was not long after Maireid had contacted her: Maireid had never made the promised visit. Kay hadn't been surprised – Maireid was still angry.

But . . .

Maireid had never turned up, and Shaun Turner – someone she barely knew, if she knew him at all – had left a message for Kay, Maireid's foster-mother.

A few days after that, a girl was attacked on the caravan site.

And Shaun was on the phone to Kay again the next day.

Maireid . . . Oh, God.

And there was more. He'd presented himself as a colleague of Matt's who'd only just heard about his death. Had he known Matt at all, or was that story of their working together a lie from start to finish? She wanted it to be a lie. She didn't want Matt's memory tarnished by any contact with something she could barely bring herself to imagine.

She had to get out. Her gaze shot to the door. It was heavy and solid, and the last time he'd looked in, she'd had no warning: she'd heard nothing through it to suggest he was coming. How long was the drug supposed to keep her under? How long before he came to check again?

She prowled the room, desperately trying to think of a way out. The bathroom was windowless, the door was locked, the skylight was out of reach. When she found herself studying the floor and walls in the hopes of finding an escape route, she knew she'd run out of options.

There had to be a way. If she could just *think*.

There was a sound from the door. It was the handle,

turning, and then the faint, sticky sound of a tight-fitting door being opened. As she slid back onto the bed, she wondered why Shaun needed soundproof doors. She squeezed her eyes shut and tried to make her breathing regular.

'Kay?'

Feet moved towards the bed, and she could sense him looking at her. Then she heard the clunk of something being set down on the bedside table, and he moved away. The door closed, and she was alone.

She sat up, noting that the near-empty water jug had been replaced by a full one, and her phone was beside it. He'd given her back her phone – did that mean she was being paranoid after all? He was on the up and up; he wasn't drugging her, holding her captive? But when she picked it up to call Maggie, she saw there was no signal. She walked round the room, trying different places, different angles, but got nothing.

Messages. Had anyone been in touch? She opened her messages folder. There was nothing new, but that didn't mean anything – a message could easily have been deleted.

Right. Shaun probably wouldn't be back to check on her for a while. Now was the time to do something. It was all starting to come together. She was remembering now. Shaun had asked about Becca the night before.

Becca had to be his target. Becca had worked at the drop-in and was somehow linked to the caravan site at Flamborough where Maireid – Kay didn't want to accept it, but she knew the unnamed girl must be

Maireid – where Maireid had been so badly hurt. Becca knew something.

It would be so simple for him to send Becca a text from Kay's phone, asking her to come here. Becca would think it was from Kay and be there like a shot, then Shaun could do whatever he wanted with both of them. Becca could even be on her way here now.

The thought made her jumpy with panic.

She pulled on her clothes, shoving money, keys and her phone any old way into her pockets. Then she opened the drawers and dumped the contents on the bed – flimsy, lacy lingerie, some heavy belts, stuff she'd think about later, not now – took out the drawers and dragged the heavy piece of furniture across the room to stand under the skylight. Something small and metallic rolled off the top and onto the floor with a clatter. She glanced down. It was a key, too small to notice, too small to be the door key. She tensed, then shrugged. If he came in now, she couldn't hide what she was doing.

Then she lifted the chair up on top of the drawers. Together they would give her enough height to swing the window open, then maybe she could pull herself up and out.

She climbed up onto the drawers, then, feeling insecure and unsteady, climbed up onto the chair. Once she straightened up, she could hold onto the window frame, which gave her a bit more balance.

She gripped the latch that opened it.

It was locked.

Hell and damn. There was no way she could restore the room so Shaun wouldn't notice – she'd given herself away for nothing. What could she do? Break it? It was safety glass. She'd need a hammer. At least. Who'd be so paranoid as to lock a high skylight?

Someone with something to hide.

She stood on the chair looking round the room, then saw something on the floor and remembered the small key that had fallen off the drawers when she moved them.

She dropped down onto the floor and picked the key up. Sending up a silent prayer, she climbed onto the chair again, glancing at her watch once she was balanced and holding the frame. She guessed that it had been almost an hour since Shaun had last been in here. How long before he checked again?

The key fitted the lock and turned smoothly. The window swivelled towards her, almost unbalancing her, and the cold air rolled in. She breathed deeply, letting it clear her head, then gripped the sides of the window firmly and tried to pull herself up.

No chance. She just didn't have the upper-body strength to pull her own weight up through the open window. She could try calling out – but she was pretty sure there were no houses close by. And if there were, who paid attention to shouting and screaming these days anyway?

She could try attracting attention by throwing things out of the window, but for that to work, she'd need to know there was someone out there she wanted to attract. Otherwise, she'd bring Shaun up here again, and that would just make things worse.

And then it came to her: a plan. Maybe it wasn't the best one but it was the only one she had. Climbing down, she got the water jug and then climbed back up on top of the chair. She wound her arm back, took aim, then threw the jug as high and as far out as she could.

She was rewarded a second later with the shattering sound of breaking glass.

Jumping down, she went and stood to one side of the door and waited.

Chapter 67

'Fuck's sake,' Jared kept saying. 'For fuck's sake.'

He wanted to go straight to the police, even though they didn't have the pictures, but Becca wouldn't. 'They won't believe us,' she said.

'Look,' Jared said for about the fifth time, 'we've got the photo of the girl. If we tell them about the mine, they've got to check it out. And they'll stop that little scrote before he disappears. You want that, don't you? If we don't go to them – now – it's going to happen to another girl.'

Becca knew that, but after what had happened in York, everything in her was saying no, or at least not yet. She couldn't trust the police. Not after the way they'd treated her. She had to talk to Kay first. Kay would know what to do.

'I want to go and see Kay. She asked me to and I said I would.'

'And what can she do? Come on, Becca. She's hurt, she's old – we have to go to the police.'

'You go. I'm going to see Kay.'

'Oh for— Look, it isn't safe for you to be running round on your own.'

'Fuck you! Who made you God?'

'No one. Jesus, will you stop being so touchy? It isn't safe for either of us to be round here on our own, right? Greaseball and his mates are out there. And your friend Liam. If he gets into a bad situation with Greaseball, do you think he'll keep quiet? He'll save his own skin and sell us. He'll probably do that anyway.'

She didn't want to admit he was right. 'Paige won't grass us out.'

'Paige will do exactly as she's told. That little shit is pimping her, and she's just sitting there and going *Yes Liam, no Liam*, so don't expect any loyalty from her.'

Becca was determinedly packing her stuff into Kay's car. Her own car, with the taped windows, might attract too much attention. She wouldn't look at Jared – she didn't want to let him persuade her. He was wrong, she knew he was wrong but she couldn't explain it. 'Kay will want her car back. I'll go and see her, then we can go to the police.'

'Yeah, yeah, we see Kay and then you'll think of another excuse not to go to them. For fuck's sake, Becca, this is dangerous.'

'Come with me. Then we won't be *running round* on our own.'

'For God's sake, Becca!' He seemed really angry, took a breath. 'Right,' he said, more gently. 'We'll do this. But I'm following you on the bike, because whatever happens, after you see Kay, I'm going to the police, OK?'

She opened her mouth to object, then closed it. Part of her thought Jared was right. But another part – the part that kept remembering that police cow Call-Me-Mandy's face with that disbelieving smile – that part *knew* the police were the last people to go to now. If they'd got the pictures, it would have been different, but . . .

She needed to see Kay, talk to Kay. Kay would know what to do. Jared following on the bike was a good idea. If that scary caravan guy – what did Jared call him? Greaseball? – if he found them, they'd be in trouble. It would be easier to get away on the bike. Jared said it was powerful and fast. 'OK,' she said, to show she had heard him. 'You can follow on the bike.'

Jared wasn't happy, but he gave a brief nod. She slid into the car, then hesitated. She had no idea where to go. The address Kay had sent her was in Whitby, but she didn't know where.

She reached for her phone to open the map app, then stopped. She couldn't. Not without Liam knowing where she was going. Did Kay have a map book? How did you get around if your phone wasn't an option?

Jared was beside the car, straddling the bike. She pressed the button to wind down the window.

'Is sitting here all day part of the plan?' he said.

She muttered, 'Fuck off,' under her breath, and saw Jared roll his eyes. She turned the key in the ignition and shoved the car into gear. She'd get to Whitby and find the place. She'd manage.

But Jared was leaning in through the open window, stopping her from driving away. 'Where are we going?'

'Whitby.'

'OK, that's a start. Where in Whitby?' He waited, then said into her silence, 'You do have an address?'

'Yeah. Course. What kind of . . .?'

'Look, she's got built-in satnav, your friend. Use that.'

She'd never used one of these satnavs. She waited for Jared to go on being arsey and patronising, but he leaned in further, muttering, 'Can never sort these things out. What's the post code? OK, let's try . . . there you go.'

The screen lit up, the road rolling away in front of her. 'You want the voice?' Jared said, fiddling with the buttons so he could see the whole route.

Her confidence came flooding back. 'No. Let's go.'

Chapter 68

The door opened. Kay stood behind it, waiting. Hardly even breathing.

'Kay?' Shaun was standing in the doorway. 'Kay? Are you ...' He must have seen the construction under the skylight because he broke off and strode into the room, looking up at the open window. She heard him curse under his breath as she slid round the door and out.

There was a flight of stairs in front of her. She fled down them, moving as silently as she could. As she went, she realised she should have closed the door behind her – the key was probably in the lock, she could have trapped him.

Too late now.

She made it to a carpeted landing with a corridor leading to another flight of stairs. There were doors along the corridor, closed and silent. Run? Find a hiding place?

Decide, she told herself. Pick a direction. No hiding, just get out, get out.

There was a shout from above her. 'Bill! BILL!' and the sound of feet on the corridor below.

Someone was coming up the stairs. They'd see her just standing there. She had to do something!

She pushed open the door on the left and slipped into one of the rooms, a bedroom, holding the door shut behind her as feet pounded past along the corridor, towards the stairs she'd just come down.

How much time did she have? How long before they realised she couldn't possibly have got out of the skylight? All her instincts made her want to huddle in a cupboard or under the bed, but they'd find her in minutes. She had to get help. She had to find other people.

She checked her phone. The signal was back, just barely. She pressed the emergency button, but she could hear feet on the stairs above her.

No time! She ran down the stairs and found herself in the entrance hall at the front door.

The way out.

Quick! she barked instructions to herself. Don't panic! The door looked heavy, with stained-glass panels and brass hinges and bolts. There was no key in the lock. She tried the handle: it didn't move. She was locked in. Trapped.

The sound of pursuit was close.

Decision-time again. Run and hide? Or spend the time trying to open the door?

Get out! She had to get out.

She pulled the bolts and unlatched the Yale. Her

gamble paid off. She didn't need the key. The door swung open. Then she was in a porch; with another door in front of her – more bolts; she fumbled with them, and then she was outside.

Almost safe. Keep going. She stumbled down a flight of stone steps onto a gravel drive, looking round for the nearest house, the nearest road, anywhere she could get help.

There was nothing in sight.

There were no houses, no neighbours, nothing.

But she could hear the sound of a car. There was a road. She had to get to the road!

Behind her, someone shouted.

Then she was running, her feet slipping in the loose gravel, no plan anymore, just the mantra *the road, the road, get to the road*. She could hear feet pounding behind her, closer and closer and then something snagged her ankle and she fell, her face smashing down onto the gravel. The pain flared, instantly, across her face and body, everywhere the sharp stones cut into her.

She raised her head, half stunned, watching blood drip onto the ground. She put her hand up to her face. It came away red. She couldn't get up – she couldn't move.

A pair of booted feet came into view. One of them lifted, and she braced herself for the kick she knew was coming.

'Leave her!' Shaun's voice, sharp.

'We can't let her go.' Another male voice. *Bill*, Kay thought.

'I know.' Shaun sounded almost sorrowful. 'Just . . . keep it clean.' She heard crunching, saw a second pair of feet, then Shaun knelt down beside her and spoke almost tenderly. 'I'm sorry, Kay,' he said, his voice tinged with regret. 'I tried to keep you out of it, but you just kept getting involved.' He stood and spoke to the other man. 'Enough. Deal with it.'

She heard the sound of feet moving on the gravel and struggled to get to her knees. She could see what must be Shaun's feet moving away. The other, booted feet took a wider stance, as if the other man – what had Shaun called him? Bill? – was steadying himself. She couldn't fool herself. She knew what *deal with it* meant.

He was going to kill her.

She looked up at him. He was pointing a gun at her, at her head.

He was going to shoot her; she was going to die.

Everything was moving slowly, with a clarity and brightness she had never known before. She could hear a high-pitched cheeping not so far away – a meadow pipit? This early in the year? Matt would have loved that.

That soft susurration: that was the sound of the wind blowing through the dry winter grasses. How many times had she heard that whispering breath, walking the moors with Matt? They must be in open country, far away from the town. The air tasted clean and fresh and cold.

The feet moved slightly, taking a firmer stance.

Remember! This is what the world is like. Beautiful and peaceful, with birds calling and the grass singing in the distance. Kay ached with yearning for it, to see it again, to be on those open moors, not here, sprawled on the gravel like some broken-down old woman.

The screech of tyres and the *bang!* came together. Something hit her – hard – on the head. She struggled for clarity, to make some sense of what was happening, but there was just darkness, confusion, noise. Pain. She was rushing down a dark tunnel. *Stay!* She told herself. *You have to stay here!*

But the tunnel was too powerful; the darkness was too strong. It carried her inexorably away.

The turn was sudden and sharp. Becca felt the back wheels skid in the gravel as she turned up into a steep drive. And it was there in front of her, a scene out of her worst nightmares.

One man, on the phone, by a house.

Kay lying on the ground.

The man Jared called Greaseball standing above her, a gun pointed at her head.

She didn't even stop to think. She floored the gas and the car smashed into him, throwing him back against the house. Becca was thrown forward, over the steering wheel, then back, hard, against the seat. Everything went dark for a moment, the world spinning. She opened her eyes, tried to pull herself together. Greaseball was staggering to his feet, pulling himself up against the brickwork of the house. Her foot stamped

419

on the gas again and drove the car straight towards him, into the wall. The impact threw her forwards, the seat belt biting into her, her head smacking into the steering wheel and bouncing back.

Then there was silence, and then someone was screaming.

Chapter 68

Becca's head hurt, her body ached, the car horn was blaring, someone was screaming. Nothing made sense. She eased herself back from the steering wheel, wincing at each movement. *Kay.* She had to get to Kay. Her fingers fumbled as she unbuckled her seat belt, pushed open the door, climbed shakily out of the car.

Kay was hurt. Becca didn't look at the man she had rammed. She ran across the drive to where Kay lay on the ground with blood pouring from a wound on her head, deep cuts on her face and hands. Becca pulled off her jacket and put it over Kay, using her scarf as an improvised pad to try and stop the bleeding.

Had Greaseball shot Kay before Becca crashed into him? She didn't know. Everything was confused. Things were happening around her. A man was shouting into a phone, running between the crashed car and Kay on the ground. Gravel crunched under moving feet.

And after some time, maybe a few seconds, maybe an hour, there were sirens and blue lights flashing. Paramedics eased her away from Kay's side and knelt down where Becca had been. Two of them were over by the car, and then one came across to her and helped her over to a low wall, helped her sit. Asked her questions about what hurt and where, if she could breathe.

Another man joined them, 'You were driving?' he asked.

She nodded.

He made her blow into something – and that was when she realised the police were here. She had to tell them about the dead girls in the cave, about Greaseball and the caravan parties. Jared had been right. They should have gone to the police straight away. But if they had, Kay would be dead.

Oh God, Kay.

'He was going to shoot her,' Becca said. 'I had to stop him.' She kept trying to explain about the mine, about coming to see Kay, about Paige and Liam, but it all came out in a confused babble, and she could see the familiar look of suspicion on the man's face.

He didn't believe her.

And where was Jared? He'd been right behind her on the bike, hadn't he? But there was no sign of him. She reached for her phone that she'd dropped onto the gravel. 'I'll call him.'

'You'll have to leave that there for now. They're checking the area. We need you to come with us, Becca.'

'I can't. I won't. You've got to find Jared. He was here!' She pointed at the man who had been talking on the phone when the other man was pointing a gun at Kay. 'He saw it!'

'If this Jared did anything, we'll find him.'

'Not Jared. He didn't do anything. He knows what's happened. He can explain. He's on his way. He's coming.' She tried to stand up. She had to find Jared.

'Becca, just stay here. You need to tell me what happened. Now—'

'I told you. Kay—'

'Listen to me. Listen. You drove up the drive. Now tell me from there.'

'I saw him. He was going to kill Kay! I had to!'

'What did you have to do, Becca?'

'Stop him. I had to stop him.'

'OK. How did you stop him?'

They were lifting Kay into the ambulance. She was lying very still but there was a mask over her face so she must still be alive. They didn't put a mask on you if you were dead, did they?

She swung round to the man questioning her. 'I have to go to the hospital with her. My mum . . .'

'She's in good hands. You have to come with us.'

She jumped to her feet. 'Fuck that! Kay's hurt. I'm—'

The policeman shook his head. 'Rebecca Armitage, I'm arresting you on suspicion of causing death by dangerous driving. You do not have to say anything. But it may harm your defence if you do not mention when questioned something which you later rely on in court. Anything you do say may be given in evidence.'

She stared at him, her mouth falling open. She hadn't planned to kill Greaseball – there hadn't been any plan – she just had to get him away from Kay.

And she'd *told* the police – he was going to shoot Kay like Jared saw him shoot the girl in the mine. 'What about everything I told you? What are you doing about that? What about Jared? You've got to find Jared, he'll tell you. They tried to kill Kay! His gun must be here somewhere. He had a gun. That's why I hit him. With the car.' She had to get away, had to find Jared so he could tell them what happened.

She saw the man who'd been on his phone when she first drove up. He was talking to one of the other policemen, all serious, shaking his head, talking, talking. But he knew what had happened. He'd been there.

'He knows!' Becca shouted. 'Ask him!' The policeman was holding her arm as she struggled to get free. She kicked back, felt her foot make contact, then her legs were swept from under her and she was down on the ground, her face pressed painfully into the sharp stones. She could barely breathe. Fuck them! Fuck them!

'I have to go with Kay!' she screamed, struggling, but the words wouldn't come out and her mouth filled with fine gravel and dirt. She felt her arms held in an immovable grip and then the cold touch of something going round her wrists, and she was trapped.

She heard footsteps, then saw feet – the man who'd been on his phone, the man who had been there when Greaseball was holding a gun on Kay.

'Officer, I know this girl,' he said, his voice level. 'She's Mrs McKinnon's foster-daughter. She's a very troubled young woman but Bill . . .' His voice choked.

'My God. He was a good friend. I can hardly believe she'd kill him.' For the first time, his gaze moved to Becca as she glared up at him. 'You might be able to pull the wool over Kay McKinnon's eyes,' he said to her, 'but I'm not such a pushover. Officer, this is the second time in just a few days this girl has tried to harm Kay. Two days ago there was a fire at Kay's cottage. She was lucky to escape with her life. Your people think this girl was involved, and Kay thought so too.' He looked at Becca. 'Well you've got what you wanted, haven't you?'

Becca was pulled to her feet. She spat at the man and he recoiled.

'Liar,' she screamed. 'Fucking liar.'

'That's enough of that.' The policeman pushed her down into the back of the car where his colleague sat waiting behind the wheel.

She could see the man watching her as she was driven away.

The expression on his face – it had been all concern as he talked about his friend, as he talked about Kay, but now . . .

Now it was triumph.

Becca tilted her head back so the tears wouldn't spill over. They weren't going to see her cry. They pulled away from the house and Becca kept her silence during the drive, forcing herself not to cry. They wouldn't see her cry.

She started telling her story as they booked her into the custody suite, told them again and again. Asking over and over about Kay, asking where Jared was. She never thought about what would happen next.

Until they pushed her into a cell and locked the door behind her.

That was when she started screaming.

Chapter 69

The motor cut out suddenly. One moment, Jared was moving smoothly along the road, Becca in his sights, the next, the engine stopped, and the bike rolled slowly to a halt.

Jared leaped off, swearing. The fuel gauge was registering zero. What the fuck? Then he saw the fuel line hanging loose, detached from the carburettor. It hadn't been like that when he started – no way he could have missed it, so it had worked loose while he was ... but that didn't happen. Unless ...

Liam standing by the bike, checking it out as they talked, his parting shot. *And you won't be following us, right?*

Liam hadn't been offering advice, but making a statement of fact. Jared and Becca wouldn't be following because their vehicle had been damaged. It would have only taken seconds to loosen the screw, let the tank start to drain.

Fucking hell!

He had to do something. Becca probably hadn't

noticed he'd fallen away – she had been speeding, too set on getting to this Kay woman to see much at all. He was angry with her for her stubbornness. They should be with the police now, telling the part of the story they'd managed to piece together. Instead, they were driving – well, she was, he was stuck – through the countryside to get the blessing of some old biddy Becca was fixated on before they could go to the police.

Some kind of fucked-up cavalry charge this was.

He took out his phone and called her number but it went to voicemail.

Fuck! The battery. He'd taken the battery out himself to stop Liam tracking them. The sea was on his left, grey and restless, and behind him in the distance, he could see Sandsend Bay and the dark bulk of Kettleness looming behind it.

He closed his eyes and pictured the route he'd seen on the satnav after Becca had keyed the address into it. He thought they might be pretty close. There was a turn off – probably the next one, then maybe another half mile to another turn off, the same distance again to the actual location – middle of nowhere.

If he followed the satnav route, he'd have to go round three sides of a square, but on foot, he could cut across the fields. As the crow flew, it was probably not much over a mile.

He pulled the bike up onto the verge – there was no way of making it safe if someone wanted to nick it – and climbed over the wire fence and into the field beyond.

As he crossed the rough ground, he tried to put the

information they had into some kind of order. OK, it starts out as small-time prostitution in Bridlington, taking advantage of the displaced kids shipped out there for the cheap accommodation. Then someone sees the potential and moves in, taking control, bringing in more girls, from further away. More girls with no one to look out for them, no one to ask questions on their behalf.

Start small, with a brothel in a caravan park in the off-season. Move into bigger properties, with more girls. Make more money. Bring over even more girls.

And then you come up with a very special line in hardcore videos, and that's when you really start minting it. And if the girls kick off?

No one would ask questions about missing girls if no one knew the girls were missing.

But the *brutality* of the murders. Why would they do that? Why would they tear their faces off, leave them to die, trapped in a mine in the middle of nowhere? Because to them, the girls weren't people – they were just commodities who had lost their value.

He was halfway through the field when he heard the sound of a siren. It was hard to locate which direction it was coming from, but it was getting closer. Then there was a second one coming from the same direction, following the same route. He stopped to listen. They were both converging on the point he was heading for.

Jesus. Becca.

He started running – a slow jog was the best he could manage across the rough ground. It was like one of those dreams where you try to run through treacle, but worse, because he wasn't going to wake up. After ten minutes of painful running, a road came into view, and then a house, standing by itself; a big stone house with a red-tiled roof. He was on slightly higher ground, and he could see down into a drive and a turning space. The sirens had stopped wailing some time ago, but he could see two police cars and an ambulance parked in the space, and lights flashing, and people milling round.

And – *oh Jesus* – there was a car smashed into the house wall. What the fuck had happened? It looked as though it had hit with real force. And there was . . . His binoculars were in his pocket. Moving into the shadow of a tree, he crouched down to steady himself and slipped them out to take a closer look. Vague grey shapes blurred his vision, then the scene jumped into focus.

It was as bad as it could be.

The car rammed against the wall was the car Becca had been driving, and there was worse. A figure was slumped over the bonnet; a figure the paramedics were doing nothing about. They were loading someone into the ambulance. Becca? Jared focused. It was a grey-haired woman, who seemed to be unconscious.

Jared's glasses swung back to the crashed car. The figure slumped over the car bonnet was all too familiar.

GBH. Becca must have driven her car straight into GBH.

He'd promised to look after her. He should have been in the car with her – if he couldn't stop her going to see this Kay woman, then he should have been with her, instead of following behind.

And then he saw Becca – she had been on a low wall, that's why he hadn't seen her at first, she'd been surrounded by police. Now she was on her feet, was fighting the police, and as he watched they threw her down onto the ground. He jumped to his feet – she needed him down there – and then realised he was too late.

Far, far too late. He was too far away. Even so, he started moving again, more of a slow stumble than a run. Every part of him hurt. He'd never get there in time. Slowly, painfully, he began to make his way down the hill towards the house, watching as they hauled Becca off the ground and bundled her into the back of a police car.

Then they were gone.

Jared leaned against a tree, trying to get his breath, then he lifted the binoculars to his eyes again.

A uniformed figure was putting tape around the crash site.

Because it was a crime scene. A murder scene.

There was one more person there, besides the police; a man dressed in a suit who was pacing backwards and forwards, a phone pressed to his ear. He stopped to talk to a police officer; they seemed friendly. Like mates. There was something familiar about him. Then the man turned and looked in Jared's direction. His face jumped into focus, and Jared almost dropped the binoculars.

It was the man who'd been walking up the hill with GBH that night they had tried to kill him – tried to run him down in the road. Oh, Jesus, Liam had hinted at important people being involved. This guy had been chatting with the police like . . . like best mates or something. What if he was involved with the police? What if he was some kind of senior officer?

That would explain what had happened to Becca in York. He'd turned the police against her because he *was* police.

She'd been right – going to the police was the wrong thing to do. But even going straight to Kay meant she'd walked into a trap that neither of them had seen and now she was under arrest. And all she had was an impossible-sounding story that she had no way of supporting. She had the photograph of Maireid, but it wouldn't be enough, not on its own. The only solid proof of what they had found lay in the mine, and GBH had brought the roof down as he left.

He should have listened to her.

He'd fucked up. Again. He had to do something. Now.

He turned and jogged back towards the road. Every step hurt. But he had one idea: he had to get to Whitby, to an internet café. He had almost no money, no wheels . . . it would take him about half an hour to walk into Whitby, and that was too long.

As the road came into sight, he saw there was a bus stop on the opposite side and for once, luck was with him. A bus was approaching.

He put on a burst of speed, his body screaming in agony, grabbed his backpack as he raced past the bike, sailed across the road in front of the bus that was about to pull away and leaped on board. He gave the driver what amounted to half his remaining wealth and the bus trundled down the hill towards Whitby.

Maybe it wasn't too late. Maybe there was still time.

Chapter 70

Kay opened her eyes, rising up out of blackness into a strange room.

Not again!

'Where am I?' she heard herself say. 'What happened?'

'It's all right, Kay,' someone said in a soothing voice. She turned her head. She was lying on a narrow bed and everything was bumping and rattling. There was a man strapped into a seat beside her head. He smiled at her. 'You banged your head. We're just taking you to A & E to give you a bit of a check over.'

Kay looked at him in bewilderment. Banged her head? Where had she been? What had she been doing?

He was asking her questions now – did she know what day it was? Did she know what year it was? Did she know who the Prime Minister was?

'Unfortunately, yes.'

He grinned. 'Don't think there's much wrong with you, Kay. Still, better get you checked out, eh?'

Her head was aching, but something else was wrong.

What was the last thing she could remember? Lying on a bed in a strange room with the same sense of *where am I?* And before that ... a fire? There'd been a fire and she'd ended up in hospital.

Becca. There was something about Becca ...

Legal advice. Shaun said she needed legal advice. He'd been so helpful, but her stomach clenched with dread when she thought about him. Why?

There was something she needed to do, something urgent, and time was running out. She closed her eyes and tried to remember.

It only took ten minutes for Jared to get to Whitby. He jumped off the bus outside the station and looked round.

The things he needed to do – *now*; there was no time to waste – crowded in on him. He needed an internet connection. There were a couple of cafés down near the river where they had Wi-Fi – he could just go there, talk them into ... *No.* If they said no, that would waste time.

He had to get some money.

The station? A bank? He dithered, then saw a Co-op across the road. They sometimes had ATMs. He ran across and yes, there was a machine; a woman was using it. He waited with barely concealed impatience behind the woman, who put her card in, took it out, stared intensely at the screen for what seemed like hours before she finally completed her transaction, and glared suspiciously at Jared before she walked away.

He threw himself towards the ATM, shoved his card in the slot and keyed in his pin. His fingers were clumsy on the keyboard and his first request was rejected because he'd entered it wrong.

Get a grip! Get a fucking grip! He started again, making himself concentrate. He asked for fifty pounds. There was a long pause, then the words appeared on the screen: *Insufficient funds.*

Shitfuckhell! His credit-card bill must have gone through. He leaned his forehead against the wall, thinking fast. How much did he need? The price of a cup of coffee would get him an internet connection. OK. He tried again, this time asking for ten pounds, sending up a silent prayer as he waited.

A ten-pound note slid out of the slot. Jared released the breath he didn't realise he'd been holding.

He went into the first café he came to, which had a wireless sticker on the window.

'You've got to order food,' the girl behind the counter said when he asked for the Wi-Fi code.

'Oh for ...' He looked for the cheapest item on the menu. 'Chips.'

She took his money, counting out the change slowly, then finally gave him a small card with the code on it. He found a quiet corner where he could set up his tablet without anyone looking over his shoulder. OK. Think carefully. No more fuck-ups. Becca needed him to get this right.

What was the best way forward? What was the best way to help Becca? Take the whole story to the police?

He'd have done it, if it wasn't for Becca's experience in York and Liam's broad hints – supported by what Jared had seen himself – that someone high up was involved. With the mine entrance collapsed, where could they find the evidence they needed, to get the police looking in the right places?

Hang on, hang on, hang on. He'd been assuming the people who dumped the bodies had dug the mine out, but the mine wasn't crucial – it was just convenient. Digging it out was a big job and you'd have to know what was in there to know it would be worthwhile – and no one did. The mine had been buried for decades.

Who dug out the mine?

Urbex. Urban explorers.

They made it their business to find out about lost places, buried places. There were internet forums with pages dedicated to old mines and tunnels. So some of them would have come looking for sure. And when they found the blocked entrance to the mine on the cliff face?

They'd have dug it out. They'd do it for – this was what they always said on the forums if anyone bothered to ask – they'd do it for the lolz. For the fun of it. To go into the mine, just because they could. They would have explored it, taken pictures and left, leaving no trace apart from an obscure opening in the cliff.

He knew this, because he was one of them. And if they'd done it, he could find them.

The girl from behind the counter dumped a plate on the table beside him, along with a knife and fork. She muttered something about ketchup and waved a vague hand behind her, then shuffled off.

He suddenly realised he was hungry, and dug his fork into the chips, which were lukewarm and rubbery, but good enough. He crammed them into his mouth as he worked out the best way to do this. He uploaded the original video, the one from the tablet Becca had found that had guided them through the tunnel, and added a description of the chambers.

Then he downloaded a TOR browser onto his phone and went to the dark web forums where he was known – explorers were secretive people. They didn't give away their locations or their identities, or not often. He posted a link to the video and his message: *Need to confirm location. Urgent. Phoenix.*

He wasn't sure how this would help him, but if he and Becca were going to get corroboration of their story, their first hurdle was proving the mine still existed. Then he sat back. Nothing to do now but wait.

That's what he was doing, several cups of coffee and two hours later, when his phone rang. He checked the display: unknown.

'Yeah?' He spoke cautiously, wondering if someone was tracking him.

'Is that … Jared? Becca's friend?' A woman. 'My name is Kay McKinnon, and I think we need to talk.'

Chapter 71

By the time the ambulance got to Scarborough Hospital, Kay's memory was returning. She still couldn't remember anything about that morning and whatever had happened to knock her out – the paramedic said something about being knocked over by a car, but that triggered nothing at all. Her recollections of the previous day were hazy – Shaun had picked her up from the hospital, she could remember that – but every time she thought about Shaun, thought about contacting him to let him know she was OK, to find out what had happened, her whole system went on alert, telling her not to.

If Kay trusted anyone, she trusted herself.

What she did know was that Becca was in trouble. Becca, apparently, had driven her car straight at a man, crushing him against a wall. The man was dead. She, Kay, was supposed to be collateral damage from that event. Becca was now a major suspect in the fire at her cottage.

It was all nonsense, of course. It was time Kay stepped in. Even without all her memories back.

439

As soon as the paramedics wheeled her out of the ambulance and into A & E, she told them she was leaving. OK, she'd been knocked out; OK, she probably had concussion, but if she waited for the medics to give her the all-clear, it would be too late. Becca had been arrested, and if there was one thing Becca couldn't cope with, it was being locked up. But given the charges against her, it was going to be tough getting her out.

To help Becca, Kay needed her contacts, and she needed information.

Telling herself she felt fine – her head was aching, but she could get something from the chemist for that – she checked herself in the mirror in the loo. What she saw almost sent her back to A & E. Her face and hair were a mess of dried blood and dirt. It was impossible to see what was injury and what was just the aftermath of the accident. No, it hadn't been an accident. That she did know.

She tried cleaning her face with a damp towel, but all that did was spread the mess around. In the end, she washed her face using the harsh hospital soap, then dunked her head under the tap, scrubbing her hair with her fingernails to free it of all the muck. The wound on her head stung and ached like something that shouldn't be ignored, but it didn't start bleeding again. It could wait.

Just cleaning herself up made Kay feel better. She no longer looked like the walking wounded – more like a bag lady. Good enough. She tidied herself up as best she could, then checked her pockets to see what she had with her. Her handbag was probably on the ground at Shaun's somewhere.

Oddly enough, all her stuff – her money, her phone, her cards – was in her pockets. Now why would she have done that? She had a sudden memory flash of running, of urgently pressing the emergency button on her phone, and then it was gone.

It was a simple matter to get a taxi from the hospital to the nearest car-hire firm. After about half an hour of box ticking, she left in a Megane with the fiercest braking system she had ever encountered.

OK, she had transport. Now she had to decide what to do next.

She wasn't herself, that was the problem. Her mind kept slipping away and her head was still aching fiercely. She had concussion and shouldn't be driving, she knew that, but she had to find out what had happened. She should go to the police, but something inside her was saying no. Where would they have taken Becca? Whitby, surely. She turned the car north, still not sure of where she was going or what she was going to do.

There was something she knew, something she'd forgotten, and until she worked out what it was ... The frustration made her bang her fist against the steering wheel. The horn sounded and several people looked round. The driver in front of her raised a finger.

She pulled into the side of the road. She couldn't drive and sort this out at the same time. Calm down. Think! What she really needed to do was talk to Becca, but Becca wasn't accessible. Kay had tried her phone and it had gone straight to voicemail.

She checked her messages, to see if there was a new one from Becca. There wasn't, but there was a text that gave her a contact number for this Jared person.

Kay tapped the phone against her teeth. What role did this man have in Becca's latest debacle? Reluctantly, she clicked on his number. It rang for so long, she thought he wasn't going to respond, then a cautious voice said, 'Yeah?'

'Is that ... Jared? Becca's friend? My name is Kay McKinnon, and I think we need to talk.'

Chapter 72

There was only the terror. It was dark – she knew it was dark even though her eyes were tight shut. If she opened them, she'd see Him coming towards her. It would be dark but she could always see Him.

She had to stop Him. She had to stop Him. She'd screamed so much her throat was burning but she couldn't stop. If she stopped, He'd come, but her voice was raw and thready – once the barrier of the screaming had gone, He'd be there. She dragged her nails down her face and banged her head against the wall.

Stop Him! Stop Him! Stop Him!

There was a rattle and a clunk, and a voice said, 'Come on, Becca. This isn't helping. We'll have to restrain you if you don't quiet down. It's for your own good.'

It's for your own safety, Becca, your own safety, Becca, your own safety . . .

You know that's not true, not true, not true . . .

She slammed her head against the wall to shut the voices out.

And then the door was open and she could breathe again, and two people were forcing her to her feet, their voices a meaningless jabber. There was only one thing that mattered. The door was open. It mustn't be closed. It mustn't be locked again.

She's bleeding . . .

. . . bloody nutter . . .

. . . did you see . . .

. . . come on, Becca, this won't . . .

. . . who's on duty . . .

She couldn't be locked up, not again, not anymore. There was only one thing she could think of to stop them. 'I did it,' she said. 'I did it.'

Jared recognised the woman who came through the door as Kay McKinnon immediately. She was a small woman with red hair shot through with grey and she came into the café like a one-man SWAT team, glaring at Jared as he rose to introduce himself. Just the kind of woman who could have coped with an adolescent Becca.

'Right,' she said, her voice abrupt and business-like. 'You've got a lot of explaining to do. This had better be good.'

He'd opened his mouth to protest, but she was right. He did. He started with his experience in the tunnel, the caravan site parties, the attack and the apparent pursuit of Becca. Her lips tightened when he mentioned the attack on the girl.

'Maireid,' she said. 'My foster-daughter. Yes, I guessed. Go on.'

444

He explained about Becca's insistence on going to see Kay before they went to the police. 'I thought she was being paranoid.'

'With Becca, paranoia's not impossible.'

He nodded in acknowledgement. 'This time, though, she was right. I should have got in the car with her – I should have driven, I knew she was upset. I got there too late, but there was this guy marching around like he was in charge. I saw him act like he was mates with the police that were there. I know him. I don't know who he is, but he was there that night they tried to run me down – him and the guy we call Greaseball. The one Becca hit with the car.'

'The one Becca killed. Just a minute. You said …' Her face had gone white and she sat down suddenly. 'Shaun. It's coming back. Oh good grief … I …'

Alarmed, Jared leaned forward. 'Are you all right? Do you want me to get you some water?'

She stood up abruptly and pushed past him, heading for the ladies' toilets. Ignoring the sign on the door, he went in after her. She'd been knocked cold this morning, and she looked awful. The cubicle door slammed shut behind her and he heard sounds of retching.

He waited until there was silence, then he tapped on the door. 'Kay. You need to see a doctor.'

There was silence, then he heard the sound of the cistern flushing. She came out of the cubicle, pushed past him and went to the basin, where she rinsed her mouth and washed her face. He hovered, feeling clumsy and useless. When she had finished, she looked up at him.

'I remembered,' she said, her voice empty. 'I know exactly what happened.'

Brushing aside his offer of assistance, she marched back into the café. Jared saw the waitress watching them with an expression of deep suspicion. 'It's OK,' he said, deliberately inexplicit. The last thing he wanted was an officious manager descending on them. He ordered more coffee, getting Kay a cappuccino and spooning sugar into it with vague recollections of the best way to treat shock in the elderly.

Then he listened as Kay told him what had happened to her.

'The last thing I remember,' she said, finally, 'is that ... that *thug*, pointing a gun at me. I was on the ground and he was pointing a gun at my head. Shaun came over, told him to do it. And then he tried to kill me. And Becca ...' Her eyes reddened and she shook her head impatiently. 'She must have seen what he was going to do. She drove the car straight into him. She saved my life.'

This was the evidence they needed. 'We can go to the police,' he said. 'You can tell them what happened.'

He expected her to jump at the idea. Instead, she hesitated, then shook her head slowly. 'Shaun will have had time to tidy up by now, inside the house at least. Look, he was a senior officer for years. That will be why the emergency services responded – and fast. He still advises them sometimes.'

'Are you sure?'

She shook her head impatiently. 'Not sure, no. I'm

just going by what he's told me, but we can't take the risk. Don't you see? I'm an old woman, I've been widowed recently and I've been injured twice in the past couple of days. At best they can call me delusional, say I'm suffering from concussion. You? Is there any reason they might have to think you'd be lying? Have you got a police record?'

OK, that was telling it like it was, but he could see where she was going, and she was right. 'No, but I'm not exactly a respectable citizen.'

'Then we need more. Tell me the rest.'

He stifled his impatience – all the time they were talking, Becca was … He didn't know what was happening, but he remembered her fear as she talked about being locked up, and his promise to her, the night they spent together. He ran through the story as quickly as he could. 'I see why they wanted me off their patch at the caravan site. They weren't sure how much I'd seen that night. But I don't know why they went after Becca – the emails, driving her off the road – they didn't just want her out of the way. They wanted her dead.'

Kay McKinnon sighed. 'I think I do. I was the one who started asking questions – and I got Becca the job at the drop-in. It must have looked as though I had an idea of what was going on and put a spy in there just around the time Maireid found that video. Then Becca started asking questions as well. When she turned up at the caravan site with you, they put it together and they decided we all knew too much.'

'The drop-in? The place Becca used to work? So these traffickers sent the emails to get her thrown out?'

'I don't think they did. I think it was that lad Liam. You said he was pimping a couple of the girls, then Becca befriends one of them. So Liam put a stop to it. Also, the way he must have seen it, Becca out of work would be a recruit for his sordid little business. This coffee is disgusting,' she added. 'If I wanted a cup of boiled milk and sugar I'd ask for it.'

'Sorry.' She reminded him of all the head teachers he'd ever encountered – great if they were on your side, terrifying if not.

'You say the mine's inaccessible?'

'It is now.'

'And Liam and his crony have run off with Paige? That's another loose end needs dealing with.'

'I think the girl, Paige, might be talked into telling the police what she knows, if we find her.'

'I don't think so. She'll just do what she's told. So, what was your plan?'

'Whoever dumped those girls – it wasn't them who dug the mine out in the first place. That's hours – days – of work, and you need to know what you're doing. You need to know it's there, for starters. I've put out an internet call – I think I can find out who did. They'll have pictures. If they have, it will help to prove those chambers exist. But that's all. There's no way anyone else is going to get back in.' The cliff was too unstable for any more digging.

Only the mine, and the dead girls in there, one with

a bullet through her head, couldn't be explained away. Kay had her story of being imprisoned, but there was only her word for it and she had concussion. It could all be seen as the delusions of a lonely old woman. The man with the gun? There was no concrete proof of anything. Jared's story of going into the mine, backed by Becca – they couldn't check it either, and both he and Becca had dodgy pasts.

A good defence team would demolish a case that was as thin as that. And Becca was trying to defend herself against a possible murder charge.

The tablet chimed. A message. He brought up the screen.

--Phoenix wldnt tell anyone els but jst 4 u we dug it out 2 yrs ago flooded but water drained did u use cliff entrance check out the map & pix we think anther entrance is open cos of draft but couldn't find Chem6

There were attachments and a URL. Jared clicked on it and found himself looking at a page of cave maps. Slowly, he scrolled down – they were the kind of maps that would mean nothing if you didn't know the terrain. He stopped as one of them came up on the screen. *Unnamed mine, Kettleness*, from a survey done in 1975.

That was the one.

There was the cistern, there was the entrance on the cliff – marked *blocked* on the map, and beyond that was a further tunnel.

Jared traced the map with his finger. There was the chamber behind the cistern, the place where the dead girls lay. According to the map, the tunnel ran past the chamber and deeper into the cliff where it came to a dead end. He and Becca had only gone as far as the chamber. What lay beyond that, what might be hidden further down the tunnel, he had no idea.

He tried to mentally overlay it on the landscape he remembered. The map was rudimentary. It gave no real indication of distance and the direction wasn't pinpoint accurate – you wouldn't be able to get a compass bearing from it – but even so, an idea was starting to form in his mind.

He went on to Google Maps and found Kettleness. Kay watched him in silence. He zoomed in until he was close to the cliff, and tracked the path he and Becca had followed. The cliff face wasn't visible, but he could locate the point where the mine entrance was. A few hundred metres inland, he could see the shadow of the cutting where the tunnel entrance lay. In his head, the map of the mine hung in the air; he adjusted it for scale, rotated it a bit to fit the landscape, then let it drop onto the map . . . sink into the landscape, and . . .

Gotcha!

The mine fitted like the missing piece of a jigsaw puzzle into the land between the tunnel portal and the sea. The mines were closing as the railway was built. The last alum mine at Kettleness closed in 1871. The railway opened in 1883. How much had the railway engineers known about the work of the Kettleness miners?

The side shaft from the railway tunnel Jared had

explored not so very long ago ran straight out towards the cliff, and running inland from the cliff towards the tunnel was the alum mine where he and Becca had found the bodies of the girls. At some point, the two crossed, the side shaft crossing underneath the shallow mine.

He remembered the old wooden ladder that had drawn him in, the ladder that had looked as old as the mine timbers themselves. Had the side-shaft workers known about the mine and cut themselves an escape route against the collapse of their fragile tunnel, giving them access to the mine above?

And one night not so long ago, had something from the mine fallen through?

He looked at Kay. 'There's another way in,' he said.

Chapter 73

They left the café immediately but it took time, frustrating time, to find a solicitor to act for Becca. Hours later, when they did, Kay insisted they hand their evidence over to him, not to the police. 'He needs to make the case. He'll give it to them then. This way, they won't have time to argue.'

Jared's vision of going to the nick and walking out triumphantly with a freed Becca didn't quite happen. Becca was being held in Scarborough – there were no custody cells in the police station at Whitby – and would have to appear in the magistrate's court there before she could be released. The solicitor told them, with a shake of his head, that she had confessed to the charge of causing death by dangerous driving, and that was complicating everything. The hearing was scheduled for the following afternoon. Kay clearly didn't want Jared to be involved. She dealt with all the paperwork herself and left Whitby without contacting him.

But he wasn't here for Kay. He was here for Becca.

His bank account was empty, so he had, finally, to draw on the money his mother had been sending him to buy fuel for the bike, which, miraculously, was still where he'd left it, and to leave him with a bit of ready cash in his pocket. He drove down the coast on it – after all, he needed to return it to Kay – and was there in court, to Kay's evident displeasure, when Becca was finally released the following afternoon.

The charges still hung over her. She left custody on police bail to appear in the magistrate's court the following week.

But it wasn't Becca who came back to them, or not the Becca Jared remembered. She wouldn't look up, kept her gaze firmly fixed on the ground. When she finally did look at him, he saw cuts and bruising down one side of her face. What the fuck had they done to her?

Kay put her arms round Becca and hugged her. Becca just stood there, unresponsive, and Jared's first impulse, to lift her up and swirl her round in triumph – because it was a triumph, kind of – faded as he watched her.

'Thank you,' Kay said. 'You saved my life. You know that, don't you?'

Yeah.' Becca's voice was hollow, empty.

'All right,' Kay said after a moment. 'Let's get you out of here and go and get something to eat.' She looked at Jared. 'I can give you a ring when Becca's—'

He deliberately misunderstood her. 'I'll come with you. Becca and I have got stuff to sort out, right, Becca?'

Becca glanced at him. Her nod was barely

453

perceptible, but it was enough for Jared. She wanted him there. He was staying.

Kay sighed. 'OK. But Becca and I are staying in Scarborough tonight. You'll need to get back up the coast.' Jared almost smiled at her determination to get rid of him. OK, he got it. She thought she was protecting Becca.

'I brought your bike down from Whitby. It's in the car park.'

She frowned as if this was one complication too many. 'I suppose you'd better hang on to it for now.' She turned to the solicitor. 'Are you coming with us, Richard?'

'I think . . .' The solicitor surveyed the group. 'I think I'll love you and leave you. I'll sort out the paperwork and give you a call.' He smiled at Becca. 'Try not to worry. We have a strong case for self-defence, and a lot beyond that.'

Becca nodded, but didn't reply.

Jared wanted to shake her to try and get some response. What had happened to her, that day she'd been locked away? Where was the Becca who'd practically flattened someone who barged him outside the police station? The Becca who'd got into a burn-up with a van after driving his car for about ten minutes? The Becca who'd smashed Greaseball against the wall with a car when he threatened the woman she thought of as her mother?

What the fuck had they done to her?

Kay marched them into a café. She seemed resigned

454

to Jared's presence, for the moment. 'This table here, nice and quiet. Jared, go and get us tea, and –' She looked at Becca – 'bacon sandwiches.' Becca shook her head. 'Don't be difficult, Becca. Here.' She thrust some cash into Jared's hand.

He used his own money to pay for the order and returned Kay's to her, which she took without comment. They ate in silence. Becca kept her head down, but she did eat.

'Right,' Kay said once they'd finished. 'Richard thinks they'll drop all the charges at the hearing next week. It's a mess, but it'll get sorted. Becca, you did the only thing you could.'

He was beginning to understand. Becca knew she'd saved Kay's life, but the way she'd had to do it ... Despite the promises people had made to her, the promise *he'd* made to her, come the time, she'd been on her own. Not many people could bring themselves to smash a car into another person and crush them to death against a wall, and Becca wasn't one of them – it was her anger that had driven her.

And then she must have felt that they'd all abandoned her as the police took her away and locked her up.

As if she could read his thoughts, she looked up and met his gaze. 'Where were you?'

The thousand-dollar question – where had he been? *You don't have to worry with me*, he'd told her. Like fuck she didn't. The first thing he'd done was let her go off on her own because he hadn't trusted her judgement.

'Not where I should have been,' he said. 'I'm sorry.'

Kay's lips tightened. 'I don't know about you, but I'm tired.' Rather pointedly excluding Jared, she turned to Becca. 'You're coming back with me tonight – we'd better get moving.'

Jared saw Becca reach listlessly for her jacket. He understood that Kay wanted to protect her, but she couldn't. None of them could. Becca carried her anger with her, the anger that seemed to be part of her, an anger that must have grown more and more intense over the years. All the time he'd known her, she'd been fighting that anger, keeping it held in.

And then she let it go, and that anger had exploded across the walls and grounds of that house, and across Becca's mind in a way that would leave scars. Forever.

'It's still early,' he said, standing up. 'We've got things to pick up, up the coast, right, Becca?'

'That doesn't matter now.' Kay gave him the full force of her glare.

Becca hesitated, and seemed about to follow Kay, then she lifted her head. 'I'm going with Jared,' she said, with a hint of her old spark.

Jared looked at her. 'Ever driven a bike?'

'A bit. In Leeds.'

'Now's the time to really learn.'

Chapter 74

The bike terrified Becca. The first couple of goes round the empty car park, she'd nearly fallen off, nearly run it into the wall. Jared stood watching and shouting instructions until she'd got to grips with the gears and had learned how to ease the throttle open slowly so the bike didn't run away with her. She could feel the power under her hands.

'OK,' he said, climbing on the bike behind her. 'Let's get going.'

She edged the bike out onto the road, the headlights reflecting back from the wet tarmac, ready to chicken out, to tell him You do it. I've changed my mind. Only she didn't. An idea was starting to form in her mind. She settled herself and felt Jared's hands on either side of her waist.

She was cautious through Scarborough, taking it slowly. It was early evening, but the sun had already set. The streetlamps created pools of light in the darkness.

She'd lost. They'd won. They'd locked her up and they'd charged her and they said it would be over and the charges dropped, but they were wrong; soon that door would close behind her forever. *Bye-bye Becca, it wasn't nice knowing you.* The solicitor might say that it was all going to be OK, but what did he know? That's what they always said. Now they were going to lock her up for years, forever, and that meant...

That meant they'd won. *Anger is useful, Becca. Use it the right way.*

But she hadn't. She hadn't.

She was through the town now and the countryside was all around her. The road lay ahead, empty, vanishing into the distance and the winter dark. She opened up the throttle, then more, then more, and the road was racing by and the wind was whipping past her ears. Then they were in Whitby, where dimly lit houses flashed by, and then onto the coast road where the sea glittered in the moonlight.

She was terrified, but she was flying. More. And then more. How fast could this thing go? Fast enough to escape from all of it, from all of them?

She felt slight pressure from Jared's hands and he said calmly in her ear, 'Bridge with a tight bend ahead.'

She said 'OK' before she realised he wouldn't be able to hear her over the noise of the engine and the wind blasting past them. She knew this bend – she'd driven it twice recently. It was sharp – a double bend that took the road across the narrow bridge at Sandsend and then up the valley side towards Lythe.

And the spark of an idea she'd had back in the car park suddenly burst into her head fully formed. If she wanted to, she could keep up this speed, head for the bridge, let them go crashing straight through it, into the icy river, into cold water that would make her feel clean and she wouldn't have to think about it ever again, trapped, waiting for the door to close behind her forever.

So they could never lock her up again.

And Jared?

He felt this way too, she knew it. Deep down, that was why he did all this climbing, all this crawling down into dark places, because one day it would kill him.

Because deep down, he wanted to die.

And he knew what she was thinking. That was why he was on the back of this bike now.

Kay had tried to stop him. Kay knew as well. Kay understood.

Or did she? Kay wanted to treat her like someone who was weak.

Jared treated her like someone who could take it.

As they swept towards the bridge, she still didn't know what she was going to do. The engine roared as she fumbled the gear change – how did you get round the bend when it was as tight as this? Jared was suddenly gripping her firmly and leaning with her as the bike cornered, skidded, righted itself, then they were shooting up the hill and she could hear Jared's triumphant yell and feel his body shaking against hers – he was laughing.

And she was too.

She opened up the throttle. The sea was on her right,

the dark bulk of Kettleness somewhere up ahead, and the road going on forever in front of her. Their speed was something she couldn't control. If anything moved into their path, if anything unexpected happened, they were dead, both of them.

Sheer terror filled her like joy. For the first time in her life, she felt free. Nothing mattered, just this moment in time.

And she understood. *This* was what Jared meant. This was what Jared went looking for, this was what he felt.

It wasn't death. It was life.

Then they were on the familiar Kettleness road. She slowed the bike down with a real feeling of regret. The gate to the field where they'd camped was just on her right. She turned the bike through and came to a stop. Her legs felt shaky, and she was out of breath as if she'd been running.

Jared swung himself off the back and came and stood beside her. 'Good?' he said.

'It was all right.'

He grinned. 'The tent's still here. And all my stuff. Want to stay?'

'Yeah. OK.'

He put his arm round her and they stood together looking out at the moonlight over the sea.

Chapter 75

The first spring warmth was in the air as Becca walked through the town centre. Bridlington seemed to be waking up from its long winter sleep. Visitors were starting to appear on the streets, the shops and cafés were opening and the down-at-heel inhabitants of the winter were fading into the background or had gone.

It was two months since she'd driven her car into the man Jared called Greaseball, and she still had the occasional nightmare, but she was getting her life back on track. She'd found a job in a local pub, and another in a supermarket, and was just about managing to pay her way through her day-to-day life. Once she'd have called them loser's jobs for a loser – only it didn't feel like that, not really. Not anymore. It felt like ... waiting.

A few days after her release, a caving team finally made their way into the mine via the Kettleness tunnel. What they found there confirmed at least part of Becca and Jared's story, including the dead girls. They also found an airshaft above the chamber, hidden with turf and scrub but which provided easy access for dumping

461

the dead or the terminally hurt. The metal grill covering it lifted smoothly, and ropes in the shaft suggested it had been used to access the mine more than once.

A further police search located a bullet at Shaun Turner's house, which put a gun at the scene – forensics would tell if it was the same gun that had been used in the mine. After this, the charges against Becca were dropped.

Kay had offered her a room in the house where she was living while the cottage was repaired, but Becca knew that if they lived together, they'd end up killing each other. And Kay was trying to get over the death of the girl in the hospital, finally identified as Maireid O'Neill. Her last foster-daughter.

Kay had thought there would be a future for Maireid.

Becca had always known there wasn't.

And that was the difference between them. Kay believed the world was basically a good place where sometimes bad things happened.

Becca knew different.

Shaun Turner had left the country. He'd gone to Qatar 'on business' when news came out that they were searching the old mine. His current location was unknown.

'Handy,' the solicitor commented. 'If he chooses his country well, they won't be able to get him. But they've frozen all his accounts. He'll be broke and he can't come back.'

It wasn't enough for Becca.

And Jared was gone too. He'd found some work

in Germany for a few months, some site where they needed climbers. His back was improving, and he was off the pills, so he decided to take it. 'It's what I need now,' he had told her. 'Build myself up, make a bit of cash. And then . . .' He'd frowned, looking uncertain.

'What?'

'I thought I might go and see my parents.' He looked away, shrugged. 'I dunno. Maybe – just, you know. Then I can get back to . . . what I do.' But his face looked lost, confused.

Becca understood. She didn't know either – what she wanted to do, where she wanted to be. She could have gone with Jared. He'd asked her to, but she needed to sort her life out for herself. They Skyped a lot and texted – they planned to meet up later that summer after his job finished. Maybe he'd go back to his life of exploration and danger, maybe he wouldn't. But if he did, the time would come, she knew, when he would fall silent, his phone become 'no longer in use', email messages drifting back from cyberspace, address unknown.

So was she OK?

Yeah. More or less. She was dealing with it.

Her aimless route had taken her close to the drop-in. She hadn't been there since the day Neil told her to leave. On impulse, she turned down the side street towards the bus station, down the familiar road where the old church hall stood.

It was locked up and silent. The pavement outside where groups of kids had hung about was empty. She looked towards the end of the road, half expecting to see Liam and Terry circling on their bikes, but there was no one there

It was strange to be standing here, where Paige had shivered in her clubbing gear that morning. It felt so long ago. *It's freezing,* she'd said. *Come on, let us in.* Where Alek had wished Becca well and closed the door behind her.

She went round to the back of the building, to the yard where Alek worked on his old engines with the drop-in lads. There was obviously some kind of renovation work going on but there was no sign of anyone. The back door was standing open. She hesitated, then entered.

The main room was empty. The snooker table and the screens were gone and the air carried the faint scent of dust and desertion. She wandered into the café, expecting the same emptiness, but the serving counter was still in place, the tables and chairs still set out, as if it was just waiting for her to arrive and start work. If she went behind the counter and switched on the hob, the users would emerge from the shadows, line up to be served and gradually the sound of their talk and laughter would fill the silence.

This was where she'd sat with Paige, playing games on her phone and texting. This was where Liam had threatened her, his smile all charm, his eyes malevolent. This was where Alek had made Liam leave Paige alone, and where he had said, *Keep an eye on her.*

Alek knew. She'd worked it out once she'd had a bit of

time to think. He'd known bad things were happening, but he hadn't been able to do anything. Or not much, anyway. He was illegal. He'd probably been afraid that if he went to the police with his suspicions, they'd deport him. But he'd trusted her. He'd kept watch. He'd recorded the things he had seen. She remembered him whistling to himself as he went about his work and realised it must have been him whistling that old song, the one she'd heard at the drop-in, the one that was on the video. And he'd left her the video, the tablet with BECKA written on the case. She'd thought it was Paige who was trying to stop what was going on, but it wasn't. It had never been Paige.

Why hadn't Alek spoken out? Because of his immigration status. As soon as the police were involved with the drop-in, he'd vanished. He couldn't risk being arrested and deported, because what would happen then to his daughter, the severely disabled girl who was doing so well at university? But he'd tried to protect the kids at the drop-in. He'd done his best for the kids who were left to make their own way as best they could.

Like Paige.

Like Maireid.

And like Becca had been, before Kay. Before Matt.

Wherever Alek was, she wished him well.

She heard the sounds of voices from further back in the building, and the tramp of heavy feet. Someone was coming, probably the people working on the renovations.

It was time to go.

465

Outside, the sky was blue and the air itself seemed full of possibilities. Becca felt her spirits lift with a kind of excitement. It wasn't a bad place, Brid. OK, it was at the bottom of the pile, but then, so was she, right now.

Maybe that was the best place to be when you were starting all over again.

ACKNOWLEDGEMENTS

With many thanks to all the people who helped and supported me through the writing of this book, especially my agent Teresa Chris for all the support she has given me, my editor at Simon & Schuster, Anne Perry who gave me so much help in shaping this book into its final form and Fraser Crichton for his copyediting.

Many thanks to writers Jenny Ryan, Janet Blackwell, Sue Knight and Penny Grubb for their critical reading and feedback, which helped to keep the book on track.

To Annie McKie for her wonderful writers' retreat and for the manuscript discussion we had in the early days of writing this book.

And finally – but not least – to Ken for his support and for keeping me supplied with endless cups of coffee.